Praise for *New York Times* bestselling author B.J. Daniels

"Forget slow-simmering romance: the multiple story lines weaving in and out of Big Timber, Montana, mean the second Montana Hamiltons contemporary (after *Wild Horses*) is always at a rolling boil."
—*Publishers Weekly* on *Lone Rider*

"The first book of Daniels' new Montana Hamiltons series will draw readers in with its genuine characters, multiple storylines and intense conflict set against the beautiful Montana landscape."
—*RT Book Reviews* on *Wild Horses*

"Truly amazing crime story for every amateur sleuth."
—*Fresh Fiction* on *Mercy*

"Daniels is truly an expert at Western romantic suspense."
—*RT Book Reviews* on *Atonement*

"Romantic suspense that will keep readers guessing. If you like Longmire, this is the book for you."
—*RT Book Reviews* on *Forsaken*

"Will keep readers on the edge of their chairs from beginning to end."
—*Booklist* on *Forsaken*

"Action-packed and chock-full of suspense."
—*Under the Covers* on *Redemption*

"Fans of Western romantic suspense will relish Daniels' tale of clandestine love played out in a small town on the Great Plains."
—*Booklist* on *Unforgiven*

B.J. DANIELS

LUCKY SHOT

HQN™

HQN™

ISBN-13: 978-0-373-78855-2

Recycling programs
for this product may
not exist in your area.

Lucky Shot

For questions and comments about the quality of this book,
please contact us at CustomerService@Harlequin.com.

® and TM are trademarks of Harlequin Enterprises Limited or its
corporate affiliates. Trademarks indicated with ® are registered in the
United States Patent and Trademark Office, the Canadian Intellectual
Property Office and in other countries.

www.HQNBooks.com

Printed in U.S.A.

This one is for Susie Higgins. When I moved to a very small town in north central Montana, my writer friends worried that I wouldn't have any other writers to inspire me. While we are short on writers up here, no one is more creative than my quilting friend Susie. She inspires everyone around her with her laugh, her generosity and her fun-loving, happy disposition. She has talked me off the ledge more than once. Thanks, my friend.

CHAPTER ONE

MAX MALONE SCRATCHED his shaggy sandy-blond hair and squinted at the sunrise that cast the awe-inspiring Crazy Mountains in a pale pink glow. He'd camped just outside the Hamilton Ranch, sleeping in the back of his pickup and hoping it wouldn't rain.

He needed a haircut and he also had a couple days' growth of beard. *All part of the job*, he thought as he surveyed the news vans parked outside the Hamilton Ranch gate. There'd been more vans parked here nine months ago when the senator's first wife had returned from the dead. Now only two vehicles remained, along with a few reporters who drove out some mornings after a hot shower, a latte and a night in a warm bed. Like him, they lived in hope of getting something newsworthy on the days they heard the senator was back from Washington.

Max had met the other reporters and photographers the first day he'd shown up here. They would have looked down their noses at him even if he hadn't been driving an old pickup and sleeping in the back of it under the camper shell. He was a freelancing investigative journalist, one of a dying breed.

But he had a reputation that preceded him, so he hoped he made them all nervous as they worried about what he was up to. Anyone who had ever read his articles would know that this wasn't his kind of story.

Which meant he might know something they didn't.

He smiled to himself. Let them wonder. If he was right… Well, he wasn't going to let himself go down that trail of thought, not yet. He didn't want to jinx it.

The only one of the news bunch waiting at the ranch gate who'd given him more than a nod was an old-timer newspaper journalist named Harvey Duncan. It was Harvey he stood with this morning at the fence.

"Is it true there are no photographs of Sarah Hamilton except for her high school yearbook and her driver's license mug shot from years ago?" Max asked about the senator's first wife, Sarah Johnson Hamilton.

"Rumor is the new wife disposed of all the photos, photos of Sarah, including the wedding photos," Harvey said and took a gulp of his coffee from a cup that said Big Timber Java on the side.

Just the smell of the coffee was almost enough to send Max hightailing it into town. He could go without food for several days. But coffee, that was a whole other matter.

"Surely someone's seen her and gotten a recent shot, at least a candid one," he said as if merely passing time.

Harvey shook his head. "No one knows where she is. She couldn't move back in here at the ranch after her unexpected return from the dead, not and live with the senator and his current wife. And after the story came out about her…memory loss…" He pulled a face.

No one believed anyone could forget twenty-two years of her life. "I heard all six daughters have scattered to the wind, as well," Max said.

"So it seems." Harvey took another drink. "Abandoned the ranch as if it was a sinking ship."

Hamilton Ranch was far from a sinking ship. Just as Senator Buckmaster Hamilton's bid for the presidency was a far cry from the disaster everyone had predicted when his dead wife had shown up. He was a front-runner in the polls, and the gracious way he'd handled his first wife's return had only garnered him more popularity.

"I've been struggling to get a bead on Sarah Hamilton. No one seems to know anything about her," Max said. "With a maiden name like Johnson and a married name like Hamilton, it makes it hard to get much background, other than what is already known about her. Not that she was probably using either name in the past twenty-two years. That is, if she was trying to hide and really didn't lose her memory."

Harvey chuckled. If he knew anything, he wasn't giving it up. Max had used all of his resources and had come up empty, but apparently so had everyone else. Not that anyone in the world would care about the woman if she hadn't been married to the future president of the United States—if you could believe the polls and he didn't do anything to screw up before election day.

Still, Max was fascinated by the woman and more than a little curious about what she might be up to. Sarah Johnson had come from a two-parent, affluent home with a squeaky-clean past. She'd been the golden girl, high school cheerleader, valedictorian and had apparently glided through college without making a ripple, coming out with a bachelor of arts degree in literature. She'd married well, had six children and then one winter night, for some unknown reason, she'd driven her car into the Yellowstone River. Her body was never found. Because there were no skid marks on the highway, it had looked like a suicide. Foul play had never been suspected.

That was twenty-two years ago. Now she was back—with no memory of those years or why she'd apparently tried to take her own life.

Max wanted this story more than he wanted a hot cup of coffee this morning. Even better would be a current photograph. Right now a photo of the back-from-the-grave Sarah Hamilton would be worth…hell, he could name his price.

At movement down at the ranch house, the reporters and photographers in the vans hopped out and got ready. Word was that the senator had flown in last night for a short visit. He'd been gone for months and only returned for quick visits between his job and his campaigning. Unlike some of the others, who hadn't declared their candidacy yet, Hamilton had jumped into the ring early.

"I think I'm going into town for coffee," Max announced, even though that wasn't his plan at all as he walked back to his pickup. While the senator often came and went from the ranch with his current wife, this morning Buckmaster Hamilton was alone as he drove toward the gate.

Max crossed his fingers as he started his pickup. Maybe luck would be with him. He'd tried to follow the man before but had lost him. Buckmaster was a Montana rancher at heart. Being a senator hadn't changed that. Nor had money. He didn't own a private jet, he didn't have a large staff while at the ranch and he certainly didn't have a driver. On top of that, the man drove like a bat out of hell and had the luxury of knowing the roads. If that didn't make it difficult enough to follow him, add the dust that boiled up behind the senator's SUV. Because of that Max hadn't seen where the man had disappeared to during his other attempts to follow him.

This morning, while he would have loved to actually go in to town for coffee, he was determined to outfox the man. On a hunch, Max took off down the road that led to the old mining town of Beartooth, Montana. If he was wrong and the senator headed the other way, then he still had nothing to lose. He'd go have coffee and breakfast at the Branding Iron. Maybe he'd pick up some gossip he could use.

But as he glanced in his mirror, he saw the senator's SUV behind him and grinned. Max drove slowly like many of the local ranchers, his window down, his elbow out. The smells of fall blew in. He breathed deeply. He'd grown up in California, and this kind of fall was new to him. He loved the scents, as well as the spectacular leaf show the aspens and cottonwoods put on this time of year in Montana against the snowcapped Crazy Mountains backdrop.

He'd been a lot of places over the years with this job that he loved. As an investigative journalist, he got to delve into other people's lives. It was like digging through their garbage, which admittedly he'd done a few times when the situation necessitated it. And because he freelanced, he didn't have a boss he had to answer to either.

Max was going slow enough that he knew the senator would eventually pass him to get out of his dust.

Sure enough, Hamilton finally did, blowing past without a sideways glance. Max was betting the man hadn't noticed him or his old truck parked away from where the other reporters hung out by the ranch fence.

A news van came flying up behind Max. He moved to the middle of the road and ignored the driver blasting his horn. The driver was a hotshot newsman who looked down his nose at him. Let him eat some dust.

Meanwhile, Max could see the senator's dust dissipating in the distance. Just a little farther.

He'd followed Buckmaster Hamilton several other times when he'd left about this time of day and headed in this direction. Max was betting the senator was going to the same place he had before. What had thrown him previously was that there hadn't been any ranches or houses near the spot where he'd lost him.

Since then, Max had had plenty of time to explore the area. He had an idea where the senator was going. He moved over and let the news van pass him, knowing the van would never be able to catch up to Hamilton now. The newsman flipped him off as he went by.

Max smiled and slowed, turning at the next dirt road, and hoping his instincts paid off. Sometimes at night, with nothing to do, he would just drive back roads. He'd found this one quite by accident and had been surprised to end up on a tall rocky outcropping. The view had been incredible. He figured teenagers knew about the spot because he'd seen rock fire pits and a lot of smashed, empty beer cans.

Driving up the road, he stopped short of the top of the rocky hill. Getting out, he grabbed his camera case and, closing the door quietly, headed up to the pinnacle. He'd almost reached the top when he heard a vehicle on the narrow dirt road below him. He recognized the senator's SUV as it came to a stop at the edge of the tree-lined creek.

He smiled to himself, pleased that he'd been right as Hamilton got out. Fifty-nine, the senator was a large, distinguished-looking man with thick salt-and-pepper hair. No one had been surprised when he'd thrown his hat in to the ring for the presidency. The Montana rancher was well liked and moderate enough that he had friends on both sides of the aisle.

The senator exited his vehicle and walked down to the water and paced as if waiting impatiently for someone. Max was betting that *someone* was Sarah Hamilton, the wife who'd only recently come back from the dead. As he watched the senator, he reminded himself that he could be spying on the next president of the United States. That was, if nothing happened to derail the man's run for the top political seat.

Five minutes later a pickup truck came down the road from the other direction and began to slow to a stop. Max took a photo of the dust trail the truck had left across the canyon and up into the pines of the foothills. It wouldn't be easy, but maybe he could track down where that pickup had come from—and find Sarah Hamilton's hideout.

Excited now, he was betting it all on who would climb out of that truck. It had to be the senator's first wife, the woman who'd left behind six daughters, the youngest twins and only a few months old, to plunge her vehicle into the icy Yellowstone River.

When her body was never found, Buckmaster Hamilton had had her declared dead and had also apparently buried her memory before marrying Angelina Broadwater fifteen years ago. Needless to say, Sarah's return had caused an uproar even before everyone found out about her memory loss.

There wasn't a reporter worth his salt who didn't want her story, which had forced her underground. Even the man she'd been staying with, a rancher named Russell Murdock, refused to say where she was hiding.

As the pickup came to a full stop, Max had his camera ready. Everything about this clandestine meeting in the middle of nowhere told him it was going to be worth the hours he'd spent driving these back roads.

With the telephoto lens, he snapped a shot of the driver behind the wheel, recognizing him as Russell Murdock. Russell, who was about Sarah Johnson Hamilton's age, had been the one who'd found her. The story was that she'd stumbled out into the road a few miles out of Beartooth in the middle of nowhere with no memory of where she'd been the past twenty-two years.

Max quickly focused on the other side of the truck as the passenger side door opened. A blonde woman in her fifties stepped out and he knew he'd hit pay dirt.

Sarah Johnson Hamilton? The only other photos he'd seen of her were from her high school yearbook and her 1993 driver's license mug shot. Strangely enough, there were no photos of her from college that he'd been able to find. Obviously, she'd changed in the years since those photographs were taken. But he told himself this had to be her.

He snapped a half dozen pictures of her as she headed down to the creek. The senator looked up, frowning as she approached him. *Snap. Snap. Snap.* He took several shots of the two of them. Even through the viewfinder he could read their body language and see the tension between them.

Max wondered what it would be like to think that no time had passed, only to return home to find your children all grown and your husband married to someone else.

The woman looked around as if worried that she was being watched. She glanced in his direction. Although dozens of yards away, Max froze. After a moment, she turned back to the man she'd obviously come here to meet.

What had driven her to leave behind her husband, six daughters, money and a huge ranch? That was the question everyone was asking. That, and why had she returned *now*—right when Hamilton was making a run for the White House with his current wife, Angelina?

The media had jumped on the lovers' triangle angle. But that was getting old. Everyone was looking for another angle, something more. He wished he could hear what was being said, but they were too far away and talking too softly. He watched them, snapping photos, intrigued by the way they were acting. Not like strangers. They'd known each other too well for that. He could almost feel the chemistry between them. Good or bad, he couldn't quite tell.

Hamilton might have remarried, but there were definitely some old feelings still between these two. Max could see it even through the viewfinder. He couldn't wait to get the photos on to his computer so he could get a good look at them. Maybe the tabloids were right, and the current wife, Angelina Broadwater Hamilton, *did* have something to worry about.

Everyone wanted to know the real story.

Everyone but Max Monroe. Right now he couldn't care less about why Sarah was back, where she'd been or if she'd end up getting her man back. He was too pleased with himself. If he was right and this woman was indeed Sarah Hamilton, what he had in his camera was money in the bank.

CHAPTER TWO

KAT HAMILTON DUCKED into a small café on the main street of Bozeman, Montana. She waited by the door as she watched for the tall, dark man she'd seen following her. Her heart was pounding even though she tried to assure herself it was probably just a reporter. The press had been dogging her and her sisters ever since her mother had turned up and her father had announced he was running for president.

"Would you like a seat or are you waiting for someone?"

Kat jumped at the sound of the waitress's voice behind her. She turned to see an older woman with a menu and an impatient expression. She shook her head and looked back to the street. The man who'd been following her hadn't walked by. Had she just imagined that he'd been tailing her?

"No, thank you, I've changed my mind," Kat said and pulled open the door. Stepping outside, she scanned the street. Maybe she was just being paranoid. But all her instincts told her that wasn't the case.

When she'd spoken with her older sister, Ainsley had also complained that there'd been a man following *her*. Ainsley had taken a job scouting movie set locations in Montana for film companies. Apparently,

Ainsley's shadow had been tracking her from town to town.

The thought gave Kat the creeps. She did everything possible to blend into her surroundings. The last thing she'd ever wanted was this. Her father's political career had never been this much of a problem—until it became clear he was looking at the presidency. The fact that he had six daughters he'd raised alone for years before marrying Angelina Broadwater had made the press interested in them.

Kat searched the street. She had decided that if she caught him following her again today, she was going to confront him. The thought terrified her. The last time she'd confronted a man… She pushed the thought away as she had in the years since, telling herself she was stronger now.

Just when she was starting to doubt her own sanity, she spotted him.

There, across Main. He'd been standing in front of the bank, looking in this direction, but when she'd seen him, he'd quickly stepped behind a group of women coming out of the quilt store and had now disappeared around the corner.

She hadn't imagined it. The man *was* following her. So why didn't he try to corner her like all the other reporters who'd gotten in to her face demanding answers? As if she had any answers. She didn't know any more about her mother than the general public since she'd been eight when her mother had allegedly died. She'd been a difficult child—at least that's what she'd been told. So her memories of Sarah, as she now thought of her, were clouded.

Kat considered confronting him. There was too

much traffic this time of day to get across Main since it was the main highway through town. She waited until there was a break in the traffic and ran across the street, telling herself she would be safe in public, but he was gone. Had she really been ready to confront him? She could feel herself trembling at the thought. For years, she'd told herself she'd put the past behind her, but at moments like this, she knew it was a lie.

More than likely, the man had been following her, hoping she'd get together with her mother. She and three of her sisters had met with their mother when she'd first returned. Since then, she'd talked with Sarah a couple of times on the phone, but that was it.

No one wanted to lead the press to Buckmaster Hamilton's first wife. Russell Murdock hadn't just saved their mother that day he'd found her months ago. He'd given her a place to stay, since Sarah Hamilton couldn't return to the ranch and the husband who'd remarried fifteen years ago.

It was a mess, not that Kat hadn't seen her friends go through their parents' divorces and affairs and financial problems. But none of them had believed their mother dead for twenty-two years to have her suddenly return.

"Why are you so angry with Mother?" Livie had wanted to know the few times she and her sister had discussed Sarah. "It isn't her fault that she can't remember what happened."

For Kat, it was complicated. She wanted to trust the woman who'd come back to them, but for some reason, she couldn't. Maybe her mother had a good reason for leaving them. Or maybe she didn't. That was the problem. No one knew—including her mother.

"We don't know what would make her do what she did," her sister Bo had said in their mother's defense. "Maybe it was a bad case of postpartum depression. We really shouldn't judge her until we know all the facts."

"And when exactly are we going to get all these… facts? Mother says she doesn't remember anything. Not one day of the past twenty-two years. Not to mention driving into the river, surviving that and calling someone to pick her up." Kat had shaken her head. "It isn't that I'm not compassionate and even understanding. But I'm sorry, I don't…trust her. Maybe in time…"

Kat had often wondered if the reason she was thought to be difficult by her mother as a child was because she resembled her father with her dark hair and gray eyes. Or maybe her anger at her mother just wouldn't let her believe Sarah Hamilton had loved her.

Ainsley, who was blond with blue eyes like her mother, had been ten, so she had the most memories of their mother. Their sister Bo had been five. Blonde with green eyes, Bo was always the cute one. Kat was sure her mother had adored the child. Same with Olivia, the blue-eyed brunette in the family. Livie had been three when their mother had left them.

The twins, Harper and Cassidy, had been only months old, so they had no memory of their mother. They both resembled Sarah. As far as Kat knew, neither of them had laid eyes on their mother yet, though. With the press dogging them all, they'd stayed away at their father's request.

Kat pulled out her cell phone and called Ainsley. Her big sister had practically raised them all, so was it any wonder that they all went to her when they needed help?

"Have you had any more reporters following you?" she asked without preamble.

"Kat?"

"Has Sarah done something that I haven't heard about?" She groaned, realizing she'd been out of touch for a while, camping in the woods while she shot more photos for her upcoming exhibit. "The press coverage *was* starting to die down. What has she done now?"

"I don't believe Mother has done anything," Ainsley said patiently. "At least not that I've heard. You sound strange. Are you all right?"

"I've had a man tailing me the past few days, so I just assumed something new had happened. I've been off the grid."

"If it makes you feel any better, the man tailing me has been doing it for weeks now off and on."

"He hasn't tried to talk to you?"

"No. He just seems to show up in whatever town I'm in," Ainsley said. She had dropped out of law school, breaking their father's heart, to scout movie and commercial locations in the state.

"Where are you now?" Kat asked.

"East Glacier. They're shooting a commercial here and hoping it snows, so we're waiting. How about you?"

"Bozeman."

"That's right—you have your photograph exhibit coming up soon, don't you?"

"Not until closer to Christmas. I wasn't happy with the photos I had so I had the date extended. Dad is determined to fly back for it. I tried to talk him out of it."

It would be her first exhibit. She wanted it to be good. What she didn't want was a media circus. Maybe it was foolish, but she didn't want that kind of exposure. She wanted her photographs to speak for themselves.

"I'll be there, too. Just text me the date and time."

Kat wanted to tell her sister it wasn't necessary, but she hadn't seen Ainsley in months and she missed her. "Thanks."

"You could go to the police," her sister suggested, steering their discussion back to the more concerning topic.

"And end up in the police reports? No, thanks." Kat looked back up the street but didn't see the man. "He'll eventually corner me and want the whole story on Sarah, and I'll kick him in the—"

"I would advise against that. I had enough law school to know that he could have you arrested for assault." She laughed. "When I told Dad about the man following me, he suggested that he might be a nice man who just didn't know how to ask me out."

"Is *yours* handsome? I don't think mine is. I only got a glimpse, but it would be just like you to get the handsome reporter."

"Actually, he is. I don't think he's a reporter, though. I almost suspect he might have been hired to keep an eye on me."

"Dad's doing?" Kat asked suspiciously. "You think that's what this is?"

"I wouldn't put it past him. He wouldn't tell us because he knows we would demand he call them off."

"That *does* sound like Dad, now that you mention it. I wonder if I've had one tailing me for months as well and I just didn't notice." Kat thought about contacting her father to verify it.

"Don't bother Dad with this," her sister said as if

reading her mind. "He's got a lot on his plate right now with the primary only months away. Also, if he didn't hire the men, then he's going to be upset that reporters are tailing us. If Dad had his way, he'd lock us up until all this blows over."

"As if that's going to happen." Their father was headed for the White House. They would never be free of the press. But Kat knew her sister was right. "Okay. Have you talked to Harper or Cassidy?"

"They're both fine. They have been running around Europe, pretending to continue their educations, but Harper called to say they were flying back to spend a few days in New York City. Neither has mentioned anyone following them. Oh, it's finally starting to snow up here in the cold north. Gotta go."

Kat looked down the street again as she disconnected and wondered if her father had hired someone to tail her and...what? Keep her out of trouble? Or keep the press away from her?

I feel as if I live in an aquarium full of bottom feeders, Kat thought as she headed down the street toward the art gallery. She hated it, wishing she was invisible. But she was one of the "Hamilton Girls," as they had been known as far back as she could remember. With her father in politics, she'd done her best to stay out of the limelight. Now with him running for president, a mother whom the press had dubbed unstable and with Angelina Broadwater Hamilton, their stepmother, caught in what the press liked to call a hopeless love triangle, Kat feared all of this was never going to end.

MAX COULDN'T WAIT to get to a computer and upload the shots he'd taken. He'd looked at what he had on his camera, heart pounding with excitement. He might have the only recent photo of the senator's first wife.

But the really good shots were the ones of Sarah and the senator together. He'd managed to capture the chemistry between them. Lovers' triangle indeed.

While most of the media were making her out to be mentally unstable, Max thought she looked normal. True, he told himself as he drove back to town, looks could be deceiving. The senator hadn't spent a whole lot of time with her at the creek. Max would have given anything to have heard what they said to each other.

But he had the photos. He'd captured something explosive in their expressions. There was…heat between them. These two let off fireworks when they were together—and it showed up even in the distant shots he'd taken.

He couldn't contain his excitement. The question was who would want the photos badly enough to start the bidding.

Big Timber Java had great coffee—and free Wi-Fi. He opened his laptop, took a sip of his coffee and uploaded his photos.

An older woman came in, a local who seemed to know everyone in town. After she settled in, he approached her table and showed her the photo he'd taken of the man in the pickup—the one who'd brought Sarah Hamilton out to the creek to meet the senator.

"I was taking a photo of a doe down by the creek early this morning, and this truck and driver drove by just as I took the shot," he said chuckling. "I thought you might know him."

She squinted at the photo on his laptop for a moment. "That's Russell Murdock. He has a ranch outside of Beartooth. Used to work for W. T. Grant. Russell had to be a saint to work for that man."

"I figure he owes me a beer since he ruined my shot," Max joked.

"I'm sure he didn't mean to," the woman said cheerfully. "Russell is a sweetheart." She took a good look at him then, eyes narrowing. "Are you one of those journalists in town?" Immediately she didn't seem as friendly.

"Amateur photographer." That much was true enough.

She seemed to relax. "Well, I think it is a fine shot of Russell. Did you get one of the deer?"

He shook his head. "The truck scared the deer away."

"Too bad. We have several fine photographers in the area." She rattled off three or four names. "Sometimes they offer classes." Only one name caught his attention.

"Kat Hamilton? Any relation to—"

"Senator Buckmaster Hamilton?" She nodded. "One of his daughters. I've heard she's quite talented."

"I'm sorry, your coffee is getting cold because of me. May I buy you another cup?"

She declined, said she was meeting her granddaughter and had to go anyway. "It was nice visiting with you. Maybe I'll see some more of your photographs one of these days in a gallery."

"Maybe," he said, hoping more for the front page of a nationally syndicated newspaper.

RUSSELL MURDOCK HADN'T been looking forward to telling his daughter that he'd asked Sarah Hamilton to marry him. He was no fool. He knew Destry would be shocked—just as everyone else in the county would be once it was announced. He'd expected the arguments Destry would make. What he hadn't anticipated was how upset she would be.

"You can't be serious!" Destry West spun away from him, turning her back as she stormed into the kitchen. He followed her, seeing her shake as she poured herself a mug of coffee and cupped it in her two hands. It didn't stop her trembling as she turned to him again. "Sarah Hamilton? Have you lost your mind?"

He tried to find the words to explain how he'd felt from the moment she'd stumbled out of the trees and in front of his pickup. Fortunately, he'd gotten the truck stopped in time. But when he'd leaped out and seen her face… Well, it was like seeing a ghost. He'd been to her memorial service twenty-two years ago.

"You know I've been looking out for her since her return," he said as calmly as he could. He needed his daughter to understand. "I fell in love with her."

Destry shook her head, looking at him as if in amazement. "Sarah Hamilton? Doesn't it bother you in the least that her return is surrounded by mystery— let alone her past?"

"She has *amnesia*. She's not crazy."

His daughter cocked her head at him. "*Really?* How can you be sure? She doesn't know where she's been for the past twenty-two years? Dad!" The word came out a plea.

Sarah had tried to warn him that his daughter would be upset. "Why wouldn't she, Russell? Like everyone else in the world, she's heard the stories about me."

"Once she gets to know you—"

"Please, Russell. Let's give it a couple more months before we announce."

"Is this Buckmaster Hamilton's doing?" He'd demanded, even though he could tell by her expression that it was.

"He will take a short break soon and come home," she'd argued. "He wants to be here for our daughters when you and I announce our engagement. That isn't too much to ask, is it?"

All he'd been able to do was shake his head. "If I were a suspicious man I might question if you were sincere about wanting to marry me or if this was just a ploy to win your husband back."

Sarah had stepped to him and kissed him. "You know better than that. I'm nothing but a liability to Buck."

He hadn't been convinced. "Because if he left his wife and came back to you, it would hurt his political career. But if Angelina wasn't in the picture—"

She shook her head. "Maybe you're right, and he did something so horrible that I drove my car into the Yellowstone River that winter night so many years ago. Maybe I'll never know the truth. But, for whatever reason, I see no future for me and Buck."

Russell had taken her in his arms and held her, praying it was true but knowing Sarah still loved the man. If Buckmaster were free—

Fortunately, Buckmaster wasn't free. Not only was he married to Angelina Broadwater Hamilton, but also he was wed to the idea of being the next president of the United States. Which meant Sarah was inconvenient. A liability, just as she'd said.

Russell was determined to give Sarah the life she deserved. "I understand why you're upset," he said now to his daughter. "Destry, I've gotten to know this woman. For her to leave her children like that…well, she had a good reason, just as there is a very good reason why she can't remember."

He didn't dare tell her about his theory that Sarah's brain had been wiped clean of the memories because Senator Buckmaster Hamilton didn't want her to remember. "She's the victim here, sweetheart."

Destry shook her head. "Are you sure you aren't just making excuses for her?"

Maybe he was. Late at night sometimes, he argued the same case with himself. He knew things about Sarah that would horrify his daughter. Like the way Sarah had returned to Beartooth. She'd parachuted from a plane at low altitude. She had no memory of it, but he was convinced that whoever was behind her memory loss was using her. If he had to name that person, it would be Senator Buckmaster Hamilton.

Since Sarah's supposedly untimely return, his standings in the presidential race had only improved tenfold. He was a shoo-in for the Republican nomination now. His allegedly "crazy" first wife had taken a beating in the press, while Buckmaster had garnered all the sympathy.

"I just need you to trust me on this," he said, stepping to his daughter. Destry hadn't known that he'd fathered her until a few years ago. He'd worked as ranch manager at the W Bar G Ranch, so he'd seen her grow up. She'd always come to him with her problems instead of the man she believed to be her father, W. T. Grant. Russel and his wife, Judy, had never had any children. But now with her gone, he was lonely. He saw Destry and his grandchildren as often as he could, but it wasn't the same as having a partner to share the rest of his life with.

"I want to get on with my life. Can you wish me well?"

Destry searched his gaze for a long moment. "I know you've been lonely since you lost Judy, and I can even understand how you might have fallen for this woman, but are you sure you want Sarah Hamilton around your grandchildren? Think about that, Dad."

"YOUR DAUGHTERS HAVE been in my jewelry again," Angelina complained as Senator Buckmaster Hamilton walked into their bedroom.

He groaned inwardly. "I really doubt—"

"My watch is missing. You know the one with my name engraved inside it. It was the first present you gave me. Don't you remember? You said it was because I'm never on time."

"I doubt you'll miss it since you never looked at it. You're still never on time," he said.

"Why would one of them want that watch unless they knew how much it meant to me?" she asked, sounding close to tears.

"None of them would take your watch, especially with your name engraved on it. I'm sure it will turn up. Your missing things always do."

"That's because one of your daughters finally returns whatever she took."

He sighed loudly, sick of this and the other arguments they kept having.

"It's true," she said, turning, hands on her hips. "You always take up for them."

"And you always blame them for everything."

His wife narrowed her gaze as she studied him. "You've been to see Sarah."

He should have known that Sarah would be next. If Angelina wasn't complaining about his daughters, she was complaining about his former wife. He wasn't sure how much more he could take.

"Angelina, we just got home. I have barely gotten unpacked and I had a meeting this morning with some constituents." He was doing his best not to lie. But if he told Angelina, they would have a huge row. If she had her way, he'd never see Sarah again.

She was eyeing him suspiciously. "If you haven't seen her, then how do you explain that hangdog look you always get after one of your secret rendezvous? Come to think of it, you've had that look pretty much since the last time we were home." She stepped toward him. Her gaze was like a laser as she prodded at him. "What's going on?"

The woman was much more intuitive than he'd ever imagined. Sarah had also brought out a suspicious nature in Angelina that he'd never known existed. He knew she'd keep after him until he told her. He also knew how she'd take the news. That's why he hadn't told her about Sarah's engagement to Russell Murdock.

In truth, he was hoping that Sarah would change her mind. He'd been shocked when she'd told him and had had a terrible time hiding how upset he'd been ever since.

His first love, Sarah still seemed like his wife. True, since her shocking return from the dead, he felt as if he had two wives. Legally, he had only one. But tell that to his heart.

Now Angelina would be over the moon with joy

when she found out Sarah would be getting married to Russell. Angelina wouldn't have to be worried about the other woman in his life anymore. In the fifteen years they'd been married, the woman had never shown even the slightest bit of jealousy.

That was until his first wife had returned. The worst part was that Angelina had every reason to be jealous. He'd thought he'd gotten over Sarah's death and the anger he'd felt when he'd learned that it hadn't been an accident. But the moment he saw her again, he knew he'd only been lying to himself. He still loved her. He'd never stopped loving her.

"Well?" Angelina was impatiently waiting for an answer. Just the mention of Sarah always set her off. Hell, she'd even hired a private investigator to try to discover not only where Sarah had been the past twenty-two years but also to dig up dirt from even before Buck had met her.

"Sarah has decided it's time she gets on with her life," he said carefully, knowing that if he showed his true feelings about this news, things would turn ugly.

"Really?" Angelina asked suspiciously. "She told you this?" Her tone couldn't have called Sarah a liar any clearer than if she'd said the word. "So she's leaving Montana?"

He braced himself. "No, she's getting married. She and Russell Murdock will be announcing their engagement soon."

To his shock, Angelina's face went taut with fury. Her blue eyes narrowed dangerously, and she let out a very un-First-Lady-like curse. "The conniving bitch. And *you* believed her?" She stormed over to the window, only to swing back around. "So that explains the way you've been acting. How long have you known this?"

He thought he'd been hiding his feelings well. Apparently not. "For a couple of months."

"But you never said anything."

He simply stood there, looking guilty and wishing they didn't have to ever talk about Sarah again.

"You actually *believed* her. Of course you did. Just as she knew you would. Buckmaster, you can't be that naive. Don't you see what she's trying to do? She's playing you."

"I don't see how marrying Russell—"

"She's never going to marry Russell Murdock," she snapped with a wave of her arm.

He hated the surge of hope he felt at her words. He quickly squashed it because it was only a matter of time before Sarah remarried. He couldn't expect her to sit around waiting for him to…to what? Angelina was his wife now, his future, his only hope if he wanted to win this election.

While it shouldn't matter whether a candidate was married, single or divorced, or had a mistress, it did when it came to the voting public. So much had already been made of Sarah's return from the grave. If he left Angelina for her…

"She's trying to force your hand," Angelina said, sounding sad that he could be so easily fooled. "She wants you to choose her over me. Why else would she just happen to mention this before you left on the campaign? And let me guess, she's waiting to announce it to the world, right? Giving you some time."

"Yes, but only because I asked her to wait," he said

with a sigh. "I'm afraid this is going to upset our daughters, so I asked her to wait until I came home again."

She cocked her head at him. "Why would it upset the girls? They don't even know her. Why would they care who she marries? She was just giving you time to let it sink in, so you will try to stop her."

He shook his head. "You give her too much credit. She doesn't sit around plotting like…"

"Like me?"

He raked a hand through his graying hair. Nothing he could say would make this situation better. Wasn't that why he'd waited as long as he could before telling her?

"Sarah wants to destroy you. Destroy your career."

"You're wrong. She thinks marrying Russell will help me."

Angelina laughed. "So she's really just doing this for you. Seriously, Buckmaster, you bought that?"

"Away from me, the press will forget about her. All the focus will be on the campaign instead of the three of us. Sarah will be forgotten like any other former wife."

"What a martyr she is," Angelina said, her words as tart as vinegar.

"She cares about Russell. She trusts him, and I think he cares about her."

"Always the saint, that Sarah, huh?" She moved away as if trying to hide her anger, but her body had gone rigid with her rage.

That's why he was surprised when she turned back, and this time, he saw tears. She'd always been so strong, so self-assured. His daughters called her the

Ice Queen. But since Sarah's return… "Angelina," he said, stepping toward her.

She took a step back and shook her head. "If you choose her, you'll lose the election."

He swore. "It isn't always about the damned election." He dropped his arms and started to turn away.

"Don't you think we should discuss this?" she demanded of his back.

"I thought we just did," he said and kept walking.

MAX HAD WANTED to ask the elderly lady in the coffee shop if she recognized the photographs he'd taken of the woman he believed to be Sarah Hamilton. He just needed a simple verification. He already knew it was Sarah, but he hadn't become the journalist he was by assuming anything.

He couldn't have asked the woman, though, without blowing his cover. Not to mention, she probably wouldn't have helped him anyway. He'd seen her expression when she'd asked him if he was a reporter. He had a feeling that she wouldn't have talked to him if he'd admitted it.

Fortunately, he'd managed to get her talking—it usually wasn't hard to get people to open up in small towns—and she'd told him about Kat Hamilton.

He went back to his computer and searched for a Kat Hamilton, photographer. He found her website and let out a low whistle as he studied the self-portrait photo she'd taken of herself. She didn't look terribly approachable. Her long dark hair was tightly pulled back from her face and wound into a knot at the base of her neck. Her piercing gray eyes looked into the camera as if in challenge. Everything about her told him she was a difficult woman and one he should probably stay away from.

While he seldom took his own good advice, he might have this time if he hadn't seen that she was going to be having a one-woman exhibit at a gallery in Bozeman. Feeling the need to verify that the blonde he'd photographed was indeed Sarah Hamilton before he tried to sell the shots, he headed for Bozeman.

The gallery was on Main Street in a narrow building with old brick walls and lots of spot lighting. The moment he walked in, the owner came out of the back.

"Is there anything in particular you're looking for?" she asked.

"I understand Kat Hamilton will have an exhibit here soon?"

She instantly looked wary.

"I saw one of her photos." He described one he'd seen on her website. "I was interested in buying it."

The shop owner seemed to relax a little. Bozeman, because of the university there, had an almost Bohemian feel to it. So he fit right in, even looking as he did. "We don't have that particular one here…" She led him over to a black-and-white photo taken in a rainstorm. Max knew enough about photography to realize the moment he saw the photo that it was nothing short of amazing.

"You like it?" she asked, even though she'd clearly seen his reaction.

"I *love* it. I can't wait to see more of her work. That's an incredible photograph. I do a little shooting myself. I'd love to pick her brain as to how I can improve my photos, but I'm sure she gets a lot of that."

"She'll be here for her exhibit. It's coming up soon." She rattled off a date near Christmas.

Not soon enough. He sighed. "I'm not sure I'll be in town then. Maybe I can catch her some other time. I definitely am interested." He looked again longingly at the rain photo.

The woman seemed to hesitate, and he knew he had her. "You know…I'm expecting her later today. She said about four. She's coming in to do some work to get her photographs ready for the exhibit. Maybe you could catch her then."

He couldn't wait to meet Kat Hamilton.

CHAPTER THREE

MAX MADE A FEW calls to see what kind of interest there was in the photos of Senator Buckmaster Hamilton with his first wife, the back-from-the-dead Sarah Johnson Hamilton. There was always skepticism with something this big. But not one of the people he called told him to get lost.

"Where can you be reached?" they each asked in turn. "I'll have to get back to you… Is there any chance of getting an exclusive if these photographs…?" The questions came.

Not one to count his chickens before they hatched, Max still couldn't help feeling as if the money was already in his pocket. He could already taste the huge steak he planned to have as soon as he got Kat Hamilton to verify that the photos he'd taken were of her long-lost mother.

Then it was just a matter of waiting for the calls to start coming in and the bidding to begin. All he had to do was wait around until four for Kat.

He'd parked his pickup down the street so he could watch the art gallery, and see who came and went. A little after four, he spotted Kat Hamilton. She looked just as she had in her photo on her website. He watched her climb out of a newer model SUV, pull a large folder from the back and head across the street toward the gallery.

As he got out of his pickup, he admitted that he was flying by the seat of his pants. He wasn't sure how he was going to play this. He just hoped that the Max Malone charm didn't let him down. Passing a shop window, he caught his reflection and stopped to brush back his too-long hair. He really needed a haircut, and a shave wouldn't hurt either, he thought as he rubbed a palm along his bristled jaw.

Well, too late for any of that. He straightened his shirt, sniffed to make sure he didn't reek—after all, he'd spent the night sleeping under the stars in the back of his truck. He smelled like the great outdoors, and from what he could tell, Kat Hamilton might appreciate that. Most of her photographs he'd seen were taken in the great outdoors.

Still, he knew this wasn't going to be easy. Kat Hamilton wasn't just a rich, probably spoiled artist. She was a rich, probably spoiled artist whose daddy was running for president and whose birth mother was possibly unstable. He had no idea what it was going to take to get what he wanted from the unapproachable Kat Hamilton.

When he pushed into the gallery, the bell over the door chimed softly and both women turned in his direction. The gallery owner looked happy to see him. Kat? Not so much. He saw her take in his attire from his Western shirt to his worn jeans and boots. He'd left his straw cowboy hat in the truck, but his camera bag was slung over one shoulder.

"This is the man I was just telling you about," the shop owner said.

Kat's gray eyes seemed to bore into him as he sauntered toward her. Mistrust and something colder made
her gaze appear hard as granite. She was dressed in
an oversize sweater and loose jeans, that approach-at-
your-own-risk look welded on her face.

"Max Malone," he said extending his hand. "I'm a
huge fan of your work, but I'm sure you hear that all
the time."

Her handshake was firm enough. Her steely gaze
never warmed, just as it never left his. "Thank you."
Her voice had an edge to it, a warning. *Tread carefully.*

"I was especially taken with your rain photo," he
said, moving in that direction, hoping she would take
the hint and follow.

"You should show him your latest ones you brought
in today," the gallery owner said.

Kat didn't jump at that.

"Would you mind if I took a photo of this? I want
to show it to my wife. This would be perfect for her
office."

"That would be fine," Kat said, clearly not invested
in his company. He was reminded that she came from
a wealthy family. She didn't need to make money from
her photographs.

He snapped the shot of her rain photo and then
walked back to where he'd left her standing. Every
line of her body language said she'd had enough of
him. He felt as if he was chipping away at solid ice.
Charm wasn't going to get what he wanted. He hoped
he wouldn't be forced to buy one of her photographs.
The prices were a little steep, and he doubted cash
would warm her up.

He was tempted, though, to buy the one she'd taken

of the pouring rain. There was something about the shot… "I hate to even show you the photo I took, " he said, stopping next to her to show her a scenery shot he'd taken on his camera while he'd been waiting for her to show up at the gallery.

She gave the photo a cursory glance and started to turn away when he flipped to the one he believed to be of her mother.

Kat Hamilton froze. Her gaze leaped from the camera to him. She took a step back, her gray eyes sparking with anger.

"I'm sorry," he said innocently, even though he felt a surge of pleasure to see some emotion in her face. "Is something wrong?"

"Who are you?" she demanded. "You're one of those reporters who have been camped outside the ranch like vultures for weeks."

That pretty well covered it, while at the same time confirming what he already knew. The photo was of Sarah Hamilton.

"I guess I don't have to ask you if the woman in the photo is your mother," he said as he put his camera away.

"Do you want me to call the police?" the shop owner asked as she stood wringing her hands.

"No, this man is leaving," Kat said, glaring poison darts at him. She looked shaken. Clearly, he'd caught her flat-footed with the photo.

"For what it's worth, I really do like your photos." With that, he left. She hurled insults after him. Not that he didn't deserve them.

He was just doing his job. He doubted Kat Hamilton had ever had a real job. But even though he could and would defend his to the death, he was always sorry when innocent people got hurt.

It was debatable how innocent Sarah Hamilton was at this point, though. Unfortunately, her daughters would pay the price for her notoriety.

"WHAT DO YOU mean you're finished with the job?" Angelina Broadwater Hamilton demanded of the private investigator after taking a seat across from him. She had flown in this morning after he'd told her he had to see her. "What did you find out? I know Sarah Johnson Hamilton is hiding something. Did you find out what it is or not?"

"I hit a dead end."

The fifty-something Mike "Moose" McCallahan was tall and strapping with a full head of blond hair. Right now, though, the big, tough-looking man was avoiding her gaze.

"Why are you lying to me?" she asked calmly. "Did my husband buy you off?"

He quit fiddling with the papers on his desk to look up at her. "No."

"If you're worried because he's going to be the next president—"

"It's not that." He took a breath and let it out slowly. "I can tell you this. Your husband's former…wife, Sarah Johnson Hamilton, was involved with some… undesirables. One of them paid me a visit."

She studied him. "He roughed you up? Not much as far as I can tell, because you look fine."

Moose chuckled at that. "Look, I've dealt with a lot of scary people in my time." He met her gaze. "You need to drop this."

Angelina let out a bark of a laugh. "Maybe this… undesirable scared *you*, but I don't scare that easily. Tell me what you found out."

"Nothing, that's the problem. I didn't find out anything, but apparently some friends of your husband's—"

"Sarah. Her name is Sarah. She is no longer my husband's anything, all right?"

"Fine. Sarah Johnson Hamilton has some friends who are very protective of her."

"From which past? The one before my husband met her or during the twenty-two years he believed she was dead?"

"I have no idea, and, quite frankly, I don't care. Whatever your husband's—Sarah might be hiding, it isn't worth it to me to find out."

"Well, it is to *me*," Angelina snapped. She couldn't believe this man had been scared off so easily. Clearly, she'd hired the wrong person for this job. "Did this undesirable threaten you? Surely, it wasn't the first time someone wanted to—"

"Chop me up into little pieces and feed me to a pit bull? No, not the first time. Just the first time the person threatening me was more frightening than *being* chopped up and fed to a pit bull."

She studied him, realizing he had to know who the man was, what Sarah had been involved in. Otherwise, he wouldn't be so afraid. "I paid you an exorbitant amount of money to—"

"Here." He shoved a check across the desk at her. "All of your money back."

Angelina stared at him, finally seeing just how terrified Moose was. She wanted to pummel the coward with the first thing she could reach, but she saw that it would do no good.

"Fine," she said, snatching up the check as she rose to her feet. "I'll hire someone with more...guts."

"Good luck with that," he said as he stood. "Before you leave, wouldn't you like the message Sarah's friend left for you?"

She had already started for the door but now turned. "By all means."

"He said he'd destroy your husband...after he killed you."

She'd expected a threat, but the simplicity of this one definitely hit a nerve. Had she ever doubted that Sarah would do anything to get Buckmaster back?

Straightening her back so Moose didn't see the tremor of fear that pulsed through her, she walked back to the private investigator's desk. "Who are these... friends of Sarah's? Organized criminals? Gang members? Terrorists?"

Moose clamped his jaws shut and shook his head.

"But you believe they're capable of these threats."

It wasn't a question, but he nodded anyway.

"So Sarah *does* have something to hide, just as I suspected."

"Maybe they're just protective...friends. But if I were you, I'd drop this. You don't want to make men like them your enemies, let alone your husband's."

"*Men?* You said only one paid you a visit."

Again he gave her his mum look.

"I'm going to find out the truth. I'll hire someone who won't be scared off as easily as you."

He shook his head almost sadly. "You hire another PI and you'll only get him killed—and start a shit storm

that is going to rain down on not only you but also
your husband and his daughters. You sure it's worth it
just to get some dirt on your husband's former wife?"

MAX HAD PLANNED to drive back to Big Timber. But as
he crossed Main Street, he realized that he was starv-
ing. His productiveness had left him ready to call it a
day. Stopping at a hotel with a restaurant on the lower
level, he decided he'd stay in Bozeman for the night.
He was about to leave his camera bag and laptop in his
pickup, but changed his mind.

He knew he was being paranoid, but just the thought
of someone breaking in to his pickup, and stealing
them and the photos on them, made him take the equipment with him. Earlier at Big Timber Java, he'd put
the photos on a thumb drive and stuck it in his pocket.
Still, he didn't want to take any chances.

He'd just sat down in the restaurant after getting a
room, when the calls began coming in. He let them go
to voice mail. He'd go through them in his room later.
If he seemed too anxious, it would make him look
as if he didn't have the goods. He'd just ordered the
restaurant's largest T-bone steak with the trimmings
when he saw a pretty brunette sitting alone at a table,
perusing a menu.

She looked around as if a little lost. They made eye
contact. She smiled, then put down her menu and got
up to walk over to him. "I know this is going to sound
forward…" She bit her lower lip as if screwing up her
courage. "I hate eating alone and I've had this amazing
day." She stopped. "I'm sorry. I'm sure you'd prefer—"

"Have a seat. I've had a pretty amazing day myself."

All her nervousness seemed to evaporate. "Thank

you. I've never done anything like that before. I'm not sure what came over me," she said as she took a seat across from him. "It's just that I noticed you were alone and I'm alone…"

The woman looked to be a few years younger than his thirty-five years. After the day he'd had, he was glad to have company to celebrate with him.

"Max Malone," he said holding out his hand.

"Tammy Jones." Seeing what was going on, the waitress set up cutlery at the table and took her order.

Tammy explained that she was a retail buyer for a local department store. She was in town visiting from Seattle. "I'm only in town tonight. I normally don't invite myself to a stranger's table. But I'm tired of eating alone and today I got a great raise. I feel as if I just won the lottery."

He told her he was on vacation and just passing through town. He'd found when he told anyone that he was a reporter, it made them clam up, too nervous that they might end up in one of his articles.

"I saw your camera bag. So what all do you shoot?" she asked, leaning toward him with interest.

"Mostly scenic photos," he said. "It's just a hobby." He didn't want to talk about his job. Not tonight. He didn't want to jinx it.

Their meals came, and they talked about movies, books, food they loved and hated. It was pleasant, so he didn't mind having an after-dinner drink with her at the bar. She had a sweet, innocent face, which was strange because she reminded him a little of Kat Hamilton, sans the gray eyes. He kept thinking of those fog-veiled eyes. Kat was a woman who kept secrets bottled up, he thought.

"Am I losing you?" Tammy Jones asked, touching his hand.

"No." He gave her his best smile.

"You seemed a million miles away for a minute there."

"Nope." Just at the gallery across the street where he'd seen a light on in the back. Was Kat Hamilton still over there? She'd brought in new photos, if that large, flat portfolio she'd been carrying was any indication. He wished now that he'd asked to see them before he'd gotten thrown out.

"I know it's awful, but I'm not ready to call it a night." She met his gaze with a shy one. "A drink in my room?"

How could he say no? They took the stairs to her room on the second floor.

What could one more drink hurt? With a feeling of euphoria as warm as summer sunshine, he reminded himself of the photos he would be selling tomorrow.

When he woke the next morning, he was lying in the alley behind the hotel. While he still had his wallet, his camera and laptop were gone.

CHAPTER FOUR

As HE STUMBLED through the stupor of whatever he'd been drugged with, Max tried to figure out who'd set him up. He knew why he'd been so stupid as to fall for it. He'd wanted someone to celebrate with last night. As much as he loved his job, he got lonely.

Now, though, he just wanted his camera and laptop and the photos on them back. Maybe Tammy Jones— if that had even been her real name—had just planned to pawn them for money. But he suspected that wasn't the case once he checked his wallet and found he had almost a hundred in cash that she hadn't bothered with.

His head cleared a little more after a large coffee at a drive-through. He put in a call to the department store where Tammy Jones said she worked as a buyer, hoping he was wrong. He was told no one by that name worked for the company, not in Bozeman, not in Seattle.

He groaned as he disconnected. Whoever the woman had been last night, she had only one agenda. She was after the photos.

But how did she even know about them? He'd made a lot of calls yesterday and quite a few people were aware that he had the shots. All the people he'd called, though, he'd worked with before and he trusted them. That left… No way was that woman from the restaurant hired by the senator to steal the photos. If the future president had known about the photos he would have tried to buy them if not strong-arm him, Max was sure.

That left Kat Hamilton.

He drove back downtown. It was early enough that the gallery wasn't open yet, but the light was still on in the back. He parked on Main Street and walked down the alley. The rear entrance in the deserted alley had an old door and an even older lock. One little slip of his credit card and he was inside, thankful for his misspent youth.

The first thing he saw was a sleeping bag in one corner of the back area with a battery-operated lamp next to it and a book lying facedown on the floor. The woman clearly didn't appreciate the spines of books.

He found Kat wearing a pair of oversize jeans and a different baggy sweater. Clearly, this must be the attire she preferred. But he thought about bottled up secrets. Was she hiding under all those clothes? She stood next to a counter in the framing room of the gallery, her back to him, lost in her work. "I want my camera and laptop back."

At the sound of his voice, she spun around, gray eyes wide as if startled but not necessarily surprised. If he'd had any doubt who'd set him up, he didn't any longer. She'd known she'd be seeing him again.

"I beg your pardon?" she asked haughtily.

He enunciated each word as he stepped toward her. "The woman you hired to steal my camera and laptop? Tell her I want them back along with the photos of your mother and—"

"I have no idea what you're talking about."

He laughed. "Did anyone ever mention that you're a terrible liar?"

She bristled and looked offended. "I don't lie. Nor do I like being accused of something I didn't do."

"Save it," he said before she could deny it again. "I show you a photograph of your mother, and hours later my camera and laptop are stolen, and you have no idea what I'm talking about?"

Kat shrugged. "Maybe you should be more careful about who you hang out with." She turned her back to him as she resumed what she'd been doing. Or at least pretended to.

"Look. Someone is going to get a photo of your mother sooner or later. Why go to so much trouble?"

She turned to face him. "Exactly. If not you, then someone else will get her photo. Do you think I really care that you took a photo of my mother with plans to sell it to some sleazy rag? I didn't and I still don't. I've lived in a fishbowl my whole life. I've had people like you in my face with cameras since my father first ran for office. It comes with the territory. My mother is just another casualty."

He took off his hat and scratched the back of his neck as he considered whether or not she was lying. He'd been bluffing earlier. "I'm not buying it. I saw your expression when you recognized your mother in the photograph."

She sighed. "Think what you like."

"Let's talk about another woman, the one you set me up with last night."

Hand on one hip, she turned to study him openly for a moment. "What did this woman look like?"

He described her. "Don't pretend you don't know her."

"I know her *type*." She smiled, noticeably amused. "Come on, weren't you even a little suspicious when she hit on you? She did hit on you, right? That's what I thought, and you fell for it. Whoever set you up must know you."

Max laughed. Kat had lightened up, and he liked her sense of humor. "I'll have you know, women hit on me all the time."

She rolled her eyes. "Chalk this up as a learning experience and move on." She started to turn away again.

"You really don't think I'm going to let you get away with this, do you?"

She sighed and faced him once more. "What option do you have? Even if you had a shred of proof, it would be my word, the daughter of a senator, against your word, a…reporter."

Okay, now she was ticking him off. "I happen to like what I do, and it puts food on my table." He glanced at the photos she was working on. "Who keeps food on your table? I doubt your…hobby of taking pictures is your means of support." He cocked his head at her. "Then again, you don't need to stoop to having a real job, do you?"

KAT HAD KNOWN she would see Max Malone again after he'd ambushed her yesterday. He would want a story about her mother. He would use the photos he'd gotten to bargain with her. This wasn't her first rodeo.

But she hadn't expected him to come in the back way accusing her of stealing his camera and laptop with the photos of her mother. If she'd known how easy it would have been, she might have considered setting him up just for the fun of it, though.

No, she had expected him to come through the front door and make a scene once the gallery opened. She'd been prepared to threaten to call the police on him.

But he'd surprised her in more ways than one. Not many men did that. So she'd let him have his say, waiting to see what his game was. She'd even found the man somewhat amusing at first, but now he was starting to irritate her.

"I'll have you know I take care of myself."

"Is that right? You pay for that fancy SUV you drive?" He laughed. "I didn't think so. Now about my camera—"

"If you think I'm going to replace your camera— What are you doing?" she demanded as he pulled out his cell phone and keyed in three numbers. She'd planned to *threaten* to call the police, but she wouldn't have done it because she didn't want the hassle or the publicity.

"Calling the cops."

"They'll arrest you for breaking in to the gallery." She heard the 911 operator answer. He was calling her bluff. He knew she didn't want the police involved.

"I'd like to report—"

"Fine," she snapped.

He said, "Sorry, my mistake," into the phone and pocketed it again. He eyed her, waiting.

"But I don't have your camera or your laptop."

He studied her for a long moment. "Okay, if you want to play it that way, then what do you have to offer me?" he asked as he leaned against the counter where she'd been working.

She gritted her teeth. Hadn't she suspected that he hadn't really lost his camera or laptop and that he was playing her? She no longer found him amusing. It was time to call a halt to this.

"Even though I had nothing to do with the loss of your camera or laptop, I'll write you a check for new ones just to get rid of you."

He shook his head slowly, his gaze lingering on her long enough that she could feel heat color her cheeks. He made her feel naked, as if he could see her the way no one else could. "*My* camera, *my* laptop, *my* photos. That's the only deal on the table, unless you have something more to offer."

"I just offered you money!"

He shook his head, his gaze warm on her.

She felt her cheeks flush as she realized what he was suggesting. "I have *nothing* more to offer you."

He raised a brow, shoved off the counter and closed the distance between them. "Either I get my camera back, or you're going to have to make it up to me in another way." He was close, too close, but it wasn't fear he evoked. She could smell the scent of freshly showered soap on him. Her gaze went from his blue eyes to his lips and the slight smirk there. The man was so cocky, so arrogant, so sure of the effect he was having on her.

As he brushed his fingertips over her cheek, she felt a tingle before she slapped his hand away. "If you think I'm going to sleep with you—"

"I said something that I would like *better*," he said.

Better than sleeping with her? "You really are a bastard."

He shook his head. "Untrue. Both my parents were married and to each other."

"You're enjoying this."

His smile belied his words. "It's purely business, I assure you. But I appreciate you considering sleeping with me."

She fought the urge to slap his handsome face. "I never—"

"I'm sure you have never," he said. "But we can deal with that later. Right now, I suggest we discuss this over breakfast. I'm starved." He moved away, finally giving her breathing room. "You're buying."

"I don't think so." She was trembling inside, her stomach doing slow somersaults. The man threw her off balance, and he knew it. That made it even worse. She took a couple of deep breaths, shocked that some reporter could get this kind of primitive response from her.

Finally she turned to face him. He was going through her photos with an apparent critical eye. She wanted to grab them from him. The last thing she needed was a critique from him about her art.

"Call the police." She crossed her arms over her chest. "If you think you can blackmail me—"

"These are good, really," he said, turning to look at her as if surprised. "You have a good eye."

She hated how pleased she was but quickly mentally shook herself. What did he know about photography anyway? Just because he carried around a camera and took underhanded snapshots of people who didn't want their photos taken…

"I'd hoped we could discuss this over pancakes," he said as he stepped away from her photos. "I know something about your mother that you're going to want to hear before you see it in the media."

"There is nothing you can tell me that I would—"

"Your mother isn't just lying about the past twenty-two years. She's been lying since the get-go, and I can prove it." He smiled. "But first I want breakfast. I'm starved."

LYNETTE "NETTIE" CURRY found her husband out by the barn, talking to his crows. The crows, a long line of them, teetered on the phone line, cawing down occasionally as if conversing.

"Am I interrupting, Frank?" she asked.

Her husband, the long-time sheriff in Sweet Grass County, Montana, laughed. He was a big man with graying blond hair, a drooping, old-timey gunfighter mustache and bright blue eyes. She'd been in love with him for more than fifty years and often still couldn't believe that they'd finally found their way back to each other.

The crows cawed down at her as if in greeting. Ask Frank and he'd report that's exactly what they were saying. He'd always been fascinated with the birds and clearly loved them. But even as skeptical as she'd been when she'd first moved in, Nettie now believed that they were equally as fond of him.

"I found something I thought might interest you," she said, flapping the papers she'd printed off the computer. "It's about that tattoo. The one on Sarah Hamilton's behind. I might know what it means."

She saw that she had his attention. Frank had been trying to solve the mystery of not only Sarah's miraculous and oddly timed return from the dead, but also her missing twenty-two years. The fifty-eight-year-old woman hadn't just secretly parachuted back into the county, she'd come with no memory of where she'd been, what she'd been or why she was back now. At least that was her story.

All of it, according to Frank, added up to trouble. And that was before he'd found out about the strange tattoo Sarah Hamilton had gotten on her butt cheek during those missing years.

Frank walked her back to the porch and waited until they'd both sat down before he asked what she'd found.

"We agreed that the tattoo appears to be a pendulum that left a circular pattern beneath its point," she said and picked up papers she'd printed out from the computer. She began to read what she'd discovered. "'There is nothing new about pendulums since they date back eight thousand years. While often associated with predicting the future, they were used by the Egyptians four thousand years ago for spiritual healing with the energy of that particular pendulum. Not all pendulums have the same energy.'"

When she looked up from her papers, Frank looked about to roll his eyes.

"Bear with me," she said and hurried on. "'Along with reportedly detecting imbalances in energy fields for healing, pendulums have been used to find missing objects, unmarked graves, buried treasure, even underground water sources.'"

"So Sarah was using her ass to find water?" Frank laughed and got to his feet. "Lynette, it might be just a stupid tattoo that she really did get while drunk on tequila."

"Is that what she told you?" Nettie could tell he didn't believe it any more than she did. "It means something, and I, for one, am going to find out what."

He shook his head but he was smiling. "I have to go to work."

"Still no word on that missing reporter?" she asked, putting her papers aside for the time being. Chuck Barrow had been covering the Sarah Hamilton story when he'd disappeared. His car was found at the bottom of a ravine along with his bloody coat. It was assumed that he'd crashed his car, and, hurt and disoriented, he'd wandered away into the woods and died.

"No. I'd hoped either he or his body would have turned up by now."

"You don't think he merely took the opportunity to walk away from his life, do you?" It wouldn't be the first time a person had done that.

Frank shook his head. "I think he's dead." He glanced over at her. "It's just a feeling." His gaze went to the information she'd printed out. "If you decide to take up pendulum divining, see if you can locate a spot for another well out here on the ranch." He grinned before leaning down to kiss her.

"Laugh, Frank Curry, but I just might do that." As she watched him go, she realized that he'd given her an idea. All she needed to do was get back on the computer and find out where she could buy a pendulum.

FRANK CURRY PRIDED himself on never having an unsolved murder since taking over as sheriff of Sweet Grass County. Homicides were rare in Montana, and yet his county seemed to have had more than its share recently.

And now he had this missing person's case involving one of the reporters who'd been hanging around outside the Hamilton Ranch. Chuck Barrow had disappeared back in late June. His vehicle had been found later at the bottom of a ravine. A bloodstained coat was found inside, leading him and the other investigators to believe Barrow had been injured when he'd left on foot and apparently had gotten lost in the mountains.

The search had been called off after several weeks, but the lack of a body still bothered Frank. Barrow wasn't the first man to get lost in the Crazy Mountains. The body of a hunter lost last fall still hadn't been found either.

Much like the reappearance of Sarah Hamilton, the cases felt like loose ends that he needed to tie up. Only Sarah wasn't an official case. He'd called in the FBI, and they hadn't found any reason for continuing investigating her disappearance or reappearance. So Frank had taken it on outside of his official cases.

What made Barrow's disappearance interesting was, according to the television news department he worked for, he had been going to talk to Sarah Hamilton. Sarah had denied giving the man an interview, but Frank couldn't shake the feeling that Barrow had found her and, not long after, had met his fate.

When he returned to his office, he called his undersheriff in. "Are you saying you think she killed him?" Dillon Lawson asked after he'd shared his theory with him. "And then she pushed his vehicle into a ravine."

"After leaving his bloody coat in the rig, yes." He could see how skeptical Dillon was of his theory. Sarah was fifty-eight years old and, while in great shape for her age, wasn't capable of dragging the dead weight of a man the size of Chuck Barrow anywhere. "She had help."

The undersheriff's eyes widened. "Russell Murdock?"

Frank shook his head. "Someone from her past."

"Wait a minute," Dillon said, leaning back in his chair across the desk from Frank. "That would mean that she's lying about not remembering her past."

"If she was in on it, yes."

Dillon frowned. "You think someone from her past is running interference for her without her being aware of it?"

It had crossed his mind. "It's possible. If, and it's a huge *if*, she really doesn't recall jumping or being pushed from a plane, parachuting into a tree, changing clothes and stumbling out to the road for Russell Murdock to find her...then she might not know she isn't alone."

The undersheriff rubbed a hand over his jaw. "This is quite a theory. I suppose you also have a theory about their purpose in doing this." Before Frank could answer, Dillon said, "The senator."

"Soon to be our next president if the polls are even partially correct."

Dillon let out a low whistle. "Say you're right. If Sarah's purpose in coming back here, along with her cohorts, is to keep him from being president, then why not stop him now? Or maybe they want him to be president and plan to use him. The bad publicity against Sarah has only strengthened his standing in the race."

Frank nodded.

"Or maybe Chuck Barrow had a car accident and, injured, wandered off into the mountains to die."

"Do you know what bothers me the most? Whoever wanted Sarah Hamilton back here could have just dropped her off beside the road. But they dropped her from a plane. They had to know we'd discover that. They *wanted* us to know."

Dillon was frowning again. "Why?"

"Because they think they're smarter than we are."

"And Sarah? What's her role in all this?"

"She's Buckmaster Hamilton's Achilles' heel."

The undersheriff shook his head. "The senator is on the campaign trail, his current wife at his side. I'd say Sarah has lost."

Frank laughed. "Don't ever underestimate a woman with a mission, let alone this one. Sarah Hamilton is up to something, you can count on it."

MAX DIDN'T THINK the senator's daughter could surprise him. He told himself he knew her kind only too well. That's why he didn't expect to get too far with her. The truth was, he needed her help to prove what he suspected about her mother. He'd bluffed his way this far. He was thinking that if he could convince her he knew more than he did—

"Here, take this," she said as she came back from getting something out of her SUV. "It's one of my old cameras I've kept as a backup."

Max stared at the camera bag, too surprised to reach for it.

"I'm only lending it to you until you can afford to replace yours. Sorry, but I don't have an extra laptop."

He took the camera bag and peeked inside before his gaze shot up to hers. It surprised him how touched he was by this kind gesture. "This is an awfully nice old backup."

She shrugged and looked embarrassed. He could see

she felt guilty about her privileged life. She shouldn't have, but he understood. He liked her better for it.

"I still want mine back. It had sentimental value."

"I'm sure it did," she said with a hint of sarcasm.

It was hundreds of dollars cheaper than the "loaner" she had given him, and they both knew it. "It was my lucky camera."

"Like those are your lucky boots?"

He looked down at his worn boots and laughed. "Actually, they are."

She shook her head. "Maybe you'll get lucky with this camera," she said, then instantly regretted it if the color that warmed her cheeks was any indication.

"Maybe I will," he said with a wink.

She groaned. "Let's get this over with, though I don't know why I would care what you have on my mother. But I am hungry and it is time for breakfast."

"Hey." She stopped to glance back at him as if to say, now what? "Thanks," he said, slipping the camera bag strap over his shoulder. "I appreciate it."

"Take better care of it than you did yours."

Max smiled at her retreating back. It was a nice rear view. What surprised him was that he was actually beginning to believe that Kat Hamilton *hadn't* been behind stealing the photos. Which brought him back to who, then, if not Kat?

He was considering that question as they left by the front of the gallery and started across the street toward the small café next to the hotel. He hardly heard the roar of the big engine; he'd been concentrating so hard on how to get this woman to help him with his story. He was surprised she'd even agreed to have breakfast with him. Maybe he *would* let her pay.

Or maybe he'd try a different approach. Maybe he'd tell her the truth, which would mean paying for breakfast himself.

The engine roar filled his ears, jerking him out of his thoughts. He looked up as a large SUV came around the corner and headed right for them.

CHAPTER FIVE

Max didn't have time to think. He acted instinctively, surprising himself as much as Kat. He grabbed her and threw them both back out of the way as the giant SUV roared past. The vehicle had missed them by mere inches. As the dust settled, he listened to it thunder away, the shock of the near miss hitting home. Had whoever was behind the wheel purposely tried to run them down?

"Excuse me?"

He felt Kat's body under him, surprised that there were more curves than he'd expected in a woman as fit as she was. She dressed in a way that hid her attributes well. Why was that, he wondered again idly as he realized that one of his hands was resting on her full, nicely rounded left breast.

"Get off me," Kat said, shoving his hand away.

"That was purely accidental," he said as he rose and offered her a hand up.

She ignored it as she got to her feet. "Sure it was." She brushed at her jeans and sweater. "What was that about anyway?"

"Uh, I just saved your life."

She shot him a disbelieving look.

"Did you not see that SUV that was speeding directly at us only moments ago?" He looked around for someone on the street to verify his story, but it was early on a Sunday morning, so there were no other people out yet.

"Us?" She looked away from him in the direction the vehicle had gone. "If the driver of that SUV really was trying to kill one of us, I'm betting he was aiming for you."

He appraised her. "Why would someone want me dead?"

"Are. You. Serious?"

"Not everyone hates reporters."

She scoffed at that before starting across the street. He suspected she was more shaken by the near hit-and-run than she was letting on. But then again she hadn't gotten such an up-close-and-personal look at the chrome grille on the monster SUV as he had.

Still it appeared Kat Hamilton didn't scare easily. He filed that information away for the future and followed her. Unlike her, he glanced around in case the SUV came back to try again. He was still surprised she'd agreed to breakfast. He chalked it up to curiosity. She had to be as interested in her mother's past as he was. Maybe more.

Then again, she could just be hungry like she said.

As he held the café door open for her to enter, he looked back out into the empty street. Had that just been some irresponsible kid driving that SUV who hadn't even seen them?

KAT STUDIED THE MAN across the table from her as she questioned her sanity. She'd had a delayed reaction from their near accident in the street and now felt herself shaking inside. Not that she believed someone had been trying to kill her. Maybe Max, though, she thought as she considered the handsome, arrogant reporter sitting across from her. *I bet it was a woman behind the wheel.*

"I'm not sure this was a good idea," he said as he rearranged the napkins and salt and pepper shakers.

She sighed. "I'm buying, so order whatever you want." Had her legs not felt so weak right now, she would have walked out. She just needed to sit for a few minutes.

He quit fooling with the items on the table to meet her gaze. Max didn't seem like the nervous type, but when she met his eyes, she saw that he appeared to be anxious. Or at least he wanted her to think that.

"This could be more dangerous than I originally thought," he said.

Kat gave him an impatient stare. Why had she agreed to this? She certainly couldn't trust anything that came out of his mouth. Look how he'd taken advantage of a close call on the street just now. Or had he set the whole thing up? Either way, she could still feel the heat of his hand from where he'd held her breast.

And now he appeared to be trying to scare her.

"You really don't have anything on my mother, do you? This was just a ruse to get me to what? Buy breakfast? Or just scare me into telling you something about her?"

He gave her an innocent, hurt look. "You think I had something to do with what just happened?"

"I suspect you'd stoop to just about anything to get what you want."

"I'm shocked you would think that of me. Seriously, I thought you and I were becoming friends."

She laughed. "Does that work on other women?"

A waitress in her late teens appeared with two menus, two cups and a coffeepot.

"Good morning," Max said, turning on his charm and immediately rattling the poor girl.

"Good morning," the girl stammered and sloshed coffee onto the table. She hurried away to get a dishrag to clean up the mess.

He shot Kat a grin as if to say, "See, all women find me irresistible."

Kat groaned and disappeared behind her menu.

The waitress returned, sopped up the spilled coffee and apologized profusely.

"It's all right," Kat assured her. "It could have happened to anyone."

Max shot her another grin before picking up his menu.

Kat waited for the young woman to finish filling their coffee cups as Max continued to peruse his menu.

"We'll both have bacon and eggs, hash browns and a side of pancakes," Max said.

"No," she said and tried to stop the waitress, but Max shooed the girl off with a wink. Kat had been planning to have nothing but coffee and toast like she usually did to also make this breakfast as short as possible. "I don't eat pancakes, let alone bacon or hash browns or egg yolks for that matter."

Max lifted an eyebrow.

"What?" she demanded.

"I hadn't taken you for one of *those*."

"One of *those*?" she repeated, feeling her blood begin to heat.

"Why do you deny yourself one of the pleasures of life?"

"Bacon?"

"Eating." He leaned on his elbows on the table to study her. "What other pleasures do you deny yourself?"

"I really don't have t—"

As she started to rise, he reached over and put a hand on her arm. "Sorry, didn't know you were that sensitive about life's…pleasures."

She shot him a daggered look. "Just tell me what I'm doing here."

"I hate doing business on an empty stomach."

"Start talking or I'm walking."

He nodded and leaned back, suddenly all business. It startled her for a moment at how quickly he could turn off the charming but inept, arrogant cowboy reporter, and become serious and seemingly competent. It made her wonder who the real Max Malone was.

"How much do you know about your mother's past before she married your father?" he asked.

Kat shrugged, a little embarrassed to admit even to herself that she knew little. Her father had never talked about their mother. Even as a child, when she'd asked about her mother, he'd been vague. It wasn't until her mother returned that she understood why. For years, her father had believed that Sarah had committed suicide. He would have seen that as the ultimate betrayal—as well as his own failure. Add to that his broken heart…

Once Angelina had come into the picture, all evidence of their mother had disappeared, and her mother was never mentioned again. That was, until she'd shown up all these years later, alive but with no memory of the past.

"Why don't you tell me what *you* know," Kat suggested.

He gave her a look that said he saw right through her veiled attempt to hide what she didn't know, but he didn't seem concerned about it. "Your mother had what appeared to be a privileged childhood," he began as if reciting from notes. "Two loving parents, a nice house in a nice neighborhood, friends and picture-perfect high school years. So I ask you, why are there no photographs from college? Your mother has been all over the news. By now friends would have come forward with candid shots, which would have been worth a nice chunk of change."

"Maybe her friends aren't as mercenary as you."

"It's just a fact of life. If not for the money, then for fifteen minutes of fame. It looks to me like your mother just dropped off the radar in college after being so popular and so involved in high school. It doesn't add up."

"So what?" Kat said, frowning. "I know she graduated."

"According to her transcripts."

She stared at him. "What are you saying?"

The waitress reappeared with their food. Max dug in as if he hadn't eaten in days. Maybe he hadn't. There hadn't been many vehicles on Main this morning because of the hour. She assumed that the old pickup parked down the street from the gallery with the California plates must have been his.

"I can't find anyone who knew her," he said between bites. "Not a professor who remembers her, a roommate, *anyone*."

"It was a large university, and she probably could afford not to have a roommate," Kat said.

He continued as if she hadn't spoken. "Add to that the fact that she wasn't a member of any organizations, sororities or even campus clubs, or involved in any campus-sponsored extracurricular activities."

Absentmindedly Kat picked up a strip of bacon and took a bite. It had been so long since she'd had meat—let alone bacon—that she was shocked at how good it tasted. She quickly put it down.

"That isn't that unusual," she said wiping her hands on her napkin. "I wasn't interested in any of that either and at a large campus…" She watched him slather butter on his pancakes and then drown them in syrup, recalling the taste for the first time in what seemed like forever.

He was right. She hadn't quit eating things that she loved for health reasons. She knew exactly when she'd begun denying herself any pleasures and shuddered inside at the memory.

"So you really don't have any proof," she said. "You're just fishing."

MAX DIDN'T LET her words affect his appetite or his confidence in what he had to tell her—or her desire to hear it.

Looking up, he jabbed his fork into the air as he ticked off what he'd discovered about the early Sarah Johnson pre-Hamilton.

"Think about it. Your mother was pretty and popular in high school. There were tons of photos of her in all kinds of organizations, at dances, with her girlfriends in the yearbooks. She was a cheerleader and in every kind of after-school activity there was." He noticed that she was buttering her pancakes. Not missing a beat, he slid the syrup over to her. "Then she goes off to college and...*nothing.*"

"Maybe college was harder for her, and she had to study more," Kat said and took a bite of her pancake. She closed her eyes for a moment, her face a picture of euphoria. He tried to concentrate on her words, telling himself she was beginning to question her mother's past, as well.

But at the back of his mind, he kept asking himself why Kat Hamilton had given up the food she loved. What else had she given up, he wondered as he considered her apparel.

"A person as outgoing as your mother was in high school is the kind to pledge a sorority, to get involved in the school paper or university politics, have her photo all over that campus." He shook his head. "Who changes just like that?" He snapped his fingers. "Something happened."

He stabbed his fork into his pancakes. Like Kat Hamilton, he thought. He'd met women on diets. Others who wanted to eat more healthfully. But Kat was different. She seemed to be in a battle with food. Or was it with herself? Why was that?

"Something happened that changed your mother's life, changed her." He'd bet his lucky boots on that.

Kat sat back, as if trying to distance herself from what he was saying. "Like what?"

He chewed for a moment. "That's what I don't know and I'm trying to find out."

"I think you're making too much out of this."

He considered her for a moment. "And I think you're just as curious as I am. Too bad we can't ask her."

"Oh, I see what you're up to. You want me to ask my mother what she was doing in college besides studying?"

He leaned his elbows on the table as he bent toward her. "Why not? Supposedly those were years she should be able to remember, right?"

Kat shook her head, and he saw that he'd made her angry again. "You think she's lying about not remembering the past twenty-two years?"

He shrugged and took another bite of his pancakes. "What do you think?"

"I think breakfast is over." She started to rise, but he caught her hand with his free one.

"I'm being honest with you. How about being honest with me?"

"I didn't take your camera and laptop," she said, pulling loose of his touch.

"I believe you. Who did you tell about the photo after I showed it to you, though?"

Kat's gray eyes widened for an instant. She slowly sat back down. "I'm not sure I even believe you lost anything."

He put down his fork and pushed his plate away before wiping his mouth with his napkin. "Yes, you are, and I think you know who was behind stealing them and the photos." His gaze captured hers. "So who did you call?" To his surprise, he saw the answer in her expression. "You called your mother."

"You can't think that my mother…"

"Would she call your father? Or would she call Russell Murdock?"

"This is ridiculous," Kat snapped. "You can't think that my father or Russell—"

"No," he said, frowning down at his nearly empty plate. "Unless..." He looked up at her. "What if her phone or wherever she is staying is bugged?"

She gave him an angry look. "You're just saying all this to scare me. Why would anyone bug the cabin where my mother's staying?"

"*Seriously?* The first wife of the possible future president. Even if she wasn't missing the past twenty-two years, there's a story there. The other reporters are chasing the love triangle, but I think the real story started back in college."

CHAPTER SIX

KAT COULDN'T HELP but stare at him. He'd tricked her into coming to breakfast with this crazy story about her mother's college years and now he was trying to make her think that her mother's cabin was bugged by...by people who would hire some woman to steal the photos he'd taken.

It was just crazy enough to have a ring of truth to it, she thought, then quickly pushed the idea away.

Max picked up his coffee cup, took a sip and put it back down as if lost in thought. "If that SUV that almost ran us down wasn't an accident..."

"Do you really think I am that gullible that I'm buying any of this?" Kat demanded, trying to keep her voice down. She worried enough about her mother without having some...some reporter try to fill her head with complete nonsense. "You dig into other people's life for dirt, and if you can't find it, you make it up out of thin air? I can't believe you do this for a living, because I can see that you clearly enjoy it."

He didn't even look offended. She suspected he'd heard it all before. "People fascinate me. I try to figure them out, learn their deep, dark secrets, reveal the real person behind the mask." Max shrugged. "Like you." He cocked his head as he surveyed her openly. "I bet you have a few secrets of your own."

She held up her hand. "Don't start. What you see is what you get."

He laughed. *"Really?"*

"You know what I mean."

"I just don't believe you. Everyone has something to hide. You're no different."

She got to her feet. "You're wasting your time."

"Maybe." He was still studying her, still grinning.

"Obviously my mother went to that college and graduated—"

"Records can be doctored."

"Then she came out here to work in Yellowstone Park."

"But she never did work in the park."

"That's because my father swept her off her feet and—"

"She never even applied for work in the park. Instead, she was hanging around a corral, no doubt aware your father would be delivering horses that day."

Kat stared at him. "Is there no end to your devious theories? You have no way of knowing if that is true or not."

"But you have to admit, it is all very…suspicious."

She shook her head. There was no dissuading him. "Well, if you don't have more to do than this, I do." She reached for her purse, figuring he really was going to let her buy breakfast.

He rose slowly to his feet. The man annoyed her on so many levels. Like the way he dressed, as if he really didn't give a damn that people thought he was homeless. Like the slow, laid-back way he moved. Like the way his blue eyes pierced through the wall she'd built around herself.

On top of that, she noticed that she'd eaten most of the breakfast he'd ordered her.

"If I'm wrong, then help me prove it," he challenged as he shifted that blue-eyed gaze to her. "Your father would have your mother's things—you know, the usual stuff we hang on to in safety deposit boxes—diplomas, photos, transcripts of grades from college, anything to convince me your mother really did attend that university. Maybe you've even seen some of these things."

She hadn't and she was pretty sure he was counting on that. He'd established doubt in her mind, and now he was daring her to prove him wrong.

"I see what you're doing," she said.

He gave her that innocent boyish look of his, another thing about him she didn't like. "If I'm wrong, I won't bother you again."

"Fine." A part of her couldn't wait to prove him wrong. "Where can I find you?"

"I'm staying in the back of my pickup outside the ranch gate."

"Of course you are. How glamorous."

"I'm pretty low maintenance when I'm working."

Was he implying she wasn't? She took a breath and didn't take the bait. While she was at the house proving him wrong, she would take the opportunity to do a little digging into Max Malone's life as well and see how he liked it.

She pulled out her debit card.

"Breakfast is on me," he said, sounding almost amused as he picked up the bill from the table.

"How gallant."

"I'm glad to see that you enjoyed your meal," he said, a grin in his voice.

She refused to look at him as she put her card away. "I just want to see your face when I prove you wrong."

MAX FOUND HIMSELF whistling as he walked to his pickup. He'd enjoyed breakfast. He'd enjoyed Kat Hamilton. She was talented, quick-witted and smart. Hopefully, she would also be useful.

He had thought it odd when he couldn't find out anything about Sarah Johnson Hamilton's college years, other than her transcript. But after talking to Kat, he was more convinced than ever that he was onto something. Had she seen anything that proved Kat had even gone to college, she would have said something.

He'd seen from her expression that she didn't know any more about her mother's time at college than he did. Maybe Kat would produce more documents from those days, but Max seriously doubted it.

Sarah had been a straight A student in high school, even though she'd been involved in every activity known to man. Her college transcript, on the other hand, was filled with Bs and Cs.

On the surface, that hadn't seemed that strange. College was often harder. Also, as he recalled, it was a time to spread your wings and have some fun. So the grades hadn't triggered any red flags. If he was right, though, and her records had been manipulated, then whoever did it wouldn't have given her all As. Straight A students attracted attention. Professors would have remembered *that* Sarah.

He shook his head. Maybe he really was looking for a story where there wasn't one. It wouldn't be the first time he'd let his imagination loose only to come back to earth with a thud, disappointing himself. But if a man didn't dream...

As he reached his pickup, he saw that someone had stuck a small piece of paper under the windshield wiper. He slowed and looked around. The paper was ragged on the edges, as if quickly torn from a larger sheet. He didn't see anyone watching him, but he had the distinct feeling eyes were on him.

Carefully, he pulled the note out, trying not to touch more than the edge in case he had need to check it for fingerprints at sometime in the future. It was a cautious behavior that was familiar to him. His favorite stories were those involving people who didn't want their secrets revealed. Because of that, he'd had his share of threats—not to mention the times things had turned violent. He was often thankful for the years he'd spent in martial arts training.

The piece of paper was folded in half. Opening it, he saw the apparently hurriedly scrawled words: *Back off or you will lose more than your photos.*

Max smiled, opened his pickup and carefully put the note into the glove box. Apparently, he was making someone nervous. That was always a good sign. It was time to dig deeper into the years Sarah Johnson had spent at college back East, because he was onto something. Too bad he didn't know what. Yet.

KAT TOLD HERSELF that she'd never met a more irritating man. She returned to the studio feeling as if she'd just been in a three-ring boxing bout—or just had angry sex.

Where had that thought come from?

She shook her head as she tried to get her head

back into her work. But she couldn't wait to prove Max Malone wrong. Smiling, she thought of the look on his face when she shot down his theory. Not that he would stop stalking her mother, she thought, her smile fading. But Sarah could take care of herself.

Another thought from out of nowhere.

She had no basis for it. She didn't know her mother. Worse, she hadn't made an effort to get to know the stranger who'd returned.

But Buckmaster certainly saw his first wife as weak, broken, vulnerable. Kat could tell it drove him crazy that he couldn't take care of her and have her totally dependent on him. She could imagine how Angelina hated that he was now supporting both of them.

But Kat sensed that her mother was stronger than her father thought.

She shivered as she remembered the things that Max had said. Did her mother have something to hide— other than the twenty-two missing years?

Realizing she wasn't going to be able to get anything done until she proved Max Malone wrong, she left the gallery and drove to the ranch.

At the gate, she looked around for Max's old pickup. No sign of it or him. She couldn't help but wonder where he might be. He had to know she would come back to the ranch to look for the information on her mother right away. She'd thought for sure he would be anxious to hear what she'd found.

Was he that convinced that she wouldn't find anything?

The thought made her all the more determined to discover proof and squash his crazy theory.

As she pulled up in front of the main ranch house,

she was surprised to see that her father and stepmother had returned.

"That will make this easier," she said as she got out and hurried inside.

"Kat!" her father said the moment he saw her. He'd been standing at the breakfast bar, but now put down his coffee cup to give her a hug. "I was hoping we'd get to see you while we were home. How are the photos coming along?"

"Fine." She glanced toward her stepmother. Angelina hadn't said a word of greeting. Kat picked up tension between them, but then again, there'd been tension from the moment the first Mrs. Buckmaster Hamilton had come back.

"I need to talk to you," Kat said to her father as he offered her coffee or breakfast. She declined, saying she'd just eaten. "Could we step into your den?"

"If this is about your mother…" Angelina said.

"Actually, it is," Kat said and heard her father sigh.

"Then by all means, Angelina should join us," he said.

Once the three of them were settled in the den, Kat got right to it. "I was wondering if I could see some things of my mother's from her years in college. I'm sure she must have saved something."

Her father shook his head. "Maybe she did, but I don't have—"

"There must be photos or yearbooks or something from her earlier life." Kat noticed that Angelina seemed to be listening with interest.

"I'm sorry, but anything of that nature was probably destroyed in the fire," Buckmaster said.

"Fire?" Kat and Angelina echoed.

He glanced at both of them in surprise. "I thought I might have mentioned…" He brushed that off. "A fire destroyed Sarah's family home not long before she came out West. From what Sarah said, she lost everything but the clothes on her back. Both her parents died in the fire."

Kat stared at him in shock. "I can't believe this is the first time I've heard about this." She'd known that both sets of her grandparents were gone, but that her mother's side was killed in a fire? Worse, she could well imagine what Max was going to say when she told him why there was nothing of her mother's from college, since she was thinking the same thing. *How convenient.*

He shook his head, looking miserable. "There really is no reason either of you would have known about it. It happened so long ago—"

"Still, those were my grandparents," Kat said.

Her father nodded. "I'm sorry that you never got to know any of your grandparents."

Stunned, Kat tried to get her head around this news. "But surely any important papers would have been kept in a safety deposit box at the bank."

Again he shook his head. "Her parents were in the process of moving. Downsizing since Sarah had graduated from college and wouldn't be living at home. They'd packed up everything, closed their bank accounts… I'm sorry, but why are you so interested in things from your mother's earlier life?"

Kat pushed back her hair. The last thing she wanted to tell her father was that she was looking for the information because of an encounter with a reporter doing a story on Sarah.

"I thought maybe something from her past might help her remember," she said lamely. While the explanation was possible, she knew what it would sound like to Max.

Angelina's expression was one of disbelief. "Something from her college years? Why would you think that would trigger memory of the past twenty-two years?"

Kat shrugged. "It was just a thought. I was especially interested in photographs of her from back then for an album I thought about putting together."

"How sweet." Her stepmother's words dripped with sarcasm. "Better put some current snapshots in it, so that way you girls can remember what she looked like when she disappears again."

Her father ignored Angelina. Either that or he'd heard it all before and was desensitized to her remarks. "I think that is a wonderful idea, but I'm afraid there are no photographs either. Over the years they've been either lost or somehow misplaced."

Angelina looked away. They all knew how the photos had gotten *lost*. "Well, it was worth a shot. I'd better get going." Kat turned toward the door.

Her father walked her out to her SUV. "I'm glad you came by. We're only home for a few days, then it is off again, but I'll be back for your photo exhibit."

She started to tell him it wasn't necessary, but he didn't give her a chance.

"Have you seen your mother?" he asked, worry furrowing his brows.

Kat shook her head. "I've been so busy with the exhibit."

"Then you haven't heard the news."

She felt her stomach drop. "The *news*?"

"I probably should wait and let your mother tell you herself. I just assumed she would have by now."

"What?" Kat demanded. She'd never liked secrets and had a feeling she wouldn't like this one either.

"She told me that she's getting married."

Kat could see that this was tearing her father up. "*Married*? To whom?"

"Russell Murdock."

IT WAS ONE of those clear, crisp fall mornings with Montana's big sky a splendid blue. While a few puffy white clouds hung over the Crazies, the sun caught on the needles of the pine trees and made them glisten.

Russell had driven up, taken out several sacks of groceries he'd brought and come inside the cabin, bringing the smell of the cold fall day with him.

"So you talked to your daughter," Sarah said after Russell had put the groceries away in the small cabin where she'd been hiding out for months.

He nodded without turning around. But she'd seen his expression when he'd driven up, his real emotions before he'd quickly covered them up with a smile.

"She's not happy about it, is she?" Sarah said with a nervous laugh.

He turned quickly and took her shoulders in his big hands. "She's concerned that we haven't known each other very long."

"She's right."

"She just needs to get to know you."

"Too bad I don't know myself." That wasn't quite true. She'd been experiencing—not memories, but... fleeting though odd, disturbing images. Russell thought she was starting to remember. He said it didn't worry him. But then Russell liked to believe that everything would turn out for the best.

He really seemed to believe he could handle whatever might surface from her past. Maybe he could. More than likely he would be shocked, horrified, repulsed and, if the past were half as bad as the images, it would probably get them both killed.

She'd tried to reason with Russell, but he loved her and wanted her, and he knew that she needed him. Maybe he needed her even more. Why else would he want to marry her?

Anyway, what was the alternative? To just hang around Beartooth until...until what? Buck was married to Angelina and campaigning day and night for the presidency. When Russell had suggested marriage, she'd told herself she couldn't do that to him.

Later, she'd given it more thought and realized it might be the answer. Russell loved her. She cared about him. Mostly, though, she'd seen it as a way to free Buck and maybe herself. Buck needed to concentrate on his election campaign. She needed to let him go. Not that she thought she could ever stop loving him.

Russell, on the other hand, believed that one day she would remember why she'd driven her car into the iced-over Yellowstone River in a suicide attempt. He was convinced it had something to do with Buckmaster, and once she remembered there would be no love lost between them.

The last thing she remembered was giving birth to her twins, Harper and Cassidy, both of whom had now graduated from college. She had no memory of why she would have tried to kill herself all those years ago.

Buck had sworn he didn't know. The press had decided she'd been desperate with postpartum depression and mentally unstable. She thought the truth, if it ever came out, might be closer to what the press believed.

What she hadn't considered when she'd agreed to marry Russell was how hard Buck would take the news. She'd thought he might be relieved. He'd seemed caught between her and Angelina, and the press had certainly made the most of the lovers' triangle stories, whether true or not.

Buck had pleaded with her to wait until he returned to Montana before she announced her engagement to Russell.

She had agreed, even against Russell's protests. But now he was back. Yesterday, when she and Buck had met, though, he'd begged for more time.

"We'll get you your driver's license and a vehicle so Russell doesn't have to bring you every time we meet," Buck had said.

"He's the man I'm going to marry."

Buck had held her gaze. "No. You're still my wife."

"Not legally. You're married to Angelina now."

He'd groaned as if in pain. "I can't let you go, Sarah. Please, I'm trying to work this out."

"There is no way to work it out, Buck. If you leave her to be with me…the voters will turn on you. If you have any hope of being our next president…"

"I can't lose you," he said. "Two weeks. Surely you can give me that much more time, yes?"

"Two weeks or even two months, what will it accomplish? There is no way we can be together."

"Let me see what I can do."

Now, as she looked into Russell's handsome, trusting face, she knew what she had to do. "Buck wants us to wait another two weeks before we announce our engagement."

Russell looked upset but not surprised. "Why two weeks? I don't understand why we're waiting. What will be different in two weeks?"

"Maybe it has something to do with the campaign." She had no idea what Buck was thinking or what he might do. Probably nothing, because he was caught, and there was no way out.

Russell shook his head, his look sympathetic. "Sarah, if he was going to leave Angelina, he would have done it already."

She hid the sting of his words, willing herself not to show how much the truth hurt. "Buck just needs a little more time to accept it." She stepped to him and cupped his jaw in her hand. "That isn't too much to ask, is it?"

He weakened at once, just as he always did. He loved her. She had no doubt of that. Loved the woman he thought he knew.

"What's two weeks? We will have the rest of our lives together." Even as she said it, she didn't believe it. Her life felt too tenuous to plan more than a few minutes ahead. In truth, she felt as if she was waiting—not for Buck to do anything—but for her past to show up and destroy any future she'd planned.

Russell took her into his arms. He was a tall, strong, attractive man, and he was kind and good. She closed her eyes as she breathed in his outdoor scent.

She'd needed him from the moment they'd crossed paths that day on the road in the middle of nowhere. But was she seriously planning to marry him? If so, then why couldn't she see the two of them married and living on his ranch? Why did she keep seeing herself back on Hamilton Ranch? Back with Buck? When she knew it was impossible?

"Do you believe in fate?" Russell asked as he hugged her.

Did she? Something told her she didn't. "You think all of this is fate?" That would be just like Russell. Fate that he was the one who found her that day? Or had that been planned all along? Didn't he say he went to the cemetery the same time every week? She could see how easily a person watching him would see his routine.

"I believe there's a reason you came into my life."

Was he a fool? Or were they both fools? She drew back to look into his eyes, and suddenly she knew she couldn't keep hoping that Buck would find a way back to her. "You're right. We shouldn't wait. Let's announce our engagement. Do we put a notice in the newspaper or—"

"Leave it to me," Russell said, sounding happier than she'd ever seen him. "I'm going to take care of you, Sarah. You'll always be safe with me."

MAX DROVE TO Big Timber Java, got a cup of coffee and opened his new laptop. He'd considered buying a new camera, but he liked the idea of using Kat's for the time being.

Before coming to Montana, he'd done as much research as he could on Sarah Johnson Hamilton. Now, though, as he stared at the empty screen, he remembered everything he'd said to Kat. It had been a good argument, one he'd never verbalized before, so he must have been thinking about this for some time.

A stirring in his gut told him that there was something there. Something he'd missed. Something... He realized with a start that he needed to look at in the bigger picture.

If Sarah hadn't been attending college classes, then what had she been doing? Whatever it had been, it was something she had kept from her parents—and as it turned out, something she'd hidden well from everyone. Every reporter worth his or her salt had looked into her past and found...nothing.

But that didn't mean it wasn't there. It just meant she'd managed somehow to keep the rest of the world from finding out what it was. So she hadn't dropped out of college and gotten a job. There would have been a record.

Nor had she run off with some boy. All of that would have come out by now with hundreds of reporters digging into her past—and some now-fifty-something old boyfriend looking to make a few bucks.

He had a sudden thought. Where were all of Sarah's old boyfriends from college? The high school boyfriends had already been vetted by the press. None of them had produced anything of interest. In fact none of them had even professed to having taken her virginity.

Max mulled that over, frowning as he considered why a beautiful woman—she had been a beauty back then and still was a knockout—hadn't had a bevy of boyfriends at college. One of them would have come forward by now for his fifteen seconds in the limelight. But none had.

He felt himself getting more excited as he realized he *really* was onto something. Another question popped up in his thoughts. Let's say Sarah Johnson had something to hide when she'd met the son of an up-and-coming politician. Would she have known about the extent of Buckmaster's political ambitions all those years ago when they'd married? Maybe not. Maybe she hadn't realized that her life would be thrust under a microscope. That her secrets would no longer be safe.

The next thought made him let out a low whistle. Fortunately the coffee shop was empty and the barista was busy in the back. The thought had come on the heels of two others. Buckmaster's father had been a senator who had started to run for president when Sarah had married into the family. Buckmaster hadn't himself been involved in politics back then.

Max was almost too excited to type. What year was that? As the answer came up on the screen and he sat back, the realization made it hard to catch his next breath.

He felt as if he had one of those two-thousand-piece puzzles in front of him. But he'd managed to put together at least part of the border.

Six children and twelve years later, Buckmaster made his first run for state government. Only a matter of months later his wife had driven into the Yellowstone River.

"WHERE ARE YOU taking me, Frank?" Nettie asked that morning as he turned onto a dirt road that led up into the foothills outside White Sulphur Springs. Peering ahead, she could make out a dilapidated old building through the trees. "When you suggested driving up here on your day off, I just assumed you were taking me to lunch." She looked over at her husband and saw the intensity in his expression. "This has something to do with an investigation. I know you, Frank Curry."

"Not officially an investigation, and I promise you we will get lunch—just not yet." He pulled up in front of the large old structure. She could make out what was left of the faded print on the sign: Spring Creek Sanitarium.

"You brought me to a *sanitarium*? Thinking of having me admitted?"

"Fortunately for you, it's closed. But it once housed the mentally ill. Let's take a look around," he said as he opened his door and exited.

Curiosity alone would have made her get out of the SUV. Why had her husband brought her here? It had something to do with his work. It always did. As much as he threatened to retire, Frank Curry couldn't give up snooping and solving any more than she could. The fact that he'd brought her along could mean only one thing.

"You need me," she said, sounding as happy as she felt as she caught up to him. "You thought I'd come in handy. But I can't help unless you tell me what this is about."

He wiped a small portion of dirty glass that had been missed at one of the partially boarded up windows. After peering in for a moment, he turned to her. "Along with enjoying your company on such a beautiful fall day, I admit I do need your…talents. I thought this might be right up your alley."

"Crazy people? That's what you think is up my alley?"

"I did some asking around. I was surprised to find

out that a man by the name of Dr. Ralph Venable worked here. A few years before that, the good doctor had published an article in a medical journal about brain wiping."

"Brain wiping?"

"He believed he could take the bad memories out of the brain—and put them back—or replace them with false memories. It was rumored at the time that he was doing his research on real patients instead of rats."

"Here?"

Her husband nodded. "Until the place closed about twenty-two years."

She stared at him. "Twenty-two years ago?" Even though she knew, she still asked, "Who is it you think was a patient here? If the place closed that many years ago, it couldn't have been Sarah Hamilton."

"I said *about* twenty-two years ago. It closed only a matter of days after Sarah went into the river."

Nettie looked at the building. It was far enough from town, no one would be the wiser if patients were brought here in the middle of the night. "There would have been nurses, though. One of them…" She turned back to Frank. "You found one of the nurses who worked here?"

He smiled. "She might be hesitant to talk, though. But since you definitely have a talent for getting people to tell you their most well-kept secrets, I was hoping—"

"What is it you want to know other than if Sarah was brought here?" she asked. Then she answered the question herself. "You want to know who brought her here."

"Like I said, right up your alley."

"But if the place closed within days after her arrival…
then where did she go?"

"That will probably be a question that not even the
nurse can answer."

CHAPTER SEVEN

MAX COULDN'T BELIEVE the path his mind had taken—or more important, where it had led him. All his instincts told him he was onto something. Something big.

From what he and the rest of the media had been able to find out, Sarah Johnson had attended NYU from 1974 to 1979, graduating with a bachelor of arts degree in literature. Had she been planning to get her masters? Maybe teach?

No, he thought, he wasn't buying it.

Think big picture, he reminded himself.

He mentally ran through what was happening in the country from 1974 to 1979 and then looked up some details. In '74 a first-class stamp sold for eight cents, the median household income was around nine thousand dollars and the Oakland A's beat the LA Dodgers in the World Series.

He scrolled down. It was also the year that Patty Hearst was kidnapped by the Symbionese Liberation Army and President Richard Nixon resigned.

He checked 1975. The Vietnam War ended, President Ford escaped two assassination attempts, stamps went up to ten cents and Cincinnati beat the Red Sox.

By 1977, stamps were up to thirteen cents, nuclear disarmament was the big news, along with President Carter pardoning the Vietnam War draft dodgers. Jim

Jones's followers committed mass suicide in Jonestown in 1978 and the Yankees beat the Dodgers.

Max swore. This was getting him nowhere. He clicked on the year 1979. Ohio agreed to pay $675,000 to families of dead and injured in the Kent State University shootings, the nuclear power plant accident at Three Mile Island released radiation, first-class stamps went up to fifteen cents and the median household income had risen to over sixteen thousand.

What was he missing? Maybe he needed to reduce his scope. That's when he realized he hadn't been thinking colleges and universities. Hurriedly he typed in *Social Unrest* and then hesitated. Whatever had happened to Sarah Johnson probably hadn't happened her first year at school. He typed *1975* after *Social Unrest* and hit Return.

As he scrolled through articles, he felt as if he was blindfolded and throwing darts at a map, hoping something would stick.

Sarah could have gotten involved in any number of underground groups. He found a variety of radical activists with causes ranging from antiabortion, racism and animal rights to ecoterrorists and white nationalist neo-Nazis.

He quickly checked to see the life cycle of the various groups. Most had sprung up and died off quickly. Some were pacifists, others more radical. One caught his eye. A group he'd never heard of had taken credit for bombing a courthouse in Pittsburgh. Apparently, it was a small anarchist group that had taken responsibility for a series of bombings and bank robberies, modeling itself after the urban guerrilla warfare group, the Symbionese Liberation Army or SLA, that had kidnapped newspaper heiress Patty Hearst in 1974—the same year Sarah had started college.

This group called themselves the Prophecy, and, after two of the members had been arrested in 1979—the year Sarah Johnson reportedly graduated from the university—the group was never heard from again. That summer, Sarah met Buckmaster Hamilton in Yellowstone Park, and a year later they were married.

Max could hear Kat saying that he was making up a wild tale where there wasn't one. But the timing was right, and the story he'd concocted for her lack of participation in college added up. The problem was tying Sarah Johnson Hamilton to the group.

And then a snapshot taken by one of the members of the organization came up from some small weekly newspaper. The photograph was of poor quality. But right away, he spotted the only woman in the group and felt the hair rise on the back of his neck.

REGISTERED NURSE BECCA THORSON got off for her break at two. Dressed in her scrubs and her comfortable white shoes, she stepped out the back door of the small hospital and reached into her pocket for her nicotine gum. She popped a piece into her mouth and opened the cold can of cola she'd bought from the machine.

Nettie waited until the nurse had taken a long drink before she approached her.

As Becca lowered the can, she didn't seem surprised or concerned. "You must be the friend the cop said wanted to talk to me. Well, you've wasted a trip. I only worked at Spring Creek a few weeks toward the end. I was a nurse's aide. I worked nights. I cleaned bedpans, so I can't tell you anything about Dr. Venable or the sanitarium, other than they were cheap and let us all go without any warning."

Nettie nodded. "Sounds like a delightful place to work. I suspect, though, that you're like me. You're smart. You notice things."

Becca took another sip without comment.

"I'm interested in one night in particular. It would have been a little more than twenty-two years ago, only days before the place closed for good. A patient would have come in late that night," Nettie said, watching the nurse.

"You expect me to remember one patient?"

"I suspect this one was kept away from the others." She saw something in the other woman's expression. "Am I right?"

"I didn't see her," Becca said and took another drink of her cola.

"But you know it was a woman?"

The nurse seemed to realize her mistake. "All right, I saw someone bring her in, okay?"

"A man or a woman?"

"A man. I didn't get a good look at him, before you ask."

"But you have an idea how large he was," Nettie prodded.

"Larger than average, okay?"

"And the woman?"

"I told you, I didn't really see her. Dr. Venable came out, and they rushed her into a room at the end of the hall. She was all wrapped up in a blanket or coat or something. She was small," Becca said before Nettie could ask. "I didn't see her again."

"Not even to clean her bedpan?"

"No. Several of us were curious about her because she seemed to be special, you know."

"Special, how?"

"Dr. Venable made her his priority right away. Just like he made it clear that she was not to be bothered. One of the nurses said he kept her room locked when he wasn't in there with her, but most of the time he was in there."

"So you can't say if she was a brunette or a blonde—"

"She was a blonde." She sighed. "I only know that because after she and the doctor left, a company came to clean out all the furnishings. I happened to be up at the place to get my last check. I went into the room." She shrugged and looked away. "I was curious, all right?"

Nettie smiled. She knew curious inside and out. "You found a blond hair."

"She left behind a brush. It had blond hair in it."

"You don't happen to—"

"No!" she said and mugged an unpleasant face. "I was curious, not…weird. Why would I want her brush?"

Nettie couldn't hide her disappointment. If they had the brush, they could have proved who the mystery patient had been through DNA. Not that there was any doubt in her mind that the blonde had been Sarah Hamilton.

"So the closing came fast after this woman's arrival at the sanitarium," Nettie said. "What happened to the other patients?"

"What few we had were moved to the hospital until a place could be found for them. It wasn't a big deal. We didn't have that many real patients."

"What do you mean *real* patients?"

The nurse looked at her watch.

"Please. It's important. The doctor was experimenting on people, right?"

She looked up in surprise and then looked around to make sure no one from inside was listening. "He said he was *helping* them forget the bad things in their lives, homeless people he picked up on the highway, vagrant types who hitchhiked through the state and needed a little extra money, anyone willing to let him use them as guinea pigs. He *paid* them to let him mess with their minds." She shook her head as if she couldn't believe what people would do for money. The woman was naive, unlike Nettie, who felt nothing about human nature could surprise her anymore.

"Why didn't someone report him?" she had to ask.

"And lose their jobs? Not just that," she said as if still feeling guilty she hadn't turned him in. "The people he experimented on all agreed to it, and they seemed fine when they left so…" She shrugged again. "And to be truthful, most of us thought he was a crackpot and that his experiments were harmless because they didn't work."

"How do you know they didn't work?" Nettie asked.

The nurse shrugged. "The people seemed the same when they left."

Apparently Becca had expected them to come out like zombies. "What did he do to this special patient?"

"Who knows? Once she arrived, he spent all his time with her in her room, and a few days later she was gone and so was he."

"Do you think they left together?" Nettie asked.

She shrugged. "Beats me. I was busy looking for another job to pay for nursing school. We're supposed to give two weeks notice when we quit, but a doctor can just up and decide to close the entire hospital without even telling us until the last minute."

"Did you ever see the man who brought the woman in again? Or hear the doctor call either of them by name?"

"No, and before you ask, the doctor didn't make a chart for her." The nurse finished her cola and tossed the can into a nearby waste bin.

"You got a feeling about the relationship between the doctor and the man who brought the woman in, right?"

Becca gave that a moment's thought before she asked, "You mean like, did they seem to know each other?"

Nettie nodded.

"I suppose the men must have known each other, but not as well as the doctor knew the woman. He was a lot older than her, but I got the feeling they were old friends."

"Was it something either of them said that gave you that impression?"

"No," she said slowly. Nettie saw the flash of memory in the woman's eyes and waited. She'd found that once a person got talking, the memories came flooding back.

"That night when the man brought her in and the doctor came out to admit her, the woman held out her hand to him, and he took it in both of his. I couldn't hear what they were saying, but I got the impression she was glad to see him."

ANGELINA FINALLY FOUND a private investigator to take her case. Most of them had refused when she told them who she was. No, it was more because of who she was married to and that she wanted dirt on Buckmaster's first wife.

She'd always thought that once she and Buckmaster were in the White House—or even on their way like they were now—that people would fall all over themselves getting her what she wanted.

Apparently not, if she wanted information that might upset the soon-to-be president.

This knowledge did little to improve her mood. Not that her mood had been good for months. Not since Sarah Johnson Hamilton had come back into Buckmaster's life. Angelina woke most mornings in a funk at the mere thought of Sarah. Buckmaster mooning around all the time about his first wife hadn't helped matters either.

If she could have gotten away with it, Angelina would have killed the woman—anything to get her out of the picture. She'd thought about paying someone to do the job, but since she couldn't take the chance, she'd have to find another way to eradicate Sarah from their lives.

She'd already had to deal with one blackmailer.

"What exactly are you looking for?" The PI asked when she met him at his office to give him his first installment. Curtis Olsen looked more like an accountant than a private investigator. But she'd made the mistake of thinking Moose could handle anything because of his size. She was willing to give Curtis a chance. Also, he was the only one who'd give her the time of day after she told him what she wanted.

"I want the dirt," she said, tired of pretending otherwise. "I know there is something to find."

"Like what?"

She shook her head. "Sarah Johnson Hamilton is just too squeaky-clean. She's hiding something. Something that she's kept hidden not only from my husband but also from the press. I hope you're the man to find it."

"Let me see what I can do."

As Angelina left his office, she hoped Curtis would come through for her. She'd thought about telling him that PI Mike "Moose" McCallahan had pretty much told her there was something to find—before he'd chickened out. But she feared Curtis would quit before he even started if he knew that another PI had bailed already.

She could feel the clock ticking. She couldn't let Sarah win because she knew what the prize at the end of this race was—Buckmaster Hamilton and the White House.

KAT HATED THAT she hadn't been able to prove Max Malone wrong. Now at her computer she typed in *Journalist Max Malone*. Given the truck he drove and the laid-back way he lived and dressed, she hadn't been expecting much to come up.

Not for the first time since she'd met Max did she get a surprise. The first story she stumbled across was about a national newspaper award he'd been given for investigative reporting. She found another where he'd been nominated for a Pulitzer for an article he'd done on crooked politics and politicians in Georgia.

This couldn't be the same Max Malone. She looked for something that included a photo and found one. He was grinning at the camera, much like he'd grinned at her earlier across the table at the café in Bozeman.

She scanned the article, tripping over the background material at the end. His real name was Maximilian Malone? *Seriously?*

If that wasn't shocking enough, he apparently was the son of Wallace Maximilian Malone, the famous financier. *That couldn't be right.* Why would the son of Wallace Maximilian Malone be sleeping in the back of his old pickup outside the Hamilton Ranch gate?

Kat growled to herself. Max had wanted her to think he was dirt-poor, living hand to mouth, just another of the many journalists looking for a story. And she'd fallen for it. She hadn't taken him seriously. She'd played along just to humor him. She realized he probably used this same approach on everyone—including the people he was investigating.

Shaken by what she was seeing, she scrolled down the listings of the many articles the man had written. Even more shocking was how much acclaim he'd been awarded by his young age of thirty-five.

Closing the computer, Kat sat for a moment, letting it all sink in. It came down to one simple fact: Max was more than just good at what he did. He got stories where other reporters failed.

And now he was determined to get her mother's story.

Kat stood, thinking she should warn her father, but she quickly sat back down again. She couldn't imagine anything the senator could do that would stop Max in his pursuit—given the freedom of the press. Also, what little she now knew about Max, if her father tried to stop him, it would only make him more determined.

The senator's interference—if he would get involved—would only make things worse. Max already believed he was onto something big. All Kat could hope was that the man was wrong. Meanwhile, she would stay in his confidence and play along, so she'd know if he really did have anything explosive about her mother. Then, she would warn her father.

Her cell phone rang, making her jump. Even before she checked it, she knew who it would be.

"So?" Max said, sounding much too confident.

Kat closed her eyes and groaned inwardly. "There was a fire and—"

He interrupted with a bark of a laugh. "What a coincidence."

Even though she'd thought the same thing and knew he would, too, it still rankled her. "People do have house fires!"

"And all of her belongings were lost, right?"

Kat wanted to argue that her mother had just returned from college with all her things, that her parents had been in the process of downsizing, that… She knew he would think the same thing she did, so without a decent defense, she fell silent.

"I'm not surprised. Luckily, I found something. You need to see this."

She had a feeling that whatever it was, she really wasn't going to want to see it. "Where are you?"

"I'm leaving Big Timber. Why don't we meet at the Branding Iron in Beartooth? Isn't it lunchtime yet? I'm starved."

"Apparently you're always starved." She thought of Max's wealthy father. Was it possible he'd done something that had gotten him disinherited? It would explain the old truck and Max's current lifestyle. Maybe there was more to Max's story than she was giving him credit for. "Shall I assume I'm buying?"

He laughed. "Why not?"

Because you're some famous journalist who apparently lives hand to mouth. Why was that? Surely he made good money. Or was his job all acclaim and little cash?

Kat put her curiosity about Maximilian's finances out of her mind as she drove toward Beartooth. She had greater concerns. What if he had found out something damaging about her mother? Something that would also hurt her father? She couldn't let that happen if she could help it. Her father was going through so much right now already. But if so, how was she going to stop Max from exposing it?

CHAPTER EIGHT

MAX REACHED THE Branding Iron before Kat and ordered them both cheeseburgers, fries and chocolate milk shakes. She walked in just moments after the waitress had brought out their order.

"What is this?" Kat asked, looking at all the food.

"Lunch."

"After that huge breakfast you put away?"

He grinned at her as she slid into the booth opposite him. "You didn't do such a bad job of cleaning your plate this morning either, as I recall."

"I told you, I don't eat—" she wrinkled her nose as she picked up one of the French fries and dropped it again "—food like this."

"You can always order a salad."

She eyed the food as he began to eat with gusto while watching her out of the corner of his eye. He tried not to laugh when she picked up another of the fries and ate it. Apparently she hadn't had one in a very long time, if the pleasure-filled expression on her face was any indication.

She daintily cut the burger into quarters, picked up a portion and took a bite.

This time he could not hold back the laugh.

"I hate you," she said and took another bite.

"I still don't get why you would give up food that

you obviously love," he said, sincerely curious. "My motto is—if it feels good—" he grinned as he held her gaze "—then I do it."

"I'm sure it is your motto," she said, her gray eyes going dark as a midnight fog as she narrowed them at him. "I, however, believe in...restraint."

He laughed. "You really need to let your hair down."

She touched the knot at the back of her neck, looking uncomfortable. "My hair is curly and unruly. It tends to go wild if..." Her gaze met his. "Not that that it is any of your business."

Without thinking, he picked up his napkin and reached across the table to wipe at a dab of ketchup at the corner of her lips. She had a full, generous mouth that looked so damned kissable...

Her eyes opened wide, their gazes locking. What passed between them felt way too intimate. He quickly drew back the napkin and concentrated on his meal. He had one hard and fast rule that had served him well: *never get involved on the job.*

Kat concentrated on her food as well for a few minutes. "So, what did you have to show me?" she asked without looking at him. Her voice sounded strange, making him realize whatever had just happened between them hadn't been one-sided.

Keep it strictly business, he warned himself. But Kat Hamilton intrigued him. She didn't keep her hair bound back like that because it was curly. If anyone could afford to have it straightened, it was her. He wanted to peel away the layers of protection she'd wrapped around herself until he reached the heart of her. He'd never been able to resist digging for what made someone tick. And Kat Hamilton definitely had some odd ticks.

He found himself studying her, wanting to strip away more than those layers of protection. He wanted to peel off those oversize clothes, let her hair go wild, introduce her to every pleasure he could think of. He already had a pretty good idea something—or someone—had made her like this. So what would it take to release Kat Hamilton from her self-imposed prison?

"Eat and then I'll tell you everything," he said.

The tension he'd felt only moments before eased some as they ate in a companionable silence, both clearly enjoying their food. He couldn't help but wonder what else besides food Kat Hamilton had deprived herself of—and for how long.

When the waitress came to clear their plates, he noticed that Kat had made short work of her food.

"Enjoy your lunch?" he asked with a grin. "How about a piece of that banana cream pie they just put out?"

She glared at him. "You really are the devil."

"You have no idea."

KAT WATCHED HIM spread out copies of articles systematically on the table after their dishes were cleared. The waitress refilled their coffee cups and brought Max a piece of pie. The café was warm and empty now that the lunch crowd had cleared out.

"I realized that I'd been thinking too small," Max said. "If I was right and your mother had been up to something else during those university years…then I had to look at the big picture."

She listened, watching him as he provided her with

one set of articles after another. The grinning, joking
Max Malone was gone. This man was a deadly serious journalist, and from what she could see, he'd done
his homework.

"A newspaper in Los Angeles ran a photo of the
group back in 1978," he was saying. "I talked to someone in archives, and they still have the original," he
said as he picked up all the copies of the articles and
started to put them back in a weathered leather satchel
that looked as if it had been around the world. From
what she knew of Max's work from the pieces she'd
seen online, it probably had.

"Here, you have to try this," he said reached across
with a fork full of banana cream pie.

Without thinking, she took a bite and licked her lips
at the creamy, buttery dessert. As she met his gaze, she
was struck by the intimacy of the act of him offering
her a bite. As if he realized what he'd done, he quickly
drew back the fork.

"There's a flight to LA tomorrow afternoon from
Bozeman," he said as if nothing had just happened between them—just like earlier. "Pack light. It's warm
down there. I have a friend who's letting us use his
place on the beach, so you'll want to bring your swimsuit. It isn't every day that you get a chance to swim
in the Pacific."

"Wait, what?"

He finished putting the papers into his satchel and
looked at her. "Have you been listening to anything
I said?"

"You think my mother was part of some radical
group that bombed buildings from 1974 to 1979."

"No, from 1975 to 1979. I don't think she got involved right away. More than likely she met some man who saw that she was ripe for the picking. She came from a very conservative, well-off family. She was probably more than a little susceptible to someone with big ambitions and change-the-world ideas all in the name of helping the downtrodden."

Kat shook her head. "You have no idea what my mother was like. You just make assumptions as you go."

"The photo of the group will prove it. The newspaper has the color photo in archives. All I've seen is a bad black-and-white version. We need to see the original. *You* need to see the original."

She shook her head. This was all moving too fast. "First off, there is no way my mother was part of this... group. What did you call it?"

"The Prophecy. No doubt they envisioned a different future than the one that befell them since two of them went to prison and the rest scattered, never to be heard from again."

"Nor can I fly off to California. I don't fly."

He laughed. "Of course you don't."

"I'm also in the process of preparing for my first photo exhibit. I've already put it off several times."

She'd already put it off several times? He studied her again. Fear of success? Or fear of failure, he wondered. "Your exhibit isn't until Christmas, and from what I've seen, you have more than enough photos."

"You really don't know anything about it," she snapped. She had a million things to do and resented him making it sound as if her photo exhibit wouldn't be all that much work. She said as much as calmly as she could.

"I didn't say it wasn't important." He leaned toward
her, seeming to take over the space. "I've known you
how long? Not even forty-eight hours and I know that
you have more photographs than you can possibly hang
for this show, that you need to stop shooting and worrying. Your artwork is great. Have a little confidence
in yourself."

"I have confidence in myself," she retorted. Even
though it was true she had too many photos and that
had become the problem, she still wanted to argue that
he didn't know what he was talking about.

He placed his hand over hers, making her catch
her breath at the surprise of his touch—and the jolt
that swept through her. "I can understand you being
afraid." Before she would assure him she wasn't afraid,
he continued. "This photo in LA is going to be of your
mother. You and I both know you are going to have to
see the original or you aren't going to believe it's true."

"You're wrong."

He merely looked at her with all that confidence and
conceit. "Only one way to prove it."

She shook off his hand. "Fine. You're wrong. But
if you are planning to trick me, anything I might say
is off the record."

Max smiled. "Fine. I hate to break it to you, though.
I am seldom wrong. However," he added, "for your
sake, I almost want to be wrong."

"Liar." She got to her feet. She couldn't remember
being this full. Why had she let him goad her into eating all the things she'd given up? She wished she could
regret even one bite. Damn this man.

He was leaving her no choice. She did have to see
this photo, because if he was right…then none of them

had ever really known Sarah Johnson Hamilton. But, she assured herself, he would be wrong this time. She definitely wanted to be there for that.

"I'll pick you up at the ranch. That is, if you let them know at the gate."

She could tell that he'd been hoping to find a way to get past the guards at the gate probably since he'd arrived in Montana. "I'll meet you at the airport."

He grinned. "Spoilsport. But let's at least share a car to the airport. Meet me at the gate. We can take my truck."

"We'll take my SUV."

His grin broadened. "Have it your way, but if you don't bring your swimsuit, you're going in the ocean clothes and all."

SITTING IN FRONT of a fast-food restaurant in White Sulphur Springs, Lynette said, "This is your idea of taking me on a dinner date?"

The sheriff smiled as he handed over her fish burger and fries. She had related to him everything the nurse had shared with her on the way into town. He'd listened, laughed and pulled the SUV over long enough to hug her. It always amazed him how people tended to open up to this woman.

He hadn't seen her this excited since the news about Sarah's tattoo. The woman could get a confession faster than a priest. Once people saw a badge they tended to get tight-lipped. Nettie had a way of making them relax. People had confessed the damnedest things to her over the years. He laughed, thinking they needed someone like her down at the sheriff's office.

He'd known he would need her today and had debated if he was making a mistake by bringing Lynette in on this. But this investigation, if he could call it that, was on his own time and unofficial. Not that he wasn't aware that this was about the first wife of Senator—and very possibly soon President—Buckmaster Hamilton.

While the FBI hadn't found any reason to investigate Sarah Hamilton further, Frank had no intentions of stopping.

"So?" Lynette said impatiently as she opened her fish burger wrapper. "What do you think?"

"I'm not sure." She had repeated her conversation with Becca Thorson, no doubt close to verbatim. Along with everything else amazing about his wife, she had an incredible memory when it came to details of conversations.

He looked over at her as he dug his double cheeseburger and onion rings out of the greasy paper sack. "I don't have to remind you that all of this is just between you and me, do I?"

She waved a hand through the air in answer. "You think it was the senator who took her to the funny farm, don't you?"

Lynette worked on assumption and rumor. In his line of work, he needed that little thing called proof. "The nurse didn't give much of a description," he said noncommittally.

"It was winter. He would have been bundled up, was probably even wearing a hat. The nurse said he was big, and Buckmaster is definitely that."

It made sense, just as Russell had speculated. Russell Murdock had come to him with what at the time had been a crazy theory about not just brain wiping. Russell believed Sarah had been taken to a clinic or hospital by her husband that night after she'd crashed into the icy river.

He had to admit, it made sense. After what they believed to be a failed suicide attempt, Sarah would have called someone she trusted. But would she have trusted her husband? If only they knew why she'd tried to kill herself.

"Come on, Frank. The timing is right. It had to be Sarah."

Frank shook his head. "All this is speculation without proof. Also, whoever the woman was, according to your nurse, she seemed to know the doctor."

"Is there any way to find out if Sarah had been admitted to the loony bin before that night?"

"Patient-doctor confidentiality, so probably not."

"Wouldn't the senator know?" Lynette asked.

That was one conversation he wasn't looking forward to—if it ever came to that. The senator had been on the campaign trail and busy in Washington. Frank had heard he was back at the ranch for a few days, but without any proof...

"Even if she was the woman who was admitted that night, it doesn't mean this Dr. Venable wiped her brain. He couldn't erase memories she hadn't made yet. And even if he could wipe away whatever memory led her to suicide, it doesn't explain the past twenty-two years."

"Unless he got his hands on her again," Lynette said. "You haven't been able to find him?"

"I had Dillon looking for him, but I pulled him off this. I don't want it to be an official investigation. He has better things to do than chase this anyway."

His wife didn't seem to be listening. "This brain

wiping is interesting, but there could be a simpler explanation."

He grinned over at her. "That Sarah Hamilton is lying."

Lynette laughed. "You and I make a pretty good team, Frank Curry."

"That's exactly what I was thinking."

KAT AND MAX were able to get two first-class seats on a jet to Los Angeles, thanks to Max reserving them the day before.

"You were that sure I was going with you?" she asked as she produced her credit card.

"Nope. I figured if I had another first-class seat, I could find someone who wanted to share it with me."

She shook her head at his apparent arrogance and conceit. "Who are you really?"

He took a step back and swung his arms wide. "What you see is what you get," he said, a twinkle in his blue eyes.

Those were the same words she'd used about herself. She didn't believe it any more than she figured he had. How much of what this man told her *could* she believe? One moment he was self-deprecating, the next he was so arrogant it made her teeth ache. One moment he was joking and grinning, the next he was all business.

"I did some research on you," she said once they were seated and the flight attendant had brought her a glass of sparkling water and him a beer.

She took a sip of her water and gave him a challenging look. "You didn't tell me you'd been writing for quite a while."

"You didn't ask. Anyway, writers are the most boring people in the world." He shrugged. "If we aren't writing, we're thinking about writing."

"Is that why you've never married?"

Max seemed to freeze for a moment. He took a drink of his beer before he looked over at her. "Who says I've never married?"

She glanced at his left hand. No ring. No faded spot where there had been a ring. Nowhere in the research she'd done was there anything about a wife. Nor had there been one standing next to him when he'd received his awards. "Are you married?"

"Would it make a difference?" His blue eyes shone with either amusement or irritation. He shot her the grin he used against her whenever he felt uncomfortable, she realized.

"Stop doing whatever it is you're doing right now," she snapped, keeping her voice down.

He looked away and took a deep breath, letting it out before he answered. "I was married." He turned to her again. "I'm not anymore. End of story."

She lifted a brow, thinking about all the traveling that Max would have had to do to write all the stories he'd written beginning when he was twenty-two. What wife would have wanted to be married to a freelance journalist who was gone all the time?

But she couldn't help being curious. Maybe Max was the one who had ended the marriage. Too many interesting women to meet on the stories he did. Or maybe it had been the woman who'd found someone else while he was off gallivanting and that's why he didn't want to talk about it.

"I take it marriage didn't suit you?" she said, thinking he shouldn't get to dig into other people's secrets if he didn't want his own dug up.

He looked straight ahead, his voice sounding strange. "Marriage suited me just fine. It was the best two years of my life."

When she realized he wasn't going to say any more, she started to ask what had happened, when he cut her off.

"I'm not going to talk about my past with you," he said.

She couldn't help but laugh. "Other people's lives are fair game, but yours is off-limits?"

"That's right."

"That hardly seems fair."

He cocked his head at her as if surprised. "Life isn't fair. I suppose there is no reason that you would have learned that yet, since yours seems to have been pretty cushy so far."

It was her turn to look away. "You know nothing about my life." She could feel his gaze on her.

"I doubt you've even had your heart broken."

Turning to face him, she said, "My life is also off-limits."

He nodded slowly. "Okay. At least that is something we can both agree on."

But she could still feel his penetrating gaze on her. She wished she could take back her words. Now he was probably wondering what she had to hide. Just as she was wondering the same thing about him.

CHAPTER NINE

MAX DOZED ON the two-hour flight to Los Angeles. Or at least pretended to. He had a lot on his mind. From the first time he'd met Kat, he'd suspected she didn't like men. Not that she wasn't heterosexual. She just had a closed-for-business way of dressing and acting. His instincts told him that someone had hurt her and badly.

He told himself it was none of his business. They'd agreed to stay out of each others' pasts. And since it didn't have anything to do with the story he was working on… And yet he couldn't help but be curious. It was his nature. He liked ferreting out the close-held secrets people kept, especially after he got to know them a little. He'd gotten to know Kat just enough that he couldn't let it go.

Did her sisters know about whatever had happened? Or had Kat kept it to herself? Somehow, he thought that was more like her. He'd seen an independence in her. She liked going her own way.

He'd found out a long time ago that what made people interesting and worth-his-while subjects was the painful things they'd been through. It was why he liked to do articles on those over a certain age. Most twenty or even thirtysomethings often hadn't lived long enough to experience life's hard knocks, let alone had time to process them and come out the other side.

Kat, though, he suspected had. But what in her seemingly perfect life could have happened to her? Even as he told himself not to, he was wondering how he could find out. With Kat, he would have to get closer to her. Really close.

Now he checked his watch as a car was brought around.

"You rented this?" Kat asked taking in the convertible sports car.

He grinned as he dumped their overnight bags into the trunk. "Only the best for you."

"You charged it to me," she said and shook her head.

He didn't tell her different. Kat had been subdued— or was it worried?—the rest of the flight. Yesterday, she hadn't seemed to be listening when he laid out this theory about the radical group the Prophecy for her. Now she patted nervously at her hair as they waited. He could see that her hair was curly. He couldn't wait to free it from that damned knot and let it flow around her shoulders.

Who was the woman she kept locked up? He thought back to the plane ride. She'd caught him off guard when she'd asked him about being married.

Normally, he let people think he'd never been married. Otherwise, they wanted the whole story in every detail. It was one story he wasn't ready to tell. Maybe he never would be ready.

"I think it would be best if you let me do the talking once we get to the newspaper," Max told her and caught her irritated expression as he opened the passenger-side door for her. "I'm not being a male jerk. If they know who you are, then it could open a Pandora's box that I don't think you're up for. Also it could make them suspicious as to why you wanted to see this particular photo. I don't want them digging into places I don't want them to go."

"For a moment I thought you were actually being considerate," she said as he slid behind the wheel. "I should have known it was only about your story."

"It's always about the story," he said as if reminding himself as he started the engine. "Don't ever doubt it."

They said nothing the rest of the ride to the newspaper office. Kat didn't do anything more than nod when he introduced her to the archivist as his girlfriend who was just tagging along.

"You do that on purpose," she said, though, after they'd been led to a small room and told to wait.

"Do what on purpose?"

"Make people think you aren't a serious journalist. The laid-back way you act and dress and joke around, and now bringing your girlfriend along to the newspaper as if you weren't on an important story. The same way you asked for a half dozen photos to cover up for the one you're really after."

Max had to hand it to her. She'd nailed him pretty well.

The archivist came in with the photos he'd requested. "I can let you look at them, but I'd prefer you don't pick them up because of their age." He spread them out on the table and stood over them.

"Thanks. My kid sister has been doing a paper on social unrest in the 1960s and '70s." Max didn't rush. He stepped slowly to the table and looked down at the photos. Kat was right. He'd requested a variety of photographs pertaining to unrest during those years.

So he took his time, looking at each before he got to the only one he was really interested in. It was a color snapshot taken almost forty years ago by one of the members of the Prophecy. Eight people, seven men and one woman, stood against a brick wall. They all held weapons, mostly automatic weapons and assault rifles. It reminded him of a photo he'd seen taken of the SLA, which confirmed his suspicion that the Prophecy had modeled themselves after the earlier SLA.

The other thing about the photo that struck him was their expressions. It made him doubt this was the first shot the photographer had taken. All in the group seemed to be trying to look serious as if reminding themselves that were involved in serious business. And yet several of them looked as if someone had said something funny and they were trying hard not to laugh.

That told him that the group was close. At least some of them knew each other well. He studied the faces, noticing how young the majority of them were. All but a couple were in their teens or early twenties. The two older members were male, one maybe in his thirties, the other older, maybe early forties. He looked distinguished. A former professor?

As he studied the two older males, he wondered which of them had brought Sarah Johnson, now Hamilton, into the fold. The distinguished professor type, he thought. Or the other older one?

Finally he let his gaze focus on the only woman in the group. The black-and-white copy of the photo he'd seen had excited him. The original confirmed it. The woman was none other than Kat Hamilton's mother. He'd bet his truck on it.

KAT WANTED TO shove Max out of the way and get this over with. But her feet were rooted to the floor. Suddenly the room felt too small. It was as if all the air had been sucked out, taking even the oxygen from her lungs.

She clutched a hand to her chest. A trickle of sweat ran down her back, making her shiver even though it was too hot in the room.

"Want to take a look?" Max said and reached for her hand. The touch of his fingers made her jump. His gaze shot to hers, and she saw something reassuring in his eyes as if he was trying to tell her that everything was going to be all right now.

It wasn't her mother. That's all she could think as his warm hand enveloped hers and drew her toward the table and the photos lying on it.

Still, she didn't want to look. She wanted him to just tell her he'd been wrong. To admit it, then the two of them could get out of here.

But he pulled her closer until she couldn't help but look down at the array of photos. Her eyes skimmed over them, seeing nothing familiar. She assumed given what he'd said that there would be a woman in the photo who looked like her mother.

Her gaze fell on a small color snapshot of eight people, all holding guns and looking… Her gaze went to the woman, and she felt a jolt. "Her hair is *red*," she said aloud.

Max laughed. Out of the corner of her eye, she saw him wink at the archivist. "All of the rest of them, just like the Symbionese Liberation Army and other groups of that time, went by nicknames. Hers was Red."

Kat swallowed and took a step back.

"Any chance I could get a copy of these for my sister? It would make her day," Max was saying.

The archivist told him he'd have to sign a form and that it would cost him two dollars a photo. He agreed, and the man hurried out with the photographs, closing the door behind him.

Kat moved to lean back against the wall, wishing she could have gone with the archivist. She put a hand on her stomach as she tried to keep from throwing up. Her heart was pounding too hard, and each breath was a labor.

The woman in the photo wasn't her mother. Sarah was a blue-eyed blonde. She closed her eyes and tried to calm herself or she really was going to be sick. This wasn't like her. She didn't have panic attacks. She stayed in control. She didn't... She felt the first tear slide down her face as she heard the man come back into the room. Quickly wiping her eyes, she swallowed back the emotion that had closed off her throat.

It wasn't her mother.

She clung to those words like a mantra as she tried to relax. All this foolishness was over. So why couldn't she catch her breath?

"Is she all right?" the archivist asked.

"Her lunch didn't agree with her," Max said.

The other man nodded and looked worried that she might lose her lunch before he could get them out of the room.

It wasn't until they were on the street that Kat finally was able to take a deep breath. Even smoggy air was better than that stuffy little room.

"Take deep breaths," Max said. "You're all right."

She nodded, feeling foolish. All the way here she'd told herself that she was fine. She wasn't worried that the photo would turn out to be her mother's. There was no way her mother... She shook her head now.

"It was just too hot and close in that room. That's all," she said, not wanting him to see how afraid she'd been and yet knowing that he did see.

He gave her a sympathetic look as they walked to where he'd parked the convertible. "What you need is a swim in the ocean."

"What I need," she said as she continued to take deep breaths and got into the car, "is the next flight back to Montana."

"That won't be until tomorrow morning," he said and started the engine. "So we might as well enjoy Southern California, don't you think?"

He was way too chipper, she thought, as he drove on to the freeway. Maybe he was hoping that she wouldn't force him to admit he was wrong. "I'm sorry this trip was a waste of time," she said over the roar of the wind.

"A waste of time?" He sounded confused.

"You were wrong about my mother being a member of that group, the Prophecy."

Max didn't answer as he passed a large truck. Wind whipped around her. Her hair came loose from the knot at the back of her neck and twirled around her face. She gave up trying to get it under control and leaned back into the seat. The California sun bored down on her, making her head ache.

"You better have brought your swimsuit," he said over the roar of the wind and the engine. "And your appetite, the real one. Tonight we're feasting on authentic Mexican food, not that stuff they make in Montana."

She closed her eyes against the sun and his words,

surprised how tired she felt. The day had taken its toll on her. She hadn't realized how anxious she'd been. Now that it was over…

RUSSELL KNEW EXACTLY how to get word out about his engagement to Sarah Hamilton. As he drove toward Beartooth General Store, he told himself that he and Sarah would be happy. He would make sure of that.

The first step was getting Senator Buckmaster Hamilton out of their lives. Not that he didn't expect a backlash. The engagement would send the press into overdrive. But he could handle the press. It was Buckmaster who had him concerned. The man clearly didn't want to lose Sarah—and yet he was married to another woman. If he dumped his current wife for Sarah, it would destroy his political career.

Surely he wouldn't give up the presidency for Sarah. The man wasn't that big of a fool. But even as Russell thought it, he couldn't help worrying. What kind of effect would the announcement of the engagement have on Buckmaster, given that he had asked Sarah to wait and now she wasn't?

Pulling into the parking spot in front of the store, Russell couldn't wait to tell Nettie Curry. He'd checked to make sure she was working today. Once he told her…

The bell tinkled over the door just as it used to in the old Beartooth General Store. The place had been restored after the fire to its original blueprint. Nettie was behind the counter. He had thought about pretending he was there to buy something, but this morning he wasn't up to subterfuge.

"Nettie," he said in greeting.

She was watching him with interest as he came toward her. "Russell."

"Mr. Murdock. How are you this morning?"

He hadn't seen the other woman until she spoke. Mabel Murphy, a busybody who was actually worse than Nettie in her prime when it came to spreading gossip. He felt as if he'd hit the mother lode.

"Morning, ladies."

"What can we get you?" Nettie asked, looking curious, but not as curious as Mabel.

"A cup of coffee to go and…" He glanced around, spied the fresh homemade fried turnovers and said, "One of those. Raspberry, if you have it."

"You're quite chipper this morning," Mabel commented, studying him openly.

He gave her his biggest smile. "I'm getting married."

That raised two sets of eyebrows and left both women momentarily too stunned to speak.

"To whom?" Mabel asked, her voice breaking with surprise.

"Sarah. Sarah Hamilton."

Their shock was priceless.

"*Sarah Hamilton?* The senator's *wife*?" Mabel asked.

"His…*former* wife and, yes, Sarah Hamilton."

"Congratulations," Nettie said as if finally finding her voice.

Neither woman spoke as he paid for the coffee and turnover and, wishing them both a good morning, left. Just before the door closed behind him, though, he heard Mabel say, "Can you believe it?"

He didn't hear Nettie's answer. He glanced at his watch as he climbed into his pickup. He doubted it would take five minutes for the news to circulate around the county. Taking a big bite of the turnover, he smiled to himself. It was done. No going back.

But by the time the turnover was gone, along with half his cup of coffee, his stomach was roiling. His daughter, Destry, wouldn't be happy. Nor would the senator. But who else from Sarah's recent past might have an objection? He didn't know, but he feared he might soon be finding out.

MAX HAD BEEN glad when Kat had fallen asleep in the car on the way to the beach house. He'd liked watching the city he'd known so well rocket past as he drove up the coast.

"Where are we?" she asked beside him, waking with a start as he parked next to the beach house.

Max was looking out at the ocean. He couldn't believe how much he'd missed this view. He stared, trying to memorize it, because he didn't know when he'd get to see it again. Or if he ever would. With his job, he never knew.

"We're at the ocean, sleepyhead." Opening his door, he took a huge gulp of sea air and began to laugh at the briny taste that tickled his throat as it brought back the best memories of his life.

"Come on," he said to Kat and popped the trunk to get their overnight bags. He slung his over one shoulder. He always traveled light, finding that the more stuff you carried, the more problems came with them.

"You said a friend lives here?" she asked as she climbed out and looked at the beach cottage. He admired it as well for a moment, seeing it through her eyes. It was a beauty, small but obviously expensive.

Her eyebrow shot up questioningly as he carried their bags to the door and then climbed partway up a rock wall to feel along the ledge for the key. When he produced it, she seemed to relax a little.

"What did you think? That I was going to break in?" He shook his head. "You really need to have more faith."

Once inside, he saw her eyes widen in awe at the view. Like him, she was drawn immediately to the windows that filled the front wall and overlooked the Pacific. The sun, now a glowing orange ball, hung just over the horizon.

"Change into your swimsuit. We have to hit the beach so we're there for the sunset. Hurry," he said handing over her overnight bag and pushing her down the short hallway toward the spare bedroom.

Going in the opposite direction, he entered the master bedroom, threw his bag on the bed and quickly changed into his swimsuit. He'd grabbed some towels, a couple of beers and a small cooler by the time she'd come into the kitchen.

She wore a large shirt over what he assumed was her swimsuit and a pair of jeans rolled up capri-style. Her long curly dark hair was pulled up in a ponytail.

He wondered again what she would be like if she really let her hair down and relaxed. Or if that was even possible.

"Let's take the elevator. It's faster." He drew her over to a wooden panel in the wall that opened at the touch of a button to expose a small lift.

"I take it this is a *close* friend?" she asked as they stepped in and he hit the button to take them down.

"Very. We grew up together right on this beach."

She glanced over at him as the elevator descended. "I didn't know you grew up in California."

"My parents divorced when I was young." He shrugged. "I ended up living out here with my cousin's family."

"Not your mother?"

"Nope." Fortunately the elevator door opened just then, dumping them out on the beach. "Come on."

He dropped the small cooler along with the towels and began to take off his shirt that he'd pulled on over his swimsuit and jogging pants. The air was cooler with the waning sun. But October in Southern California was still plenty warm, especially compared to Montana.

Kat dropped her jeans and began to unbutton her shirt. As anxious as he was to hit the water, he waited for her. She'd been through a lot today, and it wasn't over, even though she seemed to think it was.

"Ready?" He smiled at her. Her face glowed from the sun, now level with the horizon. In the light she looked more beautiful than ever standing there. He felt a pull like the tide and had to swallow back the lump in this throat as he turned to look down the beach now cast in gold. "Last one in's a chicken!"

He turned back toward her in time to see her shrug out of her shirt, the fabric fluttering to the ground around her feet, and for a moment he was too stunned to move. She had an *amazing* body. Even more amazing than he'd thought from feeling her up after the near hit-and-run.

"Damn," he said under his breath.

CHAPTER TEN

Max's HESITATION WAS just enough to give Kat the edge. She was halfway to the water before he got out of his jogging pants. She'd never been competitive, so this was really unlike her, she thought as she splashed into the surf.

"Last one in," she said as he caught up before she was waist deep. "Chicken."

He grinned before he dived in next to her, and she felt the salty spray. A wave hit her, rocking her on her feet. She dived in deeper and came up only inches from Max. Water droplets beaded his pale lashes. His blue eyes shone in the waning sunlight. He smiled over at her, reaching out to flip her wet ponytail off her shoulder.

"You like?" he asked.

She felt the silky, warm, salty water wash over her. "I love." Her voice broke with emotion she couldn't explain. She hurriedly ducked under the crest of a large wave and, surfacing, swam out farther into the sea. For a Montana girl, born and raised, it felt surreal swimming in the ocean in October.

Actually, she'd felt like another woman from the moment she'd put on the swimsuit. It was one of her sister Bo's castoffs, since she hadn't owned a suit since college. When she'd first pulled it on—after not bothering to try it on back at the ranch—she'd been afraid it would be too tight.

But the royal blue one-piece fit perfectly. Kat had stood in front of the mirror in the beach house bedroom, captivated by the woman she saw reflected there. She couldn't remember the last time she'd stood before a full-length mirror this scantily dressed. It had been years.

Then she had heard Max in the kitchen. For a moment, she'd almost taken the suit off and told him she'd forgotten hers. But she'd known he would still try to make her go swimming, no matter what. She had looked again in the mirror and felt a tiny tremor of excitement. The smell of the sea coming in one of the windows and the sound of the waves had drawn her, as well as the thought of Max in nothing but a swimsuit. At least she hoped he would be wearing one. Knowing him…

Her body had almost ached to go in the surf—ached to just let go as if she'd been locked up for too long.

She had quickly pulled on the large shirt she'd brought, the jeans and the pair of flip-flops, the only extra clothing she'd packed for the trip.

Now as the waves washed around her, she was thankful she hadn't changed her mind. She floated in a sea of shifting water and light as the sun began to sink into the Pacific.

"Glad you brought your swimsuit?" Max asked, suddenly appearing next to her. His long blond hair was wet and brushed back from his forehead to curl against his suntanned neck. The water droplets that clung to his eyelashes looked like tiny jewels. He couldn't have looked more like a bronzed sea god.

She swallowed, only able to nod in answer.

"I've missed this sunset," he said, his face turned to the horizon.

They swam, bathed in the golden light, until the sun dipped below the horizon and was gone.

Kat had a sudden pang of sorrow at its passing. Her gaze met Max's and saw her own regret mirrored in his eyes. She breathed in the salty air, the water lapping around her, caressing her skin, and felt free and alive in a way that she hadn't in years.

That alone scared her. Then there was Max. She felt the intensity of his gaze as a wave rocked her and he grabbed for her, pulling her against him. His warm, wet skin brushed against hers, and then his arms were around her, his mouth on hers as he tangled his legs with hers.

Kat lost herself in his kiss, in his mouth, in his touch, as the ocean waves gently rocked them and the sky paled into twilight. A rogue wave dropped over them, driving them underwater—and apart. Kat kicked her way to the surface, coughing on the salt water.

Max came up looking as surprised by the kiss as the wave that had almost drowned them. "I didn't mean for that to happen. But you looked so damned…kissable."

The memory of his mouth on hers, his warm skin pressed against hers, the caress of his hands over her, had left her feeling shaken—and worse, vulnerable. She knew better than to let down her guard, especially with a man like Max.

Turning, she swam back toward the beach, telling herself that once back in Montana, there was no reason she'd ever have to see Max again.

To her surprise, that thought didn't make her feel better.

THE SHERIFF LOOKED up as his wife stepped into his office and closed the door behind her. "I was just getting ready to head home," he said, surprised to see her. "What's wrong?"

"Sarah Hamilton is getting married," Lynette announced.

"To whom?"

She laughed as she took a chair. "That does seem to be the first question that comes to mind. Russell Murdock."

Frank shook his head, dismissing the rumor she'd driven all the way to Big Timber to share. "You really shouldn't believe everything you hear," he said, looking again at the expense sheets on his desk. He loved his job—except for the paperwork. When he retired, he wasn't going to miss this part at all.

"Even if I heard it straight from the horse's mouth?" his wife demanded.

He looked up to her. "Sarah told you this? Sarah, who is in hiding from the press?"

"Russell told me—and Mabel Murphy."

He let out a low whistle. "So it's all over three counties by now."

"That's why I wanted you to be one of the first to hear." Her good cheer seemed to leave her. "Russell is so happy about it." She met her husband's eyes. "He can't have any idea what he's getting into."

Frank shook his head in both wonderment and worry.

"Don't you think you should tell him what we found out about the brain wiping?" Lynette asked.

"It was Russell who came to me with the theory." Russell was already convinced that the reason Sarah couldn't remember the past twenty-two years of her life was because her brain had been wiped. He was also convinced that Buckmaster Hamilton was behind it.

"But shouldn't he be told he was right?" she argued.

"Not until I have proof. I've been trying to track down Dr. Ralph Venable without much luck."

When he'd first heard this theory, he had been more than a little skeptical. *Brain wiping?* While it sounded like something out of a sci-fi movie, he'd soon discovered that scientists could actually now wipe a brain of certain memories. They could also restore them.

As far as Frank knew, the method had only been tested on rats. But once he'd found out that there'd been a doctor doing the research more than twenty-two years ago, it had led him to White Sulphur Springs and Dr. Venable.

Not only did they learn that the good doctor had been experimenting on humans, but also they had a pretty good idea that Sarah Hamilton had known the doctor and had been at the sanitarium only hours after her SUV had gone under the ice in the Yellowstone River. To add to that, the sanitarium had closed a few days later, and Dr. Venable and the blonde woman had both disappeared.

"But if Russell is right, it was Sarah's husband, the presumed soon-to-be president of the United States, who had her brain wiped," Lynette said.

"Your point?"

"Wouldn't Buckmaster be worried that Sarah is going to remember whatever it was he was trying to cover up?"

"That's all supposition. We have no proof—especially

that Senator Buckmaster Hamilton was even involved," Frank said.

"What if Buckmaster isn't behind the brain wiping? What if someone else knows what happened to make Sarah try to kill herself?"

"You mean if she called someone from her past to pick her up that night and not Buckmaster?" he asked.

Lynette nodded. "If they really did wipe her brain, couldn't they also retrieve those memories whenever they wanted to?"

Frank frowned. "What are you getting at?"

"Couldn't those same people have a reason they want her to remember at some point?"

"You mean, remember why she tried to kill herself that night in the Yellowstone River?"

She nodded. "If her husband really does have something to hide, as Russell claims, then what if it came out right before the election?"

Frank smiled at his wife. "Or right after. I love the way your mind works."

"But it would mean that whoever stole those memories would have to put them back. You might not have to keep looking for Dr. Venable much longer. If any of this is more than supposition, I would think the good doctor will be returning to Montana soon."

"I'm sorry you didn't like dinner," Max said after he and Kat had returned to the beach house. They'd taken the convertible to his favorite Mexican restaurant. She'd been quiet throughout the meal. Now she looked pale as he ushered her into the house.

"It was fine," Kat said. "I just wasn't very hungry." After their swim, she'd changed back into the slacks,

blouse and jacket she'd worn on the plane. The out-
fit hid her amazing body—just as, he suspected, she
wanted it. As if that wasn't sufficient, she'd pulled her
hair back into a tight knot again. The entire look was
like hanging a closed sign around her neck.

He shouldn't have kissed her. It had been one of
those spur-of-the-moment things, and admittedly he
was having trouble regretting it. He'd broken his rule.
But any red-blooded American male would have done
the same thing, he told himself, thinking of Kat out in
the surf in that swimsuit.

It had been the first time he'd seen her happy. He
wondered what it would take to get that woman back
and then quickly pushed that thought away as too dangerous to consider. *That* Kat Hamilton would make it
almost impossible not to break his golden rule again.

"Join me in a glass of wine?" he asked.

She shook her head. He could tell she was anxious
to call it a night.

"I think we should talk about earlier," he said.

"Earlier?" She seemed to shield herself. Was she
afraid he would bring up the kiss? Or the photo?

"The photo," he reminded her.

She seemed to relax. "There's really nothing to talk
about. The woman wasn't my mother. I knew that the
moment I saw her hair. It was *red*. My mother is a
blonde."

"As red as the woman in the photograph's hair was,
I'd say it was dyed." He stepped to the table where he'd
dropped the envelope earlier. "I think you'd better take
another look," he said as he pulled out the copy of the
photograph of the Prophecy.

"There is no need to. The woman isn't—"

"Humor me," Max said turning on an extra light as he held the photo out to her.

"This is ridiculous," she snapped. "Admit that you got it wrong and move on."

He waited until she stormed over to snatch the photo from him. "Look at it in the light. And this time, try to get past the red hair. Look at her face, Kat."

"I already looked at it." But she moved to the lamp he'd just lit and looked down at the copy of the photo now in her hand.

The copy wasn't as good as the original, but it was a whole lot better than the one that had run in the '70s when the group had been active.

Max saw the change in her expression and knew that she'd finally looked past the red hair to the woman's face. There was no way she couldn't see the resemblance since the woman in the snapshot was the spitting image of Kat herself.

KAT SANK DOWN into a chair and rested an elbow on the table as she stared hard at the woman in the photo. She'd been so sure when she'd seen the vivid red hair that she wasn't looking at her mother. But she'd never really looked at the woman's face. Or had she just refused to accept what was plain to see?

She had desperately wanted to believe that Max was wrong. That he was the kind of man who saw what he wanted to see and made up the rest. Now as she stared at the photo, she tried to quell the trembling of her fingers. As much as she wanted to argue that the woman couldn't possibly be her mother, she didn't bother.

Max knew. She hated that he'd been right as much

as she hated the way her stomach roiled at the sight of the woman in the photo.

The resemblance was uncanny. It was her own face, only different. She stared at the woman, still having trouble seeing her mother. Red, as she had gone by according to Max, didn't just have fiery red hair. That same fire burned in her eyes. There was a radical confidence and defiance in the way she stood, the way she held the assault rifle in her hands, the insolent way she looked into the camera.

Most people would never see meek, shy Sarah Hamilton in the redheaded firebrand in the photograph. What Kat saw was the part of herself who had kissed Max out in the surf earlier. The part of her that had cut loose so many years ago, only to regret it.

She put the photo down on the table. "There might be a slight resemblance."

He moved to the table to pick up the photo. "Like I said, lying isn't your strong suit."

"But it certainly is yours. You saw the photo before today. You knew, and bringing me to see it was just some…cruel trick."

Max shook his head, looking shocked that she would accuse him of such a thing. "After you confirmed what I already suspected about your mother not having any proof that she'd attended college those years, I just took the next logical step."

"In other words, if my mother wasn't in the university chess club, then she had to be in some radical antigovernment domestic terrorist group."

He shrugged as he pulled up a chair next to her. "It wasn't that much of a leap. The '60s and '70s were a turbulent time, and domestic terrorists often recruited members from campuses."

Max Malone was really good at this, she thought with grudging appreciation as he slid the photo over to her. "I want you to take a look at the others in the photo. Do you recognize any of the people there?"

"Seriously? I wasn't even born yet when this photo was taken."

"Humor me. Isn't it possible that the group had contact with your mother after two of them went to prison and the rest split up?"

She hadn't thought of that. Didn't even want to contemplate it, but to humor him, she looked down at the photo again, praying she didn't recognize any of them. If she did, then there would be no doubt, would there?

Moving from her mother to each of the seven men with her, she studied their faces. One woman, seven men—who had her mother been? She shuddered at the thought of what her relationship had been with the men. A part of her still wanted to rebel against this. Wasn't it possible Red was just some woman who resembled her and her mother? Didn't each of them have a double somewhere, a doppelgänger?

"You recognized one of them," Max said, startling her.

Kat hadn't realized that she'd hesitated on one of the men. She pushed the copy of the photos away. "No, I—" She shook her head, but she could see it was useless. Max saw through people in a way that made her think he knew her better than anyone she'd ever met.

That terrified her because he made her feel as if she wanted to throw caution to the wind. She'd protected herself for so long and yet she could sense Max tearing down the walls around her, brick by brick.

CHAPTER ELEVEN

"IT WAS *THIS* MAN, wasn't it?" Max said, dragging the photo over again. "This one." He tapped a handsome man standing to the left of Red.

She shook her head. "I don't know why I hesitated on him. I can't say I've ever seen him before." She could feel Max's blue gaze on her.

"He caught your eye. That's why you hesitated." He shoved the photo back over to her. "You might have seen him with your mother. You would have been young. Didn't you say you were eight when your mother disappeared from your life?"

She nodded distractedly. "Who is this man?"

"If I had to guess, given how close they're standing? I'd say her lover."

She looked again at the man in the photograph. A memory, if that's what it was, teased at the back of her mind. She tried to bring it into focus, but it instantly disappeared. "I don't...I don't remember him. I'm sorry."

Max looked disappointed. "It's okay. I was just hoping..."

Kat couldn't help but balk at all of this. It was too crazy. Anyone who knew her mother wouldn't be able to imagine her as this...Red woman.

"So other than this questionable photograph, do you

have anything that connects my mother with this... gang of domestic terrorists?" she asked.

"Not yet. But I have a plan to find out the truth."

"I figured you did. Just don't involve me in it."

"Sorry, Kat, but you were involved long before I came along. If you have a problem with that, take it up with your mother."

Angelina Broadwater Hamilton got the call on the way to the airport.

"Mrs. Broadwater?" the woman on the other end of the call asked.

Referring to her by her maiden name threw her for a moment. From behind the wheel of his SUV, Buckmaster asked, "Is everything all right?"

Belatedly she remembered that Broadwater was the name she'd given the latest private investigator she'd hired.

She nodded at her husband and said, "This is she," into the phone.

"I'm calling because you hired private investigator Curtis Olsen."

"Yes," she said cautiously.

"I'm his secretary. Was... Mr. Olsen has been killed. I'm calling all of his clients to let them know. If he was in the middle of an investigation for you, the police will be in contact with you."

Police? "What were the circumstances?" she asked, knowing that her husband was listening.

"He was stabbed during a mugging."

A *mugging*? She felt herself relax. It had nothing to do with her case.

"The police still might be contacting you to question whether or not his death might have a connection to the case he was working on for you."

"I can't imagine how there could be. You said it was a mugging."

"In any case, I wanted to let you know."

"Thank you."

"Are you all right?" Buckmaster asked. "What was that about?"

"Nothing." She looked out the side window as they neared the airport turnoff. Moose had told her that if she hired another private investigator she'd get him killed. No, she thought. It was merely a coincidence. Curtis was killed in a mugging. Moose had been scared and trying to scare her.

But, if not, she couldn't help but wonder what was buried in Sarah Hamilton's past that was so bad that someone was willing to kill to keep it quiet.

She tried to assure herself that the investigator's death might have nothing to do with her case. He could have just been in the wrong place at the wrong time. Or it could involve someone else's case.

Angelina turned to her husband, plastering a smile on her face as she did. "It is nothing for you to worry about." Unfortunately, she feared that might not be true.

MAX COULDN'T HIDE his disappointment. Kat *had* recognized the man. He'd seen that flicker of acknowledgment. But either she really couldn't remember or she hadn't wanted to share that memory with him.

Not that he could blame her. Who'd want to admit that their mother was a domestic terrorist in the '70s? He could see that Kat was having a hard time accepting that the woman who'd called herself Red was her mother. But between her mother's missing college years and this photograph, there seemed to be little doubt.

"What did this…group do?" she asked as if she didn't really want to know. Her gray eyes were large and luminous. He remembered them in the light from the waning sunset just before he'd kissed her.

"They were antigovernment terrorists," he said. "They blew up government buildings, robbed banks, defaced institutions they considered evil."

"Robbed banks?"

"Stealing from the capitalists to further their cause," he said with a shrug. "I think they stylized themselves after the SLA—"

"The group that kidnapped Patty Hearst," she said. "But they didn't do anything like that, right? Kidnap people?"

He wasn't sure how much she could handle right now. But it would all be coming out if he could find enough proof to support the article he would write. "A couple of maintenance staff were in one of the courthouses they hit. They blew it up in the middle of the night, probably assuming no one would be inside."

"The maintenance staff were…*killed*?"

He nodded. "Three more people were killed in a bank robbery that went badly, including a security guard and two bank employees. One of the tellers was pregnant. Two of the group were caught and are still doing time."

Kat looked as if she might be sick. She got to her feet and, hugging herself, walked to the wall of windows that overlooked the Pacific. "Why haven't they caught the others?"

"They're on the FBI's most-wanted lists, but no one has been able to find them, apparently. It's been… thirty-six years."

She turned. He saw the hope in her expression. "If the FBI isn't interested in my mother, then doesn't that mean she isn't…Red?"

"They probably had no reason to tie Sarah Johnson Hamilton to it. The group dissolved in 1979, the same year your mother came out to Montana. A year later she married your father and was then part of a distinguished family. The members burned down their safe house and destroyed all evidence before they disbanded."

"Except for that one photo," she pointed out.

"They released it before the deaths, before they were killers. The photo is like the one the SLA had released. I suspect the Prophecy hoped to get the same kind of publicity. They didn't. They had wanted people to know about them, wanted to make sure they got credit for the crimes they committed—until the deaths. Then they seemed to have just…dissolved and gone their separate ways. Except for the two in prison."

"So it's over. The group dissolved, so why bring it up again?" she asked, pleading in her tone.

She knew the answer.

"You can't write this story until you have proof, correct?" she said, still seeming to grasp at any hope.

"This is more than just some article, and you know it. If I'm right, then you have to ask yourself why your mother came back to Montana and your family *now*. Is it just a coincidence that a woman I believe was involved with an antigovernment group in the '70s was the wife of a man who is now running for the presidency?"

"My father…" Her voice broke. She turned back to the window. Past her he could see the silvery glow of the moonlight on the rippling sea. "You think my father is in danger."

It wasn't a question. That she even asked it meant she'd come to the same conclusion he had.

He moved across the room to her. A cool breeze blew in, billowing the sheer curtains tucked at each side of the wall of windows. "I will talk to the two men who have been serving time for the killings. They're both almost sixty now and have spent the past thirty-six years locked up after receiving life sentences without parole. I'm thinking they might want to talk."

She didn't look over at him. "If they wouldn't talk when they were arrested—"

"Even the most devout sometimes have second thoughts after that many years in prison. You look tired," he said. "You should get some sleep." He wanted to tell her what came next, but he feared she wasn't ready to hear it, not tonight.

He felt as if he was getting in over his head. Not with the story, but with his feelings when it came to this woman. He'd always been attracted to a story. Kat had a story of her own—not to mention the story surrounding her mother and family.

Max had always been able to put his feelings aside. But this time, he wasn't sure he could do that.

KAT LAY IN the bed, staring up at the ceiling, unable to sleep. No sound came from inside the beach house.

When Max had suggested that she might want to call it a night, she'd agreed, telling him she had a headache.

"We fly out at eight. I'll wake you so we can get to the airport on time," he'd said. "I know it's been a lot to take in."

He had no idea.

"Just a minute," he'd said as she'd started toward the spare bedroom.

He'd left her for a moment and come back with a couple of pain relievers and a glass of water. She'd been touched by that small kindness and had to remind herself that for him, this was only about an article that might get him a Pulitzer.

For her, so much more was at stake. Now, alone in the spare room and listening to the sound of the ocean waves on the beach below, she pulled out her cell phone. Just as she had from the time she was little, she reached out to her big sister, Ainsley, for comfort.

She dialed her number, even though it was late.

Ainsley answered on the second ring. "Kat?"

"I'm sorry if I woke you."

"You didn't. I was reading." She could hear shifting as Ainsley likely pushed her book away and sat up, giving Kat her undivided attention. That was the older sister she knew so well. "Is something wrong?"

Everything was wrong. "Do you have memories of our mother?"

If the question surprised her, Ainsley didn't show it. "Some. Not as many as I thought I would since I was ten when she…left."

"Mine seem to all be bad memories of her scolding me or me crying and upset. She was always busy. I remember our nannies better than my own mother."

"I'm the same way. I know she loved us, but she did seem…overwhelmed a lot of the time, but who can blame her?"

"Whose idea was it to have six kids, I wonder."

"Not Dad's," Ainsley said. "I know he was angry at her for leaving him with six daughters to raise alone. Of course, he knew that she'd committed suicide long before we did."

"Or apparently tried to commit suicide. I'm glad I didn't know. I would have blamed myself." When she thought of her early childhood, she had snapshots of memories. Her mother scolding her for tracking up the floor. Her mother scowling at her across the dinner table. Her mother angry at her over a birthday cake.

"Do you remember my last birthday before she was gone?" Kat asked.

"The horse cake," Ainsley said with a sigh.

Her mother had baked the cake and made a brown horse out of frosting. When Kat saw it, she'd burst into tears. "My horse isn't brown. It's black," Kat recalled crying in frustration. Her mother had followed her up the stairs. Kat had never seen her so angry. She'd been terrified of her. She'd screamed for their father, and her mother had put her hand over her mouth. Kat hadn't been able to breathe. She remembered looking into her mother's eyes and seeing…

"I'm sure you must have some good memories if you really think about it," Ainsley said.

"Do *you*?"

Her sister sighed. "I used to think so. But, honestly, the woman who's come back, I have a hard time remembering her at all."

"Me, too. Have you talked to her?"

"No," Ainsley said. "And I feel guilty about that. But that day that we met with her at the Branding Iron? It was too weird, didn't you think?"

"Yes."

"Also knowing what pain Dad's been going through because of all this. I know it's not her fault—"

"How can you say that?" Kat said. "She's the one who left us. She tried to kill herself to get away from us, and when that didn't work, she disappeared for twenty-two years."

"We don't know that. She could have been suffering from depression. All us kids and Dad busy with the ranch. Even then he was involved in local, and then state politics and gone a lot."

She hadn't thought about what it must have been like for her mother. Six daughters. That winter Ainsley was ten, Bo was five, Olivia three and Harper and Cassidy were only a few months old.

"Had it been postpartum depression? Or were we all just too much for her? Or was *I* just too much for her? I remember overhearing her tell Dad that I was irascible. I didn't even know what it meant. I had to look it up in the dictionary. Grumpy, petulant, ill-tempered. I was never the 'good one,' like you and Bo and Olivia."

She'd seen the fear in her mother's eyes that night. Her mother had quickly taken her hand from her daughter's mouth and nose. As Kat had gasped for breath, her mother had begged her forgiveness. But Kat hadn't forgotten what she'd seen in her mother's eyes. And her mother hadn't forgotten either, she suspected.

"I think I'm the reason she left." Because Kat had reminded her of a past she'd tried to put behind her?

"Kat, that's crazy. You know that's not true," Ainsley said.

"Do I?" She'd never told anyone about that night, not even Ainsley.

"Our mother had troubles that had nothing to do with us."

Kat got up and walked to the window. She had a view of the beach. The sea was silvery, the sand white in the moonlight. Maybe Ainsley was right, and their mother had more troubles than even she could have imagined before today.

"Do you think she was unhappy with Dad?" she asked.

"Who knows? I don't think *he* was unhappy. Olivia said he admitted to her that Mother is the only woman he's ever truly loved. Also he still seems mystified by her attempted suicide—and still so hurt by it."

Hurt. "You don't think she'd hurt him again, do you?"

Ainsley said nothing for a moment. "I hope not. I never thought I'd say this, but I think it's good that Dad is married to Angelina."

"He would have taken Mother back otherwise, huh." That would mean that "Red"—Sarah Johnson Hamilton—would be living on the ranch and maybe even be the next First Lady.

"Kat, are you sure you're all right?"

She thought about telling Ainsley everything. But what did she really know? And what would it accomplish at this point? She had to be sure before she laid anything about their mother's past on her sisters. But in her heart, she feared it was all true.

"I'm fine," Kat said after a moment. "I couldn't sleep

thinking about…things. I just needed to talk to my big sister."

"I'm glad you called." Ainsley sounded touched.

Kat saw a lone figure coming up the beach. She recognized Max Malone's lazy gait. He walked with his head down, the moonlight making his blond hair shine like the sun. "I should let you go. Is it a good book you're reading?"

"It is. How's the exhibit coming along? Lots of great photos?"

"We'll see." She thought of the photo of the Prophecy and the redheaded woman with Kat's features.

"It's going to be great. We're all planning to be there. I talked to Harper and Cassidy. They're having a ball in New York City, but you know how they are. They're anxious to get back to the ranch. Apparently nothing can take the cowgirl out of us Hamilton girls."

"What do you expect? Dad put us on the back of a horse before we could walk," Kat said, smiling to herself at the memories. "Thanks for the talk. I think I can sleep now."

"Good night, then."

She disconnected and watched Max walk the rest of the way up to the beach house. He'd been excited about being back here earlier. Now there was a melancholy air to him that made her suspect he was visiting with his own demons from the past.

CHAPTER TWELVE

"Sheriff Frank Curry?"

The woman's voice on the other end of the line sounded vaguely familiar.

He turned on the lamp next to the bed and saw that it was after ten. He was trying to place the woman when she said, "I'm Becca Thorson, a nurse in White Sulphur Springs?"

He felt his pulse jump with anticipation. "Ms. Thorson, of course," he said and sat up. Lynette, who'd awakened at the sound of the phone, rolled over to look at him. She'd recognized the name, as well.

"Please, call me Becca. I'm sorry to call so late, but this is the first time today that I've had a moment to myself."

"It's good to hear from you. Is everything all right?"

"Your wife said if I ever heard anything more about the things that went on at the sanitarium—" she dropped her voice "—or about Dr. Venable, that I should call you."

Frank held his breath for a moment before releasing it. "You heard something?"

"One of the women here in the rest home collects stamps. She loves showing them off, though with her dementia, I really doubt she even knows what they are anymore. I couldn't help but notice one of the postcards had an unusual stamp. That's when I saw where it was from—and *who* it was from."

"Dr. Venable," he guessed.

"Yes. The postcard was from Brazil. I'd forgotten that the doctor rented a room from this woman and that she was sweet on him. The postcard said he was doing fine and not to worry about him."

"Where in Brazil was the card mailed?"

"Santa Cruz do Sul."

He wrote it down as she spelled it. "And you said the postmark was dated shortly after the sanitarium closed?"

"A couple of months later. Does that help?"

"It just might. Thank you." He was already getting out of bed after he disconnected to get his laptop so he could look up the city on the internet. "Dr. Venable went to South America," he said when Lynette joined him after pulling on her robe. "He sent a postcard to his landlady from Santa Cruz do Sul. According to what I can find on the browser, it's a city of about a hundred and thirty thousand not far from the Uruguay border. It's a product of an immigration policy to populate Brazil."

"So they welcomed him with open arms."

Frank nodded. "A doctor from America looking for a new home? I would have imagined they did indeed."

"Not just a doctor. But his young…what would he have tried to pass off Sarah Hamilton as? Maybe his wife."

He shot her a look. "You think he took her with him."

"Why not? It could certainly explain why you haven't been able to find anything on her for the past twenty-two years. What language do they speak there?"

"Portuguese, but English has replaced French for their second language."

"So she wouldn't have had to learn Portuguese," Lynette said.

"We don't know that they stayed there. Or even if Sarah was along. It won't be easy to prove either, but on the chance that Dr. Venable is still there…"

"You're going to try to find him."

Frank knew that if he kept investigating Sarah, it would eventually get back to the senator.

"I'll help you," his wife said and held up her hand before he could tell her all the reasons it was a bad idea. "I'll just make a few calls to the hospital and clinics there. What can it hurt?"

KAT FELT BETTER the next morning, her head much clearer. She'd awakened early and was already up when Max came out of the master bedroom.

"Good morning," he said, sounding surprised to find her standing at the wall of windows overlooking the sea. She was drinking a cup of the coffee she'd made.

"This beach house? It doesn't belong to a friend of yours, does it?" When he didn't answer, she turned to look at him.

He looked only mildly guilty. "It's mine."

She nodded. "And the convertible that just happened to be waiting at the airport?"

He shifted his gaze away for a moment before coming back to hers. "Mine."

Kat sighed. "Why do you want everyone to believe you don't know where your next meal is coming from? Sleeping in the back of your pickup?" She shook her head. *Who are you?*

He shrugged. "Essentially, what you see is what you get."

"What I see this morning is a man with an expensive beach house who has an expensive convertible parked outside. So who is the destitute-looking cowboy who wears worn boots and jeans and sleeps in the back of his truck?"

"They're both me," he said as he stepped into the kitchen and opened the refrigerator. She wasn't that surprised to see that someone had stocked it.

"Really?"

"This place? It's my childhood on the beach." He glanced over at her as she joined him in the space between the kitchen island and the long counter. "I'm *sentimental*. When my cousin's family put the beach house on the market, I bought it because I wanted to hang on to those memories. The convertible? My cousin and I used to dream about owning one like that. I bought it for…us."

She heard the emotion in the last word and looked more closely at him. Her heart sank. "Your cousin…"

"Luke died before I could afford to buy the convertible for us." There was so much regret in his voice.

"But if his family had money, why sell the beach house, why didn't Luke buy the car for himself?"

"His father made some bad investments. They'd fallen on to hard times. I couldn't help them, I was just starting out…"

"But your father—"

"My father had washed his hands of both his brother and me." He shook his head. "I was barely able to buy the beach house. It needed a lot of work, but I held on to it until I could make the necessary repairs. As for my pickup, it runs good. It's the first one I ever bought, so…" He shrugged again. "We're like old friends." He grinned. "Same with my boots."

"And the camera you lost."

He nodded. "Yep. I wasn't joking about it having sentimental value and being lucky for me." There was pride in his voice. She couldn't help but admire him. "I hang on to things that I'm fond of, and I like being my own man and living life on my own terms."

Kat understood that. Max didn't discard things when they got worn or old. He cherished them. So what had happened with the wife he was married to for two years? she wondered.

"It's not that easy for some of us to live like that."

He cocked his head as he considered her. "Why not?"

"I live life on my own terms as much as I can. But I grew up as one of 'the Hamilton girls.'"

"The Hamilton girls?"

Kat knew he would have heard the expression, but she didn't call him on it. "You know, six spoiled, entitled senator's brats. Doesn't matter if it's true or not."

He looked captivated. "Is it true?"

"Somewhat," she admitted. "Growing up, we got pretty much everything we ever asked for."

"But not necessarily everything you wanted or needed," he said.

She nodded, surprised that he understood so easily. "Dad was gone a lot."

"And with your mother gone, as well…"

"Ainsley was like a mother to us," she said, smiling at the memory. "She still is. We didn't suffer."

Max didn't look convinced.

"What I wanted was to be my own person."

"Let me guess," he said, smiling. "You were the rebellious one."

"That's a polite way of putting it, yes. My family would use more colorful terms." Her mother in particular, she thought.

"There is nothing wrong with rebellion."

Kat raised an eyebrow. "That's probably what the man said who recruited my mother into the Prophecy, huh. *If* Red is my mother."

MAX REFILLED KAT'S coffee cup and began making them breakfast. He pulled out chorizo, eggs, potatoes, onions, peppers and tortillas.

"Max," she said, seeing what he was doing. "I don't—"

"You *do* this morning. You've never had my huevos rancheros. You, my sweet, are in for a treat."

She sighed and pulled up a stool at the breakfast bar as if knowing it was a waste of breath to argue with him.

"We should talk about the next step."

She took a sip of her coffee, then frowned as if she thought she must have missed something. "Next step?"

"We have to find out if your mother really was Red. The simplest approach is to just ask her."

Kat almost spilled her coffee. "I am not going to accuse my mother of being this…terrorist from the picture."

"Because you're afraid that she'll admit it."

"No, because…*I* still don't believe it."

He gave her a sympathetic look. "If you're that convinced—"

The smell of frying chorizo filled the kitchen, making her stomach growl. "Save the reverse psychology."

"I would think you'd be even more anxious than me to have her confirm that she isn't Red."

She cut her eyes to him. "Really? Come on, what's the point of asking her? You don't believe she'll admit it, do you? You said these people are still wanted by the law. So, even if she was this Red woman, she will lie."

He shrugged. "So, what harm would it do, then? The options are pretty simple. She will either not have a clue what we're talking about, she'll break down and confess all or she'll lie through her teeth. No harm. No foul."

Kat narrowed her eyes. "I know what you're up to. You think you know people so well that you'll be able to tell by her reaction to the photo. But if my mother is that much of a…psychopath, terrorist killer, then I would assume she can beat a lie detector test—let alone the Max Malone test."

He grinned. "I'm a hundred times better than a polygraph."

"Humble, as well. You are so…irritating. Fine. But it won't prove anything."

He cracked three eggs expertly into the skillet along with the peppers, onions and chorizo. "It will to me."

She shook her head, surprised that the man seemed to know how to cook.

"And it could ease your mind."

"Or not." The wonderful smell coming from the skillet was making her salivate.

"Come on, you know you won't be able to live with yourself if you don't find out the truth."

"I could surprise you." A part of her wanted confirmation for what she felt in her heart. But who wanted to believe their mother capable of the things the group had done?

His grin broadened as he glanced over at her. "You just might at that, but not about this. You would always be looking at your mother, wondering…"

"What do you think I'm going to be doing now?" she demanded as he pulled the skillet from the stove, then set about getting them plates and silverware before joining her.

"Another reason we have to find out the truth," he said as he took a tortilla, rolled it up full of filling and held it out for her to take a bite. "Taste this. I promise you won't be sorry."

"I'll be sorry when I weigh twenty pounds more than the day I met you," she mumbled under her breath before relenting and taking a bite. He took one, as well.

"It's time you stopped denying yourself. I think I'd like another twenty pounds on you." He grinned. Their eyes met for a moment, both of them now more than aware of the intimacy of his actions.

It was beyond delicious, so there was no hiding the fact from Max. "Oh, my gosh," she groaned. "Max, this is amazing."

He beamed. "That one's for you. I'll make another for myself. I made enough for seconds."

They ate contentedly looking out at the ocean. Kat could feel the salty breeze coming in an open window and wished they had time to swim again. She quickly dispelled the thought, remembering the kiss and the way that swimsuit had made her feel. If Max hadn't been a gentleman…

She put down part of a second tortilla, stuffed and

shocked by her last thought. Max *was* a gentleman. She had kissed him more than willingly. If that wave hadn't come down on them just then… But even later, he hadn't tried to take advantage of the mood she'd been in at the ocean. If he'd come after her when she'd left the water, if he'd caught her and kissed her again…

Kat had a sudden flash of the two of them making love on the secluded beach.

"Too hot for you?" Max asked.

She frowned at him, confused.

"The burrito. You were fanning yourself."

She knew she must have blushed to the roots of her hair, but, fortunately, Max didn't notice. He'd gotten up to get her a glass of iced water. She gulped it down, needing to cool off, and a cold shower was out of the question since they had to get to the airport.

"When?" she asked as Max began to pick up their dishes and load them into the dishwasher. She'd offered to help, but he'd insisted she was his guest. "When do you want to go see my mother?"

"I've found sooner is always better than later."

"I'm sure." She sighed. "If we do this, then there have to be some ground rules," she said, holding up a finger. "No interview. No photos. Nothing is on the record."

He couldn't help being amused. "Agreed, except we are going to need just one photo—one of you and your mother."

"What?"

"Look, I agree with everything you've said. We probably won't get a lot from your mother. That is why we need the photo for when I go to the prison where her former cohorts have been housed for the past forty years. I'll need the photo of the two of you, since I doubt you're going to want to go to the prison with me."

"There is no way I'm going to the prison to confront… terrorists."

"That's what I thought you would say." He grinned. "Thus the photo I'm going to need."

"Wait. Why would you need my photo?"

"Because you look like your mother when she was college age."

"You do realize this isn't going to work. Once you tell her you're a reporter—"

"You could tell her we are dating, but," he rushed on before she could interrupt, "I doubt she will believe that."

"Wait, why wouldn't she believe we're together?" She regretted the question the moment it was out of her mouth.

His grin broadened. "Because you look as if you're going to jump out of your skin every time I touch you, and in order to be convincing as lovers we'd have to do more than touch. We might actually have to kiss again."

She narrowed her eyes at him, not about to deny it. "You enjoy making me uncomfortable, don't you?"

"Not really. I did enjoy kissing you, though. Maybe you should just tell your mother we're friends. If she's Red, then she'll see through it right away anyway."

"You make it sound as if she's…clairvoyant or something."

"No, just sharp, I would imagine. Oh, didn't I mention? Your mother was the coleader of the group with that man you recognized. They *were* lovers."

"Coleaders?"

"Yep. Of course, the authorities believe she really was the brains behind the Prophecy. But I'm betting her lover would argue that."

Kat stared at him, too shocked to speak for a moment. Her mother, the brains of the Prophecy? Looking at the small, meek woman who'd come back from the dead, it was laughable. But she kept thinking about her birthday. Nor could she deny her own resemblance to Red. Or what Max had found out—or hadn't found out—about her mother.

One thought struck home. If her mother was Red, the alleged brains behind the Prophecy, then not only could her father be in danger, but also her sisters and… the entire country if her father was elected president.

She had to know the truth. What galled her was that Max had been counting on that. Without looking at him, she moved to the window overlooking the ocean again and pulled out her cell phone. Her mother had given her the new cell phone number where she could be reached.

Kat keyed in the number, hoping she didn't answer. Better yet, that she'd disappeared again for another twenty-two years.

Her mother answered on the second ring. "Hello." Sarah sounded cheerful, indicating that she'd checked to see who was calling before she'd answered.

"It's Kat," she said unnecessarily.

"Yes, Kat, how are you?"

"Good." Not quite true. "I wondered if we could come see you?"

"*We?* You and your sisters?"

She sounded so pleased that Kat hated to tell her

differently. "Just me…and a friend." She shot Max a look. He grinned. Friends, indeed.

"Of course," her mother said, although sounding a little disappointed.

"Do you want to meet somewhere or—" Max was shaking his head. Clearly he thought her mother would react differently in a public place than a private one.

"Why don't you come up here?" her mother suggested.

"Are you sure?"

"I'm tired of hiding out, and I think most of the media has lost interest in me."

I wouldn't bet on that, Kat thought as she saw how impatient Max was.

"How do we get there?" She listened as her mother gave her directions. "It won't be until later this afternoon. Will you be around?" Her mother said she would. "Can we bring you anything?"

"No, Russell dropped off groceries earlier. I have something I need to tell you, but it can wait until you get here."

"Okay." Kat figured if the news was her engagement, she'd already heard. But with her mother, it could be anything. "Then we'll see you soon."

CHAPTER THIRTEEN

WHEN NETTIE SAW the tiny box sitting in her post office box, she was almost afraid to touch it. Silly, she told herself as she pulled it out. She noted the return address. Just as she'd thought, it was the pendulum she'd ordered.

She knew what Frank would say if he found out. Complete foolishness. But what if, as the advertisement had said, she could tell the future with the darned thing? Now, wouldn't that be something?

Tucking the box in her pocket, she headed for the Branding Iron. The waitress Callie Kincaid was working, but she said the café owner Kate French would be in shortly. Nettie took a seat, feeling anxious and excited and a little sick to her stomach. Callie brought her a coffee, and Nettie invited her to sit down. As she pulled out the box from her pocket, her fingers were shaking.

"Do you believe a pendulum can tell the future?" Nettie asked.

Callie looked from her to the box. "If it really could, are you sure you want to know the future?"

"Supposedly, the pendulum will also answer questions about other people. Like if they are lying or telling the truth."

"I can tell you from experience, that isn't a good

thing," Callie said, getting up as her boss, Kate, came in. "Be careful, Nettie. You might be opening up a Pandora's box."

Nettie had the heavy gold droplet of a pendulum out of the box by the time Kate joined her.

"What did you say to Callie that has her looking worried?" her friend said as she slid into the booth.

Nettie waved that off. "Where is your adorable daughter?"

"With her father. I needed to do a couple of things down here. Is that a…pendulum?"

She nodded sagely. She'd read how to hold it and now tried to still the movement of her hand and the pendulum as she held it a few inches over the tabletop. "I'm trying to solve a mystery."

"The mystery is why you would spend good money on that…thing." But Kate was watching with obvious interest as the pendulum suddenly came to a dead stop.

Nettie swallowed. "We'll start with an easy question. Is Kate's baby a girl or a boy?"

"We already know she's a girl," Kate argued.

"But does the pendulum know?" Nettie whispered. Nothing happened for a moment, and then the pendulum began to move in a small circle. "Whoa," Nettie exclaimed. "Okay, it got that right. A girl," she said as the pendulum stopped again. She lowered her voice, even though they were the only people in the café at the moment other than Callie and the cook, and they were in the back.

"Is Sarah Hamilton lying about her memory loss?"

Kate leaned closer. Nettie stared at the pendulum. It didn't move.

"What does that mean?" Kate asked.

"Maybe yes *and* no. I'll ask it a different question." She cleared her voice. "Did Sarah really come back to be with her daughters?"

For a moment, nothing happened, then the pendulum began to move in a small circle before it stopped again. "Yes."

"Is Sarah dangerous?" The pendulum began to circle again, only in larger circles. Nettie looked up at Kate, who was also wide-eyed.

"What are you going to ask it now?" Kate said in a whisper.

Just then the café phone rang. "It's the supplier. He said you were waiting for his call?" Callie said from back by the kitchen.

Kate got up and left. Nettie had to relax her arm. She stared at the pendulum lying on the tabletop and then slowly picked it up again. What was the one question she wanted answered more than anything else?

"Is Frank going to retire as sheriff?" she asked, her voice coming out in a hoarse whisper.

The pendulum began to move slowly in a tight circle and then stopped again.

"Soon?" she asked as Kate started back toward her table.

As the pendulum circled again, Kate sat down. "Ask it if I am going to have a boy this time?" She grinned over at Nettie and put a finger to her lips. "I'm only a couple weeks late, so it is way too early to even hope."

"Is Kate going to give birth to a boy or a girl?" Nettie asked.

The pendulum began to swing back and forth. It stopped, but then to both of their amazement, it began to swing again.

"Nettie?" Kate said, her voice breaking.

Nettie smiled over at her friend. "Twin boys, if this thing can be trusted." She quickly put the pendulum back into the box, a little spooked by it. Frank was going to retire soon? She knew how much he loved his job, most of the time. She couldn't imagine he would be happy if he didn't have something more to do than run the ranch. Callie was right, she thought. Maybe she didn't want to know the future.

MAX COULDN'T WAIT to meet Red. But he knew he probably wouldn't even get a glimpse of her. Instead, he would be meeting Sarah Johnson Hamilton.

"You're like a little kid on the way to the candy store," Kat said, glancing over at him as she drove. She'd insisted on driving.

He suspected that she thought she'd have the upper hand if she drove. But then, she didn't know him well, did she?

He'd agreed to let her drive. He could tell she was nervous. Maybe driving would make her feel as if she had more control of her life—and what was about to go down.

"I won't apologize for being excited about meeting your mother," he said now as he memorized the route to the cabin where Sarah Johnson Hamilton was hiding out.

"I think you're going to be disappointed," Kat said.

He shook his head. No matter what happened, he wouldn't be disappointed. Just to get this close to a member of the Prophecy—not just a member but possibly the brains behind the antigovernment group—was more than he could hope for. While Kat might still have her doubts, he had none at all and hadn't since he'd seen the first photo.

"Thanks for doing this," he said, looking over at Kat.

"Yeah, my pleasure," she said sarcastically as she slowed for a narrow turnoff back into the pines.

He caught sight of the cabin, the green metal roof gleaming in the sunlight. He would never have found this cabin on his own, he realized. Russell Murdock had done a great job of hiding her away. But had he done it to keep her away from the media—or away from Buckmaster Hamilton?

Kat pulled up in front of a small rustic-looking house. It was too modern to really be called a cabin. Cutting the engine, she looked over at him. She was pale, and he noticed that her hand trembled as she pulled the keys from the ignition and pocketed them.

He took her hand in his larger one. Her fingers were ice-cold. "You're not betraying your mother."

She met his gaze, her gray eyes glittering with unshed tears. "It isn't my mother I'm worried about. It's my father. If any of this is true…"

"Your father is why we have to know the truth," Max said and gently squeezed her hand. He caught movement out of the corner of his eye and looked up as Sarah Johnson Hamilton, aka Red, came out onto the porch.

"Showtime," Max said, giving Kat's hand one final squeeze.

KAT TRIED TO still her nerves as she climbed out of the SUV. She heard Max get out and glanced over at him. He'd left his camera bag in the back of the vehicle. She didn't realize until that moment how much she'd worried that she couldn't trust him.

"Kat, it is so good to see you," her mother said in her small meek voice. "I was so excited when you called. And this must be your friend."

"Max Malone. Max, my mother, Sarah."

She watched as Max shook her mother's hand. She saw the way he took her mother's measure. Sarah looked fit for her age, and while small, she was strong, Kat remembered. Her mother had taken her hands, squeezing them.

They all commented on the nice fall day before stepping inside. Kat had never been in this particular cabin owned by the West family.

"This is nice," she said, scanning the well-furnished cottage.

"It *is* nice," her mother agreed. "But it gets lonely up here."

"I'm sure it does," Max said as he moved to the large window overlooking the valley. "You do have a beautiful view, though."

"Please, sit down. I put on some coffee. I would have baked something as well, but—"

"That wasn't necessary. We can't stay long." Kat laid her hand on the side of her shoulder bag, wondering how to broach the subject of the photo inside.

"Oh," her mother said, sounding disappointed. "Well, at least sit down."

"There's something we need you to see," Kat said, just wanting this over.

Sarah looked from her to Max and back again. "Something I need to see?"

"What Kat didn't mention was that I'm a reporter,

and I'm working on a story. We were hoping you might be of help."

Kat shot him a surprised look. Hadn't he insinuated that it might be better not to mention that to her mother?

Sarah's eyes widened at the news. She looked to Kat as if waiting for an explanation. "I thought you said he was a friend of yours?"

Max laughed. "Kat and I are closer than she'd like to admit to her mother," he said and gave Sarah a wink.

Kat flushed to her roots. How dare he—

"If you are looking for a scoop, there is nothing I have to say. I'm more concerned about how you might be using my daughter. So, how did you and my daughter meet?" her mother asked, still looking at Max.

"It's a funny story, but probably not one we have time for today," he said.

"I'm not going anywhere."

"Well, if you have the time…" Max said, pulling out a chair, flipping it around to straddle it, clearly ignoring the eye daggers Kat was sending in his direction. "Kat and I are both interested in photography. We met at the gallery where she will have her showing soon."

Sarah nodded. "My daughter is very talented."

"Yes, she is," he said smiling over at her before glancing around the cabin. "Nice place you have here."

"It's not mine," her mother was saying. "Russell Murdock was kind enough to let me use his guesthouse, and then when the press—" She seemed to bite her tongue as she realized what she'd said.

"I know how people love us reporters," Max said with a laugh. "They've forced you to hide out up here.

I'm sorry about that. Some reporters will do anything to get a story."

"Boy, isn't that the case," Kat said sarcastically.

He didn't look at her but kept smiling at her mother, who seemed to be falling for Max's charm. "So this story you're working on… You think I can help?" Sarah asked.

Kat felt Max's gaze on her as she reached into her purse and pulled out the snapshot of the Prophecy.

THE NEWS OF Sarah's engagement to Russell Murdock spread like a wildfire through the community. Angelina heard that the announcement had been made when she stopped at the gas station in Big Timber. Everyone assumed she already knew since it had apparently also come out in the local newspaper, along with a photo of the two of them.

When she got home, she could see that her husband had heard, as well. Buckmaster looked even more depressed. He tried to hide it, but Angelina witnessed his moods at moments when he didn't think she was watching him.

"They make a nice couple," she said, holding up the newspaper story and photograph.

"I already saw it," her husband said. Clearly, he couldn't bear to look at it again.

It was all Angelina could do not to start beating him with the newspaper, but she knew she wouldn't be able to stop. The man was an idiot when it came to Sarah.

She feared there was only one way for him to get over his former wife. She had to prove that Sarah wasn't the woman he thought she was. If only she could find out what Sarah's deep dark secret was and expose her. But didn't she already have proof?

"The private investigator I hired," she said, making Buckmaster look up from his newspaper. "He was killed. Murdered."

"You hired a private investigator?" He let out a curse. "You had him looking into Sarah's past."

They both knew that was exactly what she'd done. "The police want to talk to me."

"You? Why…"

"Don't you see? This proves that there's something she doesn't want anyone to find. My first PI quit because he said it was too dangerous. Now this one gets killed. Don't look at me like that. I didn't kill him."

"Quit hiring investigators, for God's sake," Buckmaster snapped. "You're driving yourself crazy. How do you even know what case the man was working on before he was killed? It might have nothing at all to do with this fool's errand you're on."

"How can you keep denying that Sarah isn't a threat to our marriage, our life, the presidency?"

"Sarah is marrying Russell," he snapped. "She is no longer a threat to either of us." He stood abruptly, tossing down the newspaper and stalking out of the room. "I have to get ready for the fund-raiser," he said over his shoulder.

Angelina let him leave the room without further argument. Buckmaster wanted to believe the best when it came to Sarah, "the mother of my children," as he always said in answer to her complaints about the woman. But even he had seen things in Sarah that had him doubting the woman he'd foolishly married so long ago.

"I'm not with her anymore," he said, now sticking his head back into the room as if he'd been having a private argument with himself since leaving the room. "I'm with *you*. You're the woman I love. The one I choose to spend my life with. I don't care if Sarah is the devil. She's Russell's problem now." With that, he turned to leave again.

Angelina thought it was a nice speech from the future president, but she wouldn't be happy until Russell and Sarah tied the knot. If that happened, then Sarah Hamilton would be nothing more than a footnote in history, a very small one.

Even as she thought it, though, she knew she couldn't count on that. Quietly, she debated hiring another private investigator. Maybe the third time would be the charm.

MAX STARED AT the woman as she took the photo Kat handed her, but didn't look at it for a moment. Instead, she looked questioningly at her daughter, then to Max.

"What kind of story are you working on?" Sarah asked.

"It's an investigative piece."

"As long as I'm not a part of your story." She slowly looked down at the photograph in her hand. "What is it you want me to look at?" she asked in her small, calm voice.

"Do you recognize any of these people?" Kat asked. He heard the fear in her voice. The statute of limitations never ran out on domestic terrorists like this group.

Max watched Sarah's reaction to the photo. After a moment she looked up.

He prided himself on knowing when a subject was

lying to him. He'd seldom been wrong. He felt a jolt that shook him to his core as he met Sarah Hamilton's blue eyes.

"Mother?" Kat said, clearly unable to stand the suspense any longer.

"I'm sorry, but I don't recognize any of these people." Her mother frowned. "Should I know them?"

"No," Kat said and quickly took the photo from her and put it back into her purse. "It was a long shot. Don't worry about it. Well?" Kat said to him.

"What is it?" Sarah asked. "Have I done something wrong?"

"Not at all, Mrs. Hamilton—"

She cut Max off. "Please, call me Sarah. I can see that you and Kat are close. You're obviously a good friend."

Kat made a rude sound under her breath, but her mother didn't seem to notice.

"I'm following up on a lead in a story, and I thought you might be able to help me," he said. "But since you didn't recognize anyone in the photo…"

"Who were those people?" Sarah asked.

"Not people you need to concern yourself with," Kat said.

Sarah looked a little confused but recovered quickly as she rose to see them out. "I'm sorry you have to leave so soon. But I'm glad you came to see me anyway." She smiled over at her daughter. "I have some news I want to share before you leave. Since you've been so busy with your upcoming exhibit, you probably haven't heard." After a beat, she said, "Russell Murdock and I are getting married."

Kat tried to act surprised. *"Married?"*

Sarah nodded, still smiling. "Russell has been so wonderful. I don't know what I would have done without him, and your father has gotten on with his life, so I realized it was time I did so, as well."

"Best wishes," Max said.

"Our engagement announcement should be out in the local paper. Plus, Russell told a few of the local women in Beartooth." Sarah chuckled. "He said it would be faster at reaching everyone than the announcement in the newspaper. We're going to buy the ring tomorrow, and then I'll be coming out of seclusion. I can't wait for that. This cabin is quite cozy, but I go a little stir-crazy alone up here. Not that Russell hasn't been a dear. He comes up every day, brings me food and presents…" Her voice trailed off as she looked over at Kat. "I'm sorry for running on so."

Kat seemed as if she was trying to come up with something to say. "I'm happy for you and Russell, if you're sure that's what you want."

Her mother nodded. "I appreciate that. Now tell me what you've been up to, other than this exhibit you're working so hard on."

Max grinned, "Yes, tell your mother."

She flashed him a warning look before turning to her mother. "Just getting ready for the exhibit. It should open around Christmas."

"If she doesn't get cold feet and postpone it again," Max said and got another death-defying glare.

"Well," her mother said. "Whatever you've been doing, it becomes you. The last time I saw you, you were skinny as a rail. You've gained weight, and there is a glow about you now. I'm so glad to see that."

Max grinned. "I've been taking good care of her."

"I can see that and I thank you," Sarah said. "Now, you be sure and let me know the date of your exhibit. I want to be there. That is, if it is all right with you. If you think it would be awkward for you with your father and I both there…"

Max saw Kat's expression. She knew what a zoo it would become if both her father and mother showed up. Max wondered if there would be a catfight between Buckmaster Hamilton's wives. That would be worth selling tickets to.

"I would love it if you could attend," Kat said, her voice breaking, surprising them both. Kat tried so hard not to show that soft underside. "I'll let you know the date. I'm sorry, but we really should go."

"I'm just so glad the two of you drove up to see me," Sarah said, walking them to Kat's SUV. "Thank you," she said to her daughter, reaching out to grasp her hand for a moment before she turned to Max. "It was nice to meet you. I do hope I see you again."

"It was nice to meet you, as well," he said. "Kat and I will be back. I promise. Oh, would you mind taking a picture of Kat and me? We're both photographers, and yet we have few photos of ourselves. I'll grab my camera out of the back." Max reached in the vehicle and brought out his camera.

"Kat, I hope you understand about me marrying Russell. Your father has moved on. I need to do that, too, and I couldn't have picked a kinder man than Russell."

"I'm happy if you are," she said and stepped to her mother to give her a quick hug.

"Stay just like that," Max ordered as he lifted the camera. *Snap. Snap. Snap.* "I got a great shot of you both. There is definitely a resemblance," he said checking the digital photos he'd taken. "Now, one of Kat and me, if you don't mind."

He handed the camera to her mother and then pulled Kat to him. He could see that she was trying hard not to hit him. "Smile," he said and looked toward the camera, thinking about Red and the Prophecy and the photo that one of them had taken that day.

"Say cheese," he said and squeezed her tighter against him as he grinned at the camera and heard the familiar snap.

"How could you make a promise like that?" Kat demanded the moment she and Max were in her SUV and headed down off the mountain.

"No matter who that woman used to be, and maybe still is, she loves you." He shot her a look, but she seemed to be concentrating only on her driving and the mad she had going. "She was so touched that you came to see her."

Kat shook her head, and when she spoke, her voice broke. "I know, which makes our deception back there all the more despicable. You wanted her to think we were lovers."

"Don't you think it's just a matter of time anyway?" he joked, since it was definitely against his golden rule. But around Kat sometimes, he thought it was a stupid rule.

She shot him a venomous look. "She didn't recognize any of the people in the photo." She seemed to be waiting for him to tell her he thought her mother had lied. *"Well?"*

"You're right. She didn't recognize any of them—even herself."

"What?" She hit the brakes for a hairpin turn on the narrow dirt road.

"She either doesn't remember or..."

"Or what?"

"Or she's a better liar than I am a lie detector. If so, then she's the first who's fooled me."

"Maybe you're wrong about all of it," Kat said, sounding hopeful.

"You and I both know better than that. She's Red. Now it is just a matter of proving it."

Kat groaned. "You are such a...manipulator."

He'd been called worse. "Because I got a photo of the two of you?"

"So help me, if you use that in an article—"

"I wouldn't do that."

"How do I know that?" she demanded. "How do I know that you aren't manipulating me right now, like you do everyone else, to get what you want?"

"Because if that was true, you and I would already be lovers."

KAT TOOK A curve a little too fast. She had made the mistake of glancing over at him. The look he gave her made her catch her breath. Heat radiated through her on a race to her core. It brought aches in places she couldn't remember ever aching before.

She quickly turned back to her driving, cussing her reaction to him as she warned herself not to fall for any of this. Max knew how to work people. He'd been working her since the moment they met.

When she dared look at him again, she saw that he

was back to being an investigative journalist. Which only made her angrier, since she was still in a bad mood. How could she let this man get to her like this?

"I'll take the photo of you and your mother with me to the prison," he said, clearly having moved on to his real desire—getting his story.

"I'm going with you." She was as surprised as he was.

"But I thought—"

"I've changed my mind."

"Good. You'll definitely be an asset. Nothing like Senator Buckmaster Hamilton's daughter to get us in. Mason Green is in a part of the prison that could make it dicey."

"Glad I could be of help," she said, her words dripping with sarcasm, but he didn't seem to notice.

"What changed your mind?" he asked after a moment.

Out of the corner of her eye, she could see him frowning over at her, as if perplexed by this change in her.

"No big secret," she said. "Maybe I want to be there when you talk to these men. I want to judge for myself if they recognize my mother."

"You don't trust me?"

"Not as far as I can throw you."

He grinned at her. "I'd like to see that move. Anytime you'd like to try."

"Stop flirting with me. I already said I would go with you." She shook her head and kept driving. What had she gotten herself into? She'd never been to a prison, had no desire to meet any killers behind bars there and... She shuddered as she had a thought. The two who'd been arrested? Was one of them Red's lover? This was crazy.

"Stop sitting over there thinking of ways to get out of this," Max said, clearly reading her. "You're Kat Hamilton. This might turn out to be the adventure you've been waiting for all your life."

She'd reached his pickup where they'd left it outside the fence at Hamilton Ranch and parked a ways from it. "I have not been waiting for—"

"Me to come along?" He grinned. "You really need to work on becoming a better liar."

"I'll get right on that."

"You're too honest. You'll never make a good liar."

She shook her head. "You think you know me so well."

His look turned serious again, and she realized that it was more dangerous than his grin. "I know you, Kat Hamilton. I'd like to say I know you inside and out. Maybe someday soon."

His gaze was so probing, so invasive, so personal that it made her squirm. She reached across him and opened his door. "In your dreams, Malone."

He laughed. "Yep, you've *definitely* been there." He tipped his straw cowboy hat and slid his long lanky frame out of her SUV, only to lean back in. "Sometime I'll have to tell you how those dreams ended."

Before she could react, he cupped the back of her neck, drew her to him and kissed her. "I'll call you," he said with a wink, closed the door and sauntered toward his pickup.

SARAH WAS STILL upset after her daughter and friend's visit. Kat hadn't taken her upcoming nuptials well at all. She'd hoped that her daughters would understand. Maybe the others would, she reminded herself. Kat had always been her most difficult child.

As she let her thoughts drift to the photograph her daughter and the reporter had shown her, Sarah frowned. What had that been about? Whatever it was, it had made her...uncomfortable. She'd looked into each of the faces and felt...something, but nothing she could put her finger on.

They'd all been holding weapons. Hadn't she had a sense that she'd held just such a large weapon? Not just held one, but fired one.

She thought again of the faces and felt her stomach knot. She remembered standing like that for a snapshot, only in this flash of memory she was trying hard not to laugh. She shook her head. All these flashes of what she assumed were memories gave her a headache. None of them made any sense.

But there had been a reason Kat had wanted her to see the photo, wanted her to look into those faces. Wanted her to react. Other than feeling slightly uncomfortable looking at those people, she'd felt...nothing. Did they think she knew those people? Did she?

Her cell phone rang, drawing her back from her dark thoughts. Checking the screen, she saw that it was Russell and answered.

"How are you?" he asked.

She considered telling him about Kat and Max Malone's visit. But something held her back. "I'm fine. What are you up to?"

There was a smile in his voice. "Where should we go to pick out your engagement ring tomorrow?" he asked. "I want you to have exactly what you want."

What did she want? Only the normal life that Russell was promising her, she told herself. "You say where. Can we have dinner after in town? I'm ready to get back into the world." *No matter who I knew or what I was in the past.*

ANGELINA COULDN'T BELIEVE how hard it was to hire a private investigator. The first one had quit, the second one had died, although she was sure it had nothing to do with her, and now she had to drive all the way to Butte in the hopes that the one she'd talked to on the phone would take her money. Well, Buckmaster's money, but she'd definitely earned her share of it.

Addison "Ace" Crenshaw's office was in an abandoned-looking part of town on the side of a mountain that, according to Crenshaw, was known as the Richest Hill on Earth. She found that hard to believe as she got out, stepped over a homeless man on the sidewalk and dodged a whirlwind of flying debris.

Once inside the weathered door, she was forced to climb two flights of stairs. This had been a mistake, she told herself with each step. But she'd driven almost two hours to get here. She'd hoped she and "Ace" could do their business over the phone, but he'd insisted in his deep smoker's voice on a face-to-face meeting.

"I like to know who I'm doing business with," the man had said.

"I'm Senator Buckmaster Hamilton's wife. What more do you need to know?"

He'd chuckled. "You sound uppity enough to be his wife, but I'd like to take a gander at you just the same."

She'd almost hung up right then. But she'd run out of options. Most of the investigators had been happy to talk to her, until she'd mentioned what she wanted. Then they'd passed, saying they wouldn't be interested.

At the top of the second flight of stairs, Angelina stopped to catch her breath. The stairs had been steep and smelled of decay. Looking around, she saw a door marked Crenshaw Investigations. Bracing herself, she stepped to it and tried the doorknob. Locked.

He'd told her to be here at four. It was two minutes after. Irritation set her blood to a slow simmer as she knocked hard on the door.

A moment later, she heard heavy footfalls from inside the room. The knob rattled and the door swung in. Standing before her was a woman.

"I'm looking for Addison Crenshaw," Angelina said, thinking the man probably thought he could push her off on to his receptionist.

"Just call me Ace," the woman said in that deep, gruff voice Angelina recalled from their phone conversation.

Still she said, "*You're* Addison?"

"In the flesh." Though her voice was deep and brisk, to say the least, she was a surprisingly attractive woman. The statuesque blonde was dressed in jeans, boots and a sweater that accented every curve. Her hair was pulled back in a ponytail. Angelina guessed her to be in her early forties.

"I'm not sure—"

"That a woman can handle what you need?" Ace asked, sounding amused. "Something tells me that you've knocked on a lot of doors. But if you think I can't handle it…"

"No, I mean, yes, I want to hire you."

Ace chuckled and waved her in. The office couldn't

have been more utilitarian. There wasn't even a living plant. Angelina pulled up a straight-back chair and sat, her purse on her lap. The woman made her a little nervous. She could see that whatever room Ace was in, she filled the entire space with her presence.

"I'm guessing whatever you need, it's…sensitive," Ace said, leaning back in her leather office chair.

"How long have you been—"

"My father was the original Addison Crenshaw. I used to help him with cases from the time I was little. He's the 'Ace.' I like a challenge and I usually come through. When he passed…I stepped into his shoes."

Angelina nodded, thinking that few men had ever made her feel intimidated, let alone a woman.

"So spit it out," the PI said. "It has something to do with your husband."

"His first wife."

Ace nodded. "You want her killed."

Angelina blinked. "No, I, that is…"

The PI laughed. "What *do* you want done with her?"

"I want to find out what she's hiding. Her name is—"

"Sarah Johnson Hamilton. I read the papers. She really can't remember the past twenty-two years?"

"So she says. But I think there is more to it, and whatever she's hiding goes way back. Her past is too… perfect. She is too…perfect."

Ace nodded. "So you're jealous as hell, and you're hoping there is something to dig up."

"There *is* something. Otherwise the other PIs—"

"You've had other investigators on this."

It wasn't a question. "Yes. One quit. He said it was too dangerous. The second one…was killed." Angelina stopped, realizing that she was going to scare this one off, as well. "I can understand if you don't—"

Addison cut her off with a smile. "Here I was thinking that finding any secrets on this woman was just wishful thinking on your part. But it sounds to me like you just might be onto something. I'll take the job, but I don't come cheap."

"Money is no object," Angelina said and opened her purse.

News of Senator Buckmaster Hamilton's first wife's engagement to rancher Russell Murdock had whirled around the county like the winds out of the Crazies.

It died down just as quickly. Russell had said marrying him would free her from media attention. Sarah was a little surprised, though, at how quickly the reporters lost interest in her.

Russell had talked her into a short press conference to make the announcement official. He'd had it at his ranch out front of his house in the morning before they headed out to get a large diamond engagement ring. Several dozen reporters had shown up.

"I just want to confirm that Sarah and I are getting married." He'd taken her hand, squeezing it before continuing, as cameras snapped dozens of shots of the two of them. "We'd appreciate all of you letting us enjoy the rest of our lives in peace. Thank you."

As they turned to retreat back into the house, though, reporters called out questions. "What about your memory, Sarah? Has it come back?"

"What does the senator think about this?"

"Does this have anything to do with your former husband's run for president?"

"What do your daughters think about your engagement?"

But that had been it. The reporters had all left. Sarah saw her photo plastered across the supermarket rags for a couple of weeks with headlines like Senator's Ex to Wed Rancher Who Saved Her, Lovers' Triangle Broken by Handsome Rancher, No White House For Long-Lost Mom. And then there was nothing.

"I told you that marrying me would make you no longer newsworthy," Russell had joked as they drove to Bozeman. They hadn't seen one reporter, and she doubted they would.

Sarah felt a strange pang. Angelina Hamilton's face was always on the television. People were already referring to her as the First Lady, even though Buck hadn't yet been nominated for the Republican candidacy.

Not that she wanted to be in the public eye like that. But a part of her felt...ripped off, as if Angelina had stolen what should have been hers.

She reminded herself that she was the one who'd tried to kill herself in the Yellowstone River. Had she been leaving Buck or really just depressed and wanting to end it all? With twenty-two years missing, she'd likely never know. Now she'd come back to grown children who didn't even know her and to a husband who had a new wife.

"Are you all right?" Russell asked as he parked in front of the jewelry store.

"I'm...great," she said and flashed him a smile. She'd told him that Kat and a friend had come up to the cabin for a visit. She hadn't told him about the photo they'd asked her to look at or that Max Malone was a reporter.

Not that it mattered anymore whether he did a story on her or not. The only news was her engagement. Her memory hadn't returned. Buck hadn't left Angelina for her.

"You aren't going to be sorry that you married me," Russell assured her as he hurried around to open her door.

"You're a wonderful man. No woman would regret marrying you," she said honestly. So why did she still feel as if the marriage would never happen?

"Let's get that ring. I want you to have something beautiful."

As she got out of Russell's pickup, she looked down at her left hand. With a start, she recalled that she hadn't been wearing any jewelry when she'd come wandering out of the woods and into the road in front of Russell's truck.

So where was the diamond engagement ring and wedding band that Buck had put on her finger? Long ago pawned for cash? Or lost? Or stolen? She had no idea. But wherever it was, it hadn't been on her finger in years. Maybe she'd taken it off that night before she'd gone into the river. Buck hadn't mentioned having it at the house. Maybe she'd thrown it in the river. Or maybe she'd given it to whoever had picked her up in the wee hours of the morning after she'd gone in the river.

"Sarah?"

She looked up, realizing that she'd been standing staring at her left hand all this time. After taking a shaky breath, she let it out. "I was just thinking about what kind of ring I would like."

His look said he didn't believe that was what she'd been pondering, but he didn't call her on it. "If I know you, you want something tasteful but not flashy."

Tasteful but not flashy. Was that her? "You *do* know me," she said as she joined him on the sidewalk. He pushed open the jewelry store door, and they stepped in to the sound of soft music.

CHAPTER FOURTEEN

KAT COULDN'T BELIEVE she was headed for New York and the maximum security facility where Mason Green, former member of the Prophecy, had been locked up for almost forty years.

Max had been quiet on the plane. Like her, he seemed to be lost in his own thoughts as he drove the rental car toward the prison.

"This just seems like a waste of time," she said as she fidgeted with the clasp on her purse. "He isn't going to tell us anything we don't already know."

"He agreed to see us. If he didn't want to talk, he wouldn't have agreed to see us," Max said without looking at her. "I had to pull a lot of strings to get this interview."

She looked at her watch. "What time did you say visiting hours were?"

"Kat," he said and took his hand off the wheel long enough to take her hand for a moment. "There's no reason to be so nervous."

No reason? She was about to meet a dangerous killer, possibly from her mother's past. If true, then what did that make her mother?

Max, on the other hand, looked cool and calm. She couldn't believe that she'd let him come into her life and turn it upside down. What was it about this man that she'd let him in?

"Mason Green isn't the one who was my mother's lover, right?"

He glanced over at her. "He's not the man believed to be the coleader of the group, if that's what you're asking."

She closed her eyes for a moment as she realized he, too, wondered about Red's relationship with the seven men in the Prophecy.

"Red was involved in five killings, and you're worried about her morals?" Max asked, humor in his voice.

"I was thinking more of the families they destroyed, and for what end?"

He shook his head as he turned in to the prison gate. A guard stepped to the driver's side of the car and asked for their identification. Max handed over their drivers' licenses and, after a few moments, the guard handed them back and instructed them where to park.

"Do you want to wait here?" Max asked as he cut the engine to the rental car. "You can, if this is too much for you."

She shook her head. "I'm fine."

"Then, let's do this."

Max took her hand on the walk to the entrance and the processing area, squeezing it as if he thought he could press his warmth into her icy fingers. Once inside, another guard took her purse and waved them through a metal detector. Sounds seemed to echo through the building, making her aware of her own footfalls, her own pounding heart.

With relief, the metal detector didn't go off. Max

had warned her not to wear any metal, including an underwire bra, jewelry, or even metal buttons or studs.

"If your bra makes the metal detector go off, you have to remove it and be searched by a guard. If they can't figure out what it was that made the alarm go off," Max had warned her, "then you're looking at a strip search."

"If you are trying to scare me…"

He'd laughed. "I just want to make this as painless for you as I can."

As she stepped through, another guard used a hand-held device to take surface samples from her hands, clothing and purse. Max was put through the same process.

Max had also jokingly warned her about what not to wear. "No see-through clothing, bare midriffs, no plunging neckline, short shorts or miniskirts. Oh, and try to wear appropriate undergarments."

"Very funny," she said, since this was so far from how she dressed. "This sounds worse than the airport."

Max had made arrangements so that they wouldn't be visiting in the main area. As they passed what looked like a large cafeteria with a line of vending machines against one side, Kat saw that some of the hunter green–clad prisoners already had visitors.

The windowless room where they were led was small. It had a wide table at the center with plastic chairs on each side and room for nothing more.

"I thought we'd be talking to him on phones and separated with a glass," she said, her voice breaking.

Max looked excited, while her heart was threatening to pound out of her chest.

"You asked for another room," the guard said.

Kat shot a look at Max. *Another room?*

The guard pointed to the door she hadn't noticed behind them. "Do you want me to open it for you now?"

"If you wouldn't mind," Max said and turned to Kat. Lowering his voice, he said, "Give me five minutes with Green alone. I don't want him to see you until it's time."

"And you're just mentioning this now?" she whispered back.

"Miss?" the guard said as he opened a door at the back of the small room. She could see another room much like this one, maybe smaller. She looked beseechingly at Max.

"It's for the best. Trust me," he said.

She looked into his blue eyes and felt a shock. She *did* trust him. It made no sense intellectually, but she did. With a slight nod, she let the guard lead her to the adjoining room.

"The door will be open when you want to enter the other visiting room," he said. "But the outer door is locked."

Kat nodded mutely as she was left alone in the small room where she couldn't help feeling the onset of claustrophobia. She listened for a moment, wondering what was happening in the adjacent room. Pulling out her cell phone, she set her alarm for five minutes. Then she moved to one of the plastic chairs, pulled it out and sat down. Her legs were shaking.

ADDISON "ACE" CRENSHAW, PI, had told Angelina that she would contact her when she had something.

"In the meantime, don't bother me," the gruff Ace

had said. "You'll hear from me. But I suspect this could take some time—and money."

Angelina could well imagine what Buckmaster would say if he knew that she'd hired another private investigator, this one more costly than the other two.

But she had to know the truth. *Buckmaster* had to know the truth, whether he wanted to hear it or not. He'd been moping around since Sarah had announced her engagement to Russell Murdock. He seemed to really believe that Sarah was going through with the marriage.

"I wouldn't worry about buying a wedding present just yet," she'd told her husband. "That wedding is never going to happen."

"Why would you say that?" the senator had asked.

She'd heard a little too much hope in his voice. "Because Sarah will never go through with it. She is just trying to get you to dump me and go back to her."

He'd groaned as if pained by what he called her unflattering jealousy. "Sarah doesn't sit around plotting, no matter what you think. She wants to move on with her life. It's the best thing for all of us."

Angelina had had to bite her tongue. She hated it when he defended Sarah. If she heard one more time, "You're talking about the mother of my children," she thought she would scream.

Just because she'd borne him six children didn't mean the woman wasn't the devil incarnate. Men could be such fools. Was she the only one who saw through this transparent attempt by Sarah to get Buckmaster to do something before the big wedding day? *Apparently*, Angelina thought. But how far would the woman go to get Buckmaster back? Did Sarah, who pretended to hate being in the limelight, want to be the wife of the next president that badly? Or did she have some other motive?

Angelina checked her cell phone. Why didn't Addison Crenshaw call?

MASON GREEN HAD appeared to be a good-looking jock in the Prophecy snapshot the group had taken of them thirty-some years ago. He'd been a small-town hero football player in high school and had gone to college on an athletic scholarship. But after a year, he'd flunked out and had gotten odd jobs until his arrest several years later.

The man the guard led into the prison visiting room was pushing sixty. He was still big, but his thick head of curly dark hair was gone. His head was shaved and glowed under the overhead light. While he'd clearly bulked up in the weight room, he had an unhealthy pallor, making Max wonder how many more years—if not months—he might have left.

Green was wearing handcuffs on his wrists that were connected to the thick leather belt at his waist. He jangled them as the guard led him over to a chair on the opposite side of the counter.

"You have thirty minutes," the guard said. "If there is a problem, just push that button." He pointed to a red button on the wall next to Max. There was one exactly like it on the other side of the wide table.

Green glared across at him. "So you want to do a story on the Prophecy?" He looked both smug and suspicious. "About time."

Max pulled out his notebook. "The truth is I haven't found anyone who's even heard of your group."

Anger sparked in the big man's dull brown eyes. "We started the revolution, man."

"What revolution is that?" Max asked. "I have to admit, I'm not sure I understand what the Prophecy's mission was."

Green sat back as if Max had slapped him. "To make people aware that their own government is plotting to take away their rights, man. The government is run by secret globalists aimed at taking away American freedom."

Max shook his head. "That just sounds like the same old rhetoric to me. You sound like those people who keep everyone worked up with the alleged threat that the government is poised to take away our guns so the gun and ammunition companies can make a small fortune off their fear."

"You wait until they come knocking at your door, like they did in Germany, and take your gun." Green was sweating now, spittle at the corner of his mouth. "It isn't just a few radical groups anymore. Are you aware that the number of antigovernment groups have reached an all-time high? Hate groups have also grown to unbelievable numbers. What do you think that means?"

"Look, I've heard all this before. Unless there is something new..." Max started to rise. He knew that after being locked up all these years, a man like Green would want to convince him—and himself—that the cause was worth merit. Otherwise, he'd thrown his life away, and for what?

"The rage is building, man. You better listen to what you call the same old rhetoric. It's a barometer of the explosion that is building in this country. You think it's over? It's just begun, man, and when it blows..."

He smiled for the first time, showing yellowed teeth. "It is going to make a very loud bang."

"So you're saying you have something planned?"

"We started it. Now we're going to finish it."

"Who are *we*?"

Green just gave him a knowing smile. "The Prophecy."

"Are you sure the rest of the members aren't living normal lives, having completely forgotten about you? I can't see how you're going to be doing anything from a prison cell."

Green smiled. "We're not all locked up. We've just been biding our time."

The door opened behind Max. He heard Kat step in, but he didn't turn. His eyes were on Mason Green, who looked as if he'd swallowed his tongue. His gaze went from Kat to Max and back again. He looked pole-axed, mouth opening and closing as he sucked air like a fish thrown up on the bank.

"What's going on?" Mason demanded when he found his voice.

"I see that you recognize Sarah Johnson's daughter."

The man's eyes looked as if they might pop out of his head.

"You were saying that there are more members of the Prophecy who aren't locked up?" Max asked. "Are you that sure they still give a damn about your old agenda? Maybe they are busy living their lives, just like they have been for the past thirty years, and have completely forgotten about you. Did you know that Sarah is getting married—and not to her former husband. She said she wants to get on with her life."

"Screw you, man." Green stumbled to his feet, all

his bravado gone. "You don't know what you're talking about. You wait. You'll see."

"When that big boom happens?"

"It's going to rock the world and bring all you smart-asses to your knees." Mason hit the button on the wall, and the guard appeared almost instantly.

"I'm ready to go back to my room," the prisoner said.

KAT WAS STILL shaking as they walked out of the prison. The aging man she'd seen across the table from Max had looked nothing like the young idealist who'd been in the Prophecy photo. But when he'd looked up and seen her…

"I feel so…dirty. That man…" She heard the tears in her voice and fought to hold them back. "He…he thought I was *her.* I saw the way he looked at me. The way he…"

Max stopped and turned. He quickly stepped to her and took her in his arms, holding her close. She pressed her face against his broad chest and tried to breathe and not cry. Her mother was Red. There was no doubt.

"Let it out," Max said quietly. "Just let it go."

"I don't…cry." The sobs rose from her aching chest, rattling out of her with each shuddered breath. He held her more tightly as the implications of what they had learned hit her like a fist to the gut. She sobbed her heart out in his strong arms until there was nothing left inside her but a deep sadness and a feeling of impending disaster.

Max handed her a tissue from his pocket. He'd known she would break down. He'd been expecting it. She was touched by the gesture and at the same time angered by it.

"What did that accomplish back there?" she demanded as she wiped away the tears and pulled herself together.

"You wanted proof that your mother is Red. Do you have any doubt now?"

"So, that back there was all for me?"

"No, we know now that they're planning something. Something big, according to Mason."

She stared at him. "That big bang you asked him about?"

Max nodded.

"We have to go to the sheriff, FBI, Homeland Security," she said as they walked the rest of the way to the rental car.

It wasn't until they were inside and Max had started the engine that he looked over at her. "We can't do that."

"We *have* to."

"We have no proof. Not even that your mother is Red, let alone that something as vague as 'something big' is going to happen."

She watched him back out of the lot. "You said that man just admitted that they are planning to do something…terrible."

"The man is a *criminal*. Do you really think he would tell the authorities the truth? Or that they would believe him? He isn't going to give up your mother, but I suspected that would be the case from the get-go." Max raked a hand through his thick blond hair. He'd mentioned that he needed a haircut, but he hadn't gotten one. Nor had he shaved in a few days either. Surprisingly, both looked good on him.

Who was she kidding? The man was drop-dead sexy, and he knew it.

"There has to be something we can do," she said when he looked over at her and seemed to realize she was no longer listening.

"Kat, your mom doesn't remember. Unless the FBI had Red's fingerprints or DNA at the scene of one of the bombings or bank robberies, there would be no way to prove she was involved."

"Wait, if she doesn't remember, then she won't do anything." When he said nothing, she prodded, *"What?"*

"We don't know why your mother can't seem to remember certain things," he said carefully. "But I get the feeling she might have been…programmed."

"Programmed? Like some robot that is sitting quietly right now, but push the right button and…"

"Yeah, like that." He held up a hand. "I know it sounds crazy. Another reason you would be wasting your time trying to get anyone to believe any of this."

"But you believe that she's going to do something. If she's antigovernment, though, wouldn't she and the others be glad if my father is elected? He would fight for less government."

Max shook his head. "These people aren't antigovernment. They want to destroy all government. They're anarchists who want disorder. But the good news is that I believe they'll wait until the primary or, if your father wins that, then the election."

Kat stared at him. "We can't wait that long. She has to be stopped now. You said yourself that my father could be in danger."

"It would help if we knew what she had planned—if

she has *anything* planned. Like I said, Mason Green is a hard-core criminal. He could be pulling our chain."

"I can tell that you don't believe that."

"Not to mention," he continued as if he hadn't heard her, "your mother is about to marry Russell Murdock. Mason Green can't have seen your mother for years. Who knows if they have even had any recent contact? Maybe she's not that woman anymore. Maybe there is, nothing to fear."

She gave him an impatient look. "If you're just saying all of this for my benefit—"

"I'm not. Maybe you shouldn't listen to me. What do I know?"

She tried to find some solace in that but realized she trusted Max's instincts. He hadn't gotten where he was by being wrong about things. She kept thinking about Mason Green's panicked look when he saw her.

Max said nothing as he drove away from the prison.

"I have to at least warn my father."

"He won't believe you."

She remembered what her father had told her sister Olivia. He'd said that Sarah was the only woman he'd ever truly loved.

"Kat, I saw the two of them together when I got that lucky shot I took of your mother. There was definitely chemistry between them. I could see the tension in the way they reacted to each other. Your father is still in love with her."

"Then I'm glad he's married to the Ice Queen," she said.

Max chuckled. "You call your stepmother the Ice Queen?"

"I better never see that in print," she warned. Looking up, she asked, "Where are we going?"

"To the other prison where Wallace McGill is serving time, but we can't get in until tomorrow, so I booked us a motel near the prison."

"If it is anything like an airport motel, I can hardly wait. But why do we have to see another one of these men? Didn't you accomplish what you set out to do without having to face another one of them?"

Max shot her a regretful look. "Sorry, but if I'm right, Green will contact McGill. If we hope to find out if there is anything to Green's threat... You look like a woman who could use a stiff drink."

"I don't drink alcohol."

CHAPTER FIFTEEN

"ARE YOU TRYING to get me drunk?"

Max grinned across the narrow table in the dark back corner of the bar. "Is it working?"

"I don't ever cry, let alone fall apart like I did earlier." She waved a hand through the air, still embarrassed that she'd broken down in the prison parking lot. "I've always been the strong, determined, stubborn one in the family."

"Sounds like a boring, tedious and tiring job. Have you ever thought about saying to hell with it and letting down your hair? You might be surprised what happens."

He'd ordered for her. She hadn't minded, feeling surprisingly safe with Max. The alcohol had lightened her up. She was actually having fun. It didn't hurt that she was with a charming, handsome, incredibly sexy man. Or that she was starting to like him. A lot.

That alone should have scared her. She hadn't let her guard down around a man in so long…

"There is a wild, adventurous, free-spirited woman in you who is fighting to get out," Max said.

She laughed. "Does that line actually work on women?"

"I've never said that to any woman before." He made an X over his heart with his index finger.

Kat studied him for a moment, amazed that she'd let him talk her into any of this. Even more amazed that she could laugh after everything she'd been through since making Max Malone's acquaintance.

"Are you trying to seduce me?"

He shook his head slowly, his gaze never leaving hers. "I have a rule. I never get involved with anyone connected to a story I'm working on."

"*Really?* But you want to see me let my hair down anyway?"

His smile was almost sad. "I got a glimpse of that woman a few nights ago in the Pacific. I was enchanted, so, yes, I'd love to see her again."

She felt a flush move up her neck at his words, at the memory of the kiss, the feel of his hands on her wet, warm skin. She quickly changed the subject.

"You know this would be funny, if it wasn't so horrible. I keep seeing the headline in one of the tabloids. My Mother Was a Terrorist—Senator's Daughter Tells All."

"Not a bad headline," Max said.

She took another sip of her drink as she perused him over the rim of the glass, before she said, "I sometimes forget that you're a reporter. That all this is just a story for you."

He grew serious as he looked over at her. "It's become more than that, Kat, and I think we both know it."

"Why am I helping you?" She asked the question she'd been asking herself since the beginning.

"You're helping yourself. You've wanted to know the truth long before I came along. Or am I wrong about that?"

She shook her head. "But wouldn't a loving, car-ing, compassionate daughter try to protect her mother? Her family?"

He smiled. "That is exactly what you *are* trying to do, because you know your mother is the woman formerly known as Red."

Kat felt tears burn her eyes the way the alcohol burned like a warm fire in her stomach. "You see me, don't you?"

"I do. I don't know what happened yet that made you close yourself off from not just the world but from every pleasure, every indulgence, everything you love," he said. "But I'm glad to see you coming back."

She felt the alcohol in her system warming her clear to her toes. She also felt her inhibitions take a hike out the back door as she looked at this man. He *did* see her. She hadn't even been aware of how she'd denied herself.

"This rule of yours?" she asked. "How many times have you wanted to break it?"

"A few times I was tempted."

"And how many times have you broken it?"

When he spoke, his voice sounded rough with emotion. "Never."

ANGELINA GOT THE CALL in Washington, DC. When she saw that it was Ace phoning, she quickly excused herself from the fund-raiser dinner and hurried to the powder room to take the call.

"Tell me you've found something," she said the moment she was alone.

"Where are you?"

The question caught her off guard. "At a fund-raising dinner in DC."

"How soon can you come back to Montana?" Ace asked.

Her pulse jumped. "Tell me what you found out."

"Not over the phone. It would take too long."

"Then just tell me I was right."

That deep gruff chuckle. "You were right. Call me when you get here. Are you flying in to Butte?"

"No, Bozeman. I'll drive from there."

"Watch your back."

"Sarah doesn't scare me," she said and realized it was a lie. The one time she'd confronted the woman, she'd felt on some primitive level that Sarah Johnson Hamilton was dangerous. Behind that shy, sweet, confused and helpless-seeming woman was a monster. Only before now, Angelina had had no way to prove it.

"I can handle Sarah," she said with more confidence than she felt.

"It isn't only Sarah you have to fear," Ace said and hung up.

Angelina stared at the phone for a long moment, her heart pounding. Surely the PI hadn't meant that she should be afraid of Buckmaster.

She shoved that thought away, refusing to worry about it. *Ace had the goods on Sarah.* She felt a weight lift off her shoulders. Her heart seemed to swell. She had to fight tears. She'd known there was something. She'd known, and Buckmaster hadn't believed her.

She wanted to dance around the restroom. She wanted to cheer. She could imagine herself walking back to the dinner and announcing to the world that the senator's first wife was a liar, a fraud and as far from an angel as a manipulating bitch could be.

Instead, she called the airport, got the next flight

out, fixed her makeup, put on her soon-to-be-First-
Lady smile and returned to the table to finish her meal.

"WE'D BETTER GET to the motel before they give away
our rooms," Max said and finished his drink. This had
been a bad idea.

Even though Kat said she didn't drink, he'd thought
one might relax her. She'd had a rough few days. He
couldn't imagine what she'd been going through. He
hadn't known his mother but he wouldn't have wanted
her to be a terrorist who'd been responsible in part for
the deaths of five people. Five people, so far, he reminded himself.

He hadn't forced alcohol on her, though. "I'll buy
you a Shirley Temple," he'd said to the teetotaler as
they'd entered the dim, small bar.

"I'll have what you're having."

He'd grinned at her. "You're on."

After the first one, she'd begun to relax.

"You aren't in AA or anything, are you?" he'd asked.

She'd laughed. "No, I don't drink because—"

"You like being in control."

Kat had stopped laughing. "Is it that obvious?"

"Maybe someday you'll tell me about the man," he
said now.

"What man?" she asked, sounding leery.

"The one who hurt you so badly that you dress the
way you do, don't eat or drink things you like, and
have that sign on your forehead that says Approach at
Your Own Risk."

She reached for her drink, took a long pull and set
the glass back down. "Maybe I *will* tell you someday."

"You all right?" he asked as she got to her feet.

She nodded. "Little girls' room. You are actually… fun, you know that?"

He chuckled. "Thanks. So are you."

"When I let my hair down, right?" She grabbed the clip holding her hair up, pulled and shook out the long, dark, curly locks. "Better?"

"Much. If we didn't have to be at the prison so early in the morning, I would take you dancing."

"I don't dance."

WHEN KAT RETURNED from the restroom, Max drove them to the motel. It was as bad as any he'd ever stayed in, and he'd stayed in some doozies. Kat, bless her, had tried to hide how appalled she was, and offered to stay in the car while he went in and got the keys.

"There's some kind of convention in town and with the prison so far away from everything," he said, "this was all I could get."

"I'm sure it will be fine." She sat back, smiled and closed her eyes.

He knew that had to be the booze talking. Wait until she woke up in the morning. Worse, when she found out that he could get only one room. He'd been told, though, that the couch folded out into a bed.

Still, as he went inside the motel office, he knew he was playing with a wildfire. It hadn't been the booze talking when he'd told her that he'd been enchanted with her in the Pacific. True, the alcohol had loosened his tongue, but enchanted was exactly what he was still.

He had gotten a tempting glimpse of the real Kat Hamilton, the one she kept locked up under the baggy clothes and the "Keep Your Distance" expression. He couldn't help thinking about what she would be like unleashed.

Pushing that thought away, he paid for the motel, took the key and walked back to the rental car. The night sky couldn't compare to Montana's, but still there was a sprinkling of stars and a sliver of silver moon. Nor could the cool night air, which smelled of broiled steaks from the steak house down the road, compare.

But he breathed in the night, feeling oddly happier than he had in a long time. And it wasn't the story he was chasing, which was usually the case. He just felt... good. That, too, surprised him.

He was smart enough to know the cause. Kat.

Now, if he could just get through this night without—

As he reached the car, he stopped to smile. Kat was sacked out. Even when he opened the door and carried her to their room, she didn't wake up. He pulled back the covers and laid her down. As he took off her shoes, he found himself laughing to himself.

He'd made it through another day without breaking his rule.

KAT WOKE THE next morning with a start. She sat up but then quickly lay back as her head began to spin. Where was she? She could hear water running. Blinking, she looked around the tacky, older motel room. She'd never stayed in any place this run-down. She'd always preferred her tent over a motel anyway.

Her tent would have definitely been a step up from this dump.

Looking down, she saw that she was wearing only her undergarments. She frowned, trying to recall taking off her clothes, as she sat up again. The last thing she could remember was Max going in to get the keys.

"Good morning!"

Kat jumped, startled as Max came out of the bathroom wearing nothing but a towel around his waist. She was instantly reminded of the Pacific Ocean and the feel of that wonderfully strong, beautiful body.

Her gaze flew up to his face. "What are you doing here?" she demanded, pulling the sheet up to cover herself.

"I could get only one room," he said as he stepped over to his worn leather satchel, no doubt something else with sentimental value, and began pulling out clothes.

Her voice came out unusually high as she asked, "Where did you sleep last night?"

"On the couch. I didn't bother making it into a bed." He turned to look at her. "Your honor is safe. I only carried you in and put you to bed."

"You undressed me."

"I figured you would feel more comfortable that way, but don't worry. I'm a professional," he joked.

She took a breath, not sure if she was glad about that or sorry. But if anything ever happened between them, she wanted to be wide-awake. She didn't want to miss a second of it.

That thought shook her. It had been so long and her last memory of sex… She shoved that away as she had always done. Nothing was ever going to happen with her and Max. He'd already told her he never broke his rule.

"Here," he said as he took a bottle of aspirin from his suitcase and got her a plastic cup of water. "I'll go get us some coffee and cinnamon rolls while you get ready."

She swallowed the aspirin and handed him back the cup. "I don't eat—"

"Cinnamon rolls," he said with a grin and left.

KAT, HE NOTICED, was still licking the sugar off her fingers when they arrived at the prison. "I hate you," she said without much conviction.

Max chuckled. "How are you feeling this morning?"

"Fine."

She seemed stronger today, more ready to face another man who'd known a Sarah Johnson she'd never dreamed existed. That was something else about Kat Hamilton that fascinated him. He found himself wondering more and more about the woman under that protective shell she'd built around herself.

"Well, aren't you going to tell me the plan?" she said, yanking him out of his musings.

"Today should go easier," he said as they got out and walked toward the prison entrance. "McGill will have heard about our visit with his cohort Green. Actually, when I called the warden this morning, I was only a little surprised when McGill had still agreed to see us."

Unlike Green, McGill would be prepared to see a version of Sarah Johnson as she'd been all those years ago.

They went through the same access routine as they had yesterday at the other prison. The only difference was that the room they were led to was a little larger.

Max found himself watching the door. He wanted to make sure he didn't miss McGill's reaction to Kat.

At the sound of footfalls outside, he held his breath.

Could anything prepare McGill for seeing a ghostlike version of Red? Both Green and McGill would be wondering about Kat, wondering if Red was trying to send them a message. Or if Red's cover was truly blown.

The visiting room door had opened. Max had had to get special permission for Kat to accompany him for this visit. But he was damned glad she'd decided to come along. It was one thing to be told that Kat looked like her mother. It was another thing to actually see how much she resembled the woman called Red.

The instant Wallace McGill laid eyes on Red's daughter, he stumbled and would have fallen if the guard hadn't grabbed him.

KAT HAD BEEN trying to remember what Wallace McGill looked like from the old photo. Max had pointed him out in the eight-member antigovernment group before they'd left the motel. He'd been tall and blond with pale blue eyes. What had struck her was how young he'd looked—how innocent.

When the door to the visiting room opened, she'd been so deep in thought that she jumped. Max laid a hand on her knee as a guard helped a thin, gray-haired man into the room. Kat thought there must have been a mistake. This couldn't be the man from the photo. Maybe this was the wrong Wallace McGill.

When the old man stumbled, the guard kept him from falling and helped him into a chair. He was shackled like Green had been, but he didn't look as if he could hurt a spider.

She felt his gaze boring into her, though. But unlike Mason Green, Wallace McGill looked nostalgic, as if he was caught in a time warp. Did he think it was Red herself visiting him?

"So, what is this about?" McGill asked, still looking at Kat. "I was told you were doing a story?"

"On the Prophecy," Max said. "But what is it anyway?"

McGill finally shifted his gaze to Max. "You know or you wouldn't be here." His eyes cut back to Kat.

"We're here about Sarah Johnson," Max said.

"I don't know anyone by that name," he said, his gaze on her.

"But you know Red," Max said. "This is her daughter, not that I need to tell you that. You saw the resemblance the moment you came through the door."

"You knew my mother," Kat said, her voice breaking.

McGill shook his head. "I just told you—"

"Please, we don't have much time," Kat said.

"We were with Red just yesterday," Max interjected. "We know everything."

The man smiled, exposing several missing teeth. "I highly doubt that."

Max held up the photo of Sarah and Kat. The other side of the counter grew very quiet as the elderly man studied it, something sad and regretful in his eyes.

"If you know so much, then why are you here?" Before either of them could answer, he continued. "Why bother me?"

"Did you know that Sarah is remarrying? A nice rancher, and settling down in the Sweet Grass Valley," Max said. "Or maybe Green didn't tell you."

Kat saw the man's reaction. That was something he *hadn't* known.

"She's getting on with her life," Max said. "But why would you care? You don't know the woman."

"Was it worth it?" Kat asked. "Killing innocent people? Doing what you all did back then? Look at the price you have had to pay. Life without any chance of parole."

McGill's expression turned angry. "I'd do it again. I would do anything for Red. And she would do anything for me," the man said, suddenly looking stronger, less like an old man.

"Even though she's had it a lot easier than you have the past thirty-six years?" Max asked.

McGill's jaw tightened. "She is continuing the fight."

"Sure doesn't seem like it," Max said. "She got married to a rich man, had six children with him...so what fight would that be?"

"Red knows what she's doing," McGill said.

"Fooling you," Max said. "What did any of you really accomplish other than blowing up a few buildings and killing innocent people, so you and Green could end up in prison all these years?"

"Someone has to speak up. The government is corrupt. Someone has to bring it down, by whatever means, however long it takes. And the Prophecy will, because that has been the plan all along. I played my part but now I'm happy to sit back and watch."

"This big bang Green was telling us about?"

McGill looked surprised that Green had told them.

"Sounds like nothing more than prison talk to me," Max goaded. "The two of you can't do much locked up here."

"You have no idea what we're capable of."

"The families of the innocent people you killed know, though," Max said.

McGill shook his head. "You don't get it. Sometimes innocent people have to die for a cause. Look how many of our soldiers the government has sent to die in godforsaken countries, and for what? Someone has to say, 'Enough.' That's what the Prophecy is about. A revolution of change. A new future for mankind."

The radical shine of hatred and fanaticism burning in the man's eyes made Kat shudder inside. "You sound like a man who was brainwashed."

McGill smiled at that. "I'm a man who gave his life to help this country. I will not stop until I take my last breath."

"Shouldn't be long, the way you're looking," Max said.

McGill started to reach for the button that would signal the guard to come for him.

"You know what my mother's planning to do?" Kat asked.

The prisoner shifted his gaze to her again as he hit the button. His smile had an edge to it. "It was all set into motion long before you were born. No one believed in our cause more than your mother. She led us, kept the faith, did what needed to be done, sacrificing more than either of you could know for what she believes in. It's up to her now."

"Are you that sure she still believes in this cause of yours?" Max said.

The guard appeared at the door, and McGill got to his feet, but it was Kat he smiled at. "Give your mother my best."

CHAPTER SIXTEEN

KAT HAD TOLD herself she was braced to meet another man her mother had been involved with in the Prophecy. Yesterday, after their visit with Mason Green, the truth about her mother's involvement had hit her hard. Today as they walked out of the prison, she was still shaken, but keeping it together.

"How do you do it?" she asked after taking several gulps of air.

Max looked over at her as they walked toward the rental car. "Do what?"

"Interview people like that." She motioned back past the razor wire and high concrete walls of the prison, and shuddered. "They're...crazy."

He shrugged. "They seem like lunatics. But to them, it all makes sense. So when I do their stories, I try to see it from their side."

Kat shook her head. "You give them a voice. If you didn't write about them, then—"

"Readers need to know. Not telling it from their side doesn't make any of it go away. The radicals are still out there, still making their crazy plans." He unlocked the car. "Let's get something to eat. I'm starved."

"You're always starved." But this time, she thought he'd said it to lighten the mood. Max could act as if none of this affected him, but she could tell that Wal-

lace McGill had gotten to him even more than Mason
Green had.

"I'll even let you pick the type of food you would
like," he said as he opened her door before walking
around to the driver's side of the car to get in.

Kat grabbed the top of the open door and hesitated
to look back at the prison. She couldn't shake the feeling that they were being watched. She felt as if she
needed another shower.

"When do we fly back?" she asked as she climbed
into the car and buckled up.

"This afternoon. We have plenty of time. Name your
poison."

She couldn't think about food right now. "Do you
think it's true that they have something planned and
my mother is at the center of it?"

"I think they want us to believe it's true." He started
the car and drove out of the prison lot and onto the two-
lane road that would take them back to civilization.
They'd traveled through miles of nothing but barren-
looking ground with an occasional line of storage units
or old car junkyards to get to the prison.

"But if it's true..." Kat looked over at Max. He
looked so serious. "If it is, then it will certainly make
a better story for you to write."

"I GUESS IT WILL." Max concentrated on his driving,
wondering when all of this had become so much more
than another story, another job, another investigation.
He'd adopted this golden rule because he knew in his
profession that getting involved in the story was the
worst thing he could do. It ruined his objectivity.

As a journalist, he was the fly on the wall. He was

the guy who looked at all the facts and wove an un-biased story together. He prided himself on being able to see all sides. On being fair and impartial. On not getting involved and becoming part of the tale.

Somehow, that plan had gone off the rails. He wasn't even sure exactly when it had happened. Maybe that evening just before sunset. Kat Hamilton in that electric-blue swimsuit, the smell of salty air, the feel of the silky sea, that feeling of being totally liberated.

He'd gotten to know her just enough that he wanted to know more. He wanted to see that woman he'd kissed in the Pacific again. Sometimes he glimpsed her. Kat was beginning to trust him. Maybe that was what had changed things. He didn't take that trust lightly.

Someone had made her withdraw into herself. A man. Max couldn't be another man who hurt her. He had to either back off completely or—

"Max?"

At the strained sound of her voice, he looked over at Kat. Her gray eyes were wide with alarm, and she was looking past him out his side window.

Turning, he saw a large car with tinted windows had pulled alongside them. He couldn't see more than the silhouette of the passenger, but it was clear that the driver didn't intend to pass.

For a moment, he thought the driver intended to force them off the road. He was about to either hit his brakes or gas to end this, when the passenger-side win-dow whirred down.

Max saw the dark ski mask over the passenger's face only an instant before he saw the gun. He hit his brakes, but not before a bullet was fired into his side of the rental car. The side windows exploded. Kat's

scream was drowned out by the sound of the windshield shattering.

"Are you all right?" Max cried as he pulled the car
over to the edge of the road. Through the spiderweb
of glass, he could see the car speeding away before he
could get the license plate number.

"I'm okay," Kat said, looking pale and shaken but
apparently unharmed except for a few tiny cuts from
when the glass around her had exploded.

"THE COPS THINK it was a drive-by shooting," Max said
when he joined Kat outside the police station. An of-
ficer had taken both of their statements, and then the
rental car had been impounded. "He suggested we stay
out of that neighborhood. Apparently, there's been a
lot of that sort of thing lately in that area."

"Near the prison?" Kat shook her head. "So it had
nothing to do with us visiting two members of the
Prophecy in prison?"

He glanced over at her as they waited for the taxi
he'd called to take them to the rental agency. There
would be tons of paperwork to fill out. They had already missed their flight and wouldn't be able to get
back to Montana until late tonight—if they could make
that flight.

"The police think we were just in the wrong place
at the wrong time," he said.

"You don't really expect me to believe that."

Max raked a hand through his hair. "I'm as skeptical as you are, but think about it. Why kill us? We
don't know anything."

"We know my mother is Red."

"But we can't prove it. "

"If we went to the FBI, they would see how much she resembles Red, they would—"

"Don't you think they chased a lot of women who looked like Red when they were actively hunting these guys back in the '70s? For all we know they even questioned your mother. By then, she was probably blonde again and maybe even attending a few classes at the university."

"I would think they would take more of an interest because she was Senator Buckmaster Hamilton's wife," Kat argued.

"Or maybe they wouldn't touch this with a ten-foot pole for the very same reason. Without—"

"Proof. I know." She sighed. "Max, those two men just as good as confirmed what we feared. They have something planned. Something big. You know it has something to do with my father and this election."

"Like I said, the election is still a year away. I don't believe they'll do anything until he's president. Killing a candidate is not a big bang." Just then their taxi pulled to a stop at the curb. Max opened the back door and Kat slid in. He followed. "So we have time."

"What are we going to do?" she whispered after Max gave the driver the address of their car-rental agency.

"*We* aren't going to do anything. I don't want you involved anymore."

She turned to look at him in surprise. "So you *don't* believe that was just some coincidental drive-by shooting any more than I do."

"I'm not sure what I believe. But I'm not taking any chances with your safety."

"And I have no say in this?"

"Kat, I don't have to tell you that this is more dangerous than I ever imagined. At first it was just another story. A great big story, as it turned out, that I was dying to break. But now…"

BUCKMASTER STARED OUT through the dark night at the city. In between the fund-raisers, the dinners and the strategy meeting for the campaign, he hadn't had a lot of time to think, let alone feel.

But tonight, alone in their DC apartment with Angelina gone back to Montana, he finally let himself ponder what he'd been feeling.

When he thought of Sarah marrying Russell, it threatened to double him over. He'd always been a strong-willed, determined man. But lately he felt as if he was walking a tightrope trying to keep Angelina happy and yet do what he felt was right for Sarah.

Angelina was right. If he left her for Sarah, he might as well bow out of the presidential race. The other side would crucify him in the media. Angelina would come off as the betrayed loyal wife. His political career would be tarnished, if not over.

But right now, standing here alone, staring out at the city, he didn't give a damn about any of that. He couldn't keep lying to himself. Nothing mattered without Sarah. Not the presidency, not any of this. The thought of giving it up and going home to the ranch to be with Sarah sounded wonderful. Was any of this really worth it, if the price was losing Sarah for good?

He had let months go by without making a decision and feared it was too late. Maybe Sarah wouldn't take him back. He wouldn't blame her.

As for Angelina… He had tried to placate her for

months, and all it had done was make her more angry at him. She saw him as weak because he still loved Sarah, because he couldn't turn on her the way Angelina demanded he do. He was tired of feeling guilty and making excuses for his feelings.

It was time he took a stand. This was his life. He'd let other people take it over for too long. He would leave Angelina.

Relief washed over him.

He would leave Angelina.

Taking a deep breath, he let it out. He knew why it had taken him so long to come to this decision. Sarah, for whatever reason, had left him the night she'd tried to kill herself in the Yellowstone River. He thought he could never forgive her for that. He'd been so bitter for so long… He'd filled the hole she'd left in his heart with politics, telling himself he could do good for the state and finally for the country.

But with Sarah back…he couldn't pretend he didn't love her anymore.

There would be fallout, plenty of it. But he had to follow his heart.

He stood for a moment, living with his decision, before he reached for his cell phone. It rang before he could get to it.

Probably Angelina. He frowned, realizing he hadn't really gotten a straight answer from her about why she'd had to return to Montana in such a hurry. If she had ever been a mother to his girls, he might have thought it had something to do with them. More than likely it had something to do with the upcoming election or… Or Sarah.

He frowned as he pulled out the phone, remembering that Angelina had said the police might want to talk to her about the death of the private investigator she'd hired to look into Sarah's past. He hadn't asked where she'd found the PI or where he'd been killed.

Now checking the screen, he saw that the call was from the Silverbow Sheriff's Department. He quickly answered, expecting it would be Angelina and that he'd been right about where and why she'd gone. Surely she wasn't somehow involved in the man's death.

"Senator Hamilton?" a male voice said on the other end of the line. "I'm afraid I have some bad news."

"Now what?" Kat asked, half turning in the seat to look at Max. He'd said that all of this was no longer just a story. She desperately wanted him to say the words. *This...whatever I'm feeling between us, tell me it isn't just me feeling it.* "What's changed, Max?"

His gaze locked with hers. "Do you even have to ask?"

"I guess I do since you never break your golden rule."

He chuckled as he shook his head and then cupped her face in his large palms. "There's always a first time, I guess."

The kiss between them in the Pacific was child's play compared to this one. He pressed his lips to hers and teased them apart with his tongue. She opened to him and caught her breath as she felt him slowly, tenderly explore her mouth. He moved one hand to cup the back of her neck, while the other hand found her breast.

Her nipple hardened instantly under his touch. She closed her eyes as a groan escaped her lips. His warm fingers worked at a button on her blouse, easing it open, his lips never leaving hers. She shivered at the feel of his touch on her bare skin, then flinched as she felt him take the hard nub of her nipple between his fingers and gently pull on it.

Kat felt herself sliding down in the taxi seat, completely unaware of anything but the feel of Max's mouth, his hands, his body. Like hers, his breathing sounded ragged.

"Max," she whispered against his mouth as she felt another button open to his demand. His hand moved down her ribs to her stomach to the top of her pants, and she thought she might burst with her need for him if he didn't—

The taxi came to a stop, yanking her out of the foggy, dreamlike erotic state. "We're here," the driver said, amusement in his voice.

Max disengaged his hand, making her want to groan with frustration even as she quickly buttoned up her shirt. As they disembarked, she didn't look at the taxi driver. She'd never done anything like that in her life and felt torn between embarrassment and regret that they'd been interrupted.

Max cleared his throat as they stood on the curb. He seemed as uncomfortable with their sudden interruption as she felt. "Whew," he said. "I really wish that had been a longer taxi ride." He looked over at her, his gaze locking with hers. "Maybe we'll have to do something about that."

Just the promise in his stare made Kat feel weak at the knees with yearning. "Yes."

"Yes?" Max laughed. "I thought you were going to say, 'I don't—'"

"No," she quickly interrupted. Although in truth,

it was true. She hadn't made love since… She quickly pushed that thought back into the darkness where it belonged and followed Max into the rental car agency.

He was filling out forms when she got the call from her sister Ainsley.

"Kat, where are you?"

"I'm…" She realized she didn't want to get into this, even with Ainsley, in a car-rental agency. "Why, what's wrong?"

"There's been an accident," her sister said. "It's Angelina. She's been killed. Dad is on his way home from DC."

Kat felt a wave of shock move through her. "Wait, where was she killed?"

"She'd apparently flown back from DC to take care of some personal business up by Butte. She must have fallen asleep at the wheel. They found her car in a canyon."

"Are you at the ranch?" Kat asked.

"No, I'm up by Glacier Park. I'll be driving down tomorrow. Dad's flying in later tonight, Harper and Cassidy are on their way, and Livie and Bo are both there already. With Livie pregnant… I was hoping you could go to the ranch and make sure Dad's all right as well as Livie and the rest."

"I'm not in town, but I'll catch the next flight out," she said as Max came out of the rental agency.

"What's wrong?" he asked. "You're as pale as a ghost."

"It's Angelina, my father's—" Suddenly goose bumps rippled over her skin.

"Wife?" Max said when she'd stopped abruptly.

"She's dead."

CHAPTER SEVENTEEN

MAX WAS ABLE to get them on the late flight to Bozeman. While they were waiting to board, Kat had seen
the story on national news. She and her sisters had
been sheltered from the limelight by living on a ranch
in Montana—until her father had announced he would
run for president.

Now things would get worse. For months, the media
had played up the lovers' triangle between her father,
mother and Angelina. Angelina's death and Sarah's engagement would start a whole new set of stories and
speculation. If only her mother was already married
to Russell.

She and Max didn't talk about it on the flight. They
were both smart enough to know that their conversation could be overhead, worse, recorded on a cell
phone for a sound bite on the news or end up in some
tabloid magazine.

"Would you mind driving?" Kat asked and handed
over the keys to her SUV at the Bozeman airport. She
was too upset right now to get behind the wheel, and
she felt guilty that she wasn't more upset over Angelina's death.

"Do you want to talk about it?" Max asked once
they were on their way to the ranch where he'd left his
pickup a few days ago.

"I don't mean to seem uncaring," she said. "I'm sorry Angelina's dead. But my stepmother and I were never close."

"I gathered that, by your reaction," Max said. "And by the fact that you and your sisters named her the Ice Queen."

"I'm just afraid of what will happen now. She and my father have been having trouble, ever since my mother came back into the picture. Still, I know he loved Angelina. He has to be taking this hard. And yet, I also know how he feels about our mother."

"Any idea what Angelina was doing up by Butte? I thought she and your father were campaigning."

"Apparently she told him she had some personal business to take care of and flew home," Kat said.

When they reached the ranch, Max stopped at the gate. "It appears everyone has heard," he said, motioning toward the news vehicles parked near the gate. There were ten times as many as there had been when they'd left.

The guard, recognizing Kat's vehicle, opened the gate. Max started to get out to let her drive, as several of the reporters moved toward the SUV.

"Keep going," Kat cried. "I can't face this alone. You and I are the only ones who know the truth about my mother."

He glanced over at her. "Kat—"

"Please."

He quickly shifted into gear and drove through the gate, which closed quickly behind them. "You aren't going to tell him tonight."

"No," she said as the house loomed ahead of them.

"But I'm going to need you to back up my story when I do. And I need you right now."

MAX SAID NOTHING, but he couldn't help being touched that she needed him and wanted him to be with her at this moment.

As for him backing her up with her father, Kat wouldn't want to hear that it was going to take more than his word to get the senator to believe them. He was just thankful he had the photo of the Prophecy. Even with that, he figured Buckmaster Hamilton would be skeptical. Look what it had taken to convince Kat.

As he pulled up in front of the large sprawling ranch house, meeting the family was the last thing Max had expected to do. The journalist in him couldn't believe his luck. He'd gotten into the inner sanctum when none of the other reporters stood a chance. But the man who'd come to care about Kat knew there was only one way he could do this.

"Everything, once I cross that threshold, is off the record," he said.

She looked over at him as if she'd forgotten who he was. *What* he was. "I am making this hard on you, aren't I?"

He let out a chuckle. "Yeah. But I'm here for you."

She smiled at him. Her trust meant everything to him. Getting out, they headed toward the front door. Kat took his hand and held it as she opened the door, and they stepped in. He felt her hand clutch his and looked over to see the expression on her face when she saw her father.

All thought of his damned story was forgotten as Kat rushed to her father.

Senator Buckmaster Hamilton looked as if he was still in shock as he took his daughter in his arms. Max stood at the edge of the living room, taking in the other women gathered. He'd seen a few photos of the senator's daughters that tabloid photographers had taken since the senator had thrown his hat into the presidential ring. The photos hadn't been good—slightly out of focus, only in-passing shots or ones taken from their yearbooks.

But he could easily recognize most of them. Ainsley was the oldest sister, the blonde beauty with the intelligent blue eyes who also resembled her mother. Bo was also blonde, freckled and more girl next door with emerald-green eyes. The very pregnant one was Olivia, or Livie, as he'd heard Kat refer to her. She was the blue-eyed brunette who'd recently married a horse trainer named Cooper Barnett, who worked for her father.

The only ones he couldn't tell apart were the twins, Harper and Cassidy. Kat had said they'd been in New York when they'd gotten the call. Another senator had offered them his jet to get them back to the ranch. They were now huddled on the couch, one on each side of Ainsley. They were all talking in low whispers and hadn't noticed him.

All of them looked shell-shocked.

"I'm sorry," Kat said as she turned to see Max standing at the edge of the room. She held out her hand. "Dad, this is Max Malone, a friend of mine, but also a reporter."

All her sisters turned then to look at him. Apparently Kat didn't bring many friends home, from their surprised expressions. But a reporter?

Max stepped forward to shake the senator's hand.

"I'm sorry to hear about your loss, Senator. I'm not here as a reporter. I'm only here as Kat's friend. She asked me to bring her."

"Thank you. So I can assume…"

"Everything is off the record. Also, I'll be taking my leave, now that she's home with her family."

The senator nodded. The door opened, and two cowboys came in. Max was introduced to Livie's husband, Cooper Barnett, and Bo's fiancé, Jace Calder.

"Kat, if you're all right, I should go and leave you with your family," Max said when she joined him.

She hesitated, but only for a moment. "Take my car."

He shook his head. "I can walk back to the gate to my pickup. The cold night air will do me good."

She took both his hands in hers, her gray eyes large and misty. "Can we talk tomorrow?"

"You have my number," he said, his gaze locking with hers. That spark between them took a hot, fast joyride through his veins before she let go.

Smiling, she said, "I think I do have your number."

BUCKMASTER COULDN'T BELIEVE Angelina was dead. Just hours ago, he'd decided to leave her. Awash with guilt now, he looked at his beautiful daughters, the family he'd made with Sarah, and felt as if he'd caused his wife's death. He'd wanted her gone, and yet, he'd loved her as much as he'd been able.

All these months of putting up with her jealousy, her plotting, her paranoia, he'd still loved Angelina. He'd owed her. She'd gotten him through the past fifteen years without Sarah. And now she was gone, and he felt such a mix of conflicting emotions that the guilt was killing him.

His cell phone vibrated. Since the news had come out about Angelina's death, he'd been getting calls from campaign staff, contributors, friends and other politicians, even one from the president. He'd taken a few of the calls at first, but had finally let the calls go to voice mail. He was too shaken to even accept condolences right now.

But this time, when he checked his phone, he saw that it was from Sarah. He quickly stepped out of the room to take the call.

"Sarah?"

"I just heard, Buck. I'm so sorry."

Suddenly he was so choked up he couldn't speak. He hadn't shed a tear since getting the news, but now the flood of emotion overwhelmed him. "I was going to leave her, Sarah," he said through the heart-wrenching sentiment. "Just moments before I got the call, I'd decided to leave her." He tried to pull himself together. "Did you hear what I said?"

"I don't know what to say, Buck."

"Say you won't marry Russell."

"Buck." There was pleading in her voice. "This isn't the time to make any kind of rash decisions."

"On either of our parts," he managed to say. "I can't let you marry him, Sarah. I want you. It's always been you."

"But the election—"

"I don't give a damn about it. Being president means nothing if you aren't at my side."

She sighed. "Buck."

"Dad?"

He turned to see Harper standing in the doorway. "I'll be right with you," he said to her.

"I would imagine the girls are home?"

"Yes. Harper and Cassidy were in New York for a visit when they heard the news. They flew in earlier. I know you want to see them. I'm sorry I've kept them from you."

"They don't know me. I've missed so much of their lives. So much of yours."

"There is still time, Sarah."

"You should go."

"We will talk soon," he said. "In the meantime—"

"I know."

He stood for a long moment after the call ended. Outside, the fall leaves on the aspen trees shimmered in the starlight. He told himself that everything was going to get better. But first he had to get through Angelina's funeral. Then…then, he would deal with the rest of his life.

"You look tired," Nettie said that evening when the sheriff came home. She'd seen the change in him since he'd been trying to track down Dr. Ralph Venable, the man who'd been experimenting with brain wiping at the clinic in White Sulphur Springs.

The last anyone had heard from Dr. Venable, he'd sent a postcard from Santa Cruz do Sul, Brazil, but that had been twenty years ago. Nettie had been placing calls to every hospital and clinic in the area, but with little luck.

As talk of the upcoming election next year increased, she could see Frank worrying more and more.

"Any news on the missing journalist?" she asked, even though she would have heard something if Chuck Barrow had been found.

Her husband shook his head as he hung up his Stetson. His gunfighter mustache tickled as he gave her a kiss. She looked into his blue eyes and wondered how long it would be before he turned in his badge and retired. She knew, though, that he would hate retirement. But she didn't know how to stop him. He was becoming more and more frustrated with the rules and regulations, the paperwork and how slow everything seemed to move in law enforcement.

Her cell phone rang. She thought about letting the call go to voice mail, but when it rang again, Frank said, "Go ahead. It could be the latest gossip. I can use a good laugh."

She slapped his arm playfully as she pulled out her phone. The connection wasn't great.

"Senora Curry?" a woman asked in what sounded to Nettie like a Spanish accent.

She realized it was probably Portuguese. Her heart leaped in her chest. "Yes, yes, this is Nettie Curry."

"One moment," the woman said. "The administrator would like to speak with you."

"Senora Curry?" a man asked, static on the line. "This is Manuel Ramirez at the Santa Maria Clinic."

"Yes." She looked up at Frank. He was watching her with interest.

"I was told you were trying to reach Dr. Venable?"

"Yes, does he work at your clinic?"

"I'm sorry, but the doctor has left."

"But he did work at your clinic?" she asked quickly.

"Yes, he and his assistant worked here for the past twenty years."

"His *assistant*?"

"Senora Johnson."

Sarah Johnson Hamilton? "You don't happen to have a photo of the two of them, do you, Senor Ramirez?"

CHAPTER EIGHTEEN

KAT WENT WITH her sisters to the condo complex her father had built for the six of them, but none of them were ready to go to sleep yet. They'd stayed up talking after Livie and Bo had left.

It was nice to have Harper and Cassidy back, although Cassidy said she was leaving right after the funeral.

"She met a man in France. He's interning in New York," Harper had explained.

"It isn't serious," Cassidy said. "We're just having fun."

The twins had been studying abroad, but Kat could tell that they were both restless. "What do you want to do, now that you've graduated?" she asked them as they sat around the separate living area.

Both shrugged. "I'm staying here to be with Dad," Harper said. "I don't want him to be alone."

"He's hardly alone," Ainsley said. "I'm sure he'll be going back to DC after the funeral."

Harper looked surprised. "I thought he'd drop out of the race."

"I wish he would," Kat said without thinking.

"Oh, you've always been antipolitics," Cassidy said. "You're worse than mother."

"You've been in contact with her?" she asked in surprise.

Cassidy shrugged. "We've been chatting online, and I've talked to her a few times on the phone. I don't really know her, but I think she's sweet."

Sweet. Wasn't that what Kat used to think? "She told you she hates politics?"

"It's obvious that she doesn't have an interest and she hates being in the spotlight. But she's very supportive of Dad being president. She's proud of him."

Kat bit down hard on her tongue for a moment. "It sounds like you've communicated with her a lot."

"She picked us up at the airport," Harper said. "It wasn't as weird as I thought it would be. She looks like all of us, more like you, Kat, and definitely you, Ainsley. But I can see each of us in her."

Kat was surprised to hear that their mother had picked the twins up at the airport and brought them to the ranch. "Did she come in the house?"

All three of her sisters looked over at her.

"It isn't as if she's going to come in and steal our silver," Ainsley said, frowning at her.

"I was just curious," Kat said in her defense. The thought of her mother being in this house again terrified her.

"We invited her in, but she declined," Cassidy said. "I felt sorry for her. What would it be like to lose more than twenty years of your life like that and then to come back, and your husband has married someone else and she's living in your house?"

"Well, he's not married anymore," Ainsley said.

"Do you think Dad wants to get back together with Mom?" Harper asked.

"There's nothing stopping them now," Cassidy said, sounding more than accepting of the idea.

Kat couldn't let that happen. "I would hope he doesn't do anything for a while."

"The media would annihilate him if he got married again too soon," Ainsley said. "But I know he still loves Mother. Remember what Livie told us? Dad confessed that Mother is the only woman he's truly loved. Would it really be so awful?"

Kat got up and excused herself, unable to listen to this kind of talk any longer. She and Max had agreed not to tell her sisters. They would talk to her father first, show him the photo and what evidence they had. He could then break the news to her sisters.

But they had to do it soon, before Sarah found a way to get back into their father's life.

WITH A SINKING FEELING, Russell Murdock listened to the news as he drove toward his ranch. The senator's wife was dead. He slowed his pickup and pulled over beside the road. Angelina was dead?

For a moment, he couldn't breathe. The pain in his chest wasn't a heart attack, but he almost wished it was. Buckmaster Hamilton was free. There would be nothing stopping him from getting Sarah back.

"Except for political suicide," Russell said to the empty truck cab. He tried to tell himself that the senator wouldn't give up everything he'd worked for—not for a woman. But Sarah wasn't just any woman. She was the mother of his six daughters. She was quite possibly the love of his life.

"You can't have her," he said, his voice breaking. "She's mine." But even as he said it, he knew that everything had changed. It wouldn't matter that he'd put a diamond engagement ring on Sarah's finger. Buckmaster could buy her a ring ten times as big. Buckmaster could give her a larger ranch. Maybe he could even give her the White House.

"But I can give her love," Russell said and slammed his palm down on the steering wheel. "Love that she can count on."

He thought again of Sarah, so desperate that she'd tried to kill herself that winter night years ago when she'd driven her SUV into the freezing Yellowstone River. Russell was still convinced that Buckmaster had been the cause.

"So how can she go back to him?" The empty truck cab seemed to echo his words. "Because she loves him."

Russell let out a bitter laugh. It was that simple. And that complicated. Sarah loved Buck. She would probably always love him. And vice versa.

"You're going to have to let her go," he said quietly over the gentle throb of the pickup engine. The thought broke his heart.

But trying to hold on to her would only cause them both more pain.

Shifting into first gear, he pulled back on to the narrow two-lane dirt road. He wanted to turn around, go back to the cabin where Sarah was still staying. She would have heard the news by now. Buck had bought her a car. For all Russell knew, she might have already packed up and left.

He might have driven up to the cabin where she was still staying until the wedding, but the moment he saw her face, he would know, and there would be nothing either of them could say. For now, he could hope he was wrong.

MAX HAD WALKED down to the gate, gotten in his pickup and driven into town. He'd told himself all he needed was a big beefsteak at the Grand and a good night's sleep in a soft bed.

But he couldn't help worrying. Angelina Hamilton's death was like a rock thrown into a still pond. It would cause a ripple effect, changing everything. Kat was right. They had to tell her father. With the senator's wife dead and gone, there would be nothing stopping Sarah from working her way back into Buckmaster's life.

It would be an uphill battle convincing the senator, though. Max had seen firsthand Sarah and her former husband together. Now there was nothing standing in Buckmaster's way. If he wanted his first wife back—and Max was positive he did—then there was nothing stopping him, especially Sarah's engagement to Russell Murdock.

The senator would have to wait a discreet time after the funeral, though. But that didn't mean that Sarah and the senator wouldn't be in contact. Knowing Kat, she would want to talk to her father right away.

He thought about calling her. But it would have been just to hear her voice. Not only that, it was late, and she was with her family. It could wait until tomorrow. He felt antsy, though. But it had nothing to do with the secret he and Kat had uncovered.

Just the thought of what had transpired between him and Kat in the back of the taxi—he let out a frus-

trated groan as he parked and went into the Grand.
First food, then a motel. He took a seat and ordered
dinner and a beer.

The waitress had just set a cold bottle in front of
him when his cell phone vibrated in his jacket pocket.
Seeing it was Kat, he smiled and picked up. "How are
you?" he asked the minute he heard her voice.

She sighed. "I'm okay."

"You don't sound okay."

"It's just hard knowing what I do. When will we talk
to my father? Max, I know you wanted to wait, but I
don't see how we can now."

"He can't go to her right away."

"Emotionally, I think he already has. He took a call
earlier. It was my mother. My sister heard him say that
he'd made the decision to leave Angelina just before
he'd gotten the call about the accident. He also said that
my mother couldn't marry Russell now. I don't know
what she said, but if we're right about all this, then she
was never going to marry him anyway."

Max swore under his breath. "When do you want
to talk to him?"

"Tomorrow?"

"I'll bring the copy of the photo. You do realize
that's pretty much all we have except for our word
about what was said by the two men we met with."

"You still don't think he's going to believe us."

"All we can do is try. I'll drive out in the morning?"

"What? You aren't sleeping in the back of your
truck?"

He heard the intimacy in her voice and felt long-
ing stir in him. "I'm splurging and staying in a motel.
But first, I'm going to have a steak. You know me."

He wanted to say, "I wish you were here with me," but she cut him off.

"Yes, I know you. You're probably starved."

"You do know me."

Silence filled the space between them.

"Kat, did your dad say why Angelina was back in Montana by herself?"

"No. Why?"

"Just curious."

"Max?"

"Yes?"

"You're not writing about all this, are you?" The intimacy he'd heard before was gone.

He swore under his breath. "I won't write anything without telling you first."

"I trust you. I'll tell them to let you through the gate in the morning."

His steak arrived, but he'd lost his enthusiasm for it as they said goodnight. He was a reporter. He believed in what he did for a living. He was sitting on one hell of a story. But he couldn't write it without proof to back it up. He told himself it had nothing to do with how he felt about Kat.

He swore and took a bite of his steak. On the television over the bar, he saw the news come on. Senator Buckmaster's face flashed on the screen, then a photo of Angelina.

He heard some locals at the bar talking about the news. He couldn't hear everything they were saying, but it was clear that a lot of people who had met Angelina wouldn't be shedding any tears over her death.

Max ate what he could, his appetite gone. The night air as he left the restaurant was cold. October in Montana could be an Indian Summer or like winter with a foot of snow. Tonight felt as if snow wasn't that far in the future.

He was angry with himself as he started down the nearly empty street toward his pickup. He'd broken his golden rule. Worse, he couldn't wait to do it again. He just hoped he got the chance. At the mere thought of getting Kat naked—

The dark figure emerged from the alley so quickly that Max didn't have time to react. The blow to the side of his head pitched him forward. Through glittering stars, he saw the sidewalk coming up. It was the last thing he remembered.

CHAPTER NINETEEN

BUCKMASTER THOUGHT THINGS couldn't get any worse until the Silverbow sheriff called. "Any idea why your wife might have been on that particular road at that time of the night?"

"No." He realized how little he knew about what Angelina had been up to. That alone caused him concern. Worse, it seemed strange the kind of questions the sheriff was asking. "It *was* an accident, wasn't it?"

"Our investigation has raised some questions. Apparently your wife tried to make a call possibly right before her car went off the highway. Did she reach you?"

The call was to him? "No, I…" He realized that he'd gotten a call earlier that night. He'd seen it was Angelina calling, but he hadn't picked up because he'd been in a meeting with his staff. He'd thought that whatever it was, it could wait. Now, he felt as if the earth beneath him had given way. "I saw that she'd called, but she didn't leave a message."

The sheriff didn't ask why he hadn't taken the call. He probably picked up whenever his wife called.

"I was in a meeting," he said, wanting to add that as a senator, especially one in the middle of a campaign for the highest office in the country, he was a little busy.

But he knew he was just making excuses. He hadn't wanted to talk to Angelina.

If he had, though, he might know what had been going on. What if she hadn't been paying attention to her driving when she called him and—

"The call before that on her cell phone was to a private investigator named Addison Crenshaw. Do you have any idea what that was about?"

"No." Buckmaster let out a sigh. So she'd hired another one? Now more than ever, he wished he'd picked up when Angelina had called. What if this investigator had found that deep, dark secret that his wife was determined Sarah was hiding?

"My wife had hired several investigators over the past few months," he said. "It was for a personal matter."

"Our attempts to talk to the investigator have been unsuccessful. I have to ask. Were you and your wife having any…problems?"

Buckmaster wanted to laugh. *You mean like when your dead first wife shows up after twenty-two years?* "If you read the tabloids, I don't think I have to tell you that we've been going through a rough patch lately."

"Was it possible your wife thought you were having an affair, and that's why she hired the private investigator?" the sheriff asked.

Buckmaster let out a curse. He could see where this was going. He saw no way around it but to tell the sheriff why Angelina had hired numerous PIs. "No, sheriff. She had it in her head that my former wife, Sarah Hamilton, was a threat. That there was something in her history that might impact my election results."

"I see."

"I'm sure when you find this Addison Crenshaw, he will verify what I've told you."

"Ms."

"I beg your pardon?"

"The private investigator. Addison is female."

Why hadn't Angelina been able to just leave things alone? Why had she felt compelled to keep digging and digging into the past? He realized there was a bigger question to concern himself with here. "I don't understand why you're asking all these questions."

"Like I said, there is evidence at the scene that has raised some questions."

"What kind of evidence?" he demanded.

"The lack of skid marks. It appears that your wife didn't hit her brakes before she went off the road."

He had such a feeling of déjà vu that he had to find a chair and sit down. Sarah hadn't hit her brakes either, indicating that she'd purposely driven into the Yellowstone River in an attempt to kill herself. "Are you telling me—"

"It's too early in the investigation to have any definitive answers. Once we have the brakes checked on the vehicle, we'll know more."

"You think someone tampered with her brakes?"

"As I said, it's too early to know. You were in DC at the time of the accident, isn't that correct?"

"Yes, just as I already told you. I can provide names of people who will verify where I was, if I have to." No wonder the sheriff was asking about their relationship. Just because he was in DC at the time of the accident, if someone had tampered with her brakes, that wouldn't necessarily clear him of suspicion. "You'll let me know once you have more information?"

"I will, Senator. In the meantime, again, I am sorry for your loss."

RUSSELL HAD BEEN RIGHT. The moment he looked into Sarah's eyes the next morning, he knew.

"You're reconsidering," he said, surprised by the disgust in his voice.

"Russell—"

He held up his hand. "Don't bother making excuses for him. I've heard them all. You still don't know that he wasn't the one who stole not only years from you but also robbed you of your children."

"I love him."

He shook his head. "You sound like you're sixteen."

"Maybe that's how I feel. I never lied to you about my feelings for Buck."

She had him there. But he'd thought that his love would make her forget. What a fool he'd been.

He felt anger burn red hot just under his skin. "Aren't you even a little suspect of the timing?" he demanded. "He couldn't bear the thought of you marrying me. You knew he would do something before it was too late, didn't you?"

He saw the answer in her face and hated the fury that made him want to shake some sense into her. He'd never been a violent man, but something in her made him feel capable of it.

"I wouldn't be surprised if he had her killed," Russell snapped. "But that would be okay with you, right? Anything he does is okay with you."

Sarah gasped, her eyes narrowing as she looked

at him. "You hate him so much that you will believe anything of him. I'm so sorry. I'm the one who made you this way."

Russell shook his head. Did he really believe that the senator would have his wife killed so he could be with Sarah? He thought of how much he wanted the woman and knew that murder wasn't necessarily out of the question. Except it wasn't for him. He knew better than to try to hang on to something that wasn't his, no matter how badly he wanted it.

"You're right. I'm sorry." He looked at his boots for a moment, not trusting his voice. "You know I only want the best for you."

She stepped to him and touched his arm. "I know. You're the best man I've ever known. That's why I don't want you to change because of me."

He nodded and removed her hand from his arm.

Her face clouded for a moment. "I'm so sorry I hurt you."

"I'll survive." Right now it didn't feel like it. But he would. "Goodbye, Sarah."

"I'm sure we'll see each other—"

"I doubt that. I'm thinking I might take a vacation. Winter's coming. I'm not up to another one right now. I'm heading south, how far is debatable."

"I don't know what to say."

"Say goodbye." With that he turned and walked out the door, his heart breaking. But he refused to look back. Sarah was gone, but then again she'd never been his.

SHERIFF CURRY WAS leaving the hospital after checking on mugging victim Max Malone, when he got the call about remains being found back in the woods at the base of the Crazy Mountains.

As county sheriff, Frank was still dealing with the mugging. He couldn't remember ever hearing of anyone being mugged on the main drag of Big Timber. "What was taken?" he'd asked.

"My wallet, my keys. He got into my pickup and took my notebooks and a camera that didn't belong to me."

"You're one of those journalists here covering Senator Hamilton?"

Malone had nodded, although it had been clear it hurt to do so. "I didn't get a good look at whoever hit me. That's why I'm surprised you're here."

"The doctor called me. He said when you were brought in, you said you were mugged."

The reporter had frowned. "I don't remember."

"Well, the good news is that you only have a minor concussion. I'm sure everything else is covered by your car insurance."

"Except for my notes," he'd said almost to himself.

"If you remember anything about the attacker, give me a holler," Frank had said. As he was leaving, he saw one of the Hamilton girls coming down the hall. He recognized Kat only a moment before she slipped into Max Malone's room.

The sheriff had raised a curious brow, but didn't give it any more thought as his cell phone rang.

Remains found at the base of the Crazies, the hunter had said. After the hunter described the clothing with the remains, Frank realized he might have found missing journalist Chuck Barrow's body. It matched the description of what Chuck Barrow was last seen wearing before he disappeared three months ago.

Barrow's vehicle had been found in a ravine, the driver's side door standing open. It was believed that the injured Barrow had been confused and wandered off into the Crazies thinking he was going for help.

"I'd say a bear got to him," the hunter said. "The remains are strewn over a pretty wide area. Looks like the bear tried to bury what he couldn't use."

"Where'd you say you are again?" Frank asked.

The hunter told him. The location was miles from where Barrow's vehicle had gone in the ravine.

"I'll be right there." Frank called the coroner, Charlie Brooks, and asked him to meet him at the location.

Two journalists. One dead, another mugged. He doubted there was a connection, though, as he called his undersheriff and asked him to meet him at the office.

Undersheriff Dillon Lawson was just coming in the office as Frank pulled up. "Take a ride with me," Frank said and explained about the remains the hunter had found and about the mugging last night.

As he drove, he also updated Dillon on the news about the brain-wiping experimenting that Dr. Venable—and his blonde assistant—had been engaged in. "We're waiting on photographs of the two of them from Brazil."

Dillon shook his head. "So you think it's really possible that Sarah Hamilton's brain was wiped clean of the past twenty-two years?"

"I'm still skeptical about all of it, but at least we have a lead on where she's been and possibly who she's been with."

"So, what was she doing down in Brazil?"

"Apparently she was acting as the doctor's assistant. If true, then it substantiates what Lynette and I learned in White Sulphur Springs. Sarah knew the doctor and she was the blonde who was brought to that clinic the night after her car went into the Yellowstone River. But we still don't know who took her there that night."

Dillon rubbed his jaw for a moment. "So you're waiting for a photo that will tie Sarah to the doctor in Brazil."

"We're getting closer to the truth."

"And then what?" Dillon asked. "I'm sorry to say it, but even if we can put her in both places, where does that leave us?"

"I'm not sure, since Sarah swears she can't remember anything."

"Living in Brazil for the past twenty years isn't illegal," Dillon said as if talking to himself. "Apparently not even brain wiping is illegal. It leaves the big question unanswered. What brought her back now?"

"She says her children. But what if I told you that the doctor has also left Brazil?"

"You think he's in Montana?"

"I think at some point, he is going to give Sarah back her memory," Frank said. "And then we'll know why she tried to kill herself. Russell Murdock is convinced that the senator is responsible for all of it."

"There's a hot potato, if there ever was one. Hamilton is one of the most respected senators in the country," Dillon said. "He's powerful enough right *now*. If he wins the presidency… We are going to have to be very careful with all this."

"I don't think we're going to have to wait too much

longer," Frank said. "I suspect Sarah will get her memory back about the time Buckmaster Hamilton becomes president."

KAT QUIT LYING to herself the moment she got Max's message. She had turned off her phone last night before she'd gone to bed. Everyone had been calling with either condolences or curiosity. She'd needed sleep, so she hadn't turned it back on until she'd come out of the shower this morning.

When she'd heard his voice, heard that he was in the hospital, heard that he was in pain, she couldn't deny how she felt any longer.

All the way into town, she'd argued with herself about her feelings. He was a reporter. Her family was a story. Only a fool would fall in love with a man like Max Malone. He'd never be happy staying in one place. He would be chasing the next story as soon as he was through here. Through with her.

But all those arguments didn't change the way she felt.

She passed the sheriff coming out of Max's room and rushed in, shocked to see how pale he was against the white sheets. His head was bandaged, but his eyes were bright when he saw her hurry to his bedside.

"Are you all right?" she asked, taking his hand and pressing it to her chest.

"I feel better already," he joked, smiling up at her.

She looked into his blue eyes. "I couldn't believe it when I got your message. You were *mugged*?"

"At least that's what my attacker wanted me to believe."

"What?"

He motioned for her to close the hospital room door, before he spoke again. "Whoever attacked me last night wasn't after the money in my wallet. He wanted my keys to get into my pickup. He took all my notes and your camera. I'm sorry, I'll replace it with any camera you want."

"I don't care about the camera," she cried as she pulled up a chair next to his bed. "I'm just worried about you."

"Oh, yeah?" he asked, grinning again.

"Be serious for once. You could have been killed."

"It's just a minor concussion. He didn't want to kill me or he would have. I'm guessing he just wanted to know how much I knew." Max rubbed at his temples.

"Your head hurts, huh? Can I get you something?"

He smiled at her, even though she could tell it hurt. "Last night when you called, I was wishing you were with me. I'm so glad you weren't." He held her gaze. "How are you doing?"

"Dad's making arrangements for the funeral Friday."

"That soon?" He sounded as surprised as she'd been.

"He wants it over as quickly as possible."

"The doctor said he'd release me later this afternoon. We'll talk to him as soon as I get out of here. But there's a problem. As soon as I came to and realized what had happened…my attacker took the photo."

"We can always get another copy, right?"

He shook his head and then winced in pain. "I called the paper this morning as soon as the archivist got in. He said the original is missing."

"How is that possible?" she demanded.

"The only way, given the paper's security, is for someone to pay to have the original disappear. Kat, that photo has been in the archives since 1978. It wasn't until we took an interest in it that it suddenly disappeared—along with our copy of it."

"The only other person who knew about the photo was my mother." Kat sat back as that sank in. "If she told one of the members from the Prophecy, then that would mean—"

"That she remembers a whole lot more than she is letting on. Let's assume she really doesn't remember. That means either someone at the paper tipped them off about my interest in the photo or I was right about her place being bugged."

"Max, this is scaring me. These people…they have resources… How can we possibly stop them?"

"Your mother is still the key. And if we're right, it's tied in with your dad's election. Is he going to continue running?"

"I don't know. He hasn't said anything. But I fear if it came down to him either running for president or getting my mother back…"

"He'd choose your mother. But if she needs him to be president, she won't let that happen. Okay, don't worry. We'll talk to him."

"But without the photo…"

Max sighed. "Yeah, your father won't believe us. I doubt anyone would."

"What about your story?"

He shook his head. "There's nothing I can do until—"

"Until the Prophecy does whatever they have planned, and by then, it will be too late."

He reached over and took her hand. "You're freezing," he said, rubbing her fingers to warm them. "Maybe we can't convince your father, but if we can put enough doubt in his mind… Also, I think we need to go to the sheriff. I met him this morning. He seems like a good man."

She nodded. "I've known him all my life. He *is* a good man."

"Then we'll tell him our story. He might not believe us either, but we have to try."

"But Sheriff Curry won't be able to do anything," Kat said. "We still have no proof."

"I'll keep looking for it. Maybe I'll get lucky." He let go of her hand. "But I have to do this alone. It's too dangerous for you to be involved."

"That must have been some knock on your head," Kat said as she got to her feet, "because you should know I'm in this with you, one way or the other. You should get some rest. I'll come back this afternoon. I don't want you driving until you're better."

She bent over the bed and kissed him before he could argue.

As she started to pull back, he cupped his hand around the back of her neck and pulled her down for another kiss; this one curled her toes. Her gaze locked with his as he let go.

"What happened to your golden rule?"

"That baby is permanently broken," he said. "If a nurse wasn't apt to walk in here at any moment, you know what I'd do?"

She couldn't help but laugh. "Save it, Casanova. I'd say you aren't up for much of anything right now."

"I might surprise you."

Kat laughed again. "Nothing you could do would surprise me."

"Now, that sounds like a challenge to me. I do love a challenge.

She sighed and started to leave when he grabbed her again. "Kat?" he said, turning serious again. "Be careful. I'm so sorry I dragged you into this."

MAX COULDN'T WAIT to get out of the hospital. His head still hurt, but he was anxious to get to Kat.

He told himself that she should be safe on the ranch. His attacker last night had gotten what he wanted. He shouldn't have any reason to come back.

But Max didn't want to take any chances with her safety. Once they talked to her father and then the sheriff, it would be out of their hands.

Well, at least out of Kat's. No matter what she said, she was done. He would have to keep digging. While he'd told Kat that the Prophecy might be bluffing about having something big coming down, he tended to believe it.

And if he had to put his money on what it was, he'd bet on Buckmaster Hamilton as the target.

He reminded himself that he was just a reporter. He had no business playing cops and robbers. But if they couldn't get anyone to believe them, then he had no choice. He couldn't stand back and let Kat's father die—and the country take the hit—if he could help it.

The election was still a year away, he reminded himself. He was convinced they wouldn't do anything until then. But if he could uncover the truth before then…

He looked up to see Kat coming down the hallway, and all his grand reasons for helping her went out the window. He was falling for this woman, plain and simple. Seeing her made his day.

"Ready?" she said.

He nodded and put his arm around her as they walked out of the hospital, as if he needed her to keep him upright. He suspected he did, which should have scared him off.

They spoke little on the drive to the ranch. "Did you tell your father we needed to talk to him?"

She nodded as she drove. "He gave me the impression he thinks you are going to ask for my hand in marriage." She laughed as she looked over at him. "Don't panic and bail out of the car."

He laughed, too, since bailing out was the last thing he wanted to do.

THE SENATOR WAS waiting for them in his den. He looked up and smiled as they entered. Max noticed that he'd seemed to age in the past twenty-four hours.

Buckmaster shook his hand and offered him and Kat a drink. They both declined, so he made a drink for himself, and they all sat down.

"You have something you want to tell me?" the senator asked, looking expectantly from Kat to Max and back again.

"This may come as a shock," Max said.

Buckmaster laughed as if he still thought this was about Kat and Max getting married.

"We have discovered something disturbing in your former wife's past," Max said.

The older man's face fell.

"I forgot for a moment that you're a reporter," the senator said, all friendliness gone.

"I found a photograph of Sarah Johnson when she was in college," Max said as if the man hadn't spoken. "She belonged to a radical group called—"

"Let me stop you right there," Buckmaster said getting to his feet. "I don't give a damn what Sarah might have—"

"You must listen to us," Kat said. "Max and I talked to two of the members of the group. They're behind bars and have been since 1979. They told us that they have something big planned. Dad, we think they plan to kill you or at least compromise you in some way once you're—"

"Enough," Buckmaster snapped. He set his half-empty drink down too hard on the coffee table. "I'm going through enough right now without this."

"I know the timing couldn't be worse, but these people mugged Max last night to steal the photograph we had of the group. If you had seen the shot of Mother—"

"You're trying to tell me that your mother was involved in a mugging? You're worse than Angelina about this. I don't give a damn about Sarah's past, and I don't want to hear anymore." He started for the door.

"Mother called herself Red and dyed her hair," Kat said to his retreating back. "They blew up government buildings, robbed banks and ended up killing five people. They call themselves the Prophecy, and Mother was one of the ringleaders."

He seemed to stumble at the doorway. But he hesitated only a moment and was gone.

For a few moments, neither of them filled the silence that hung in the den.

"I'm sorry, Kat," Max finally said. "I knew he wouldn't want to believe it. Even if we'd had the photo…"

She nodded. "I know. Look how long I was in denial. He loves her," she said simply. "And I'm afraid it's going to get him killed."

CHAPTER TWENTY

Sheriff Frank Curry had his hands full with one dead reporter and another who'd been mugged. So he wasn't exactly excited when he got the call that Max Malone and Kat Hamilton were waiting at his office. "They said it is important."

"Great," he said into the phone. "Tell them I'm on my way." He disconnected and asked his undersheriff if he had everything under control. The area had been secured after the remains had been identified as those belonging to Chuck Barrow.

"It will be next to impossible to give you a cause of death," the coroner had told him earlier. "Had his body been found a few months ago before the bears got to it—"

"I get the picture," Frank had said.

"What's up?" he said now as he stepped into his office to see the two young people waiting for him.

"You might want to close the door," Max said.

Frank did. He was both curious and strangely anxious. Their expressions were so serious. "If this is about your mugging—"

"It's much bigger than that," Max said. "We have information about Sarah Hamilton."

Now they had his attention. He moved behind his desk and sat down, trying hard not to look too eager.

"I stumbled across a photo," Max said and proceeded to tell him a remarkable story that ended with his mugging and the original picture missing from the newspaper in Los Angeles.

At some point in the story, Frank felt goose bumps break out as his heart began to pound. He'd been right about Sarah Hamilton being up to something.

When Max finished, Frank said carefully, "That is some story."

"I was with Max when we talked to the prisoners. They told us to our faces that the Prophecy is planning something big."

"And you say Sarah was the leader of this group?" Frank asked.

"Coleader, but my sources say she was believed to be the brains behind it," Max confirmed.

Frank thought about the way Sarah had returned to Beartooth—parachuting into an area far from everything. The memory loss. The good Dr. Venable and his brain-wiping experiments. Even the tattoo. It all made sense.

"Have you told anyone else about this?" he asked.

"We talked to my father earlier," Kat said.

"And?"

"He didn't believe us."

The sheriff nodded. "This is all very interesting."

"It's all true," Max said. "If we had the photograph… Red, as she was called, was Sarah."

"She looked just like me at my age," Kat put in. "I didn't want to believe at first, but the men we talked to at the prison confirmed it."

"But she was never caught, nor was there any proof

your mother was involved, or she would be in prison," the sheriff pointed out. "You talked to her about this?"

"We showed her the photo," Kat said.

Which was why they no longer had it, Frank thought. And why Max had a knot on his head and a minor concussion.

"How did your mother react?" he asked, wishing he'd been there.

"She didn't recognize herself or anyone in the photo," Max said.

"She didn't see the resemblance to this woman, Red?"

He shook his head. "I believed her," Max added. "I don't think she remembers."

Frank nodded. The brain wipe wasn't just the past twenty-two years, then. Or Sarah was a great liar.

"If you had seen the photograph," Kat said, sounding close to tears.

Frank nodded. "But without hard evidence…especially given who we're dealing with here…"

"We think that she and the others may be planning to harm my father or worse, once he is president," Kat said, her voice breaking.

Max reached over and took her hand.

"If there is any kind of attempt on your father's life—or even a rumor of possible harm, the government will protect a candidate for president," Frank said.

Max looked up at him, deadly serious. "Sheriff, you may want to see that a security detail is put in place as soon as possible."

"Let me see what I can do."

"What about exposing my mother and her crazy friends?" Kat demanded.

"That's a little trickier," the sheriff said. "Even if

you went to the FBI or Homeland Security right now, they would be hesitant because of who your mother is. Without proof…"

"Then we'll find proof," Kat said with conviction.

"I fear that could be dangerous if you're right about all this, which I'm not saying you're not," Frank said. "I would just be careful, if I were you two."

"HE BELIEVED US," Max said as they were driving away from the sheriff's department.

Kat looked over at him in surprise. "How can you say that?"

"My guess is that he'd already been suspicious for some reason. He didn't seem hesitant about getting protection for your father."

"I don't know."

"He wasn't shocked enough," Max argued. "But I do think the Prophecy was news to him. I'm betting he's finding out everything he can about it right now."

"Do you think he will be able to get some sort of security for the rest of the campaign?"

"I'm not sure your father needs it just yet, but he might as well get used to it. Once he's president…"

"We don't even know he'll still run," Kat said as she looked out the window at the country blurring past. It was fall in Montana. The cottonwoods and aspens were still golden, because there hadn't been a hard frost yet.

"Also, your mother might go ahead and marry Russell."

She shook her head. "I'm betting that she was looking to Russell for support and that he wasn't exactly the love of her life."

"I can't help but think this was all part of the plan," Max said. "Once Angelina was out of the picture—"

"You think they killed her?" Kat knew she shouldn't have been shocked. They'd attacked Max last night on the main street in Big Timber.

"I'd like to think they're too old for this, that there are only a few of them left, that after killing five people, they realized what a waste it had all been. They hadn't accomplished anything. Ask anyone on the street, and they would never even have heard of the Prophecy."

"But you think they've recruited younger members?"

He shook his head. "I sure as hell hope not. But those two in prison are certainly just as rabid as they were back in the '70s. It makes me wonder what the other ones have been up to."

She looked up and realized they were headed toward Beartooth. "Where are we going?"

"The Branding Iron. I'm—"

"Starved? *Really?* At a time like this."

He looked over at her sheepishly. "Sorry. I'm a man ruled by his needs." He grinned. "You should be glad I'm only hungry right now."

Kat thought about the night in the taxi. He'd been ready to break his golden rule. But today…he'd probably come to his senses, which she should be thankful for. Was she really ready to go there?

The café was empty this late in the afternoon. Kat spotted the owner, Kate French, with her baby and said over her shoulder to Max, "I can order for myself. I want to see Kate's little girl."

Callie, the waitress, broke away from the baby to

come take his order and Kat's. As the bell over the door jangled, an elderly couple came in, and Callie went over to talk to them.

"Cute baby?" Max asked when Kat rejoined him.

"Adorable."

He was watching the waitress and the older couple.

"That's Callie's grandparents she never knew until a few months ago. It's a long story, but nice to see that they found each other. She's married to the former US marshal Rourke Kincaid. They have a ranch outside of town. Max?"

"Sorry, I was thinking." He turned his gaze on her. "After we have lunch, I thought you wouldn't mind giving me a ride back to town, so I can pick up my truck. Then…"

She felt the full impact of his look. He wasn't just hungry for food apparently.

"When you were a teenager, where did you go to make out?"

"Seriously?" She laughed nervously. "Aren't we a little old for that?"

"I certainly hope not."

Their food arrived. Kat had ordered a cheeseburger, fries and chocolate milk shake, and Max had grinned in approval.

"You are a bad influence," she said as she dug in.

He smiled. "Just wait."

SARAH HEARD THE roar of an engine and stepped quickly to the front of the cabin. She'd been packing. Now that she and Russell were broken up, she couldn't continue to stay in his daughter's cabin.

She feared it was probably Russell coming back and

braced herself. He'd been so angry earlier. Not that she blamed him. But she couldn't see what further discussion would accomplish.

To her surprise it was Buck's SUV that came to a dust-boiling stop in front of the cabin. She watched him get out and stomp toward the porch.

She opened the door and stepped out.

"Buck, you shouldn't be here. What if one of the reporters followed you?"

"Like I give a damn. We have to talk."

She motioned him into the cabin and stood for a moment watching the road, hoping he hadn't been followed. She could well imagine what the media would make of him visiting her so soon after his wife's death.

Finally she went inside the cabin to find him pacing up and down like a caged animal.

"What on earth has gotten into you?" she demanded.

He stopped pacing to stare at her. "I was going to leave Angelina for you."

Crossing her arms over her chest, she nodded. "I know. You told me."

"Are you still engaged to Murdock?"

"No." She met his gaze. "He knows that you're the only man I've ever loved."

"As far as you can remember."

"Buck." She sighed deeply. "Did you come racing out here to argue with me about my memory loss?"

"Sarah…" His voice broke. "That tattoo on your ass. It's a pendulum. Don't they tell the future with those?"

She frowned. "You're not making any sense."

"Aren't I? What is the Prophecy?"

Sarah felt a small icy chill move up her spine. "Buck, what are you talking about?"

"I'm talking about the truth. Maybe you can't remember the past twenty-two years, but you do remember college, right?"

She suddenly felt as if she needed to sit down.

"I need to know, Sarah. Were you some member of a radical antigovernment group who blew up buildings, robbed banks and killed people?"

She recalled the photograph that Kat had shown her. Now it all made sense. "I can't believe you'd even ask me such a thing."

"I can't believe you haven't answered my question." He moved to her, dropping to his knees in front of her and taking both of her hands in his. He squeezed her fingers hard enough to make her wince.

"Sarah, I have to know the truth *now*."

As soon as the undersheriff returned, Frank relayed everything he'd been told by Max Malone and Kat Hamilton.

Dillon listened with interest before asking, *"The Prophecy?"*

Frank told him what Lynette had said about pendulums being used to foretell the future. "It all adds up. Even the way Sarah arrived back in town."

What rattled him more than anything was how blatant the group had been, dropping her off by parachute.

Now he thought he understood. "They want us to try to figure it out. They're challenging us. They could have dropped Sarah off beside the road, but they'd chosen to drop her by parachute and leave the evidence for us to find."

Dillon rubbed his jaw. "That would make them pretty sure of themselves."

"They don't believe we can stop them," he said.

"They might be right. We still don't know what they have planned. But from the get-go, you've said it has something to do with the senator."

Frank swore under his breath. He'd even let the FBI have a go at it, and they had decided Sarah wasn't a threat. Even if they knew that she might have been "Red," the brains behind the Prophecy, they couldn't do much. No proof.

No proof, because Sarah couldn't remember. Her brain had been wiped of that memory, as well as the past twenty-two years, if what Max Malone had told him was true.

"Can you imagine running the brain-wiping theory past the FBI?" he said to Dillon.

"Because of the family we're dealing with, we need to be really careful here," the undersheriff said, as if Frank didn't know that.

"They showed Sarah a photograph of the Prophecy. Max said she didn't seem to recognize them, but last night Max was attacked, and that copy of the photo was taken along with his notes. When he called the newspaper that had the original photograph, it was gone, as well."

Dillon let out a low whistle. "So somehow they found out. Either Sarah told them or—"

"Or they're monitoring her. They might be flaunting the fact that we can't stop them, but they're making sure we don't get our hands on any evidence that will help us."

Frank nodded. "Worse, I fear as Max and Kat do, that Angelina's death opens the door for Sarah to get closer to the senator. With Angelina gone, there is nothing to keep Buckmaster and Sarah apart."

"But surely, knowing what he does, Buckmaster would have his reservations."

"He refused to even listen to them."

Dillon rubbed his jaw. "But the senator is a smart man. He is going to put it all together. I wouldn't be surprised if he confronted Sarah."

"But if she really doesn't remember…"

"What do we do now?"

The sheriff's cell phone jingled as a text came in. He checked it and smiled. "That clinic in Brazil? Lynette just got a photo of Sarah and the elderly doctor she was assisting for the past twenty years down there. At least now we know where she's been—"

"And why she can't remember anything."

"Buck, this is crazy," Sarah said as she moved away from him and he rose from the floor. "It's just like I told Kat and her friend. I don't know what you're talking about."

"They showed you a photo. You didn't notice a resemblance between the woman in the snapshot? Kat said it looked just like her when you were her age."

"Kat." She sighed as she turned to him. "I wasn't the woman in that photo. I didn't even see a resemblance. Maybe I can't remember the past twenty-two years, but I remember college. I would know if I was part of some antigovernment terrorist group, wouldn't I?" She took a step to him and placed a hand on his arm. "You know me, Buck. I'm the mother of your children."

He pulled away, shaking his head. "*Do* I know you, Sarah? I thought I did. But then you got up in the middle of the night and drove your SUV into the river, trying to kill yourself."

"I don't know why I did that. Honestly, I can't imagine doing it." Her voice broke, and she felt how close she was to tears. She could understand everyone else not believing her, but Buck... Buck *had* to believe her.

"Like that damned tattoo and the way you arrived back in town," he said. "How do you explain that, Sarah?"

"I can't. I've tried to remember, but..."

"The Prophecy? That pendulum tattoo. The parachute. You've got to admit, Sarah, this all looks very suspicious. Kat is convinced you are this woman who called herself Red and was involved in the deaths of five people back in the '70s."

"Buck, someone had to have done this to me. They want everyone to believe I am this woman, Red, who helped kill those people."

"Are you saying someone is setting you up?" He sounded incredulous. "Why would they do that, Sarah?"

"Because I was once married to a man who will likely soon become the leader of the free world." She saw that she'd finally reached him. "Whoever is behind this, they know how I feel about you."

"Kat believes that this group, the Prophecy, is planning to harm me or, worse, kill me."

Sarah felt her eyes widen in alarm. "No. Oh, Buck. If they're using me..." She shook her head. "I need to leave Montana. I have to get as far away from you as possible."

"No," he said, closing the distance between them.

He took a few deep breaths. She saw him calm down. He wanted desperately to believe her.

"If you're right and these people are trying to set you up somehow for this, I will protect you," he said at last.

"I'm not worried about *my* protection. What if Kat is right and they plan to kill you and use me somehow to make that happen?"

"We won't let them. Sarah, I don't want another hour, let alone another day, to go by without us being together. I want you to come to the ranch with me now."

"Buck, no. Your campaign—"

"Screw the campaign. I'll drop out. I'll resign as senator."

"I can't let you do that." She pulled away. "This country needs you even more than I do. The only way is to wait."

"I have to be able to see you."

"Isn't there a house on the ranch, one of the small ranches you've bought, that I could stay in? You still go on your afternoon horseback rides every day when you're home, don't you?"

"But if I stay in the campaign, I'll be gone more than I will be on the ranch."

"It's the only way. You can't drop out. I can't let you. I won't take it away from you. We will be together. Once you're elected…"

"I don't know if I am going to stay in the race, but I don't want to talk about that now. I can see that you're packing to leave here. Do you remember the old Morgan Place that I bought? You can stay there. I'll see that it is made comfortable for you. You have the vehicle I bought you, so you can come and go as you please. Even if the media finds out where you're staying, they can't make too big a deal out of it since you will be miles from the main house. You have every right to live on the ranch."

"Oh, Buck, are you sure about this?"

"Yes."

But he'd hesitated just enough that she knew he still didn't completely trust her. She would gain his trust. She would prove herself to him. And soon they would be together, as they both wanted.

"Just promise me. Don't drop out of the race. Promise?"

He met her gaze and held it. She could see the love in his eyes. "If that's what you want. But if I win, you're going to the White House with me as my wife."

Sarah smiled. "*When* you win, I will be by your side."

CHAPTER TWENTY-ONE

NETTIE WAITED UNTIL her husband was sitting down before she handed over the photograph of Dr. Ralph Venable and a blonde woman who was, without a doubt, Sarah Johnson Hamilton. She couldn't help her excitement. The snapshot was taken at a festival of some kind. It was clear that neither the doctor nor Sarah realized that they'd been caught on camera.

"The man who sent me the photo said it surprised him how few photos of the two he could find—especially since they'd worked at the clinic for more than twenty years."

It didn't surprise Nettie in the least.

"So what do you think?" she asked, unable to contain her excitement.

Frank didn't look up from the photo. "I think Russell Murdock was right."

"Oh, speaking of Russell? The engagement is off. His daughter, Destry West, came into the store. She said her father is going on a cruise soon. I can tell you that she wasn't the least bit upset that he wasn't marrying Sarah."

"Going on a cruise?" Frank shook his head. He couldn't imagine anything worse, but then again he was a Montana boy, born and raised. The last thing he'd want to do was to get on some big boat with more

people than lived in his whole county. "So where is Sarah?"

"Destry didn't know where she was going. Apparently Sarah has been staying in Destry's cabin up in the Crazies, but she planned to move out after she broke the engagement."

Nettie could see that her husband wasn't surprised by the news of the breakup. Buckmaster was free. Of course Sarah would want him back.

"I need to show this to a couple of people," Frank said.

"You aren't going to cut me out of the loop now, are you?" Nettie demanded, crossing her arms over her ample chest.

He looked up at her, clearly torn.

"I haven't breathed a word about the brain wiping or our visit to White Sulphur Springs. I also found the doctor and got you that photo."

Her husband smiled. "You're right. I dragged you into this." He seemed to hesitate.

She saw by this expression that he'd found out something else he hadn't yet shared with her. "What?"

He told her about Max Malone and Kat Hamilton's visit.

Nettie couldn't believe this. "Antigovernment terrorists? I never saw that coming. The tattoo! The Prophecy! It all starting to make more sense now."

He nodded. "But we still have no proof."

"What are you going to do?"

"For starters, I'm going to show this photo to Max and Kat."

"You think the doctor was one of the members of the Prophecy," she said, making him smile.

"Another reason I can't keep you out of the loop on this. I need that brain of yours. And, at this point, this is not a sheriff's department investigation. Once it is…"

Nettie nodded. "I know. Back to being nothing but a store clerk."

He got out of his chair to kiss her. "You are much more than a store clerk, and we both know it."

"I like solving mysteries with you."

"I know," he said. "I like it, too. I've been thinking about that."

"Oh, yeah?"

Frank smiled at her. "We'll talk about it one day soon."

"This is it?" Max asked as he looked out at the valley.

"Excuse me, I suppose you had a better place to make out?"

"The beach."

Kat made a face. "Sand."

He laughed. "I said make out, not—"

"I get the picture."

He turned to look out at the valley again. "It must be pretty at night up here with the lights of town in the distance."

Kat couldn't tell if he was being serious or not. "It beats where my parents first made out. They went to the West Yellowstone dump. They sat in the dark and waited for the bears to come out."

Max laughed, smiling over at her. "And then what?"

"About the time the bars in town closed, the grizzlies would chase away the black bears. Everyone who was parked at the edge of the dump would turn on their headlights and watch the grizzlies dig in the garbage."

"You Montanans really are a romantic bunch."

She punched him playfully in the shoulder, and he grabbed her wrist and pulled her to him. His kiss was pure sugar.

He drew back. "Not so sure about this making out in an SUV with a center console."

"That's why we always got in the backseat," Kat said, almost shyly.

Max laughed. "You minx, you. Come on."

They both jumped out and climbed into the back of the SUV. "I hope you pulled up the emergency brake. I'd hate to go careening off this hill in case this car gets to rockin'."

"You aren't seriously thinking—"

He made her swallow the rest as he pulled her to him and kissed her again. "We're just making out," he said, meeting her eyes.

Kat felt tears prick her eyes. He knew. Somehow, he knew; that was why he was taking it slow. That and maybe he was as scared as she was, she thought. Both ideas endeared him all the more to her.

He drew her close again. The kiss was still sweet but hot. She felt passion make a wild gallop through her veins as he deepened it. She leaned into him, into the kiss. Again desire rippled over her skin and warmed her clear to her center. It had been so long. She had wondered if she could ever feel this again. If she would ever want another man.

Max was breathing hard as he pulled back to slip his hand up under her shirt. She arched against his warm fingers as his hand slid under her bra and cupped her breast. Her nipple was hard and aching. He brushed gently over it as he kissed her again.

Her cell phone rang, and she groaned as he pulled his hand free and drew back. "You'd better take that. It could be important."

She wanted to argue that whatever it was, she didn't care. But when she checked the screen, she saw that it was the sheriff. Getting control of her breath and straightening her clothes, she sat up and hit Accept on her phone. She felt like a schoolgirl caught doing something she shouldn't be doing.

"Sheriff Curry?" she asked, a half dozen different fears running through her head.

"Kat, I think I know where your mother has been the past twenty-two years. I have a photograph of her with a man I'd like you to take a look at. Also, do you know how I can reach Max?"

"Max is right here. We'll come into your office," she said, glancing over at Max. He looked as disappointed as she felt and yet equally as curious as to what had happened now. "We can be there in twenty minutes."

MAX COULDN'T WAIT to see the photo Kat told him the sheriff was anxious to show them. "So he thinks he knows where your mother has been. Do you think the man is another...husband?"

"That would certainly make things interesting, wouldn't it?" she said as she pulled up in front of the sheriff's department and cut the engine.

Max reached over and squeezed her arm. "I loved your make-out spot, by the way." It had been the same pinnacle from where he'd gotten lucky with the photographs of the senator and Sarah Hamilton. "But I doubt you and I are going to make it back there."

She glanced over at him questioningly.

He grinned. "I don't want our first time to be in the back of a car." With that he opened his door and got out. When he looked over the hood of the SUV in her direction, she was smiling to herself. He felt his heart go out to her and again wondered who'd hurt her. Maybe one day she'd tell him.

The sheriff was waiting for them in his office. Max closed the door behind them and took one of the chairs offered. Kat took the other.

"You said you have a photo?" Kat gripped her purse in her lap as if it was a life raft and she was lost at sea. Max wished there was some way he could make all of this easier for her. His attraction to her probably wasn't helping. His timing couldn't have been worse, given everything else she was going through.

The sheriff pushed a colored snapshot across the table. Kat seemed surprised. Max had to admit, he was, too. Somehow he'd expected to see "Red," with her red hair and possibly a few assault rifles in the shot. Instead it was an attractive blonde and an older man, both dressed in white lab coats in what appeared to be a hospital or clinic.

"Is that your mother?" the sheriff asked, even though all three of them could see that clearly it was.

Kat nodded. "Who is the man?"

"Dr. Ralph Venable. I understand that your mother was his assistant."

Kat looked up in surprise. "You mean like a… nurse?"

"Probably not. Dr. Venable was a psychiatrist."

"This photograph doesn't look like it was taken in the United States," Max said.

"It was taken in Brazil."

"Brazil?" Kat shook her head as she stared again at the photo. "So this was where my mother was all these years? Working at a clinic for a psychiatrist?"

The sheriff nodded. "They'd both been there twenty years. Until recently."

"When my mother returned. And the man?"

"We don't know where he is."

Max felt the sheriff's gaze on him as he took the photo from Kat and studied it closer.

"Do you recognize the man?" the lawman asked.

"He's older than in the other photograph, but, yes, he was in the photo we saw of the Prophecy," Max said. Older than the others, he was the man who had looked like a professor.

Kat looked over at him. "I thought he looked familiar," she said, her gaze going from him to the sheriff. "This is the proof you need."

Frank Curry sat back in his chair as he shook his head. "Without the other photograph...all we have is your mother working at a clinic in Brazil with a doctor who used to work at a clinic here in the state."

Max was quickly stringing the pieces of information together. "This is the man who picked her up that night after her failed suicide attempt."

The sheriff shook his head, apparently not surprised that he knew about that. "We're still not sure who picked her up that night, but we suspect he took her to a clinic here in the state where the doctor was working. That clinic closed down just days later, and both the doctor and Sarah Hamilton disappeared. But we have no proof of that either."

He could see that the sheriff wasn't comfortable sharing this information with him, a reporter, but he had needed them to confirm that the man in the photo was part of the Prophecy.

"If this makes it any easier on you, I'm not planning to write anything about this until I can verify all of it. By then, I suspect, you'll have half of the members in jail," he told the lawman.

"I hope you're right about the terrorists being in jail soon. Also, I did some checking on you. You have a reputation for reporting facts—not rumors." The sheriff glanced at Kat and back to Max as if he suspected there were also feelings growing between them. Another reason Max wouldn't be writing about any of this.

"So we don't know where this man is or what he is to my mother?" Kat asked.

"No." The sheriff seemed to study them for a moment. Max hoped that he'd alleviated the man's fears about talking to them. "Dr. Venable could be responsible for your mother's memory loss. While in Montana, he was allegedly doing research on brain wiping."

Max let out a low whistle. This just kept getting better and better. The reporter in him began to salivate. This was going to be one hell of a story—if he ever got to write it.

"Brain wiping?" Kat asked.

The sheriff explained what he'd learned about the process. Max had heard about it and knew that it was possible, but as far as he knew, it hadn't been used on humans yet.

"The memories can be replaced?" Kat asked.

"Yes," the sheriff said. "But they can also be replaced with…false ones."

"What did my mother get herself into?" she lamented. "These people…"

Max sympathized with her, but he had a feeling her mother had been a willing participant in all of it. Hell, this all could have been Sarah's plan—if it was true that she was the real leader of the terrorist group.

The sheriff got to his feet and reached for the snapshot of Sarah and Dr. Venable. "Thank you both for coming in. I think it's best if we keep all of this among ourselves."

"You have to tell my father," Kat said. "He has to know."

Nodding, the sheriff said, "All this photograph proves is that your mother worked with a man named Dr. Ralph Venable in a Brazil clinic. If anything, I would imagine your father will be relieved to find out what she was doing those lost years."

Kat groaned as if she, too, realized how this would play out. It appeared that nothing was now standing in the way of the senator and Sarah getting back together—except for his bid for the presidency.

"Has your father mentioned yet whether or not he plans to continue to run for president?" the sheriff asked Kat.

She shook her head. "He'd planned to announce his decision after the funeral. At least that's what he told one of my sisters."

CHAPTER TWENTY-TWO

"HOW COULD THIS get any worse?" Kat said as they left the sheriff's office. "This is totally bizarre. What are we going to do?"

Out of the corner of her eye, she saw Max look at his watch. "You're going to drop me off so I can pick up my truck. Then I am going back to my motel room to shower and change. You are going home and changing into your sexiest dress—"

"I don't—"

"Have a sexy dress," he finished for her with a laugh. "Let me retract that and start again. You are going to borrow a dress from one of your sisters that makes you feel sexy. How's that?"

She swallowed.

"Then I am going to come out to the ranch and pick you up. You and I are going on our first real date."

Kat started to argue that she was in no mood for this, but he cut her off.

"We are going out to dinner and then we are going dancing."

"I don't—"

"Dance." He laughed. "You do now. My pickup." He motioned for her to drive as he looked at his watch again. "I'll pick you up at six. Blue, definitely blue."

"Blue what?"

"A blue dress. Like that swimsuit you wore in California." He grinned. "It brings out something in those gray eyes of yours. Makes them shine."

She swallowed again. The things this man could make her feel with nothing more than a few words. "Fine, but I really don't dance."

MAX WENT BACK to his motel and got on his new laptop. Both of his laptops had been stolen, no doubt for his notes. Since he had his own type of shorthand, he doubted whoever had taken them could understand any of it.

Today, the reporter in him had his mind racing. He found the article that had alerted him to the photo of the Prophecy in the first place. The photo was grainy, out of register, which made it look out of focus, and pretty much worthless as far as offering any kind of identification. But he could still make out the older of the men on the right side of the picture.

He quickly scanned the article for the names the group went by. The Prophecy had definitely stylized themselves after the Symbionese Liberation Army. The SLA had rejected their given names for revolutionary names; so had the Prophecy. The SLA had used a seven-headed cobra as its symbol, while the Prophecy had used a pendulum.

He quickly emailed the story to the sheriff with a note saying,

Here is the story and photograph I found. The photo first ran in this now extinct small free paper and was later sold to a larger paper in LA where it recently disappeared. But you will note that the paper ran the revolutionary names of the members. Your Dr. Venable was called Médico, Portuguese for doctor. Had he done some internship down there before he and Sarah disappeared?

Max sat back after he finished sending the email. His fingers itched to see what he could find on Dr. Ralph Venable, but he knew that the sheriff had already done that and had even better resources than Max did. Still, he wanted to dig. He'd always loved the investigative part of his job more than even the writing.

He reminded himself that this particular story involved a woman he cared about—and he had a date. Shutting the laptop, he headed for the shower. As the water warmed up, he stripped down, thinking about earlier, him and Kat on that hillside with the valley stretched before them. He laughed to himself, surprised at the joy he felt. He'd always loved his job and gotten a lot of pleasure out of it.

Sure he'd dated, but sporadically, since he was never in one spot for very long. It had always been easy to leave those women behind. This one…

Just the thought of her required him to turn the shower to cold as he stepped in. He had to take this slowly. For Kat. For himself. He couldn't love and leave this one. For Kat's sake. For his own. This time was different. That alone scared him. If he was serious about her…it would mean his life would change. He wouldn't want to be gone all the time, let alone risk his life in some country on the other side of the world. He would want to stay closer to home. Closer to her. Was he really ready for a job as a reporter closer to home?

KAT FOUND THE DRESS in her sister Livie's closet. Her siblings had moved out of the condo complex their father had built for them on the ranch, but they'd left behind clothes they either didn't want or didn't have room to store where they were now living.

She took the dress from the closet over to the full-length mirror and held it up to mold to her body, curious what this color blue did to her gray eyes.

"Max is full of beans," she said to the image in the mirror. Then she looked a little closer. "Well, my eyes might be a little bluer than gray." But she wasn't even sure of that.

Her heart began to beat a little faster as she slipped on the dress. She and her sisters had all been about the same size when it came to clothes. They'd often worn each others' over the years growing up—which had caused trouble among them. But right now, Kat was thankful that her sisters all had great taste in clothing.

She took a breath and looked into the mirror. Her hair, usually bound in a knot at the back of her neck, was pulled up in a loose casual way she'd seen Bo do dozens of times. She'd found a pair of silver earrings she'd forgotten she had in her own unit of the complex and borrowed just a dab of her sister Ainsley's perfume. It was citrusy and light.

Kat had felt a little silly when she'd dug through the makeup Livie had left, but now as she looked in the mirror, she felt a shock ripple through her. She looked…good. Pretty. And that alone scared her. She hadn't dressed like this in years and she couldn't help remembering where it had gotten her.

Shoving away that awful image, she thought of Max

instead. That seemed to steady her. She could trust him. At the sound of a vehicle, she stepped away from the mirror to look out the window. Max's old black pickup came up the road and parked out front. Kat took one more look at herself before she slipped her feet into high-heeled shoes.

You're asking for it dressed like that.

She shuddered at the sound of the sneering male voice in her head, the words coming back to her from that long-ago night. She had the sudden urge to rush into the bathroom, wash off the makeup, get out of these clothes and curl up in a ball.

That's what he wants you to do.

This voice, though, sounded like Max's. Kind, loving, sensible Max.

Kat straightened as the doorbell rang. *I can do this.*

THE SHERIFF LOOKED again at the photo and called Buckmaster Hamilton.

"If this is about some fool thing my daughter and her reporter friend have come up with…" the senator said, already sounding upset.

"No." Kat and Max had told him about Buckmaster's reaction to the information they'd gathered about Sarah and the Prophecy. He wasn't stupid enough to try to convince the senator of that—especially without something to back it up. The online story Max had sent him was definitely an eye-opener, but the photo was too grainy to be of help. Anyone could argue that the woman looked nothing like the Sarah Hamilton they all knew.

"I have some information that might be of help," Frank said. "Do you want me to come to you—"

"I'm on my way into town to make arrangements for the service," the senator said brusquely. "I'll stop by your office as soon as I get there. But this better not be—"

"I think you'll be pleased with what I've found out."

Less than twenty minutes later—which meant the senator would have had to break speed laws to get there that quickly—Buckmaster walked in the door.

Frank knew better than to dillydally, given the mood the man was in. He slid the photograph across the table. Buckmaster stepped forward, picked it up and started to say something but stopped. No doubt he'd recognized his wife. In the photo, Sarah looked much like she had twenty-two years ago, making Frank think it was taken soon after she was believed dead, and she and Dr. Venable went to Brazil.

"Where did you get this?" the senator demanded.

"If you would like to sit down, I would be happy to explain."

With clear reluctance, the big man pulled out a chair.

"There have been some interesting twists and turns when it comes to your former wife," Frank began. "Actually, it was Russell Murdock who came up with a possible explanation for her loss of memory."

Buckmaster made a distasteful face but didn't interrupt.

"There was a doctor in Montana at the time of Sarah's disappearance." He was watching the senator's face closely. "He was experimenting on a technique called brain wiping."

"Brain wiping." Buckmaster shook his head in obvious disgust.

"I know it sounds crazy, more like a science-fiction

movie, but there are actually studies that the brain can be wiped of memories and then those memories replaced again. Or false memories used to fill those missing ones. The man in that photograph with Sarah was running these experiments at a clinic not far from here right before Sarah disappeared."

"Have you all gone crazy?" The senator got to his feet, but he didn't leave. He paced back and forth in front of Frank's desk. "I have enough on my mind without—"

"A woman matching Sarah's description showed up at the clinic in the wee hours of the morning the night she apparently tried to kill herself. That woman knew the doctor. She stayed there only a few days, and then she and the doctor disappeared, the clinic closing. That was twenty-two years ago. That photo in your hands came from a town in Brazil. The doctor and Sarah have been working in a clinic down there for the past twenty years."

Buckmaster stopped pacing. He glanced at the photo again, before slowly lowering himself into the chair again. "Why wouldn't Sarah remember this?" he asked, looking up from the photo.

The sheriff shook his head. "I could only speculate."

"That this doctor you're saying she knew wiped her memory? Why would he do that? What would either of them want to hide?"

Frank said nothing. He could see the wheels spinning in the senator's brain.

"You think they were working on this brain wiping down there?"

"I don't know. All I know is that according to the doctor from Brazil who sent the photo, the two of them had been working there."

"So where is this doctor?" Buckmaster demanded.

"We don't know. What we do know is that he was involved with a group called the Prophecy."

The senator shot to his feet again. "I spoke to Sarah about this. She was never part of this…terrorist group."

Frank didn't have to say anything. Buckmaster was a smart man. He could put it all together just as easily as Frank had.

"For some reason these people are trying to set her up," the senator argued. "And if there was a chance in hell that she was somehow involved with them, then she was indoctrinated by the male members of the group and she only played a minor role. She was just a kid back then. She wouldn't have known what she was doing."

Frank could see that that was what Buckmaster needed to believe. "We may never know. But I think there is a reason Sarah came back. Just as there is a reason, I believe, this doctor is on his way back to the States."

"Because I'm running for president," the senator said quietly.

"Under ordinary circumstances, you would be provided with security once you were a major presidential candidate, but that security would only be for one hundred and twenty days from the general presidential election." Frank hurried on, seeing that the senator was about to decline. "I would strongly suggest contacting the Secretary of Homeland Security. It is my understanding that he can make arrangements to provide Secret Service protection to commence before that, given the circumstances."

Buckmaster shook his head. "I am not taking this

speculation about my wife…my former wife…to any Homeland Security secretary. You don't have an ounce of proof, or you wouldn't be coming to me with this. You would be talking to the FBI who have already found no reason to investigate Sarah. Isn't that what you told me?"

Frank could have argued that, yes, it was all circumstantial, but once added up together—

"Damn it, Frank, do you really think Sarah is a threat to me?" Buckmaster asked, his voice sounding as tired as he looked.

The sheriff chose his words carefully. "I believe this group, the Prophecy, is a threat, yes. I believe they plan to harm you or manipulate you or kill you either after you become the Republican party candidate or, more likely, after you are elected president."

"Based on what?" the senator demanded.

"Based on everything we know about Sarah and the Prophecy."

"Well, you're wrong about her." Buckmaster raked a hand through his graying hair. He looked older, more road worn and sad. Frank could see that he didn't want to believe any of this. "Hell, that group of misfit antigovernment radicals are in their late fifties or early sixties now. Maybe they were young and idealistic in the '70s, but they can't be organized enough to pull something like this off. Not with all the security that will be—"

"But if Sarah is at your side, Senator, when you make your acceptance speech, security won't be expecting her to be the one who kills you, though."

Buckmaster looked as if he might bust a gasket. "Sarah would never hurt me."

Frank got to his feet, seeing that this meeting was over. "Just know that you're staking your life on that. By the way, where is Sarah staying now? I understand she broke her engagement to Russell Murdock."

For a moment he didn't think Buckmaster would tell him. Frank already had a pretty good idea that Sarah would be moving back to Hamilton Ranch once Angelina Broadwater Hamilton was laid to rest.

"Not that it is any of your business, but Sarah is staying in one of the houses on the ranch where I can make sure she's safe." Buckmaster sighed, all the anger going out of him. "You have no idea how hard this is. I'm trying here."

"I know you are. You feel responsible for Sarah. I understand that."

"I love her. I've always loved her." The admission quickly embarrassed the senator. He ducked his head and turned toward the door.

"I have to ask you, Senator. Are you thinking of pulling out of the race? It might be the only way you can save your life."

Buckmaster stopped in the doorway, his back to him. "If you're right about Sarah and the Prophecy, if I quit the race, then Sarah will bail on me like I'm a runaway mustang."

Frank couldn't help himself. "She does have experience with parachutes."

"I'll be announcing my plans after the funeral."

MAX COULDN'T BELIEVE his eyes when Kat opened the door. "Wow. You steal my breath. You look beautiful."

She glanced away as if embarrassed. "Is it too much?"

"No. You're perfect." She wore a blue dress that

gently hugged her curves. It broke his heart that she'd been hiding this woman, apparently for years. He was just glad she'd let Kat Hamilton out for the evening.

He'd picked an expensive restaurant on the Yellowstone River. Only the best tonight. He hoped it would take her mind off her mother. The funeral was tomorrow. There would be media people around the cemetery, even though the service was closed to them. The senator would be holding a press conference at the ranch.

Earlier Max had run into old-time print reporter Harvey Duncan out by the ranch gate.

"I see you've found a way into the inner sanctum," Harvey had commented with a wink. "Anything you'd like to share with your former outside-the-fence buddy?"

Max had shaken his head. "Funeral and press conference tomorrow, then I would imagine the senator will return to DC and his campaign for president."

"He's not quitting, like his old man did after he lost *his* wife?" Harvey had asked. Buckmaster's father had also made a run for president, but had withdrawn shortly after his wife died. Like his son, he was said to have been a shoo-in.

"Not that I know of. I would imagine you'll know when I do." He'd given Harvey a wink back and driven on through the gate.

Now he studied the amazing woman across the restaurant table from him. "You seem nervous."

Kat started to open her mouth to deny it, but he stopped her as he leaned forward and whispered, "If you're worried about what's going to happen after I wine and dine you, don't be."

She looked up from her menu.

"It's not going to happen tonight. Though you are so beautiful…"

"If you don't mind me asking, why not?" she whispered back, making him smile.

"You should know something about me. I joke around a lot. But I'm a pretty serious guy about some things. My job. My truck. My lucky boots." Which he just happened to be wearing tonight. "Making love."

KAT FELT HEAT work its way up her throat at his words spoken so softly. His eyes were locked with hers. This was definitely the serious Max Malone.

"Because I don't take it lightly, I'm not going to rush this. If it is supposed to happen, it will, trust me. In the meantime—" he picked up his wineglass and held it up as if to toast "—I like just being here with you."

"Me, too," she said and picked up her wineglass to tap it against his. "To serious business."

He chuckled. "I like you, Kat Hamilton."

"There is one thing that bothers me. You mentioned how you take your job seriously. Max, you aren't working."

"I can afford to take a break from it."

"Come on, I know you must be going crazy, sitting on a story like this."

He smiled at her, clearly glad she understood him. "Kat, you know I can't break this without proof."

She put her glass down carefully. "Are you looking for it when you aren't with me?"

He put down his glass, as well. She regretted changing the light, fun mood, but she had to know.

"I'll admit it's hard not to chase this to find one

thing that I could write that would bust it wide-open and expose—" his gaze met hers "—your mother. But that's where it gets tricky. I don't want to hurt you or your family. The truth will eventually come out, I'm afraid, but I may not be the one who writes it."

"Maybe if you did a story, it would stop them."

He laughed. "I'm good, Kat, but not that good that I could stop terrorists. We still don't know who they are or what they have planned. At least we know the sheriff will do what he can. Meanwhile…"

Her cell phone pinged, announcing a text. She reached for it to shut it off, when she saw that it was from her sister Ainsley.

"Oh, no," she said as she looked up at Max. "It's my sister Livie. She's in labor at the hospital. I have to—"

"Get there right away," Max said and placed his napkin on the table. "Let's go."

"I'm so sorry about dinner."

He smiled. "There will be another time."

Kat groaned inwardly. "Even though you said it wasn't going to happen tonight—" her gaze met his "—I wouldn't have minded if it had."

He grinned. "I was just trying to get you to relax during dinner. Otherwise I would have had that dress off you so fast…"

She had to laugh, knowing that when it happened, Max would take his time. He knew somehow that she would be scared. "This is getting ridiculous. I feel like fate is determined to keep us apart."

"You have a point. But if I have anything to do with it, we aren't going to let fate win, trust me."

CHAPTER TWENTY-THREE

BUCKMASTER WASN'T ABOUT to tell the sheriff that Sarah was the one insisting he stay in the race. He reassured himself that he should be relieved by what Frank had told him. He now knew where Sarah had been the past twenty years. He'd imagined all kinds of crazy scenarios. She could have remarried, had other children, lived on the street, had to compromise herself to survive...

He pushed that thought away as he recalled what he'd learned about the Prophecy. According to the sheriff, she'd done worse things than he ever had imagined—and not in the missing twenty-two years, but before that.

Did he even know the woman he'd had six daughters with?

"Dad?"

He turned as he came in the front door to find Harper waiting for him.

"Where have you been?" his daughter demanded. "We've all been trying to reach you."

"I turned off my phone when I..." When he'd gone in to see the sheriff, and he hadn't turned it back on. "Why? What's happened?"

His beautiful blonde, blue-eyed daughter quickly stepped to him. "Don't panic. It's Livie. She's having her baby. We need to get to the hospital. I told the others to go ahead and I would wait for you."

His first grandchild. His and *Sarah's* first grandchild. He started to reach for his phone to call her but stopped himself. His loyalties had been divided for months now. He still didn't know where Sarah fit into their family's lives. Now her first grandchild was being born. She should be there.

He shook his head, feeling the bitterness he still felt from her betrayal. She'd left him. Left their family. Even though he couldn't deny that he still had feelings for her, she'd given up her rights.

And if what the sheriff had told him was even a possibility...

"Let's hurry," he said to Harper. "I'm going to let you drive." He was still shaken from everything that had happened over the past few days.

"This is so exciting," Harper said. "You're going to be a grandfather," she said and laughed.

Again he thought of Sarah. This was *her* daughter, *her* grandbaby. He pulled out his cell phone.

"Are you calling Mother?" she asked.

"Don't you think I should?"

Harper nodded. "Tell her to meet us at the hospital."

Of course their mother *should* be there. This was *Sarah's* daughter, *Sarah's* grandbaby. He hit her number on his cell phone. She could meet them at the hospital. She would want to be there.

Maybe more important, he *wanted* her there. He thought of all the years when he'd wished for her to be by his side when he was raising the girls. Now she could be.

How could he overcome his doubts about her,

though? He realized that when he was with her, he didn't have any reservations about them being together again. He was sick of having doubts about her.

"THIS IS FAMILY," Max said. "I'll drop you off at the hospital."

"The funeral is tomorrow. Will you go with me? I would really appreciate it."

How could he say no? "If it's what you want."

While he was a freelancer, he didn't have an editor breathing down his neck for a story. But he had been getting calls from publications that wondered what he was doing and if he had anything for them.

After he dropped Kat off, he was too antsy to go back to his motel. He'd hoped that tonight might be the night, but as he'd told her, he wasn't going to push it for a lot of reasons. Once they made love, he knew there would be no going back. Was he really ready for that?

He drove around for a while and found himself in Beartooth. He pulled into the Range Rider bar, parked and went in, needing a drink. Taking a stool at the bar, he ordered a beer. He was staring at the label when a man pulled up a stool next to him.

"I know that look. There's a woman behind it," the man said and offered his hand. "Brody McTavish."

Normally he would have preferred to be alone. But tonight he didn't mind visiting with a local. He'd seen this rancher around. "Max Malone. How'd you guess I was thinking about a woman?"

"Some say because I'm Irish, I'm a little psychic."

The bartender, a man about their age, shook his head and said, "Don't believe anything Brody tells you. It's the Irish that makes him a good storyteller."

As the bartender went to the other end of the bar to help some other locals from the looks of them, Brody said, "I'm a good friend of Jace Calder."

"Ah," Max said and laughed. "Jace, who is engaged to Bo Hamilton, the sister of Kat."

Brody chuckled. "I heard you were smart. The Hamiltons are a fine bunch. I'd hate to see any of them hurt."

Max studied him for a moment. "So which one are you in love with?" he asked as he picked up his beer.

"I didn't say—"

"I'm a little psychic myself," he said and took a drink before flashing Brody a smile. "I'm suspecting it's not Kat, or you wouldn't have been as friendly when you started this conversation. So that leaves Ainsley. Nope. It's one of the twins."

Brody laughed. "You *are* psychic. Tom," he called to the bartender. "Give my friend here another beer, and while you're at it…"

"I haven't seen you around the ranch," Max said as the bartender set a beer in front of each of them. "So I suspect that whichever Hamilton girl you're carrying a torch for, she doesn't know how you feel."

Brody laughed. "Let's talk about you and Kat."

"Right now, there is no me and Kat. We're friends. More than friends, but there's a few roadblocks."

"Which was why you were staring into your beer as if it were a crystal ball," Brody said and raised his bottle to clink it against Max's. "To knocking down those roadblocks on the way to happy-ever-after."

"An Irish romantic." Max shook his head. He liked this rancher. "You need to tell her how you feel."

Brody laughed. "If only it were that easy. Have you

told Kat how you feel? I didn't think so. To cowards," he said and took a drink of his beer.

OLIVIA "LIVIE" HAMILTON BARNETT had her baby at nine that night. A healthy baby boy named Cooper James Barnett, Jr. after his father. He became C.J. Kat couldn't believe how small he was.

"You've always had to do everything first since we were kids," Bo had joked. "First one kissed, first one—"

"Bo, not in front of my son," Livie had cried.

"—married, first one to have a baby," Bo finished. Jace had put his arm around his soon-to-be wife and said, "There is nothing wrong with second place." Everyone laughed. It was no secret that Bo and Jace would want to start their family right away.

Kat stood back from the rest of her family, just taking them all in. As sisters growing up, they'd fought like wild mountain lion cubs. But when things got tough, they'd always pulled together as a family. She felt a swell of pride, seeing them all together.

And then her mother entered the room.

She realized then that her father had been watching the door. He'd been expecting her because he'd invited her. Of course she would want to see her first grandchild, but Kat still couldn't help feeling angry. The woman had no right. Now that they knew about her...

She reminded herself that her mother didn't remember any of that. Or at least that's what she wanted them to believe.

The others greeted Sarah as her father hurried to her, taking her hand and leading her over to the bed so she could see C.J.

Kat wanted to blurt out who Sarah Johnson Hamilton really was, what she really was, as she picked up the baby. C.J. began to cry, and Sarah quickly handed him back to his mother.

"Kat," Livie called to her. "You haven't gotten to hold C.J. yet."

She shook her head. "I'll hold him some other time. I might be coming down with a cold." It was a lie, but right now, she couldn't be a part of this happy family scene—not with her mother in it.

No one seemed to notice her as she left the room. On the way down the hall, she passed a man in a sheriff's department uniform. She heard him ask at the nurse's station where Livie's room was.

"I'm actually looking for her father, Senator Buckmaster Hamilton."

The nurse told him he would have to wait.

THE MOMENT BUCK saw Sarah, all he could think about was getting her alone so they could talk.

As his daughters were oohing and aahing over the baby, he signaled for Sarah to step out of the room with him. Once out in the hall, he led her to a nearby empty waiting room.

"You're a grandmother," he said once he had her alone.

She smiled and nodded. "He's so tiny. So perfect." There were tears in her eyes. "It reminds me of the twins when they were born."

Her last memory of their life together. Buck didn't like being reminded of all the years Sarah had been gone, all that she'd missed. He felt that old bitterness. He'd cursed her to hell for taking her life. He could well imagine how he would have felt back then if he'd known that she was alive, but didn't want to be with him or her own children.

He studied her for a long moment, wondering if he could overcome all those ill feelings. More to the point, if he could ever trust her. Still, when he looked at her, love was the overwhelming emotion he felt. In time, he told himself they could make this work. They could be a family again.

"Sarah, is there anything you need? I had the house cleaned and stocked with groceries, but if there is—"

"I'm fine, Buck," she said, stepping to him and putting a hand on his arm. "All I need is you."

He flinched, her touch like an electrical shock. He quickly took her hand in his and pulled her closer. "We're going to be together. Somehow—"

"I don't mean to interrupt."

They both turned to find a man in a Silverbow County sheriff's uniform standing in the doorway, holding a cup of vending-machine coffee.

Buck knew at once that the sheriff had been standing there for some time, listening to their conversation.

"Can I help you?" he demanded as he stepped away from Sarah.

"I certainly hope so, Senator. I need to ask you a few questions about your wife. Your *deceased* wife, Angelina Hamilton." He said the last as if to remind Buck. As if he needed more reminding.

"This is Sarah Hamilton, my former wife," he said to the sheriff, hating that he felt he needed to try to explain what the man had seen. "We have just become the proud grandparents of our first grandchild."

"Congratulations," the sheriff said and tipped his

hat to Sarah. "If I could have a few minutes of your time, Senator?"

"We really have to do this now?" Buck asked, unable to hide his irritation. He'd hoped to spend a little time with Sarah away from prying eyes.

"I'm afraid so. I would have called, but under the circumstances, I drove down to do it in person."

"Under what circumstances?" Buck asked, feeling his mouth go dry.

The sheriff looked pointedly at Sarah, who quickly excused herself.

Buck swore under his breath as the sheriff closed the waiting room door and took a long drink of his coffee before he spoke. "Care to sit down?"

"No, I'd like to get back to my daughters and my new grandbaby."

The sheriff nodded. "We found that private investigator your wife hired."

"Then she told you why Angelina hired her."

"Nope. She wasn't doing much talking. She was murdered."

Buck changed his mind and sat down.

CHAPTER TWENTY-FOUR

WIND KICKED UP fallen dried leaves and whirled them through the cemetery. Clouds scudded past in a watercolor-washed blue sky. Kat breathed in the scent of the autumn day as they climbed from the funeral home's limousine.

Max had come along, although her father hadn't been happy about it.

"He's a *reporter*," he'd complained. "Do we really need one with us? They'll be all around the cemetery as it is."

"He isn't here to report on the funeral. He's here for me."

Her father had studied her as if it was the first time he'd actually seen her for a while. He'd taken in her clothing and then shaken his head as if he was confused. She'd worn a black dress she'd found in her sister Ainsley's closet at the condos, along with black pumps and a scarf. Her hair was up as it had been on her date with Max last night. Silver hoops hung from each ear. She'd dabbed on just a little makeup.

"I see," her father had said and smiled. "Then I'm happy he's here for you."

She and Max walked with the others over to the open grave where the pastor was waiting for them. Max took her hand as the graveside service started.

Only a few of her relatives from the Broadwater family had come to pay their last respects. Music had played and her father had said a few words about Angelina. What a dedicated wife she'd been. How strong and determined she was. How she'd worked tirelessly at his side.

Earlier at the church, the pastor had talked about Angelina's service to the community. Now the pastor said a prayer over the casket. Kat was glad it was almost over. None of them other than her father had been close to Angelina. The Ice Queen had been a cold woman who had never wanted anything to do with Kat or her sisters. The only thing she'd ever wanted was to live in the White House, and now she wouldn't.

That thought made Kat sad. Angelina had died before her dream had come true. She watched her father drop a handful of dirt on the casket, and they all walked away to leave the groundskeepers to it.

Her father would look sad in the shots the photographers along the edge of the cemetery would take with their telephoto lenses. To her, he looked both sad and guilty. He'd loved Angelina, but probably not enough.

"Are you okay?" Max asked. He was still holding her hand as they neared the limousine.

A gust of wind whipped a lock of his hair over one blue eye. Instinctively, she reached over to brush it aside. "Thank you for being here."

"Whatever you need."

"You know what I need," she said, meeting his gaze.

"Then you've got it."

"But first," Kat said, "there's something we have to do."

AFTER THE FUNERAL all Buckmaster had wanted was to get back to the ranch. He'd gotten a call before that from Sarah. She remembered a back way into the ranch and would meet him at the house. They had to talk, she said.

"Harper, Cassidy and Ainsley and I are going to lunch," Bo had told him as they were leaving the funeral home. "Come along."

He'd declined. "I didn't sleep much last night. I really just want to go home. But you girls have a nice lunch. The worst is over now." But even as he thought it, he worried that wasn't true. What did Sarah want to talk to him about that she needed to be waiting at the main house?

For days he'd felt as if he was in a stupor. As if he was sleepwalking through dense fog, wanting out and yet afraid of waking up and seeing what lay beyond. He was still in shock after hearing that the investigator Angelina had hired was dead. *Murdered.* How long would it take the sheriff to find out that Addison Crenshaw wasn't the first PI Angelina had hired? Or the first one to die while under her employ?

At the ranch, he called out for Sarah. Her name echoed through the house, giving him a strange chill. The short staff he now kept had the day off. He stepped to the bar in his den and poured himself a drink since Sarah apparently hadn't arrived yet.

Two dead private investigators. Both had been looking into Sarah's past.

He wanted to write it off to coincidence, but—

"Dad, are you all right?"

He turned to find his oldest daughter standing in

the doorway. "Ainsley, I thought you went to lunch with your sisters."

"I was worried about you."

"You shouldn't worry about me. I'm going to be fine." He could see that she had something on her mind. "That man who was following you..."

Ainsley shook her head. "I haven't seen him again."

"Good," he said, relieved. So that wasn't what was bothering her?

"You aren't going to pull out of the race, are you?" she asked.

He raised his drink, offering her one. When she declined, he moved over to a chair and sat down. "I have a press conference in an hour. I'd rather not talk about it until then."

"I saw you with mother," she said as she joined him.

So that was it.

"Angelina said that if you got back with Mother, you wouldn't be able to win."

He nodded. "Angelina said a lot of things. But that was before... Truthfully, Ainsley, I don't know what I'm going to do. My staff is chomping at the bit for me to announce my plans."

"What part of your decision has to do with Mother?"

He looked over at her, surprised, but he shouldn't have been. Ainsley was the smart one when it came to people. She didn't miss much. That's why she'd always been so good with her sisters. She could settle their feuds, comfort them, cajole them, chastise them, and they adored her. He'd always depended on her because of that.

"I'm still in love with Sarah," he said simply and stopped himself from saying that love was blind, that loving her scared him. "But whether we can be together again..." He shook his head. "I will always take care of her."

"If you drop out of the race, you could marry her. The rest of the world be damned."

He laughed, since her words sounded so much like his own thoughts. "I could do that. But sometimes you have to look further than your own needs. Last night I held my first grandson in my arms. I'm worried about the world he will find when he grows up. You girls are one reason I got into politics to begin with. I wanted to make a difference in your lives, in your children's lives."

"You still want that?"

"More than anything," he said and seemed to step out of the haze that had blurred everything for days.

"More than my mother?"

At the sound of the front door opening, Buckmaster braced himself. Sarah?

KAT COULD SEE that she and Max had interrupted whatever her sister Ainsley and their father had been talking about.

"I need to take off and get back to my job scouting movie locations. I'm actually really enjoying it," Ainsley said, giving her father a hug and then Kat. "It was nice to meet you, Max, despite the circumstances."

"Same here," he said.

"I have a feeling we'll be seeing more of you around here," Ainsley said, shooting Kat a grin before she left.

"What are you two up to?" Buckmaster asked, not sounding in the least happy to see them.

"I know you don't believe anything that we told

you about Mother," Kat said, seeing no reason to beat around the bush. "If you can't stay away from her, then, please, Dad, drop out of the election. Mother says she never wanted to live in the White House anyway. If true, then the two of you can live happily here on the ranch for the rest of your lives."

Her father looked sad and disappointed. "You're still that convinced your mother is…dangerous."

"Yes, I am," Kat said.

"I spoke to Sarah about all this. I'll admit there are some things that give me pause. But I appreciate you worrying about me."

Kat could see that was as good as it was going to get. "I just don't want anything to happen to you."

"I know, sweetheart." He hugged her and shook Max's hand. "Don't worry. I'm going to make the right decision for all of us."

SARAH HEARD KAT and Max leave before she came out of where she'd been hiding. As she stepped into Buck's den, he looked up.

"You heard all of that," he said, no doubt seeing her expression. "I'm so sorry."

She shook her head as she closed the door behind her. "My daughter thinks I'm a terrorist. Maybe she's right. Maybe I am that Red who was part of the Prophecy. You have to admit, it certainly looks that way."

"Sarah, if the reason you wanted to see me was to tell me you were leaving town…"

She looked at the man she'd loved for as long as she could remember. He still knew her, the person she'd been when they were lovers, when they had their daughters, when she was still *that* Sarah Hamilton. "I will destroy your life if I stay."

"No. I don't believe that, and let me tell you why," he said as he picked up his drink from where he'd set it earlier.

"You'd better give me a drink, then," she said.

He put his back down and stepped to the bar. "Wine?"

"No, I'll have what you're having."

He handed her a crystal snifter. The rich brown liquid caught the light as he turned on the gas fireplace and motioned her into a chair opposite his. "I know where you've been the past twenty years."

Her head came up with a start. "What are you talking about?"

"Sheriff Curry tracked down your past. You spent at least the past twenty working as an assistant to a doctor in Brazil."

Sarah shook her head. "How is that possible?"

"I saw a photograph of you and a man named Dr. Ralph Venable."

She felt a small jolt inside her as if her heart shifted a little. "Venable?" she repeated.

"Does the name mean anything to you?" he asked.

Slowly, she shook her head. "Who is he?"

Buck took a sip of his drink and then locked eyes with her. "Probably the man who stole your memories."

Sarah listened as he told her what Sheriff Curry had found out about the doctor. "But they don't know who took me to see this doctor at the clinic in White Sulphur Springs after I tried to kill myself?"

"No. But it wasn't me, Sarah, if that's what you might be thinking."

"Russell was so sure that you…"

He shook his head. "You called someone. You apparently knew the doctor."

She got up to pace the room. "I don't understand any of this. If I knew him, then…"

"You might have asked him to erase your memory."

Turning to look at him, she asked, "Why would I do that? *Did* something happen between us that I wanted to forget?"

"I swear to you, nothing happened. Your attempted suicide came out of left field. Unless you had postpartum depression and I didn't have any idea…"

She shook her head as she sat back down.

"I keep thinking about the way you returned to us. Parachuted in? Then there is the tattoo. The loss of memory. The fact that you look so much like this Red, who is rumored to be the brains of the Prophecy. Someone wants me to believe that you are her."

"To keep us apart?"

"I think it's more than that. They want me to pull out of the presidential race. They're using you to manipulate me. They want me to believe I can't trust you." She listened as he told her about Angelina's quest to find out the truth about Sarah Johnson's past. "Two private investigators are dead. Now the sheriff from Silverbow County seems to think I had something to do with Angelina's death and maybe the PI's, as well."

"That's ridiculous. Doesn't it seem more likely that someone doesn't want my past revealed?"

"No. If that were true, you wouldn't have returned by parachute. You would have had that tattoo removed. Don't you see? They keep adding more doubt. They're trying to push me into a corner."

"But I overheard Kat. She is convinced that I'm going to try to harm you if you are elected."

"That's because they talked to two of the Prophecy members who alluded to something big they have planned. Why tell them that? Why warn them? No," he said with a shake of his head. "I won't be pushed into a corner. Nor will I let you go."

Sarah studied his handsome face and felt tears rush her eyes. "I hope you're not making the biggest mistake of your life by trusting me."

He pulled her into his arms. "I love you, Sarah. You could never hurt me. And if the members of the Prophecy knew me, they'd know that when pushed into a corner, I come out fighting."

CHAPTER TWENTY-FIVE

"I HOPE DAD heard what I said and pulls out of the race," Kat said as they climbed into Max's truck and left the ranch. "I know he will be disappointed, but in the long run…"

"He said he's thinking about it. So that's good. Once he adds up all the coincidences, he'll see that it's too dangerous to stay in the race."

"I hope so. But even if he withdraws, I wonder if he can stay away from my mother."

"She and the Prophecy won't be able to use him if he's out of the race. I wouldn't be surprised if she disappeared again."

"What if their plan was to get him to not run?" Kat said suddenly. "What if all this was to control him, so a candidate they want in office can win?"

Max hadn't thought about it that way. "Or make him all the more determined to run and win. I guess we'll find out, once your father makes up his mind. In the meantime, there is nothing more we can do."

Kat nodded and leaned back against the seat and closed her eyes. She hadn't slept well last night, too worried about her father. He was angry at her, and that, too, made her feel awful. She felt so helpless and right now wasn't even sure that she and Max hadn't been used to either force her father to withdraw from the election or run and win as Max had said.

She must have dozed off because when she opened her eyes she realized she didn't know where they were. Max was driving up a narrow dirt road into the Crazies.

"Where are you taking me?" she asked as she sat up and looked around.

"Camping."

"*Camping?* You didn't want our first time to be in the back of a car, but you're fine with a *tent*?"

He grinned over at her. "You're a Montana girl. I thought all of you loved the great outdoors, fresh air, a nice campfire, a bedroll tossed out on the ground."

Before Kat could comment, they came over a rise and she saw a yurt in the trees. The circular tentlike dwelling glowed from the inside as if a light was on. Looking over at Max, she smiled and shook her head. "You really are the devil."

"You just wait," he said, laughing as he parked.

"It's beautiful up here," Kat said as she got out of the truck and turned to look back at the valley. The air was scented with pine and just cold enough that it was clear winter wasn't far behind. She breathed it in, telling herself that she was ready for this. She was glad they'd stopped to change into warmer clothes after the funeral. "The view is amazing."

"Almost as good as your old make-out spot?" he said.

"I had no idea this was up here." She looked over at him. The man continued to surprise her.

"It's not an actual yurt like the nomads of Mongolia used. The construction is much more solid than skins on a frame. Most yurts are portable. This one isn't going anywhere. But you like it?"

"I love it. How did you find it?"

"I asked around and found out it was for rent. I wanted to take you to some place special."

"Max, that's so romantic."

"That's me, Mr. Romance," he joked as they walked to the door, and he swung it open in a grand gesture.

Kat caught her breath. The inside couldn't have been more perfect. A fire crackled in a small woodstove in front of a large leather couch and two chairs. On an end table nearby she spotted champagne chilling and two glasses next to it. There was fruit and cheese and strawberries dipped in chocolate.

And then there was the bed. Under a sheer canopy were piles of pillows, dozens of them atop a large, wonderfully soft-looking bed. Candles burned on each side of the bed, casting everything in a golden warmth.

"Max, it's...perfect." When she looked over at him, she was surprised to see that he had been worried she wouldn't like it. She flung her arms around his neck and kissed him.

Lifting her, he carried her in, kicking the door shut behind him. When he set her down, he pulled her close and kissed her slowly as if they had all night.

SARAH FINISHED HER drink but shook her head when Buck offered to refill it. She felt antsy and couldn't help being upset. She'd come home to get to know her daughters and look how that had turned out.

"Kat apparently hasn't mentioned her suspicions to her sisters?" she asked, wondering if he knew more than she did. "They, at least, aren't treating me like I'm a pariah. Yet."

"Kat can be impulsive, but I think she's been waiting to be sure she isn't making a mistake. You can't blame her, though, Sarah. You have to admit, the so-called evidence is pretty strong."

She nodded. "Kat always was the one who wouldn't take no for an answer. I remember how she argued and pushed me to the point where I wanted to pull my hair out." She looked up, seeing the shock on his face. "Not that I didn't love her as much as the others," she said quickly. "It is just interesting to see how their personalities haven't changed since they were young."

"I hadn't realized what it must have been like for you, trying to raise so many children," Buck said.

"I was the one who wanted a houseful. I would never change any of that. Of course there were days when I was harried and felt like a failure at motherhood, but, Buck, I love each and every one of them. I'm just so sorry I missed so much. They weren't the reason I drove into the Yellowstone River that night. I still can't imagine why I would do that. I know it had nothing to do with my daughters or you, though." She prayed that was true.

Buck sighed. "I'll admit I went through hell when I found out that you hadn't tried to brake before you went into the river. I was angry with you, Sarah, for so long."

"I know," she said, stepping to him. "Buck, I don't want to cause you any more trouble. I would have taken off after Kat showed me that photo of those awful people, but I was afraid it would only make me look guilty."

"I'm glad you didn't. I can't lose you again. We're going to get through this. If I have to give up my run for the presidency—"

"No, that's always been your dream. Buck, there

has to be a way that we can be together, and you can still win the election. If there is one thing I know, we were meant to be together."

KAT WALKED AROUND the yurt, taking it all in. To anyone else but him, she would have looked excited. Max knew her, though. He could tell she was nervous.

Maybe they should have just made love in the back of her SUV at the make-out spot before she had time to really think about it.

No, he thought, he didn't want their first time to be like that. He didn't want her to have any regrets. She might have regrets no matter what he did, he realized, though. Maybe this little romantic setup he'd paid to have ready wasn't such a good idea after all. Maybe it felt too much like a seduction. Or maybe it was just too soon, no matter what she said. He mentally quit arguing with himself.

This was Kat and he was crazy about her. He could make this right. Or at least do everything in his power to try.

"Champagne?" he asked.

She nodded, but he noticed that her fingers shook a little as she took the glass he offered her before she went to sit on the couch in front of the fire. He didn't want her to be nervous. "Max, this is amazing."

He smiled as he brought his glass over and sat down next to her. "You deserve the best, Kat Hamilton."

She looked as if she might argue that.

He shook his head and leaned over to kiss her. It was a soft, friendly kiss. No pressure. Still, he felt her tense.

"You're right, we don't need this," he said, taking the glass of champagne from her and putting both glasses on the coffee table. "All we need is each other." He pulled out his cell phone. "And music, of course." One of his favorite songs began to play. "Too bad you don't dance." Before she could argue, he pulled her to her feet and into his arms. "I'll have to dance for both of us."

Her laugh wasn't as nervous. "You're crazy. What am I going to do with you?"

He pulled back to wink at her. "I have a few ideas, but right now, we're going to dance." A fast song began to play on his phone. He started dancing around her. He grabbed her hands and began to jitterbug with her.

Laughing, he said, "You *do* know how to dance. You've been holding back on me, Ms. Hamilton."

He swung her out, pulled her back, spun her around and into his arms. Then he swung her out again. She was laughing as he twirled her around and around in front of the glow of the fire. Her face was flushed, her eyes bright. She was having fun. He couldn't have asked for anything more.

Max took a mental snapshot of her, wanting to remember this moment, her hair flying out to one side, the smile on her lips, the joy in her expression.

He drew her back as a slow song began, another of his favorites.

He pulled her closer. They were both breathing hard from the exertion and their laughter. She smiled up at him, their eyes locking.

"MAX, I..." KAT SWALLOWED, realizing she'd almost said that she loved him. But she did love this crazy man. He made her feel beautiful and free and...happy.

"I know," he said. "I feel the same way about you."

He bent to kiss the side of her neck as they swayed to the music.

"You don't know what I was going to say," she protested.

He straightened to smile at her. "Wanna bet?" He went back to kissing her neck as he pulled her against him.

His body was so solid, so strong, so warm. She leaned into it, feeling safe and yet excited. His kisses dipped lower. Need ran like liquid fire through her veins. Her aching nipples pressed hard against the fabric of her bra.

If she didn't give in to these feelings for this man soon, she thought she might explode. "Max," she breathed as his kisses burned across her flesh. "Please."

He straightened to meet her gaze as another song began on his phone. "Please? Another dance?"

She could see that he was teasing her. He knew exactly what she wanted. What she desperately needed. Him. She shook her head.

"Another kiss?"

She shook her head.

"I'm here to please you. Anything you want."

She swallowed again. "You know what I want. You."

His teasing expression turned serious as he swept her up and carried her over to the bed. As he slowly put her down, he kissed her just as slowly, deepening the kiss.

She pulled him down with her until they lay side by side looking at each other. All she could think about was pressing her palms to his naked chest. She grabbed each side of the Western shirt he wore. She yanked, expecting the snaps to sing.

Instead, buttons flew everywhere.

MAX LAUGHED AT her shocked expression. "Let me guess, you don't sew on buttons either."

She covered her mouth with her hand, her eyes swimming in tears.

He pulled her hand away.

"I am so bad at this," she cried.

"No, you're refreshingly wonderful." He kissed her as he unsnapped her Western shirt a button at a time.

She wore a white bra like one he thought a very old grandmother might have worn. But on her, it was sexy as hell.

He bent toward her to kiss the tops of her breasts. Freeing first one, then the other, he kissed her hard nipples. Kat arched against his mouth as he bathed each with his tongue and felt her shudder.

Leaving a trail of warm kisses, he slowly worked his way down her body. As he unsnapped her jeans, he heard her take a breath and hold it. Slowly, he worked the jeans off as she let the breath out. He had to smile. She wore a pair of white granny panties. Damn, but he loved this woman.

He met her gaze as he slipped his hand under the fabric. Kat let out a low moan as he began to gently stroke her. He figured she hadn't done this in a very long time. Nor had she probably pleasured herself. Because she came almost at once. Whatever had happened to her had left her telling herself she never wanted this again. But her body knew better.

He removed her panties before working his way back up to kiss her again as he took off her bra. She clung to him, pressing her freed breasts against his chest. He felt his own desire spike and had to fight his growing need to move faster. He wanted this woman like he had never wanted any other. But he was determined to take it slow.

KAT THOUGHT SHE might go crazy if she didn't feel Max inside her. She wanted him, needed him, couldn't wait to feel his naked body against hers. She eased off his shirt, letting her fingers run down his muscled back. He shuddered, and when his gaze met hers, she saw the heat of his desire.

He was holding back, taking it slow for her. He knew somehow that she needed that. But right now, she needed him to make love to her.

She worked at the buttons of his jeans until he was as naked as she was. "Please," she pleaded.

Max propped himself up on his arms and looked down at her, and then he smiled as he slowly lowered himself on to her. She felt his warmth, some of his weight, and then he gradually began to enter her. She clung to him, wanting to yell, "Just do it!" but when she reached for him, he drew back.

"KAT, OPEN YOUR EYES."

She opened her eyes and looked up at him. Desire sparked and burned in those gray eyes like lightning in a snowstorm. Max eased himself into her. She let out a cry, then clutched at him, her eyes locked with his as he began to move. And then she was moving with him. Making love with him, her face filled with the same joy that he knew was on his own.

Holding her, he rolled over on his back, taking her with him. She sat up slowly, her gaze locked with his. He cupped her breasts as she began to ride him, arching against him, her head flung back. He saw her surrender, looking as wild and free as one of the horses on the ranch.

Like when they'd danced, she laughed with abandon as they rolled around on the bed and, finally spent, lay in each other's arms.

"I love you, Kat," he whispered against her hair.

"I know. I feel the same way," she said.

Brushing her hair back from her face, he smiled at her as she lifted her cheek from his chest to look at him. Then she told him about what had happened at a college fraternity party. The drug someone had put in her drink. The rape. The shame.

"You didn't report it?" he asked, fury in his voice at the men who had used her.

She shook her head. "I felt so…stupid. I never told anyone."

"Oh, baby," he said, pulling her more tightly against him. "I'm so sorry. I won't let anyone hurt you ever again."

"I confronted him…" She wiped at the sudden tears. "He laughed in my face and told me how stupid I was. He said I'd asked for it dressing and acting the way I did."

"Tell me his name, and I will kill him for you," Max said.

She shook her head. "He was driving drunk a few months later, lost control of his car and died. Because I'd wished for something awful to happen to him…"

He drew her closer. "Now I get it," he said against her temple. "This is why you closed yourself off, why you've been denying yourself. A part of you died with him because you thought you deserved to be punished. Oh, Kat, you're so wrong. It wasn't your fault. None of it was your fault."

"Max."

"Yes?" he asked sleepily. They had made love, gotten up long enough to eat something, and gone back to bed, made love again, and apparently gone to sleep. Kat had felt safe for the first time in years. Finally telling someone about what had happened had released her pain. She felt…free. Max, wonderful Max, had made her want to truly live again.

"Will you tell me about your marriage?" she asked quietly.

He hesitated only a moment. "The short version? We were high school sweethearts. We thought we had the rest of our lives together. She was diagnosed with cancer our second year of marriage. She died four months later."

"Max, I'm so sorry."

He drew her closer. "I never thought I'd ever feel like that again." Pulling back, he met her eyes. "You've made me feel joy again."

They made love once more. Daylight had waned to dusk outside the small windows, Kat saw. Inside, the fire had died to coals.

She snuggled against him, feeling the outside world starting to intrude on them. "Max, if you're right about my mother being programmed, then who pushes the button to make her turn into Red?"

"Dr. Venable."

Hadn't she known that was what he would say? The sheriff had told them that no one knew where the doctor was, but they suspected he was either on his way to the States or already back.

"It's just hard to believe they would still be so... fanatical after all these years. I wonder about the other members and what they've been doing all this time."

"There are five members unaccounted for. Several of them would be in their sixties or early seventies by now. But the others would be close to your mother's age, some I suspect even younger, and who knows if they've recruited more members by now?"

Kat shook her head, the thought giving her waking nightmares. "But they've been quiet all these years."

"Quiet in this country." He yawned. "I suspect they've been active elsewhere but might be planning to come back now because of your father's place in the polls."

She lay back to stare up at the cracked ceiling. She'd never slept naked in her life, but it felt so right here with Max. Still, she pulled the sheet up over her breasts. Max pulled it back down and kissed the tips of both breasts.

"Do you need me to take your mind off everything again?" he asked, his voice low and seductive.

She shivered, remembering their lovemaking. "Maybe he won't win the election."

"I wouldn't count on that."

"Then he *has* to drop out of the race."

"And do what his father did?" Max shook his head. "Won't happen."

"What do you mean? Do what his father did?"

"Didn't you know your grandfather had made a bid for president?" He saw that she didn't. "You do know he was a senator, right?"

"He died so long before I was born, I guess I never realized... Why didn't he run?"

Max shrugged. "No one knows. Maybe your father does. As far as I've been able to find out, there wasn't a scandal, though there was talk of another woman in his life other than your grandmother. Then your grandmother died. He resigned as senator and dropped out of the presidential race. Apparently everyone was shocked because like your father, he was the one to beat."

"When was this?" she asked, chewing thoughtfully at her lower lip.

MAX WATCHED HER, wanting to bite that same lip. For a moment, the thought made him forget what she'd asked.

He slid closer, tucked her hair behind one ear and then bent to kiss the spot right behind it. She shivered and pulled away.

"Max! You still can't be...starved. You were telling me about my grandfather. I wonder why my father never mentions him?"

He tried to focus. "It all happened not long after your mom and dad got married."

"That's odd, isn't it?"

"Hmm," he said, as he trailed kisses down her throat to her bare shoulder. "I thought so."

"Just be serious for a moment."

"I thought I was being serious."

She shook her head. He loved that they were able to laugh during lovemaking. Most lovemaking was serious and certainly not as much fun as it was with Kat. He loved seeing the pleasure in her face when he touched her.

But she refused to let him distract her right now.

"My mother would have known what kind of man my father was before she married him. She would have known my grandfather was a senator and was planning to run for president."

Max could see where she was headed with this. "You think she sought your father out, knowing who he was." He rolled up on one elbow so he could see her face. "That would mean this plan had been in the works for...years."

Kat nodded. "Just as Wallace McGill told me. Remember? He said something about it all being in the works before I was even born. And didn't you tell me that these kind of antigovernment radicals are rabid, planning far into the future?"

He let out a curse. "What if your father *wasn't* their first target? Your grandfather was already a senator. There must have been talk of him planning to run for president before your mother came on the scene. If he hadn't dropped out of the race..."

She sat up, her eyes bright with excitement. "No one has ever known why he didn't stay in the race. What if it was because he found out the truth about my mother, about the Prophecy? True, my grandmother died, and apparently he took it hard. Even if there was a mistress..." She met his gaze. "It is sounding like history repeating itself, isn't it?"

"Your grandfather quit the race and then was killed in a car wreck. That *is* a lot of tragedy so soon after Sarah Johnson joined the family. But then she didn't just stay with your father, she had six children with him. That doesn't sound like the woman known as Red."

"True, until she disappeared for twenty-two years,"

Kat said, sitting up as she became even more convinced they were onto something.

"But now we know where she's been," Max said. "Brazil."

"With some doctor who is part of the Prophecy. I wish I knew more about my grandfather. Max, if he was the first intended target, and he found out what my mother and her friends were up to, isn't it possible his death wasn't an accident? Max, are you listening to me?"

His head was cocked, his gaze on the door. "Do you smell that?"

Kat sniffed. "Smoke?"

CHAPTER TWENTY-SIX

MAX HADN'T SMELLED it before that moment because of the dying fire in the woodstove. He bounded from the bed and ran toward the front door, all his senses on alert. He picked up another scent before he reached the door. Kerosene.

Grabbing the door handle, he let out a yelp as it burned his fingers. "Get dressed quick. We have to get out of here," he said to Kat as he rushed back to the bed. "The place is on fire."

He pulled on his jeans and grabbed his shirt. Using it like a hot pad, he hurried back to the door. He could hear flames licking at the outside of the yurt. The man he'd rented it from had bragged that the structure was built like a bomb shelter with small windows and solid wood all around the outside for privacy.

Max tried the door, already suspecting it wasn't going to open. It didn't. Something had been put against it outside. He threw a shoulder into it, but the door didn't budge.

He turned back to Kat. She was dressed, looking scared. Smoke was beginning to fill the yurt. He glanced to the windows. They were too small for either of them to get out and, because of the yurt's size, there was only one door in and out.

Pulling on his boots, Max looked around for something he could use to try to bust out of there before they were both burned to death. Outside, the dry wood and fabric the builder had used to cover the structure were crackling as they burned. The walls were already beginning to creak. Once the flames burned through them, the whole place would come down on them.

Max spotted an ax over by the woodpile next to the stove. He tossed Kat a towel he'd soaked in water and told her to put it over her face and stay low where the smoke wasn't so black. Then he picked up the ax and began to tear into the far wall near where the wood-stove vented.

As he'd guessed, the wall was weaker at this spot. The first swing opened the inner cover. The second made a hole through which he could see blue sky. He swung again and again as the smoke filled the yurt. His throat ached, and each breath was becoming a labor.

The hole was almost large enough. He felt Kat's hand on his leg as she crawled closer. She was coughing as he helped her to her feet and, shoving the coffee table over, pulled her up on it and out through what was now a ring of fire. Just as he was about to let go of her hand, she pulled him after her. They tumbled out, hitting the ground and quickly rolling away from the flames that had already burned the tall, dry grass around the structure.

"Are you all right?" Max asked, his voice hoarse, as he crawled to her and took her in his arms.

Kat nodded, still coughing, as he reached for his cell phone. He had just enough bars to put in a 911 call.

Behind them, they heard a crash as part of the roof collapsed in a roar of flames. If they had stayed in there even a few minutes more…

"They tried to kill us," Kat said in between coughs. And pointed down the mountainside.

Max turned to see a black SUV roaring toward Beartooth. It looked familiar like the one that had almost hit them that day in Bozeman. "Come on," he said and helped her up. "They aren't going to get away. Not this time."

KAT PUT THE window down as Max drove. He'd told her to buckle up and hang on. She breathed in fresh air, sucking it into her lungs. Back up the mountain, the yurt glowed bright orange as the flames consumed it.

Ahead, all she could see was the dust trail that the black SUV had left.

"What are you going to do when you catch them?" she asked, her throat raw and scratchy, but most of her coughing over.

With one hand on the wheel, he reached with his free one and pulled a pistol from the glove box. "Don't look so worried," he said as he laid it on the seat between them. "I notified the sheriff. He will be looking for them. There aren't that many roads once they get to Beartooth that they will know to take. Right now, they don't even know we're after them."

No, they thought she and Max were still in that burning yurt. She shuddered. If Max hadn't gotten them out when he did...

Max's cell phone rang. He handed it to Kat so he could concentrate on his driving. The dust ahead of them was getting thicker, which meant they were getting closer to the SUV.

"Hello?" she said into the phone, her voice raspy.

"It's Sheriff Curry. Is this Kat Hamilton?"

"Yes."

"How close are you to the SUV?"

"It isn't far ahead of us now. We can't see much because of the dust it's kicking up."

"We're coming from the other way. Tell Max not to try to apprehend them by himself. Stay back until—"

"The SUV just turned on to the old river road," Kat cried as she saw the driver make a left turn that almost rolled the black vehicle.

Max had to hit the brakes to make the turn.

"Are you still with it?" the sheriff asked.

"Right behind it," Kat said into the phone.

"Stay with it, but, please, tell Max to keep back in case the driver has a weapon. I'll come around the other way."

They were going so fast! The black SUV was kicking up small rocks that pelted the windshield of the pickup and bounced off the hood.

"The sheriff wants you to stay back," she said.

"The bastard tried to kill us. I'm not letting him get away," Max said as he kept his foot on the gas pedal, refusing to let it up.

Suddenly Kat saw the flash of chrome, and the next thing she knew the driver had lost control. The huge black SUV was abruptly sideways in the road.

Out of the corner of her eye, Kat saw Max tromp on the brakes, but she knew it was useless. There was no way he could get the pickup stopped in time. She braced herself for the crash, surprised when Max turned the wheel at the last moment, taking the blunt force of the crash with his side of the truck instead of hers. She heard the crunch of metal to metal a heartbeat before the air bags exploded.

Time seemed to stop. Either that or she'd been knocked out by the impact. She shook her head, coming out of a daze filled with the smell of steam rising from the radiator and dust. Through it, she saw that the pickup had caved in the back half of the SUV.

She blinked. Through the settling dust, she could see that the driver's seat in the SUV was empty.

"Max," she turned to find him slumped against the seat. "Max!" She reached for his hand, found a pulse, and tried not to panic. There was a small cut on his temple, blood was running down, but he was breathing.

Over the pounding of her heart, she heard what sounded like the crunch of broken glass under a boot heel. Her pulse thundered just under her skin as she looked around wildly for the driver. Somehow, he'd gotten out of his vehicle. Once he saw that Max couldn't defend himself...

Kat thought about taking Max's phone from her pocket, but the sheriff was already on his way. Calling for help would only cost her time. She unsnapped her seat belt. Her movements seemed too slow, too deliberate. She hurt all over as if she'd been beaten, but her mind was racing. She looked around for the gun that Max had taken from the glove box. It lay in the floorboard at her feet. Even though it hurt to do so, she reached out and picked it up.

Her father had taught all six of them to respect guns, which meant learning how to use them. She saw that it was a revolver and it was loaded. All she had to do was pull the trigger. Shifting the gun to her left hand, she tried to open her door. It was jammed. She had to throw herself against it before it would open. It creaked loudly.

Whoever had been driving the SUV would know that she was coming, but there was nothing she could do about that. She was a sitting duck if she stayed here. Getting the door opened enough that she could slip out, she shimmied through the crack and dropped into a shallow ditch.

The pickup had come to rest on a curve. She understood now why the driver of the SUV had lost control. The road had been recently graded, so the gravel along the side was deep and loose. For a moment, she stood listening. She could hear someone moving around on the other side of the SUV.

Cautiously, the revolver grasped in both hands, finger on the trigger, she moved around the back of the SUV.

BUCK HAD HAD his staff call a press conference at the gate into the ranch. He knew Kat would be unhappy with what he was about to do. But he wasn't all that happy about the reporter she appeared to be falling for. He'd learned after this many years that they each had to live their own lives. He had Sarah back. Maybe things really would work out.

He'd seen other politicians put a spin on their relationships and pull themselves out of the media mud. He would hire the best public relations team he could. Sarah was the love of his life. He thought he'd lost her. Now they had another chance. He had to take it. For himself. For Sarah. For their daughters.

But they'd give it time. Eventually, the girls would come around. Eventually, he hoped the American public would, as well.

He reminded himself that Angelina was barely in

her grave. He felt a tidal wave of guilt at the thought of how quickly he was forgetting her. This past year had been hell on their marriage. Angelina's jealousy and his love for Sarah had made him decide to leave her. She would probably still be alive today if she hadn't been so to-hell-and-gone on finding something damning about Sarah.

His pulse jumped at the thought that the reason the two private investigators were dead was because they *had* found out about Sarah and the Prophecy. He shook his head, knowing there could be dozens of other explanations, none of them to do with Sarah.

He refused to believe she had been involved with the group. Just as he had to believe that Angelina's death was nothing more than a tragic accident. Whatever the Prophecy members had hoped to accomplish, they weren't going to force him to withdraw from the race.

As he got ready for his press conference, he thought, *Put out one fire before you start worrying about another.*

The press conference was to be short and sweet and at the ranch. His current PR person's advice. "It will remind them that you are a local rancher with a family, first and foremost. It's those roots that make you the best person to run this country. You're grieving, but you want to assure the people, you will continue in the race."

As Buckmaster drove out to the front gate, he was surprised to see how many different news sources were present, as well as supporters. He'd thought he could keep down the number by making this an impromptu event.

He climbed out of his SUV and walked to the gate.

"Thank you all for coming. I know this was spur-of-
the-moment. I'd like to make a statement. I won't be
taking any questions following my announcement." A
murmur moved through the crowd. "I have suffered a
great loss. My first thought was to withdraw from the
campaign."

The murmur this time was louder.

"But I'm standing here a candidate for the highest
office in our country because I believe it takes over-
coming even personal loss to be president. My family
and friends believe in me. They've encouraged me to
continue. As the next president of this great country,
I believe in my heart that I can make a difference."

Some of the crowd began to clap. "I am continuing
my run because my country needs me."

Cheers went up from the crowd. Reporters began
shouting questions as he thanked everyone and stepped
away from the microphone.

HAVING POSTPONED HIS cruise for a few days, Russell
Murdock stood at the back of the crowd gathered at
the gate to the Hamilton Ranch. He heard the reporters calling out questions, but caught only one reporter's
questions as Buckmaster got into his SUV and drove
back toward his house following his announcement.

"What about your first wife, Sarah? Is there a
chance the two of you might get back together now?"

As the senator left, the crowd began to move away.
Russell stood for a moment staring at the house in
the distance, wondering if Sarah wasn't already inside
there. He wouldn't have been surprised.

His daughter, Destry, hadn't been the least bit upset

when he'd told her that he and Sarah weren't getting married.

"Dad, I'm sorry, but she wasn't right for you. Too much baggage."

He'd smiled at that. His daughter had no idea.

As he started to leave, he spotted the sheriff and walked over to him.

"Russell, I heard you were on a cruise."

"I haven't really decided yet when I'm leaving. I was wondering if you found out anything about that information I gave you?"

"Why don't we step in to my patrol SUV for a moment?" Frank suggested.

Once inside, the sheriff said, "Since you're the one who brought this theory to me to begin with…"

Russell felt his pulse kick up. "I was *right*?"

"I did find a clinic in Montana where a doctor was doing experiments with brain wiping twenty-two years ago."

"On humans?"

Frank nodded. "Also a young woman who worked at the clinic saw a blonde woman matching Sarah's description brought in the night Sarah went in the river."

Russell let out a loud breath. "I *was* right." He couldn't help sounding relieved. It had seemed like such a crazy theory at the time and yet…

"We now know where Sarah has been the past twenty years," the sheriff said. "She apparently left with the doctor from the clinic and went to work with him in Brazil."

Russell felt his eyes widen in surprise.

"I thought you'd like to know before you left," Frank said.

"Thank you. Have you talked to the doctor?"

"He's missing again," the sheriff said.

With a sigh, Russell shook his head. "I'm telling you, all this has to do with Senator Buckmaster Hamilton. And as crazy as it sounds, she'll go back to him—if she hasn't already. You need to protect her."

"I'm not sure what I can do in these circumstances, but I can assure you, I'm going to be keeping a close eye on both of them," the sheriff said.

Russell nodded. He could tell Frank thought the senator was the one he had to worry about. "Sarah's the victim. I hope everyone realizes that before something horrible happens."

As Kat came around the back of the SUV, she saw the man lying facedown on the ground and froze. He looked badly hurt. Blood had soaked into the earth around his head.

She stared at him, willing him to move, the gun pointed at the center of his back. She was terrified that he might be able to rise. Hadn't she only heard him moving around minutes before?

From in the distance came the sound of sirens. The sheriff would be here soon. But she had to know if the man was dead because she wanted desperately to get back to Max.

She took a step forward, then another. She was almost to the man, the gun in her hand, wavering, nerves on end. With the toe of her boot, she kicked the man's leg. He didn't move. Didn't make a sound.

As she started to lower the gun, she heard the crunch of gravel under a boot heel behind her and belatedly realized that there'd been two men in the SUV. She swung around, raising the gun as she did. In that split second, she recognized him from the photograph of the Prophecy. He'd been one of the younger ones in the snapshot.

She pulled the trigger. The shot went wild as the man hit her, knocking her into the side of the wrecked black SUV. As her head smacked the hard metal, stars danced before her eyes.

Before she could react again, he grabbed her hand with the gun in it and wrestled the weapon away. As her vision began to clear, she saw him holding the gun on her. She must have closed her eyes. The next thing she heard was the report of the revolver. Her eyes flew open.

To her shock, she saw Max. He had knocked the gun from the man's hands and had him down on the ground. The sound of sirens roared in her ears as the vehicles came screaming up in a cloud of dust. In moments she was in Max's arms, and an ambulance was on its way.

CHAPTER TWENTY-SEVEN

"THE MAN'S NAME is Warren Dodge," Sheriff Curry said as he looked over the small group gathered in the Hamilton ranch house. "He has confessed to being a member of the Prophecy." He gave a slight nod in Kat and Max's direction, verifying what they'd already told him.

"Has he said why he tried to kill my daughter?" the senator demanded.

"No, but he *is* talking," Frank said. "He has given us the name of the other man who was with him, a fellow named John Carter."

"How does that help us?" Buckmaster demanded.

The sheriff raised his hand, asking for a chance to finish, and the senator fell silent. "Warren Dodge has agreed to a lesser sentence for providing the names of the other members still at large." He saw the surprised looks on their faces and the fear on the senator's.

"Unfortunately, we are unable to locate the three left. One of them we know is a doctor who's been working in South America. His whereabouts are now unknown. The other two, Martin Wagner and Joe Landon, are also apparently on the run. But a woman by the name of Virginia Handley has been arrested. She has also confessed as being the member known as Red."

Frank felt all the air go out of the room. The relief was palpable. Kat was shaking her head, as if she couldn't believe it. Max didn't believe it. He met the sheriff's gaze with a steady one of his own. Frank gave him a slight shrug.

"You're sure this woman is this notorious Red?" Buckmaster asked, clearly elated by the news.

"According to her and Warren Dodge. Of course, the FBI will be verifying their stories."

"So it's over," the senator said with a sigh as he got to his feet. "This calls for a celebration drink."

"I wouldn't say it's over until the other three are caught," Frank said, but the senator waved him off.

"As far as I'm concerned, the Prophecy is dead," Buckmaster said. "If I never have to hear about it again, I will be a happy man."

The sheriff held his tongue. He understood why Buckmaster wanted to celebrate. This cleared Sarah Johnson Hamilton. Or at least seemed to.

"So this Warren Dodge has confessed, right?"

Frank nodded. "Dodge has admitted killing reporter Chuck Barrow, as well as mugging Max Malone. He has also implicated himself along with John Carter, the deceased member, in Angelina's accident, the death of several private investigators and the hiring of a woman who called herself Tammy Jones to steal Malone's camera and laptop in an earlier incident, as well as attempts on Kat and Max's lives."

Buckmaster said something under his breath as he downed his drink. "Thank God we don't have to worry about him anymore."

"Have you seen a photo of this woman who confessed?" Kat asked.

The sheriff nodded. "She looks a lot like your

mother did when she first came to Beartooth all those
years ago. She's a natural blonde but dyes her hair red,
apparently."

Max got to his feet. "So it's all wrapped up in one
nice little ball."

"Sure looks that way," Frank said.

"Well, I've got a story to write." He looked to Kat.

"I have to get back to work, too," she said, getting
to her feet.

"Talk later?" Max asked, and she nodded.

Frank watched the two of them leave, just glad neither of them had been killed. He hoped they would quit
digging into the past and stay safe.

But all his instincts told him that neither of them
had bought into Sarah's innocence as easily as Buckmaster had.

Clearly they were in love. He wished the best for
them, then smiled to himself, thinking he was getting
as sentimental as Lynette.

"Here," Buckmaster said, shoving a drink into his
hand. "To happy endings."

Frank glanced at his watch. He was officially off
duty, not that it would have mattered. He could use a
drink. He took the crystal glass the senator offered. "To
happy endings." He said it like a prayer, because all his
instincts told him this was far from over.

BUCKMASTER WANTED TO shout his relief from the highest rooftop. Sarah wasn't a terrorist. Nor had she been
during the missing twenty-two years. She'd worked
for a doctor in Brazil, a doctor who'd apparently stolen her memory.

He still had no answer for why she'd left him, why she'd tried to kill herself or why these people were trying to use her. But he told himself he could live with that for now. The sheriff was looking for this Dr. Venable. They'd deal with it when the man was found.

Meanwhile, he had to concentrate on the campaign. He had to become the next president. Once he was, he'd make sure everyone involved in this conspiracy would get what they deserved.

After everyone left, he finished his drink and was about to head to the old Morgan Place to tell Sarah the good news, when his daughter Harper came in.

"I thought you'd left," he said in surprise.

"I'm staying here on the ranch. You have to get back to DC and the campaign. You need someone here to take care of things."

"What about graduate school?"

"The truth? I miss riding my horse. I miss Montana. I miss my family."

He stepped to his beautiful blonde, blue-eyed angel. She and her sister were identical so they'd often fooled him. "Honey, there is no reason for you to stay here to take care of me. As you said, I'm going to be coming and going from now until…"

"Until you move into the White House. I know, Daddy. But I want to stay for you as much as for me. I feel as if everyone has tried to get the cowgirl out of me—without any luck. This is where I belong. I won't be a bother, I promise."

"You could never be a bother," he said and gave her a hug. "There's something I need to do before I leave tomorrow. Will you be all right here by yourself?"

She laughed. "I'm looking forward to having the run of the ranch again. And I'm certainly not alone here, with all the wranglers and staff in the house. I see Cooper has brought in more wild horses. I'll have to talk to him about one for me to ride."

"You be careful." Buckmaster eyed his grown-up daughter. He couldn't help being suspicious of her motives. It was the father in him. The one thing he'd learned after having six daughters was that once they hit a certain age, there was usually a boy involved in most of their decisions. He wondered who Harper had her sights on.

"I'm glad you're home," he said to her. "I hope you spend some time with your mother while you're here. She's staying in the old Morgan Place on the ranch."

Harper brightened. "I will, I promise."

MAX HAD A STORY, an exclusive for the moment. He went back to his motel, took out his laptop and began to work. He'd missed writing, so his fingers practically flew over the keys. He didn't expect much of a reaction to his story. The Prophecy was old news.

But he needed this story out there for when the real news broke. He wasn't fool enough to believe that Sarah Hamilton wasn't Red. He wondered why a woman named Virginia Handley would confess to something she hadn't done. The only reason was to clear Sarah. He stopped writing long enough to see what he could find out about her. Little to nothing. No surprise there.

Then he went back to his story that wouldn't hit anywhere near a front page. But the fact that the senator's daughter had almost been killed might get it close. Not that it mattered. At one time, he would have been disappointed by that.

He called Kat when he finished. "I'm starved," he said when she answered.

She laughed. "I'm in Bozeman at the gallery."

"You're probably busy."

"Not that busy."

It was his turn to laugh. "I'll drive over."

"Sounds great. See you soon. I'm thinking big thick burgers, lots of fries and chocolate milk shakes."

"Of course you are."

He hung up, feeling good, considering he had no idea what the future held. As long as it held Kat. The rest he was willing to wing.

He thought about their lovemaking and smiled. He'd never felt like this. Not even with Amy, as much as he'd loved and adored her. He'd never thought he could feel like this with any other woman. Hell, he felt as if he was walking on a cloud and he never wanted it to end.

SARAH SEEMED SURPRISED to see him. "Buck?" She smiled as she opened the door. "Is everything all right?" she asked as he tied his horse to the porch railing.

"Everything couldn't be better," he said as he stepped to her and kissed her hard on the mouth.

"What has gotten into you?" she asked with a laugh as he came in and she closed the door behind him.

"I have news. Great news." He quickly told her about what had happened. "Kat is fine. So is Max. One of the Prophecy is dead, the other confessed and ratted out Red."

Sarah seemed to freeze. For a moment, he thought she might faint.

"I'm so sorry," he said rushing to her. "It's not you, Sarah. It's some woman named Virginia Handley." He helped her over to the couch and hurried into the kitchen to get her a glass of water. When he came back, she still looked pale. "I didn't mean to scare you like that."

"It's all right," she said and took a drink of the water. "I thought for a moment…"

"Of course you did. How foolish of me," he said as he sat down beside her and took her hand. It was like ice. "It's over. I was telling the sheriff that I hope I never have to hear another word about the Prophecy."

"You said one man is dead and another was arrested?"

"A man named John Carter is dead. The other one, Warren Dodge, is the one who confessed." He was watching her closely, more closely than he'd planned. She was taking this hard. Maybe too hard.

Buckmaster pushed away his doubts. "It's over," he said, more to himself than to her. He didn't mention that there were still three members at large. Three members that they knew of.

Sarah put the glass of water aside and stood to walk to the window. "I knew Virginia Handley," she said. "We were on the same floor our freshman year at college. We used to joke about how much we looked alike. How we could be sisters."

"You *knew* her?" Buckmaster heard his voice quiver.

Sarah turned, tears in her eyes. "We were friends for a while until she got involved with campus politics. After that, she dropped out. I heard she was holding sit-ins and organizing demonstrations… But I never dreamed she'd get involved with a domestic terrorist group."

"Sarah—"

"Don't look so shocked, Buck. Just because I knew her, it doesn't mean I was involved with the Prophecy."

"Sarah, don't you realize what this *does* mean?" he demanded as he got to his feet. "Your former…friend used you. She helped set you up. I'm not sure how they pulled it off, but the tattoo, the fact that you looked like Virginia, the memory loss… Sarah, they have to be behind the brain wiping. That man you apparently knew, Dr. Ralph Venable, he was an older member of the Prophecy. They were using you to get to me."

SARAH LOWERED HERSELF into a chair, no longer trusting her legs to hold her up. All this had come as such a shock. She lifted her head as she realized what he'd just said. "You didn't withdraw from the race?"

"No." He shook his head. "I couldn't."

She felt a well of relief and wondered why it mattered so much to her. Wouldn't it be better for the two of them if he stayed here on the ranch with her? "I don't know what to say."

"Sarah, you don't have to say anything. You're the victim here. All of this is somehow tied to that radical group. Now we know the connection. We know why they wanted me to believe you were Red. But you're in the clear now. Once things settle down, there is no reason you and I can't be together. That's what you want, isn't it?"

She rose to go to him. "More than ever."

"Harper is staying at the ranch. She's promised to come visit you."

"You told her where I'm living?"

He nodded. "You need to get to know your daughters."

"Yes, that's why I came back." She met his gaze, thinking how the words had become like a mantra. Or something she'd memorized, she'd said them so much. "Because of them and you."

Buck pulled her into his arms. He was still the most handsome man she'd ever known. She remembered their fevered lovemaking, the way he always held her afterward, the feeling of being safe in his arms.

"It's all going to be fine. Trust me. You do trust me, don't you, Sarah?"

"With my life."

He kissed her, and she remembered sultry summer nights behind the house on the porch swing. Long horseback rides on fall days when the breeze stirred the dried leaves over their heads. Tangled sheets in the big bed upstairs where they'd made their children.

She frowned. "I was just thinking about horseback riding with you."

"Really?" He pulled back to look at her. "I would love it if you would try again."

She stared at him. "After the twins were born, I thought you and I went on a long horseback ride that fall."

He shook his head. "Does that sound like something you'd like to do? Sarah, I would love it if you would let me teach you to ride. Maybe you won't be afraid anymore."

"I was afraid?"

Buck held her at arm's length as he studied her face. "You don't remember? It was after we first got married. You went for a ride by yourself…" He was frowning. "You really don't remember getting bucked off?"

She shook her head.

"I found you well after dark over by Horsethief Creek. You'd taken a nasty spill. You refused to get near a horse after that."

So why did she remember riding beside him through the aspens, the fallen dried leaves kicking up under the horse's hooves as the rich smells of autumn filled her nostrils? An implanted memory? Like the horrible ones that often flashed in her mind, scaring her into believing they were memories?

"I'm sorry about your friend," Buck said as if seeing that she had paled again.

"Clearly, she wasn't my friend if she did this to me."

"You still have the gun I gave you?" he asked, no doubt seeing that it was getting dark outside. He had to ride back to the ranch house where she had once lived as his wife. His only wife. But it wouldn't be the first night he'd ridden in the dark, would it?

"Yes, but—"

"The FBI is looking for the other three of the group, including the doctor who took you to Brazil." He was studying her again. "When you looked at the photo that Kat showed you of the group, you didn't recognize your friend?"

She shook her head. "She was blonde like me. I guess it was the red hair, but, no, I didn't recognize any of them. Now that Virginia has confessed, they have no use for me, right?"

Buck nodded. "I think that's the last we'll hear of them, but I don't want to take any chances. Maybe you should move into the main house."

"No," she said, stepping away from him. She thought of the memories that weren't true memories and felt one of her headaches coming on. "I'm fine here. Like you said, we need to give this time. Harper will come visit, and I'll get out more since the media will be following your campaign and not me."

"I can't wait for us to be together," Buck said.

Sarah smiled up at him and felt that old desire warm her. "You don't have to go back right away, do you?"

"Do you believe it?" Kat asked as she dredged a fat French fry through a puddle of ketchup.

"About this Virginia Handley confessing?" Max asked between bites of hamburger. "Maybe it's the reporter in me, but I don't want to. Everything pointed to your mother."

"You think they wanted us to believe it was her? That she was being used? I know that's what my father believes."

He stopped eating for a moment as if to think. "When you add it all up, it's possible. She and Virginia Handley look a lot like each other. They went to the same college. They could have even known each other."

"I was thinking about that. What if they tried to use my mother twenty-two years ago? Dad was a senator. Isn't it possible that they tried to force her to do something she didn't want to?"

"And that's why she drove into the river that night?" Max said. "It's pretty far-fetched. But if she was involved with them...then I might buy it. She'd made a good life for herself with your father, and maybe she didn't want to blow up buildings anymore. They put pressure on her, and she knew the only way she could save herself and her husband's career would be to kill herself. Pretty desperate."

Kat agreed. "But when she survived, she would call the one person she knew who she believed would help her. Dr. Ralph Venable. I wonder whose idea it was to try to wipe away her memories?"

"You're assuming she knew about his brain-wiping research."

"If she was being…blackmailed, she couldn't stay in Dad's life without destroying it and hers and ultimately her daughters', so she tried to kill herself. Failing that, she called the doctor and asked him to wipe out the memories. Then the two of them take off to Brazil."

Max laughed. "That is one hell of a theory, but it has legs, I'll admit. Then what, though?"

"She starts remembering her family, wants to come back. The doctor puts some memories back and sends her home."

Max looked skeptical, but shrugged. "Why not?"

"Then the doctor double-crosses her, and what's left of the Prophecy members decide to use her."

"I suppose it's possible," Max said after he finished his burger. "Or your mother is Red, this other woman is taking the fall for whatever reason, and the whole plan was to keep your father in the race and your mother at his side."

She studied him. This handsome, smart man. Her lover. "Why doesn't your theory sound more probable?"

He laughed. "Neither of them holds water without proof."

"So, what are we going to do?"

He wiped his mouth with his napkin and grinned over at her. "You mean after lunch?"

"I need to get ready for my exhibit. What about you?"

"Are you trying to get rid of me?"

"Don't you need to work?"

"I do," he said seriously. "There are a couple of stories editors I've worked with would like me to chase. I wouldn't be gone long, but…"

"You should go." She could feel his gaze on her face.

"You *are* trying to get rid of me."

"No," she said just as serious. "I know how I feel about you. I think I know how you feel about me."

"Which means?"

"We aren't ready for…a big commitment."

"Speak for yourself," Max said.

"My sister Bo is getting married in a few months. I'd like you to be my date. In the meantime, I thought we'd both go back to work and see each other every chance we get."

"You think we might change our minds about each other, is that it?" he asked.

She met his blue gaze. It was like falling out of a plane into nothing but sky. "No. So some time won't change anything, right?"

"Not a thing."

She smiled at him. "Good, I thought we'd…wing it for a while and just see if this is as amazing as we both think it is."

He laughed as he reached across the table to cup her

cheek with his warm hand. "I can wing it with you. But it's not going to change how I feel. You're it for me, like it or lump it."

"I like it."

EPILOGUE

MAX STRAIGHTENED HIS TIE. He couldn't remember the last time he'd been in a tuxedo. But it had been worth it to see Kat's face when she'd gotten her first look at him.

He'd gotten a haircut, just not short, and shaved all but a little of his designer scruff. He was still that Max Malone, but he had a good feeling Kat didn't want him to change.

"Wow," she'd said and smiled as she'd rushed to him.

"Back at you!" He'd caught her and spun her in his arms. He swore she'd gotten more beautiful since the last time he'd seen her. The months apart had been good for both of them, he'd thought as they moved toward each other. Kat was her own woman again. No more too-large clothing, no more fears. There was a new confidence about her.

She wore a deep red velvet dress that fit her perfectly. Her hair dropped in dark tendrils around her beautiful face. "You make a gorgeous bridesmaid." She would make an even more beautiful bride one day, he thought.

He'd planted a kiss on her cheek, so as not to mess up her makeup, and then whispered, "I can't wait to get that dress off of you later." She'd laughed as he'd put her feet back on the ground, but he'd been able to see that she was as anxious as he was to get together.

He'd been on assignment out of the country for the past few months and had only gotten back late last night. He'd wanted desperately to see her, but with her whole family home for Bo's wedding, he'd restrained himself.

Max had been honored when her fiancé, Jace, had asked him to be one of his groomsmen at the Christmas wedding. Bo did make a beautiful bride. All five of her sisters were her bridesmaids.

"Those Hamilton girls are somethin'," Max had joked.

"Aren't we," Kat had said.

He loved seeing how close they all were. They made him feel like family already.

Max saw that one of the groomsmen was Brody McTavish, the man he'd met at the bar who was in love with one of the twins. He caught him looking at Harper several times during the ceremony and had to smile.

The truth was that Max hadn't been able to keep his eyes off Kat throughout the wedding. He'd finally gotten her in his arms at the reception for a couple of dances. Bo and Jace had their reception in the big barn on Hamilton Ranch. Now he stood back as Bo was about to throw the bouquet. She'd made all her single friends and sisters join her for the traditional toss.

Kat's first gallery exhibit was next week. Max had already bought the rain photo. It was in his bedroom at the beach house. He was hoping that the two of them would be able to get away for a few days after the wedding. He had something he wanted to ask Kat.

"Ready?" Bo called, laughing as she looked over her

shoulder, then lifted the bouquet into the air and threw it behind her. The bouquet, tiny white roses with even smaller red berries, rose high into the air.

Max watched it arc upward, the bouquet skimming the barn's rafters, before it began its descent.

He watched it all as if in slow motion as the bouquet fell, not in the tight crowd of expectant women, but toward the back where Kat had moved out of the way. The bouquet literally plummeted into her hands.

Her expression was priceless as she looked down at it for an instant before her gaze shot to him. Max smiled and nodded as he mouthed, "We're next."

KAT FELT LIKE a princess at a ball. Every time she'd looked in Max's direction, she'd found him watching her, a smile on his face and a lightness in his eyes. She'd missed him desperately but she felt she'd been right about the two of them doing their own thing for a while.

She'd needed time to be sure the feelings she had for him would last. If anything, she was all the more crazy about him. As the single women congratulated her on her "catch," she took a moment to smell the roses. She could see Max making his way toward her. Behind him, the barn had been decorated in a wonderland of white.

Earlier, she'd danced with her father. She'd never seen him looking so relaxed or happy. She knew that was her mother's doing. Now Kat spotted them both talking off to the side of the dance floor. Her mother looked beautiful, her father so handsome. They looked like two people in love.

Over the past few months, she'd seen more of her

mother. She wanted to believe that Sarah Hamilton really wasn't Red. Her father was convinced that the woman now facing trial had tried to frame her mother. Kat wanted to believe that once all of the Prophecy members were found and arrested, this nightmare would be over. But she still had too many unanswered questions.

Just as she'd feared, her parents had gotten much closer over the past few months. The senator had hired a public relations firm. They'd put a positive spin on Sarah Hamilton. And when it had come out that the two were seeing each other, most of the media had jumped on the bandwagon, portraying it as two lost lovers having found each other again.

Kat tried not to worry about it. Max had said that if her mother really was Red, they still had time to stop whatever the Prophecy might have in the works. Still, Kat found herself watching her mother closely when she was around her. She kept looking for signs, but so far she'd seen none.

Maybe her father was right and there was nothing to worry about.

Pushing those thoughts away, Kat let herself just enjoy this moment. It felt so good to have her family all here. Bo had been a beautiful bride. She looked so happy with Jace.

As Kat looked around the barn, it all felt so dream-like. She couldn't remember the last time she'd felt this happy. Happy for Bo. Happy for her sisters, who all loved a good wedding. And happy for herself now that Max was here. She didn't need to catch the bride's bouquet to know that she would be spending the rest

of her life with him. She'd seen it in his expression
when he'd looked up and seen her before the wedding.

He *loved* her.

She had to swallow the lump in her throat. And she
loved Max with all her heart. She had a feeling he already knew that as he stepped to her now, laughing as
he looked at the bouquet and pulled her into his arms.
Kat closed her eyes and breathed in the scent of him.
She couldn't wait to be alone with Max.

When she opened her eyes, she caught movement
outside the barn door. A man had been standing in the
shadows, but now he stepped away, moving into the
light for an instant before he disappeared.

Kat felt her pulse jump as her eyes widened with
recognition. The man who'd been standing out there…
She recognized him. It was the same man who'd been
standing next to Red in the Prophecy photo. He was
older, more distinguished, but there was no doubt. He
was the man who Max had said was Red's lover—and
the coleader of the terrorist group.

Kat's gaze flew to her mother, who she saw was
standing nearby—staring at the now-empty, open barn
doorway and looking as if she'd seen a ghost. All color
seemed to drain from her face just before Sarah Hamilton fainted.

* * * * *

Read on for a sneak preview of
REUNION AT CARDWELL RANCH,
the continuation of the acclaimed
CARDWELL RANCH *series by*
New York Times *bestselling author*
B.J. Daniels

CHAPTER ONE

THE MOMENT SHE'D stepped into the dark house, she could feel the emptiness surround her like a void. The owners wouldn't be coming to Montana for Christmas this year. The couple was getting a divorce. The man's third marriage, the woman's first.

She'd gotten her information from a good source, but she'd learned, though, that you could never be certain of anything, especially the rumors that ran more wildly than the river ran through the Gallatin Canyon past Big Sky.

Standing stone still in the dark, listening, she waited for a few moments before she snapped on her tiny penlight. There were no other homes close to this one. The owners of these expensive spacious second homes wanted to feel as if they had the mountainside to themselves. Because of that there was little to no chance that anyone would notice if she turned on lights. But she didn't like playing against the odds when it came to the chance of being discovered.

As she moved through the house, she saw sculptures that she knew had cost a small fortune and paintings like some she'd sat for hours studying in museums back East. She hurried on past them reminded that time was never on her side. In and out as quickly as possible was her personal motto. Otherwise she knew all too well things could go very badly.

She found the painting in the master bedroom on the third floor. A twenty-by-sixteen-inch signed Taylor West original depicting a rancher on horseback surveying his herd. It was one of her favorites. She stepped to it quickly, admiring the brushstrokes and the skillful use of shading as she let the penlight move over it until she found what she was looking for.

Lifting it off the wall, she checked the time. She was running a little over five minutes on this job because of the three stories she'd had to search for this piece.

Quickly she replaced the painting with the one she'd brought, noticing that the bag she'd carried it in had torn. Wadding up the bag, she stuffed it into her coat pocket and tucked the painting from the wall under her arm.

She made her way back through the house, pleased. If only they were all as easy as this one. She'd barely completed the thought when a set of headlights washed over the room.

Laramie Cardwell mentally kicked himself for driving up this snow-packed narrow mountain road in the dark. But according to his sister-in-law, and the real-estate agent for the property, if he wanted a house in the Big Sky area, he had to jump on it the moment it became available.

"Why would you want to buy a house up here when you can stay in one of our guesthouses on the ranch whenever you come?" his cousin Dana Cardwell Savage had argued.

While he appreciated her hospitality at Cardwell

Ranch, as much time as he found himself spending in Montana, he wanted a place of his own. It had been family that had brought his brothers back to Montana. But it was love—and barbecue—that had them staying.

He often marveled that it had all started with barbecue—the one thing all five brothers knew. They'd opened a small barbecue joint outside of Houston. Surprisingly, it had taken off and they'd opened others, turning a backyard barbecue into a multimillion-dollar business. It had been his brother Tanner "Tag" Cardwell who'd first come up with the idea of opening their first Texas Boys Barbecue restaurant in Montana in Big Sky.

While some of them had balked at the idea, it had proved to be a good one. Now his brothers were talking about opening others in the state. His four brothers had all returned to their Montana roots, but Laramie was a Texas boy who told himself that he had no desire to live in this wild country—at least not full-time.

With his entire family here now, he wanted his own place, and he could darn sure afford a second home. Though he suspected the one he was on his way to check out would be too large for what he needed.

But there was one way to find out. He figured he'd get a look at the house from the outside. If it wasn't what he wanted, then he wouldn't waste his sister-in-law McKenzie's time looking at the interior.

As he topped a small rise in the road, a moonlit Lone Mountain, the peak that dominated Big Sky, appeared from behind a cloud, making him catch his breath. He'd seen the view numerous times on his other visits to the area, but it still captivated him.

He had to admit this part of Montana was spectacular, although he wasn't so sure about staying up here for the winter. While the snow was awe inspiring in its beauty, he still wasn't used to the bracing cold up here.

"You wouldn't mind it if you had someone to cuddle with at night," his brother Tag had joked. All four of his brothers had fallen in love in Montana—and with Montana—and now had wives to snuggle up to on these cold winter nights.

"I only want a house up here," Laramie had said. "I can kick up the heat when I spend time here during the holidays."

As he topped the rise in the road, his headlights caught on a three-story house set against the mountainside. Laramie let up on the gas, captivated by the design of the house and the way it seemed to belong on the side of the mountain in the pines.

That was when he spotted the dark figure running along the roofline of the attached garage.

CHAPTER TWO

LARAMIE REMEMBERED HEARING that an alleged cat burglar had been seen in Big Sky, but so far the thief hadn't gotten away with anything.

Until now.

Slamming on the brakes, he threw open the door of his rented SUV, leaped out and took off running. It crossed his mind that the robber might be armed and dangerous. But all he could think about was catching the thief.

The freezing, snowy night air made his lungs ache. Even though he'd been the business end of Texas Boys Barbecue, he'd stayed in shape. But he felt the high altitude quicken his breathing and reminded himself he wasn't in Houston anymore.

The dark figure had reached the end of the roofline and now leaped down as agile as any cat he'd ever seen. The thief was dressed in all black, including a mask that hid his face. He was carrying what appeared to be a painting.

Laramie tackled the burglar, instantly recognizing his physical advantage. The burglar let out a breath as they hit the ground. The painting skidded across the snow.

Rolling over on top of the thief, Laramie held him down with his weight as he fumbled for his cell phone.

The slightly built burglar wriggled under him in the deep snow.

"Hold still," he ordered as he finally got his cell phone out and with freezing fingers began to call his cousin's husband, Marshal Hud Savage.

"You're crushing me."

At the burglar's distinctly female voice, Laramie froze. His gaze cut from the phone to the burglar's eyes—the only exposed part of her face other than her mouth. The eyes were a pale blue in the snowy starlight. "You're a...*woman*?"

In a breathless whisper, she said, "You just now noticed that? Could you let me breathe?"

Shocked, he shifted his weight to allow her to take breath into her lungs. This was the cat burglar?

She freed one arm and wiped away the powdery snow from her eyes as she whispered something else.

He cut his eyes to her, suddenly worried that he had injured her when he'd taken her down. She motioned for him to lean closer. He bent down.

Her free hand cupped the back of his neck, pulling him down into a kiss before he could stop her. Suddenly her lips were on his, her mouth parting as if they were lovers.

The next thing he knew he was lying on his back in the snow, looking up at the stars as the cat burglar took off. Her escape had been as much of a surprise as the kiss. He quickly sat up. He'd lost his cell phone and his Stetson. Both had fallen into the snow. He plucked them up as he lumbered to his feet. But by then she was already dropping over the side of the ridge.

He took off after her, but he had gone only a few yards when he heard the roar of a snowmobile engine.

Scrambling after her, he turned the corner of the house in time to see the snowmobile roar off through the snow-heavy pines and disappear. He listened to her get away, feeling like a fool. He'd let her trick him.

She'd taken advantage of his surprise and the extra space he'd given her to breathe. She was a lot stronger and more agile than she had appeared and she had a weapon—those lips. He groaned when he thought about the kiss—and its effects on him.

As he turned back, he saw a corner of the painting sticking up out of the snow. Laramie trudged to where it had landed. The only good news was that she hadn't gotten away with the painting.

Surprisingly the frame was still intact. He carefully brushed away the snow, thinking about the woman who'd gotten away. He'd known his share of women in his life. A few had tempted him, a couple had played havoc with his heart and several had taken him for a ride.

However, none of them had tricked him like this. He could well imagine what his brothers would say.

But would he be able to recognize her if he ever saw her again? She'd never spoken above a whisper and he hadn't gotten a chance to remove her ski mask before she'd dumped him in the snow.

Those eyes. Those lips. He told himself if he ever saw either again, damn straight he'd recognize her.

She thought she was smarter than he. She thought she'd gotten away. But he had the painting. And he would find her—if she didn't find him first, he thought, glancing at the painting in the moonlight.

To the fading sound of the snowmobile, he walked

back to his rental SUV. Placing the painting in the backseat, he called his cousin's husband, the marshal.

THAT HAD BEEN too close. As Obsidian "Sid" Forester pulled the snowmobile around to the back of the cabin, she glanced over her shoulder. No headlights. No lights at all. She hadn't been followed.

She'd taken a longer route through the trees. At first she'd thought the man who'd tackled her was the owner of the house. But she'd done her research on him and knew he was much older than the man she'd just encountered.

So who was that cowboy with the Southern drawl? Moonlight on snow did strange things to the one's vision. But she had gotten a good look at him—a better look than he'd gotten of her, she assured herself. Thick dark hair. Ice-cold blue eyes. Handsome if you liked that clean-cut, all-business kind of man. She did not.

The only thing that had thrown her was his accent. Definitely from down South. Definitely not the New Yorker who owned the house.

That wasn't all that had thrown her, she had to admit. The kiss. It had worked just as she'd planned and yet… She touched her tongue to her upper lip, remembering the electrical shock she'd felt when they'd kissed. Worse was the tingling she'd felt in her belly. True, she hadn't kissed a man in… She couldn't even remember when, but she'd never had that kind of reaction. She certainly hadn't expected to feel…anything.

Her pulse was back to normal by the time she entered the cabin. The air smelled of oil paint, turpentine and linseed oil. She shrugged out of her boots and coat at the back door, hung up her coat and kicked her boots aside as she moved to the painting she'd been working on earlier that day.

She gave it a critical perusal before moving into the small kitchen. Unfortunately she hadn't been to the grocery store in several days. She was always starved after one of what she called her "night jobs." With a bottle of beer, her last, a chunk of cheese and some stale bread, she stepped into the living area, where a half dozen paintings were drying.

The cabin was small with only a living room, kitchen, bedroom, small bath and a storage room off to one side at the back. The moment the owner had shown it to her—and told her about all its peculiarities—she'd had to have it and had quickly signed the papers.

Sitting down now, she considered each of her paintings as she ate her snack and sipped her beer. It was hard to concentrate after what had happened earlier, though. She'd come close to getting caught before, but nothing like tonight. What would the man do?

Go to the marshal.

She considered that and decided she wasn't worried about the law catching up with her.

What did worry her was that he had the painting.

Taking another bite of cheese and bread, she chewed for a moment before washing it down with the last of the beer. She really did have to go to the store tomorrow.

Just the thought of going out in public made her wonder if she would run into him. That was the other thing about her cabin. It was nestled in the woods, far from urban Big Sky.

What if she did see him again? She had no doubt

that she would recognize him. She'd gotten a good look at him. He had high cheekbones, a patrician nose and generous mouth. She felt that ridiculous stirring again over that one stupid kiss.

She assured herself that there wasn't any way he could recognize her since she'd had the black ski mask on the whole time. Nor could he recognize her voice, since she hadn't spoken above a whisper.

Shaking her head, she tried to put him out of her mind. There was more than a good chance that she would never see him again. Obviously he was a tourist, probably only here for the holidays. Once the holidays were over, he'd be on a jet back to wherever he'd picked up that Southern drawl.

Still, she wondered who he was and why he'd driven up to the house tonight. Probably lost. Just her luck. What other reason could he have had to be there?

But while she'd gotten away, it hadn't been clean, which upset her more than she wanted to admit. She prided herself on her larceny skills. Worse, she'd failed. She didn't have the painting.

Losing her appetite, she tossed the crust of stale bread into the trash and put the cheese back into the fridge before she returned to her work in progress. She always did her best thinking while she painted.

"So, you didn't see her face?" Marshal Hud Savage asked as he looked up from his report at the marshal's office later that night.

"She was wearing a ski mask with only the eyes and mouth part open. Her eyes were this amazing… bluish-silvery color." Laramie frowned. "Maybe it was the starlight but they seemed to change color." He realized the marshal was staring at him. "Just put down *blue*. If I ever see those eyes again, I'll recognize her." Or those lips, he thought, but he wasn't about to tell Hud about the kiss.

It had taken him by surprise—just as she'd planned. But for a moment, his mouth had been on hers. He'd looked into her eyes, felt something quicken inside him, then her warm breath on his cheek and...

He shook his head, reminding himself that it had only been a ploy and he'd fallen for it, hook, line and sinker. He'd kissed a *thief*! What annoyed him was that he had felt anything but disgust for what she'd done.

"How about height and weight?" Hud asked after writing down *blue*.

Laramie shrugged. "Small. Maybe five-five or -six. I have no idea on weight. Slim. I'm sorry I don't have a better description. It all happened too fast. But I have the painting. Maybe you can get her fingerprints—"

"Was she wearing gloves?"

He groaned.

"And you say she got away on a snowmobile?"

All he could do was nod.

"Did you get a make or model?"

Another shake of his head.

"And she overpowered you? Was she armed?"

Laramie groaned inwardly. "Not armed exactly. She was much stronger than I expected and she moved so fast... She caught me off guard."

Hud nodded, but he appeared to be trying hard not to laugh.

"You wait until you find her. She's...wily."

Hud did chuckle then. "I'm sure she is. Here. Sign this."

"So what are the chances you'll catch her?" Laramie asked as he signed the report.

"With a description like the one you just gave me…" Hud shook his head. His phone rang and he reached for it. "Marshal Savage." He listened, his gaze going to Laramie. "Okay. Yep, that'll do it." Hanging up, he picked up the signed report and ripped it in half before tossing it into the trash.

"What?" Laramie demanded.

"I just spoke with the owner of the house. He hadn't planned to come up this holiday, but apparently McKenzie called him yesterday and told him you would be looking at the house. Seems he's anxious to sell, so he flew in tonight." Hud met his gaze. "When I called the maintenance service and asked them to check the house, they found him there. He looked around to see what was missing and found nothing out of order."

"There wasn't anything missing? Was he sure?"

"It seems he has a painting, just like that one…" He pointed to the one leaning against the wall on the floor near Laramie, the painting the cat burglar had dropped. "It isn't missing."

"That's not possible."

Hud shrugged. "The owner says he has the original—the only one of its kind. Also, he said his house hasn't been broken into."

"That can't be right. I saw her coming out of the house."

"Or did you just see her on the ridge of the garage roofline?" the marshal asked.

Laramie thought back. "Maybe I didn't see her come out of the house."

"Since the first report we received about a cat burglar, we've had several sightings. But in all three cases, nothing was taken, the house showed no sign of forced entry…"

Laramie could see where this was going. "So it was a…hoax?"

Hud studied him openly for a moment. "You didn't happen to mention to your brothers that you were going up to that house tonight, did you? They also didn't happen to tell you beforehand about a cat burglar in the area, did they?"

He would kill his brothers. "You think it was a setup?"

"Let's hope not," Hud said with a groan. "I get a call a day about a bad twenty. Someone's churning them out," he said getting to his feet. "In the old days it took a lot of expensive equipment and space along with some talent. Now all you need is a good copy machine. A video online will walk you through the entire process. The good news is that these operations are often small. We aren't talking millions of dollars. Just someone needing some instant spending money."

"Well, good luck finding your counterfeiter and, again, I'm sorry about this. You have enough going on." But as he turned to the door, he said, "What about the painting?"

"The owner swears he has the authenticated original with paperwork on the back." Hud shrugged. "I would imagine this is nothing more than a cheap prop."

"Then you don't mind if I keep it?" Laramie asked.

The marshal chuckled. "It's all yours."

Laramie considered the painting on the floor. It was what he would have called Old West art, a rancher on horseback surveying his herd. It was titled "On the

Ranch" and signed by an artist named Taylor West. The painting looked expensive to him, but what did he know?

"If someone comes looking for it, I'll let you know. But I have my doubts." Hud grinned. "If you ever see that woman again, though… I'd be curious just what color her eyes are since they seem to have made a real impression on you."

Don't miss
REUNION AT CARDWELL RANCH
by B.J. Daniels
available wherever Harlequin Intrigue books
and ebooks are sold.

B.J. DANIELS

77846 ATONEMENT   ___ \$7.99 U.S.   ___ \$8.99 CAN.

(limited quantities available)

TOTAL AMOUNT	\$ _____
POSTAGE & HANDLING	\$ _____
(\$1.00 FOR 1 BOOK, 50¢ for each additional)	
APPLICABLE TAXES*	\$ _____
TOTAL PAYABLE	\$ _____

(check or money order—please do not send cash)

To order, complete this form and send it, along with a check or money order for the total above, payable to HQN Books, to: **In the U.S.:** 3010 Walden Avenue, P.O. Box 9077, Buffalo, NY 14269-9077; **In Canada:** P.O. Box 636, Fort Erie, Ontario, L2A 5X3.

Name: _____

Address: _____ City: _____

State/Prov.: _____ Zip/Postal Code: _____

Account Number (if applicable): _____

075 CSAS

      *New York residents remit applicable sales taxes.
    *Canadian residents remit applicable GST and provincial taxes.

HQN™

www.HQNBooks.com

PHBJD1215BL

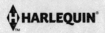

INTRIGUE

EDGE-OF-YOUR-SEAT INTRIGUE, FEARLESS ROMANCE.

Save $1.00

on the purchase of
REUNION AT CARDWELL RANCH
by B.J. Daniels,
available December 15, 2015, or on any
other Harlequin® Intrigue book.

Available wherever books are sold, including most bookstores, supermarkets, drugstores and discount stores.

- ✂

Save $1.00

on the purchase of any Harlequin Intrigue book.

Coupon valid until March 31, 2016. Redeemable at participating outlets in the U.S. and Canada only. Not redeemable at Barnes & Noble stores.
Limit one coupon per customer.

52613210

5 65373 00076 2   (8100)0 12114

REQUEST YOUR FREE BOOKS!

2 FREE NOVELS
FROM THE SUSPENSE COLLECTION
PLUS 2 FREE GIFTS!

YES! Please send me 2 FREE novels from the Suspense Collection and my 2 FREE gifts (gifts are worth about $10). After receiving them, if I don't wish to receive any more books, I can return the shipping statement marked "cancel." If I don't cancel, I will receive 4 brand-new novels every month and be billed just $6.49 per book in the U.S. or $6.99 per book in Canada. That's a savings of at least 19% off the cover price. It's quite a bargain! Shipping and handling is just 50¢ per book in the U.S. and 75¢ per book in Canada.* I understand that accepting the 2 free books and gifts places me under no obligation to buy anything. I can always return a shipment and cancel at any time. Even if I never buy another book, the two free books and gifts are mine to keep forever.

191/391 MDN GH4Z

Name _____ (PLEASE PRINT)

Address _____ Apt. #

City _____ State/Prov. _____ Zip/Postal Code

Signature (if under 18, a parent or guardian must sign)

Mail to the **Reader Service:**
IN U.S.A.: P.O. Box 1867, Buffalo, NY 14240-1867
IN CANADA: P.O. Box 609, Fort Erie, Ontario L2A 5X3

Want to try two free books from another line?
Call 1-800-873-8635 or visit www.ReaderService.com.

* Terms and prices subject to change without notice. Prices do not include applicable taxes. Sales tax applicable in N.Y. Canadian residents will be charged applicable taxes. Offer not valid in Quebec. This offer is limited to one order per household. Not valid for current subscribers to the Suspense Collection or the Romance/Suspense Collection. All orders subject to credit approval. Credit or debit balances in a customer's account(s) may be offset by any other outstanding balance owed by or to the customer. Please allow 4 to 6 weeks for delivery. Offer available while quantities last.

Your Privacy—The Reader Service is committed to protecting your privacy. Our Privacy Policy is available online at www.ReaderService.com or upon request from the Reader Service.

We make a portion of our mailing list available to reputable third parties that offer products we believe may interest you. If you prefer that we not exchange your name with third parties, or if you wish to clarify or modify your communication preferences, please visit us at www.ReaderService.com/consumerschoice or write to us at Reader Service Preference Service, P.O. Box 9062, Buffalo, NY 14240-9062. Include your complete name and address.

SUS15